www.slough.gov.uk
Slough
Borough Council

THE FLOWER SELLER

A charming and evocative tale of family and fortune from the queen of West Country sagas

Isabella Carrington has been brought up in a life of privilege in London. Her life seems perfect, until her father suddenly announces bankruptcy. To save Isabella from destitution he sends her to stay with family she has never met, far away on a violet farm deep in Devon. Isabella is horrified her uncle expects her to work for her keep, packing up the flowers and selling them in the nearby market. However she soon discovers that life on a violet farm may not be so bad, especially when she meets handsome local farmer Felix Furneaux...

THE FLOWER SELLER

THE FLOWER SELLER

by

Linda Finlay

Magna Large Print Books
Gargrave, North Yorkshire,
BD23 3SE, England.

British Library Cataloguing in Publication Data.

A catalogue record of this book is
available from the British Library

ISBN 978-0-7505-4717-8

First published in Great Britain by HQ,
an imprint of HarperCollins*Publishers* Ltd., 2018

Published in Large Print 2019 by arrangement with
HarperCollins Publishers Ltd.

Magna Large Print is an imprint of Library Magna Books Ltd.

Printed and bound in Great Britain by
T.J. (International) Ltd., Cornwall, PL28 8RW

To Pern, for your
continued encouragement and support

Chapter 1

London, September 1892

Forgetting all she'd been taught about dignified deportment, Isabella swept through the doors of Claridge's as if blown in on the autumn breeze. Her golden curls and bright blue eyes drew many an admiring glance to which she was oblivious, as she hastily smoothed down the silk of her lilac skirts and straightened the strands of pearls around her neck. With her visit to Italy only days away, she'd been shopping for accessories to complement the new outfits her dressmaker had delivered that morning, and browsing the delightful displays, she'd completely lost track of time. Not wishing to keep Maxwell waiting, she hurried between the ornate marble columns and into the garden room decorated with potted palms. He'd been so preoccupied with business recently that time with him was precious.

A waiter showed her to a table secreted behind one of the oriental silk screens that divided the room into private alcoves.

'Isabella, darling,' he greeted her, rising to his feet. He was looking especially handsome in his dark jacket with a high-necked waistcoat, and the appreciative gleam in his slate-grey eyes sent shivers tingling down her spine, although she endeavoured not to show it.

'I hope I haven't kept you waiting?' she asked demurely. Instead of answering, he glanced beyond her and frowned.

'No bodyguard this afternoon?'

'Oh Maxwell, you are terrible,' she giggled. 'You know Papa feels happier if Gaskell chaperones me. Though where she is this afternoon, I have no idea. I expressly told her I would be leaving the house at 2 p.m., yet when the clock struck the hour she was nowhere to be seen.'

'You mean you took the opportunity to slip out unaccompanied? Whatever would dear Papa say?' he exclaimed, throwing up his hands in mock horror.

'I know it was bold of me, but I had shopping that couldn't wait and, of course, I've been looking forward to our meeting. Although I have to confess Papa doesn't know,' she told him, staring at him from under her lashes. In truth, much as she hated deceiving her father, wild horses wouldn't have prevented her coming.

'Well, I can't pretend I'm sorry to have you all to myself. Those beady eyes of hers watching my every move make me nervous, I don't mind admitting. Still, here you are, and all on your own. How I shall restrain myself, I don't know.' He waggled his eyebrows so outrageously she had to laugh.

'Oh Maxwell, you are a terrible tease.'

'It's the truth, I assure you. Now before you slap my face with your lily-white hand, I have taken the liberty of ordering sandwiches, fancies and a pot of Earl Grey,' he told her becoming serious as another waiter approached, bearing a silver tray.

'My favourites,' she smiled, thinking how considerate he was.

'How is your father?' Maxwell asked, as soon as the waiter had poured their drinks and departed.

'Busy as ever,' she sighed, eyeing the food longingly. Shopping always made her hungry and the delectable fragrance of smoked salmon and cucumber was making her mouth water. However, Maxwell was staring at her intently.

'I heard there was a takeover in the offing. Your father had a successful outcome, I trust?' he asked solicitously.

'If the long hours he's been spending at his office are anything to go by, then yes he surely must have.'

'That's gratifying to hear,' he replied before adding: 'There have been rumours circulating recently.'

'Oh?' she asked.

'Nothing for you to worry your pretty head about,' he assured her, reaching across the snowy tablecloth and running one finger lightly down the back of her hand. She glanced around guiltily. Although they were screened from view, she daren't risk word getting back to Papa. Her father had been polite whenever Maxwell called for her, but they were so close she knew by the set of his face he didn't approve of their liaison. Discovering she was here unchaperoned wouldn't help matters at all, even if Maxwell wasn't to blame. As if reading her thoughts, Maxwell's hand tightened on hers.

'Isabella darling, you must know how I feel about you,' he murmured, leaning closer and staring into her eyes. 'Don't you think it's time we set a date for our betrothal?' Her heart leapt yet she endeavoured to stay composed.

'I leave for Florence next week, Maxwell,' she reminded him.

'The city that shimmers gold,' he smiled.

'You've been there?' she asked.

'Indeed, I have. Father insisted I see something of the world before taking up my position with his firm. I shall think of you on the Ponte Vecchio, the glorious green waters of the Arno gliding beneath your feet.'

'You paint a delightful picture, and of course I'm thrilled I shall be visiting Rome as well. I really can't believe my good fortune.' Her eyes clouded. 'You do realize I shall be away for over three months?'

'I know, dearest, and I shall miss you terribly,' he sighed. 'However, with your appreciation of the arts, it will be a wonderful experience for you.'

'I have to confess to looking forward to going, although I do worry...' her voice trailed away.

'Worry? What about?' he asked.

'You'll think me silly, but it's the first time I've travelled abroad and, although Gaskell will be with me, I can't help worrying something will go wrong. Suppose I don't like it?'

'Oh Isabella, you will love it, I'm sure,' he assured her. 'However, should there be any problem then I shall come and bring you home again.'

'You'd do that for me?'

'Of course, your happiness is paramount, sweetest.'

'Thank you, Maxwell,' she whispered, her heart swelling. 'I am going to miss you.'

'Then with your permission, I shall speak to your father the moment you return.' He waited for her to reply, his eyes never leaving hers. Butterflies skittered in her chest and she looked down at her plate, pretending to consider. 'We could hold a ball for your coming of age in the new year and make the formal announcement then.'

'Goodness, that soon?' she gasped, staring at him in surprise. His smile widened as he held her gaze.

'It can't be soon enough for me, Isabella, and besides as an old man of nearly thirty, I need a wife by my side,' he told her. 'I believe amethyst is the appropriate stone for those born in early February. One would be a perfect match for those beautiful cornflower eyes of yours that tinge violet when roused.'

'Stop it, Maxwell, you're making me blush,' she cried, feeling the heat creeping up her cheeks. 'Fancy you knowing my birthstone,' she added, for he wasn't usually given to sentiment.

'My grandmother told me,' he admitted with a wry grin. 'Her birthday is the day before yours and she wears such a ring.'

'Really? We shall have something to talk about when we meet.'

'You agree then?' he urged, tightening his grip.

'I suppose if we were betrothed, then we would travel together. That alone makes your proposal worth considering,' she replied, smiling so he knew she was teasing, for there was nothing she desired more. Although he returned her smile, it didn't reach his eyes and thinking he'd had enough of discussing personal matters, she changed the subject. 'On my way here, I passed a gallery displaying charming pictures by a Scottish artist. His exhibition debuts this very evening.' She looked at him hopefully.

'I'm sorry, Isabella, but I already have an appointment tonight,' he replied, releasing her hand and sitting back in his seat.

'Oh?' she frowned, disappointment flooding through her.

'A business meeting so important I cannot postpone it, even for you,' he explained. 'Now let's not waste our time together. Tell me what wicked things you've been up to whilst your keeper's been absent without leave.' Isabella took a sip of her drink, then unable to resist the appeal in his eyes, regaled him with details of her afternoon. Yet, although he smiled and nodded, she couldn't help feeling he was only half listening.

'It sounds as though you need to replace that energy you've expended,' he joked, proffering the laden silver stand the moment she paused for breath.

The bread was freshly baked, the salmon succulent and she savoured each mouthful as soft music from the pianist mingled with the murmur of voices around them. The chink of crystal glasses and clink of silver spoons against fine china added to the genial atmosphere. Cocooned in their cosy nook, Isabella sighed contentedly then darted a surreptitious glance at Maxwell. His grey silk tie brought out the colour of his eyes while his slicked-back fair hair emphasized razor-sharp cheeks. He was handsome beyond measure and she couldn't wait to become his wife. As if sensing her thoughts, he looked up and smiled.

'Next time we come here, we shall celebrate in style, Isabella,' he promised. 'Now why don't you sample these delicious-looking cakes before we leave?' She took one, toying with the purple crystallized flower on top whilst she waited for him to continue discussing plans for their future. He seemed distracted, though, even frowning at the clock on the wall. Surely he wasn't in that much of a hurry, Isabella mused, nibbling daintily at the icing. Yet, no sooner had she finished eating than he folded his napkin and smiled apologetically.

'Regrettably dearest, it's time we were leaving.' Seeing her crestfallen look, he added: 'Perhaps I may call upon you tomorrow afternoon? We could visit that gallery you mentioned.'

'That would be lovely, Maxwell, though I doubt they'll be offering the champagne and canapés advertised for this evening,' she sighed, hoping his fondness for the good things in life might change his mind.

'Then I promise to make reparation,' he assured her. 'I'm sorry I have to rush off but it really is imperative I keep this appointment tonight. However, I'm sure you'll spend a happy evening perusing all those delightful accoutrements you've bought,' he chuckled.

Outside, dusk was falling and the lamplighter was busy about his work. Seeing Isabella shiver, the doorman signalled for her carriage and Maxwell handed her inside. Then he turned to the young flower seller standing beside the hotel steps and plucked a posy of violets from her basket.

'Beautiful flowers for a beautiful lady,' he said,

presenting them to Isabella with a flourish. 'Until tomorrow, Isabella dearest,' he whispered, placing a featherlight kiss on her cheek.

As the carriage began to move, she buried her head in the flowers' satiny petals. Breathing in their sweet perfume, a faint memory stirred, hovered elusively then vanished like mist in the rays of a summer sun. It wasn't the first time that had happened and she sighed in frustration.

Oblivious to the buildings flashing by the window, she thought back over her afternoon. Maxwell was handsome, generous and charming but also, something of an enigma. One minute proposing they set a date for their betrothal, the next almost hurrying her from the hotel. Before she had time to ponder the matter, they were pulling up outside her family home, a three-storey house in Chester Square. To her surprise, the front door was immediately thrown open, spilling golden light onto the walkway and park beyond.

'Your father is waiting in his study, Miss Isabella,' the butler informed her.

'Thank you, Jenson. I'll see him as soon as I have attended to my purchases,' she told him, turning to give instruction to the driver.

'He was most insistent you go through immediately you arrived home, Miss.' Fighting her irritation, Isabella hurried inside, her heels sinking into the pile of the Persian carpet as she made her way down the hallway.

'Good evening, Papa,' she smiled, breezing into his inner sanctum where the familiar smell of beeswax and cigar smoke overpowered the gentle fragrance of her violets. 'It's ages since you were home at this hour. Does this mean we shall be dining together?' To her surprise, her usually affable father didn't answer. In fact, he looked gaunt, seeming to have shrunk in stature since she'd seen him that morning. As he stared at her from behind his highly polished desk, his hazel eyes gleaming olive in their seriousness, Isabella felt her chest tighten. 'Is something wrong? Are you not well?' she asked, taking in his pallor.

'Come and sit down, Isabella, I have something to tell you,' he said quietly.

'What is it, Papa? Has something happened?' she asked, sinking into the leather chair opposite.

'A fire has destroyed St John's in Newfoundland.'

'But that's on the other side of the world, Papa. It's a terrible shame, of course, but not of any great importance to you, surely?'

'On the contrary, my dear. I have invested heavily there and now it's all gone. My business is in ruins, Isabella. All this has to go,' he groaned, making a sweeping gesture around the room. 'Since your mother died I have done my best to keep you in the manner she wanted, but now I have failed...' his voice broke and he stuttered to a halt.

'You've been the best papa ever,' Isabella cried, hurrying to his side and throwing her arms around him. 'Don't worry, we can economize,' she said, seeking to reassure him. 'Why, Maxwell told me only this afternoon that as soon as I return from Italy, he intends asking for my hand in marriage.'

'My dearest child, you simply do not understand. There will be no Italy or friends either,' he faltered and looked away.

'But Papa, you have so many, they will all want to help...' she began.

'Alas, they are of the fair-weather kind,' he replied, grinning wryly. 'When word gets out they'll disappear faster than rats up a drainpipe, as you would find out if you were to remain here: I simply cannot put you through that, Isabella, which is why I have made arrangements for you to go and stay with your Uncle Frederick and his family in Devonshire.'

'What?' she gasped. 'But I've never met these people before,' she cried, shivering despite the fire burning brightly in the grate. 'You will be coming too?' Her father shook his head.

'That is out of the question. I have to see if I have anything at all left to salvage.'

'Then I shall stay here with you,' Isabella declared stoutly, staring at the man she so loved and revered.

'You will repair to Devonshire tomorrow morning, and that, I'm afraid, is an order.' Isabella's eyes widened. Never before had he insisted she do anything, let alone something to which she wasn't agreeable. 'If I had more time then things might be different.'

'Time, Papa? If that's what you need, then I will go,' she told him, eager to make him happy again.

'Thank you, my dear,' he said, giving her a wan smile. 'I asked Gaskell to pack your bags before she left.'

'Left, Papa? I didn't know Gaskell was going anywhere,' she frowned. 'She was supposed to be escorting me this afternoon but...,' Isabella faltered, realization dawning. 'You told her not to, didn't you?'

'I'm afraid I did. She knew which of your things would be best suited to your new life. Your uncle runs a small market garden and his homestead does not have the space you are used to here.'

'You are not painting a very agreeable picture, Papa,' Isabella frowned, wrinkling her nose.

'They are kindly people and will make you welcome,' he assured her.

'Surely you can't mean for me to travel alone?' she cried. Her father shook his head.

'Certainly not, my dear. The housekeeper's friend, Mrs Brown, is visiting family in Plymouth and will accompany you as far as Dawlish, where your Uncle Frederick will be waiting.'

'But...,' she began, still trying to grasp what he was telling her.

'Do this for me,' he beseeched, grasping her hands so tightly she had to bite her lip to stop herself from crying out. The desperation in his eyes cut her to the core, and loving him as she did, she wanted to help.

'Very well, Papa. I will go and stay with this Uncle Frederick, but only until you have sorted your affairs. You promise to send word as soon as I can return?' He reached into his inside pocket and drew out a silver locket.

'This was your dear mama's,' he murmured, pressing it into her hands. 'It is only right you have it now.'

'But you have carried it with you since she died,' she began.

'It is what she would have wanted,' he insisted.

'And give this to your uncle when you arrive,' he added, handing her an envelope sealed with his crest. 'Now go and get some rest, for you will need to be up early in the morning.' He stared down at the papers on his desk and she knew further argument would be futile.

Stunned by her papa's revelations and unable to believe he was sending her away, Isabella made her way up to her room. It felt cold and her heart sank when she saw the dressing table had been cleared of her things. The closet was empty apart from her velvet-trimmed mantle and favourite day dress. Her matching bonnet and calfskin gloves were laid out on the chaise longue, her button boots neatly positioned on the rug beneath. Fighting back the tears, she sank onto her bed and glanced down at the silver locket in her hands. It was modest in its simplicity and quite unlike the bright jewels her mama had worn. Or even the amethyst Maxwell had promised her. Maxwell! She would send him a note explaining her change of plans. The moment he received it, he would come and rescue her, she thought, her spirits rising as she remembered his earlier promise.

Chapter 2

Clutching her reticule to her chest, Isabella stared around Paddington Station in dismay. The noise was horrendous as people swarmed like ants towards the waiting trains, and porters threw luggage from their trollies into the baggage vans. Noxious smells and smuts of soot emanating from painted engines caught in her throat. Holding her handkerchief to her nose, she glanced hopefully over her shoulder. However, there was no sign of Maxwell, and her heart sank to her button boots.

'This way, Miss,' the stationmaster urged, guiding her towards the carriage where a woman of middle years stood waiting. She was wearing a brown hat, brown coat and stout brown boots, leaving Isabella in no doubt as to her identity. Even her birdlike eyes were brown as they surveyed Isabella. 'This train will take you straight through to Dawlish,' the man advised her.

'Don't worry, I'll see her safely off at the other end,' the woman told him. 'Mrs Brown at your service, dearie,' she added, turning back to Isabella and smiling. 'Sit down and make yourself comfortable, we've a fair few hours' travelling ahead of us.' Not minding the woman's lack of formality, and strangely comforted by her motherly way, Isabella settled herself onto the seat.

The banging of doors a few moments later made her jump, and glancing out of the window, she saw the stationmaster checking his pocket watch against the station clock. Surely they weren't leaving already, she thought, anxiously scanning the platform for Maxwell. He must have received her letter by now. There was a loud hiss of steam followed by creaks and groans, then with a shudder and screech from the iron wheels, the carriage lurched forward causing her to reach anxiously for the armrest. As clouds of smoke billowed past the window, the train began to pick up pace. *He isn't coming, he isn't coming,* it seemed to be saying.

'You can relax and put your bag down, dearie,' the woman said, breaking into her thoughts. 'Your father reserved us our own compartment, so it'll be quite safe.' Isabella's fingers tightened on the purse that held her travelling jewellery roll containing her mother's locket and the envelope she was to give to her uncle.

'Your first time on a train, Miss?' Mrs Brown asked. Isabella nodded.

'I'm to stay with Mama's family, although I've never met them before,' she admitted.

'It'll be an opportunity for you to get to know them then,' the woman replied philosophically.

'It's only until Papa gets his affairs sorted,' she added.

'Of course it is, dearie,' Mrs Brown smiled knowingly. Too late Isabella realized that Gaskell must have been gossiping. Eager to avoid further questioning, she turned and stared out of the window.

Tall buildings had given way to terraces of houses, smoke curling lazily from their chimneys. Washing flapped like flags in narrow gardens that led down to the railway, while allotments, chequered green and brown with vegetables, stretched beyond. The train gave another lurch then settled into its rhythm. *Going away, going away,* it seemed to be saying. Realizing it was taking her away from everyone she loved, the tears welled. Unwilling to let Mrs Brown see how miserable she felt, she closed her eyes.

Perhaps Maxwell had gone out before her note

was delivered. As soon as he received it he'd be sure to follow, her to Devonshire. Dear Papa was a clever man and she had no doubt he would soon get his affairs sorted and everything would return to normal. While her thoughts whirled like sycamore leaves in the autumn breeze, her lids grew heavy. Finally, as events of the previous day caught up with her, she slept.

The train juddering to a halt, jolted her awake and she stared around disorientated.

'There, dearie, you have had a good sleep,' Mrs Brown chuckled. 'Here we are at Exeter St Davids station and only a few stops from Dawlish.'

'Goodness,' Isabella gasped. 'I do apologize.' The woman laughed.

'No need to, I'm sure. 'Tis lucky mind, 'cos up to May this year you'd have had to change trains here.'

'Oh? Why?' she asked politely.

''Twas only then they changed the gauge from here onward so as to standardize all the railways. Means we can now go all the way through to Penzance in Cornwall, see?' the woman said, lowering her voice as if imparting inside information. 'Anyways, dearie, you must be hungry after all that sleep, so have a piece of cake,' she invited, proffering a brown bag with its brown contents. As the smell of treacle wafted her way, Isabella felt her stomach heave.

'Thank you but I have little appetite.'

'Oh shame,' Mrs Brown sighed, making to close the bag again.

'Please have some yourself, though,' Isabella said quickly.

'Don't mind if I do,' she replied, breaking off a sizable chunk and popping it into her mouth. A whistle sounded, then with another hiss of brakes the train lurched and they were on their way again.

Whilst the woman munched contentedly, Isabella stared out of the window. Before long the buildings gave way to open country and she widened her eyes in surprise.

'Goodness, those fields are red,' she gasped.

'That be the Demshur dirt. You'll have to mind not to get any on those fine threads of yours,' Mrs Brown sighed, eyeing Isabella's travelling clothes covetously. Then, seemingly pulling herself together, she added: 'And over there be the Exe.' Isabella turned to where the woman was gesturing and, sure enough, the train was rattling alongside a river teeming with sailing and rowing boats. Further along, a ferry belching black smoke was disgorging its cargo of people and animals onto the foreshore. They were so close that when the train listed as it rounded a bend, Isabella feared they might tip over and land on top of them.

'You should see the sunsets round here. Best in all the world,' Mrs Brown told her, oblivious to her concern. 'And there be the sea,' she added as Isabella gasped at the vast expanse of white-tipped water shimmering in the afternoon sun. 'You never seen the sea before?' the woman guessed. Isabella shook her head.

'No, I haven't. I was meant to be travelling to Italy later this week, though,' she replied with a pang. If she'd thought Italy far away then, surely it was nothing compared to the miles she'd travelled today. Away from everyone and everything she knew and loved.

'Ah well, I guess you'll find Demshur just as good,' the woman replied, interrupting her thoughts. Isabella was about to ask where Demshur was when the woman gestured to the other side of the carriage. 'There's the Earl's deer park. Leads right up to his castle, it does.' Isabella peered out, hoping to catch a glimpse of the building, but Mrs Brown was still chatting. 'And them dark forests yonder house wild black cats the size of panthers. One snatched up a baby and ran off with it,' she shuddered.

'Really, Mrs Brown,' Isabella tutted. Not wishing to hear any more of the woman's outrageous tales, she turned her attention back to the brightness of the sea only to find they were now passing through dark tunnels which appeared to hang over the water. Then the train slowed before shuddering to a halt.

'Doulis, Doulis, ever'one for Doulis,' a voice called.

'Here you are, dearie,' Mrs Brown announced as the door opened and the guard stood smiling up at them. Isabella frowned.

'But I'm to alight at Dawlish,' she began. The woman pointed to a sign on the platform.

'That's right, Doulis. That's how they says it here.'

'How very strange,' Isabella frowned, getting to her feet.

'Good luck, dearie,' Mrs Brown said. 'You'll have a fine time, I'm sure.'

'Goodbye, Mrs Brown, I'm obliged for your company.'

'Porter's unloading your luggage now, Miss Carrington,' the stationmaster said, hurrying towards her as she alighted.

'How do you know who I am?' she asked, surprise overtaking her trepidation.

'You be expected,' he chuckled. ''Appen your uncle'll be here drekly.' The rest of his words were lost in another deafening hiss as the brakes were released and the train chugged its way out of the station, enveloping them in a cloud of steam. As Isabella swatted away smuts of soot in annoyance, the man gave another chuckle. 'You soon gets used to that. Ah, here be Mr Northcott coming now.'

Isabella's eyes widened in disbelief. Hurrying towards them was a man of middle years wearing an ill-fitted coat with violets sprouting incongruously from his buttonhole. A large straw hat was pulled down over his head, almost obscuring his dark bushy brows. Surely this peculiar man couldn't be her mother's brother?

'Had to get the day's flowers onto the upbound train, Bert, else they'd never reach Covent Garden in time,' he explained. Then he turned to Isabella and smiled. 'You must be my sister's girl. Welcome to Doulis,' he said, proffering a huge and somewhat grubby hand.

'You are Uncle Frederick?' she asked, unable to equate this bear of a man with her ladylike mama. And yet those chocolate-brown eyes seemed strangely familiar.

'The same,' he confirmed, frowning down at the pile of luggage by her side. 'Looks like you've fetched half of London with you. Good job I didn't bring the boy or we'd have no room for it all.'

'Where is your conveyance?' she asked, peering around for sight of a carriage.

'My, er, conveyance is over there,' he grinned, pointing to a battered old trap. 'And that be Silver,' he added.

'Silver?' she replied, frowning at the donkey with its shaggy grey coat.

'I'd better 'elp ye with this lot,' the stationmaster said, bending down to pick up her travelling trunk. 'Blimey, what you got in 'ere, Miss, the crown jewels?' he asked, staggering under the weight.

'I really don't know, my chaperone packed whilst I was out shopping,' Isabella explained. The two men exchanged a look before heaving her luggage up onto the trap. Then her uncle swung himself into the seat, patting the tiny space beside him.

'Up yer come,' he called. Isabella stared at the grime-encrusted wooden plank and shuddered. Her uncle laughed. 'You'll have to get used to a bit of soil if you're to live with us. 'Tis flower growers we be.' Gingerly she clambered up beside him, but as the donkey plodded down the lane, her uncertainty turned to surprise. Ahead of them tall, elegant houses seemed to rise into the sky, and colourful shops fronted a wide green with a sparkling stream cascading down one side. Ducks swam merrily before disappearing under a bridge but before she had time to wonder where, the trap was heading away from the town and travelling alongside the sea. She could hear the shooshing sound of waves being sucked in and out of the pebbles.

'It's really pretty and the air has the clarity of crystal,' she exclaimed, breathing in deeply. 'Why, it smells of salt.'

'That be the ozone,' her uncle chuckled. 'Come spring, those pale cheeks of yours will be as rosy as the cherry blossom.'

'Oh, I'll not be staying that long,' she replied, staring at him in horror. He shot her a look but said nothing and they plodded on in silence. In the distance, she could see the rolling green of the hills Mrs Brown had spoken about. Suddenly the cart lurched as they turned into another much narrower lane.

'Nearly there,' he told her. She stared at the crooked huddle of tiny cottages, their thatched roofs almost touching. Surely he didn't live here? To her relief, they kept going until the lane opened out again and she saw mauve buds peeping from velvety leaves in the sloping hedge banks.

'They be the Devon violets,' her uncle explained, seeing her surprise.

'What a strange time of year for delicate flowers like that to be coming out,' she replied.

'Them blooms best between September and April, though we can make 'em grow longer in the shelter of our market garden,' he told her proudly. 'Here we be, and there's plenty more of them violets round the back,' her uncle chuckled, pulling up in front of a two-storey stone building with a moss-covered slate roof. To the left of this was a long brick shed half-clad with wooden boards. Although the property looked a bit ramshackle, it was bigger than her papa had led her to believe.

'Welcome to your new home, me dear,' he said, jumping down. 'Now, I believe you have something for me from your father?'

'I do?' she frowned and then remembered. Opening her reticule, she withdrew the envelope and handed it to her uncle. 'Family's dying to meet you,' he grinned. 'I mean they're looking forward to meeting you,' he hastily amended. 'Mother's been cleaning and baking since she heard you was coming.'

'I do hope your mother hasn't gone to too much trouble,' Isabella replied, carefully stepping down from the cart. Her uncle shot her a funny look, then gestured for her to go ahead, but as she made to walk down the nearest path, he held up his hand.

'Not that side, me dear. That's Grandmother's. Our door's round back.'

'You mean your property is semi-detached?' she asked. He frowned, pushed the straw hat to the back of his head and stood staring at the cottage as if seeing it for the first time.

'Reckon it is that,' he muttered, before turning back to the donkey, who was grazing the clumps of grass that appeared to serve as the front lawn. 'Right, I'll take the trap round to the yard, it'll be easier to offload all your trunks and things there.'

'Perhaps the boy could do that whilst you introduce me to your family,' she suggested, carefully picking her way along the dirt-strewn path. He started to say something but the door opened and a motherly-looking woman wearing a yellow gingham overall stood smiling at her.

'Welcome, my dear,' she said, enfolding Isabella

in a warm embrace before drawing her into the kitchen. 'I'm Mary but you can call me Auntie if you wish. Now let me take your turnover afore you meet the rest of the family,' she beamed, holding out her hand.

'My turnover?' Isabella asked. Her aunt pointed to her mantle and Isabella slipped it from her shoulders then glanced around the room. It was tiny and hung with beams so low that if she reached up she'd surely be able to touch them. Deep sills were crammed with jugs and pots while yellow curtains brightened the small windows. The flags on the floor were spread with a rag rug woven in a hotchpotch of bright colours. Finally, her gaze came to rest on the scrubbed table where five children waited, their chocolate-brown eyes gleaming with curiosity.

'Hello there,' she smiled. 'I'm Isabella Carrington.' The younger ones giggled but the older girl smiled back.

'I'm Dorothy, the eldest, but you can call me Dotty. Best to be friends if we're to share a room, don't you think?' Share a room? Isabella's heart sank.

'Me an' all,' the youngest girl piped up, her dark pigtails swinging from side to side.

'That's Alice, who's six,' Dorothy supplied. 'It'll be a bit of a squeeze but I'm sure we'll manage.' Isabella swallowed hard. Three people in one bed chamber? But she had no time to dwell on the matter, for her aunt was signalling for the boys to get to their feet.

'This is William, he's fifteen. Joseph here is twelve, and Thomas nine,' she said, pointing to each in turn. They nodded solemnly but didn't reply, and Isabella saw the eldest frowning at her clothes. Then the door swung open and her uncle staggered into the room, reeling under the weight of her portmanteau.

'Oh, I thought you were going to get the boy to do that,' she exclaimed. They all turned to her in shocked silence.

'You must mean me then,' William muttered, shooting her a glare as he stalked from the room.

'I meant your servant boy,' Isabella explained, giving her aunt a bewildered look.

'Cor, bless you dear, we don't have no servants here,' she replied.

'What, none at all?' Isabella gasped. 'Then who does all the work?'

'We do, of course. All mucks in together,' her uncle replied, looking her up and down. 'I hope you've brought some sensible clothes with you. Them fancy threads'll be no good for working the land.'

'Working the land?' she gasped.

'Ah,' he nodded. 'Come the morrow you'll be pitching in too. Got to earn your keep, girl.'

Chapter 3

As Isabella stared at her uncle in dismay, a hush fell over the room.

'I'm not sure what my chaperone has packed for me.'

'Well, don't worry about that now, my dear,' her aunt said quickly. 'You must be fair parched after all your travels. I'll set the kettle to boil and Dotty can show you where you'll be sleeping.'

'Me too,' Alice cried, springing to her feet and scurrying over to a flight of steep steps that led straight off the kitchen. Gingerly Isabella followed them up the narrow staircase and into a small room where three mattresses topped with yellow coverlets lay side by side on the floor. There was a cast iron fireplace on one wall and a small closet squeezed into the corner with a fly-spotted mirror hanging up beside it.

'Mother got Father to put that up 'specially. We've never had our own looking-glass before,' Alice proudly declared.

'He said you'd be used to tiddyvating,' Dotty said knowingly. 'And it means I can see to frizz my hair,' she added, patting her sleek braid.

'Why would you do that?' Isabella asked, staring at her in astonishment.

'To puff it up, of course. Father says he's seen thicker rats' tails,' Dotty laughed.

Charming, Isabella thought, turning towards the window. Like the rest of the cottage, it was tiny and hung with yellow curtains that, although clean, had definitely seen better days. A single candlestick stood alone and forlorn on the windowsill. She knew just how it felt, she thought, remembering her comfortable chamber at home.

'Not what you're used to?' Dotty guessed, seeing her expression.

'Don't you like it?' Alice asked. 'We've squeezed up so you can get your mattress in and Mother's made you a new cover just like ours.'

'It's a lovely room and I appreciate you making space for me,' Isabella assured her. 'Where are the facilities?'

'The facil– you mean the privy?' Dotty frowned. Isabella nodded. 'Out the back in the yard and there's a tin bath in the shed which Mother brings in each Saturday night. It's quite cosy with the range lit.'

You mean you bathe in the kitchen?' Isabella shuddered. Before Dotty could reply, William staggered into the room, set her trunk down with a thud then turned to face her.

'There's no room left in here so where would you like the boy to put the rest of your things, your ladyship?' he asked, venom sparking in his dark eyes.

'Look, I...' she began, but he was already thundering down the stairs. The two girls stared after him in dismay.

'William isn't usually rude like that,' Dotty frowned.

'It's my fault. When your father said he hadn't brought the boy with him I assumed he was referring to your servant,' Isabella explained. 'I had no idea you didn't have staff until your mother explained just now.'

'Be good if we did, though,' Dotty laughed. 'We wouldn't have to wash the dishes or sweep the floor. Don't worry about William, he'll get over it. Boy is what Father calls him, by the way.'

'Doesn't it get confusing when you have two other brothers?' Isabella asked. Dotty shook her head.

'He always called me the girl and when William came along he was the boy. Then Joe was born and Father realized he couldn't call him boy as well so had to use his name, though he always says Joseph, of course.'

'And he calls me Alice Band, 'cos he says I'm like Alice in Wonderland,' the girl added proudly. 'But I can't say Isa–, Isba– your fancy name so I'll call you Izzie.' Isabella opened her mouth to protest then saw the girl's eager expression and smiled.

'Why not,' she conceded. After all, it was only going to be for a short time. Maxwell was bound to arrive soon.

'Tay's up.' As Mary's voice sounded up the stairs, Alice turned to Isabella.

'Come on, Mother's baked Devon splits 'specially for your arrival.'

'That's the boys' room opposite,' Dotty told her, as they made their way back down the stairs. Isabella was about to ask where her parents slept when she heard her uncle's voice bemoaning the extent of her luggage.

'I tell you, Mother, I don't know where we'll put it all. The boy says there's no space left in the girls' room. She'll have to hang her work clothes in the closet and leave the finery in that fancy trunk.'

'Hush,' Mary warned when she saw Isabella. 'There you are, dear. Come and sit down,' she added, shooing a large tabby off the chair beside her. As the cat yowled in protest, her aunt laughed and returned her attention to pouring tea from the large brown earthenware pot. 'Don't mind Tibbles, he thinks it's his right to sit nearest the range. Now you maak a tay,' she added.

'Sorry?' Isabella frowned.

'Mother means tuck in, eat as much as you can,' Dotty told her.

'Hurry up, I'm starving,' William grunted. Isabella stared at everyone squashed together around the table, quickly brushed the hair-covered seat with her hand, and took her place beside them. A steaming mug was placed in front of her but the thick dark liquid made her stomach heave, and it didn't help when Dotty proffered a plate of sponge cakes spread lavishly with cream and strawberry jam. Forcing a smile, she took the smallest then looked in vain for a knife to cut it with. There didn't appear to be any napkins either. Unaware of her predicament, the others tucked in as if they hadn't seen food for weeks.

'Well, Mother, you've done us proud,' her uncle declared, licking cream from his fingers. 'That'll keep us going til supper. Come on, boys, there's still work to be done.' He got to his feet then noticed Isabella had hardly eaten anything. 'Didn't you like Mother's baking?' he frowned.

'Doesn't do to let good food go to waste,' William said, snatching it from her plate before she could reply.

'Will...,' her aunt began, but she was talking to his departing back. 'Sorry about that. There's more in the pantry if you'd like.' Isabella shook her head.

'Thank you but I'm not really hungry. Perhaps I could freshen up?' she asked, getting to her feet.

'Of course. Dotty, you show Isabella where

everything is. Alice, the teddies need boiling and bashing for supper.'

'You boil and bash teddies?' Isabella exclaimed, her eyes widening in surprise.

'How else do you get mashed spuds?' her aunt asked.

'Spuds? Oh, you mean potatoes,' she smiled.

'Of course. Goodness me, maid, I can see you need an eddy-f'cation,' her aunt tutted.

'But I want to go outside too,' Alice protested, interrupting them.

'Sorry, pet, I need your help. You know Father insists we eat on time,' Mary replied.

'See you later then, Izzie,' Alice sighed.

'Her name's Isabella,' her mother remonstrated.

'But I can't say that so she said I could call her Izzie.' Her aunt looked askance at Isabella who nodded.

'Perhaps I could have my mantle if we're going outside.'

'But it's only a few steps to the yard,' Dotty replied looking surprised.

'Isabella's used to city life, Dotty,' Mary reminded her. 'Do you have any sturdier footwear, dear?' she asked Isabella.

'Sturdier?' Isabella echoed, frowning down at her button boots.

'For outdoor wear,' her aunt elaborated.

'But these are my outdoor boots.'

'Ah. Not to worry, it'll probably be another month before we get any real rain. Gets right muddy then, it does.'

Out in the yard, Isabella looked around for the facilities but could only see a pump and a sprawl of ramshackle buildings.

'That's the privy,' Dotty told her, gesturing towards one of the sheds. Suppressing a shudder, Isabella slipped inside and carefully jammed the door closed with the piece of knotted twine which appeared to act as a bolt. Squinting in the gloom, she froze as she saw two piercing eyes glinting up at her. Then something furry brushed against her legs and with a scream, she staggered outside, an indignant-looking tabby cat flashing past her.

'Oh Izzie, you should see your face,' Dotty giggled.

'Well, how was I to know the cat was lying in wait? I shall never go back in there, ever,' she vowed.

'You'll be crossing your legs for an awfully long time then,' her cousin told her with a shake of her head. 'Bet poor old Tibbles got more of a fright anyhow 'cos that's his hiding place when he gets shooed out of the kitchen. Come on, I'll show you our violets.'

'Goodness, I had no idea you had so much land or grew so many flowers,' Isabella exclaimed as they wandered down the stone path. She seemed to be surrounded by fields of green velvet-leafed plants, many sprouting mauve buds.

''Tis the mild, damp climate. Brings them on a treat,' Dotty smiled. 'And this time of evening when there's moisture in the air you gets to smell them best.'

As the sweet, musky scent wrapped itself around her, she was gripped by a sense of déjà vu, yet she knew she'd never been here before.

'Lovely, isn't it? And definitely an improvement on the smell of those vegetables we grew before.'

'You haven't always grown flowers then?' Isabella asked. Dotty shook her head.

'Father used to farm here but when it went into depression he turned the land over to cultivating the violets that grew wild. Uncle did the same on his land over there,' she explained. Isabella looked to where she was gesturing and could just make out a line of green hedging in the distance. 'It didn't pay too well at first, then they realized there was a good demand for the flowers in London. Men buy them for their ladies to decorate their evening gowns, can you believe?' Dotty exclaimed, raising her brows in amazement.

'They are called corsages and I have worn them myself,' Isabella replied, remembering how Maxwell had purchased some from the flower girl outside Claridge's. Had it really been only the previous day?

'Coo, father said you were used to having money but you must have been filthy rich before...,' Dotty clamped her hand over her mouth. 'Sorry, I wasn't meant to mention it.' Isabella started to say they still were, then remembered her father's disclosure.

'Funny how things change, isn't it?' Dotty said, smiling sympathetically. 'Once Father couldn't even pay his bills and now we have all this,' she cried, spreading her arms out wide. Isabella frowned, surprised her cousin should be content with so little. 'And of course, you being family, we're happy to share it with you,' the girl added.

Isabella stared at her cousin, nonplussed.

Although Dotty meant well, Isabella had no desire to be some kind of charity case. Not wishing to hurt her cousin's feelings, she forced a smile.

'Thank you, that is kind.' Seeking to regain her equilibrium, she turned back towards the flowers where her uncle and cousins were moving between the plants, wielding long sticks.

'What the...,' she began.

'They're hoeing the weeds,' Dotty explained. 'You have to keep them down or they choke the plants.'

'Supper in ten,' Mary called.

'Coo, I'd no idea we'd been out here so long,' Dotty exclaimed. 'Better go, Mother'll be wanting me to take Grandmother's meal in to her.'

'Your grandmother?' Isabella asked.

'Yours too,' Dotty pointed out. 'She lives in the house next door. No doubt you'll get to meet her, though be warned, she's away with the pixies most of the time.'

Isabella stared at Dotty in surprise. Until then, she hadn't even thought about having a grandmother. Would she look like her mama? How wonderful it would be to meet this woman and find out about her.

'Perhaps you could introduce me after supper?' she asked eagerly. Dotty frowned.

'I'll speak to Mother. She'll probably say it'd be best to leave it until Grandmother's having a good day, though they're as rare as hen's teeth.'

'I must meet her before I leave, though,' Isabella insisted.

'But...,' Dotty began. Then, hearing her mother call again, she shrugged.

As they squashed into their seats round the table, a delicious smell wafted from the large pot on the range.

'Here you are, dear,' the woman said, passing her a dish of stew surrounded by a mound of mashed potatoes.

'Goodness me, I shall be enormous if I eat all this,' Isabella protested, then seeing her uncle frown, hastily picked up her knife and fork.

'Mother is a fine cook,' he said, causing her aunt to blush. 'And we need sustenance for our work tomorrow.'

'We don't usually get this much meat, so I likes you coming to live with us,' Thomas piped up.

'Actually, I'm not...,' Isabella began, but her uncle interrupted.

'No talking at the table.' Isabella blinked in surprise. Surely this was the very time for genial conversation? Obediently the others turned their attention to their food and the only noise was the scraping of cutlery on dishes.

'That was very nice, thank you,' Isabella said politely, pushing aside what she couldn't eat.

'Fancy words don't butter no parsnips, Isabella,' her uncle grunted. 'And talking of fancy, there's no room for all your luggage in here, so unpack what you need and we'll store the rest in Grandmother's barn.'

'A barn,' Isabella exclaimed.

'Perhaps her spare room would be better?' Mary ventured.

'I'll help you go through your things, Izzie,' Alice cried. 'I bet you've got lots of lovely dresses.'

'I have,' Isabella agreed thinking of her silks and

chiffons. 'Although I've left many behind in London,' she added seeing the look on her uncle's face. 'If you tell me what you do around here in the evenings, I'll have a better idea of what to unpack. Are there many balls or concerts...?' her voice trailed away as she saw their astonished expressions.

'This be Doulis not London,' William grunted.

'Even so, you must have some form of entertainment,' she persisted.

'We have a harvest hop next month,' Dotty volunteered.

'And the church put on a splendid concert at Christmas,' her aunt chipped in. 'The choir sing lovely.'

'There's the Violet Ball in May,' Dotty added.

'May? But that's months away,' Isabella said, her heart sinking.

'We don't have much time for socializing, what with the long hours we work,' her uncle told her.

'Surely picking a few flowers doesn't take all day,' Isabella replied. Her uncle gave a snort.

'You'll see, Isabella. Market gardening is more than just picking a few flowers, as you put it. It's a way of life. As well as sorting the violets into bunches and packing them up ready for market, there's the cleaning to be done, meals to be cooked.'

'Oh but...,' Isabella began. However, her uncle carried on as if she hadn't spoken.

'And you'll pitch in and help, starting with breakfast in the morning.'

'But I've never cooked anything in my life before,' she frowned.

'Then it's time you learned. When your father sent that communication asking us to take you in, we didn't hesitate.'

'But I'm only staying a short while,' Isabella pointed out. Her uncle gave a long sigh.

'For as long as you are here, you'll help Mother with the chores.' Seeing the challenge in his eyes, something stirred in Isabella.

'Of course, Uncle,' she replied. She'd show him, she thought.

'Now, go and sort some suitable clothes for the morning,' he grunted. 'Come along, boys,' he ordered, going outside.

'Don't worry, my dear, we'll show you what to do,' her aunt told her as the door closed behind them. 'Best stow those fine jewels in your trunk. You don't want them getting dirty or damaged,' she said, pointing to the pearls around Isabella's neck.

That night, sleep eluded Isabella. Although enthralled by her fine gowns and jewellery, her cousins had decided none were suited for life on the flower farm. Reluctantly, she'd packed everything away again and 17-year-old Dotty, who was of a similar height although a little broader, had loaned her a cotton frock and smock. Now they were asleep, their snorts and snuffles disrupting her peace.

She sighed and ran her fingers over the silver locket, the only piece of jewellery not packed away. *Oh Mama,* she wept, *I can hardly believe this tiny cottage is where you were raised, or that Uncle with his fastidious ways was your brother. He is so stern and forbidding while you were always so charming and gentle. Auntie has her own funny way of speaking but has been kind – and welcoming. You should see my cousins, though. William is so hostile and the younger boys, Joseph and Thomas, follow his lead. At least Dotty and Alice are friendly. One good thing to come out of this enforced holiday is that I'll hopefully get to meet your mama in the morning. Before Maxwell comes.* Maxwell! Her heart flipped at the thought of seeing him again. Imagine having to live here permanently like Dotty and Alice. It didn't bear thinking about, she thought, closing her eyes.

Chapter 4

What a frightful noise, Isabella groaned, pulling the cover up over her head. Only it wouldn't reach and the bed was rock-hard beneath her. Frowning, she opened her eyes then blinked in the brightness. Why hadn't the maid drawn her drapes? Then she remembered that she wasn't in her comfortable chamber with its feather bed and sateen eiderdown, but crammed into a poky room, with a lumpy mattress on the floor alongside her cousins. Then she heard the dreadful squawking again but, turning her head, saw she was alone in the room.

Easing herself out of the makeshift bed, she noticed the plain clothes laid out ready for her to wear. Pulling the shift over her head, she grimaced as the coarse material prickled her skin. Just as she was fastening the smock over the top, there was another shrill shriek. Hurrying over to the window, she saw dozens of small birds with glossy blue plumage lined up along the roof of the barn, their long tails wagging as they chattered away to each other. At least they were decently attired, she thought, frowning down at the shabby flaxen dress. Heaven forbid that Maxwell should see her like this, she shuddered, vowing to retrieve at least one of her silks from her trunk before he arrived.

A movement in the gardens beyond the yard caught her eye. Her uncle and William were picking the mauve flowers before placing them into large woven baskets. Goodness, they must have started work early, she thought. Then her hand flew to her mouth for hadn't she been told to help prepare breakfast? Hurrying down to the kitchen, she found her aunt rolling out pastry on the kitchen table.

'Good morning, my dear, did you sleep well?' she asked, looking up and shaking the flour from her hands.

'I did until I was woken by that dreadful din those birds were making. Am I too late to help with breakfast?' Isabella asked.

'Only by about two hours,' her aunt chuckled. 'Dotty said you were out for the count. I expect all that travelling tired you out. Don't look so worried, dear, you can help tomorrow.'

'But Uncle said...,' she began, recalling his stern look the night before.

'Don't worry, Isabella, he might sound fierce but underneath he's as soft as those beloved petals of his. Firm but fair, you'll find him,' she added, seeing Isabella's sceptical look.

'I saw him out in the garden with William, but

where is everyone else?' Isabella asked, staring around the room.

'Joseph's away helping Uncle Bill – that's Frederick's brother – pick the flowers on his land. Alice and Thomas are at school, and Dotty is seeing to Grandmother.'

'Oh yes, Dotty told me she lives next door. I have so much to ask her about Mama. May I call and see her this morning?' she asked eagerly. Her aunt set down her rolling pin.

'Grandmother's not really with us, dear. Hasn't been since the shock. Best leave it until she's having a good day.'

'But Maxwell, my intended, will be arriving to collect me shortly and I must meet her before I leave,' she insisted. Seeing her aunt frown, she smiled. 'I sent him a note explaining I was coming here instead of Italy, you see.'

'And you think he will follow you?'

'Oh yes, he said my happiness is paramount,' she explained, her voice trailing off in case her aunt should think her ungrateful.

'Well, before you go anywhere you must have something to eat, so sit yourself down,' Mary said, scurrying over to the range and lifting a plate from on top of the pan. 'There now, get that down you,' she smiled, setting it in front of her.

'Thank you,' Isabella murmured, staring down at the scramble of bright yellow egg nestling on a bed of ruby-red tomatoes. How could anyone be expected to eat all that, she wondered.

'Don't worry, the hens are laying well and we grow our own fruit and vegetables,' her aunt said, misinterpreting Isabella's look. 'Quite self-sufficient, we are. Uncle Bill reared the pig, so between us we have a goodly supply of everything we need. Those flitches of bacon and ham will see us right through the winter,' she declared, pointing to the beams above the range. Isabella stared up at the ominous dark lumps dangling from iron hooks.

'That's ham?' she asked in surprise for it bore little resemblance to the delicate pink slices she was used to. Her aunt nodded.

''Tis meat we cured from the pig. Bayliss the butcher came and did the necessary, then we all helped joint it. Took ages to clear up the mess after.' Isabella stared down at her plate where red juice from the tomatoes was seeping into the eggs. Stomach churning, she pushed it aside and got to her feet.

'Can I help, Aunt Mary?' she asked.

'Bless you, dear, I can make poverty pie with my eyes closed, we have it that many times,' her aunt smiled as she placed a large dish on the pastry and ran a knife deftly round it.

'What is poverty pie exactly?' Isabella ventured.

'Suppose you could call it leftover pie, really. Anything and everything we can get our hands on gets put into the pie crust. Them swallows had better fly off soon or they'll be going in too,' the woman chuckled.

'Swallows?' Isabella frowned.

'Those birds you heard. They're gathering ready to depart for warmer climes.'

'You mean you eat them?' she asked, staring at the woman incredulously.

'Why, bless you, no. That was just my little joke. Cors, we do bake the odd woodcock or rook but never the swallows or martins. That would bring bad luck for sure. Ah William, picked the flowers already, have you?' she asked, looking up as the boy appeared in the doorway.

'Yep. They're waiting to be bunched. Sleeping Beauty decided to join us, has she?' he asked, scowling at Isabella. Then he noticed the remains of her breakfast. 'And wasting more food, I see. Mother's got enough to do without waiting on you, and Father works hard to...'

'Now William, what did I tell you about making Isabella welcome?' her aunt interrupted. 'Why don't you show her round the violet gardens whilst I find something to go in this pie?' There was a moment's silence then he shrugged.

'Come on then.'

'You will call me when Maxwell arrives, won't you?' Isabella asked. Her aunt gave her a level look.

'Should any visitor come calling for you, you'll be the first to know.'

'Hurry up then, if you're coming,' William grunted. 'There's work to be done.'

'What else do you do, apart from growing violets?' Isabella asked, making an effort to be pleasant as she followed him across the yard.

'Pick, posy and pack 'em. Today's lot are in there having their drink of water,' he said, pointing to the big barn. She gave him a look, certain he was jesting but he continued walking down the path towards the gardens. 'Good job you're wearing decent clothing, 'cos it can get muxy bunching them up ready to take to the station this afternoon.'

'Then what happens tomorrow?' Isabella asked.

'Same again.'

'You mean you do that every day?' she asked incredulously.

'Yep, every single one,' he nodded.

'Surely not at the weekends, though?'

'Yep. 'Tis our livelihood. Flowers don't stop growing 'cos we fancies a day off,' he added, giving her a look that reminded her of his father. 'Cors they need to be perfect so we have to check for signs of disease or pests.'

'Oh, but of course,' she laughed, certain he was teasing this time. She shivered, wishing she'd brought her mantle. Although the sun was shining, there was no warmth in it for it was ridiculously early. Why, there was still dew on the grass. At home, she'd be breaking her fast in bed, although Papa would already have departed for his offices. Poor Papa, how wan he'd looked. She closed her eyes and wished for him to get his affairs sorted soon, so their lives would return to normal.

'Not interesting enough for a vurriner like you, I suppose?' Started from her musing, she realized William was sneering.

'Sorry,' she murmured.

'It don't matter,' he sighed.

'But it does,' she insisted.

'I was saying there's mildew, violet rust and smut to look out for. Not to mention slugs, snails, woodlice, aphids or more likely caterpillars and millipedes this time of year.'

'Goodness,' she murmured, her stomach churning again.

'Not squeamish, are you?' he asked, a gleam sparking in his eye.

'Good heavens, no,' she cried airily.

'Still, it's the blue mice we need to watch for.' He sighed and shook his head. 'Place is covered in them but the trouble is it's time-consuming looking out for them,' he said, hunkering down and lifting the leaves of the nearest plant.

'Can I help?' Isabella asked.

'Not from up there, you can't. Little blighters are the same colour as the flowers so you has to get right up close to spot them. And you wouldn't want to get your hands muxy now, would you?' he scoffed. Muxy? That was the second time he'd used that word, so it must mean mucky, she thought. Determined to prove him wrong, she squatted down beside him and began peering beneath the plants. The leaves felt velvety against her skin as she inhaled the heady fragrance. Suddenly something scampered over her hand and, letting out a scream, she sprang to her feet.

'What's up?' William asked, frowning up at her.

'I think one of those mice was about to attack me,' she gasped.

'Really?' he asked, his mouth twitching as he turned to where she'd been searching. With a loud snort, he got to his feet, hands cupped in front of him.

'It's only a spider, silly, and a black one at that. It's the red ones you have to look out for. They devour the flowers, see.' Feeling stupid, she resumed her search.

'I never knew you could get blue mice,' she told him.

'They be a speciality around here, like the red soil.' Hearing a shout, he jumped to his feet. 'Father's waiting. I'll have to come back later. Just hope the blighters don't eat too many afore then,' he sighed.

'I can stay and look for them,' she offered, eager to atone for her faux pas of the previous day.

'That'd be a right help,' he replied, grinning at her for the first time since she'd arrived.

Feeling happier, Isabella resumed her search. She might not be staying long, but she wanted to get along with her mother's family whilst she was here. Breathing in the sweet, musky fragrance of the violets, she felt that faint memory stir, hover then vanish. Instinctively she knew it had something to do with her mama and this place.

'What on earth are you doing, Izzie?' Startled out of her reverie, she saw Dotty frowning down at her.

'Searching for blue mice,' she replied. 'William had to help Uncle so I offered to look for them. I haven't seen any, though.'

'But Izzie, these are the blue mice,' she laughed, her sweeping gesture encompassing the plants. 'That's what violets are known as round here.'

'But why?' Isabella asked, feeling somewhat foolish.

'When the sea breeze ripples the flower heads, some say they look like little blue mice scampering across the fields. In other parts, they're called shoes and stockings.'

'How strange. And what is a vurriner?' she asked, although she suspected she knew the answer.

'It's what we call incomers round here. Why, William never called you that? Wait til I get my hands on him and Mother'll be cross when she hears,' Dotty declared stoutly.

'Please don't say anything,' Isabella said, straightening up. 'He was getting his revenge for my taking him for a servant.'

'Well, if you're sure,' Dotty shrugged. 'Better brush yourself down then, it's time we were making up the posies and Mother won't want muck everywhere.' Isabella stared at the brown clods clinging to the rough fibres of her dress.

'Oh Dotty, I am sorry,' she cried, shaking out the folds of her skirts. 'I've made your dress all dirty, or should I say muxy.'

'Coo, listen to you,' Dotty laughed. ''Tis only a bit of dung. You're lucky that's the only fertilizer father uses. He swears a bit of nature's natural is all that's necessary to produce good blooms. Along with his tailors' clippings and woollen rags, that is.'

'Tailors' clippings?' Isabella echoed.

'Take a good look between the rows.' Isabella duly studied the ground and saw bits of material and rags among the red soil.

'Goodness,' she murmured. 'Is that to keep the plants warm?'

'Oh, you are funny, Izzie,' Dotty chuckled. 'Come on, Father will go mad if we're not helping Mother.' As Isabella followed her cousin across the yard, she remembered her mission.

'Do you think we could go and see Grandmother before lunch? I must introduce myself before Maxwell arrives,' she explained, thinking she also needed to change into a decent gown. She didn't dare imagine what he would say if he saw her dressed like a peasant from the fields, and a soiled one at that. Dotty shook her head.

'Best leave it for now, she's having one of her dim and daffy days, as we call them. Now, come on,' she urged, hurrying towards the big barn.

'I just need to take a look outside,' Isabella replied. Ignoring her cousin's frown, she made her way down the side path and looked left and right, but the lane was deserted.

'You all right, dear?' her aunt asked, appearing at her side. Isabella forced a smile and nodded. 'Bit early for visitors, I'd have thought,' the woman added perceptively. 'Come and see how we bunch and pack the violets. If you're very good, we might even let you have a go.' Realizing her aunt was trying to make her feel better, she followed the woman over to the big barn.

Inside was cool, with seemingly hundreds and hundreds of violets nestling in big pails, their sweet fragrance permeating the air. Dotty was standing by a long trestle, cutting lengths of raffia from a large roll.

'These have all had a nice drink now, so we'd better start sorting them into bunches,' she said. William hadn't been joking after all, Isabella thought.

'Father and William have gone to collect more boxes,' her aunt told them. 'You show your cousin how we make the posies, Dotty, while I count out the flowers.'

As her aunt reached into the first bucket, Isabella noticed how rough and reddened her hands were.

The woman smiled wryly. 'Occupational hazard, dear.'

'What a delightful fragrance there is in here,' she replied quickly, not wishing to be thought rude. To her surprise her aunt chuckled.

'Wait another ten minutes or so and see if you still think the same. I hope when William showed you round, he explained everything we do.'

'He was most, er, enlightening,' she replied, not daring to look at Dotty. Just then they heard the rumble of wheels outside. Isabella's heart flipped.

'That's Father and William,' Dotty announced, sending Isabella's hopes sinking to her boots. Sure enough, a few moments later the two men appeared, their faces barely visible over the boxes they were carrying.

'This lot should keep us going for a few days,' her uncle declared, depositing the boxes on the floor beside them. Seeing the labels on them, Isabella's eyes widened in shock.

Chapter 5

'You never seen a corset box before?' William snorted.

'Well, I...,' Isabella began. Feeling her cheeks growing hot, she quickly averted her gaze.

'Stop goading your cousin and snap to it, boy,' Frederick interrupted. 'We've to get the rest of them boxes over to Bill's so he can pack his flowers.' He turned to go then frowned down at the pails. ''Tis high time you women were bunching these flowers an' all.'

'You're right there, Father,' Aunt Mary agreed. With another smirk in Isabella's direction, William followed his father outside.

'Shall I begin taking the labels off?' Isabella asked, eager to be of use.

'Why ever would you do that?' her aunt exclaimed. 'Everyone knows them corset boxes contain our violets, so it saves time addressing them. They be the perfect size for packing the flowers into an' all. Right useful it's been, old Mrs Pudge stocking them ready-made foundations in her shop.' Isabella stared at her aunt incredulously. Ready-made foundations? 'Cors they can be a bit hit and miss sometimes,' the woman conceded, mistaking her look.

'Do you wear them?' Dotty asked. Isabella thought of the modish Madame Mai who would stand and scrutinize her curves through half-closed eyes before producing a template cincture from her velvet-lined valise. Carefully she would fashion the garment into shape before encasing Isabella's midriff and lacing it up tightly. Isabella would then have to turn around slowly in front of her and only when Madame was satisfied, would she nod and declare her client's form feminine par excellence.

'Actually, my *corsetière* fits me in the privacy of my bed chamber,' she explained.

'Coo, how the other half live,' Dotty drooled. 'You wait til you have to resort to Pudge's. The changing-room curtains don't reach so you has to keep an eye out for nosy neighbours, and all while you're trying to wriggle into the darned thing,' Dotty grimaced, rolling her eyes dramatically.

'Right that's enough, Dotty,' her mother interrupted. 'If we don't get a move on, we'll miss the train and Father'll go mad. I've counted out the first few bunches so you can show Isabella how we arrange and pack them.' Dotty pouted but duly did as she'd been told.

Isabella watched as she picked up one bunch of the flowers and deftly enclosed them in velvety green leaves.

'They protect the flowers as well as making them smell sweeter, you see,' she explained. 'Then you tie the bunch neatly with raffia to keep the stems straight and place them carefully in one of those boxes Mother has lined. It's important to make sure the first row of heads go on this little pillow like this, see?' Isabella nodded.

'Now you try,' Dotty invited. Isabella began wrapping the foliage round the violets but it wasn't as easy as it looked and her cousin shook her head.

'You have to make sure the flower heads are facing the same way.'

'Oh,' Isabella replied, trying again.

'That's it, now pack the bunch firmly beside the others so they don't get shaken about on the train. They have to look as neat and fresh when they arrive as they do when they leave here,' Dotty told her.

'That's right, Father's built up a good reputation in Covent Garden and it wouldn't do to let him down,' Mary explained. 'We pick, pack and dispatch the same day for freshness, and it's essential that when the men in London open the boxes all they see is the mauve heads of the posies. Good selling, that is.'

'But why do you transport them all the way to London?' Isabella asked the question that had been niggling her.

''Cos of the demand, dear. High demand means better prices. Your uncle can sell them for six pence a bunch up there,' she exclaimed.

'Is that good?' Isabella frowned.

'Good?' her aunt exclaimed. ''Tis a princely sum compared to the penny ha'penny he was getting around here.'

'But if the demand is so great in London, why don't they grow them there?' Isabella asked. Her aunt finished counting her flowers then laid them on the table.

'Violets need good soil and a mild, moist climate, so conditions round here are perfect. The air in London is laden with smoke from the manufactories. And of course, the land there's being taken up with the building of houses and yet more factories. Don't know how people can live crowded together like that,' she sniffed.

'Not all London is like that,' Isabella protested loyally.

'Begging your pardon,' Aunt Mary murmured.

'Coo, you ain't done many, Izzie,' Dotty tutted, setting her full box down on the floor and lifting another onto the table beside her.

'Sorry,' she replied, turning her attention back to the flowers. It didn't matter how hard she tried, though, even when she managed to get the heads facing the same way, her bunches were nothing like as neat as her cousin's. How she wished Maxwell would arrive and take her back to civilization. Remembering the fragrant posy that he'd purchased from the flower seller, she lifted the blooms to her nose.

'Oh, these ones are no good, they have no smell,' she cried. A chuckle behind her made her jump.

''Tis you that's lost your smell girl, not the flowers,' her uncle said. 'Dainty they might be, but they produce ionine which dulls the senses. I have a theory that...'

'Oh, you and your theories, Father,' her aunt interrupted, shaking her head. 'I told you that would happen, didn't I, dear?' her aunt laughed. 'Don't worry, it'll soon come back when you go outside and breathe in the fresh air.'

'Talking of fresh air, Mother, I've been out in it all morning and I'm starving hungry and dying for a brew,' said Uncle Frederick.

'Just let me finish these then I'll go get us something to eat,' her aunt told him, resuming her counting. As her uncle grumped and stomped out of the barn, Isabella turned to her aunt.

'Would you like me to prepare luncheon?' she offered, knowing she'd been slowing their progress.

'That'd be a right help. There's bread, butter and cheese in the back'ouze behind the kitchen. Tomatoes and cucumbers as well.'

Not knowing what the back'ouze was but determined to do something to assist, Isabella hurried indoors. She set the kettle to boil then noticed a little door beside the dresser. Opening it gingerly, she smiled when she saw a scullery similar to one behind their kitchen at home.

She'd found it quite by chance when, as a young girl, she'd dared to explore downstairs. This one was much smaller though it also housed a pantry. The upper shelves were neatly lined with jars of pickled vegetables and bottles of preserved fruits, while on the marble slab below, dishes of butter and cheese glistened gold. On the lower shelf, a basket similar to the ones used for gathering flowers held tomatoes and cucumbers along with potatoes still caked with the red soil she now knew was typical of the area. Her aunt was obviously a good housekeeper, she thought, quickly gathering up the items she needed and going back to the kitchen.

As she carefully cut and buttered the bread, the tabby cat snaked itself around her legs.

'Out of my way, puss,' she chided. She couldn't understand why a pet was allowed in the kitchen. It wasn't hygienic, with all those long hairs. Cook wouldn't stand for it, she knew. Yet, as it stared hopefully up at her with bright amber eyes, she felt her heart soften and couldn't resist letting a sliver of cheese drop to the floor. The animal snapped it up then purred contentedly at her feet while she finished preparing their meal. Scooping up the crumbs in her smock, she went to the doorstep and threw them out for the birds. How she wished Maxwell would arrive now, for if they were to be married it would be good for him to see how proficient she was at running a household. The thought sent her hurrying to the front gate.

There was no sign of his carriage, though, and she wondered what could be delaying him. Perhaps he'd stopped off at her home and would have news of her papa. Dear Papa, she hoped he was getting his business sorted. Retracing her steps, she spotted a cluster of little mauve heads peering out of the grass. Impulsively, she bent and picked a few of the violets to decorate the table. As their musky scent engulfed her, she couldn't help smiling. Her aunt was right, their desensitizing effect hadn't lasted long. Hurrying back indoors, she arranged them in a jug and placed it in the centre of the table. She'd just made the tea when her uncle came in followed by the others.

'It's not Sunday, you know,' he exclaimed, frowning at the cloth on the table. Her aunt gave him a nudge, then smiled.

'You've made everything look lovely, Izzie.'

'Thank you,' she replied, proffering the plate of sandwiches.

'What's these fancy bites?' William snorted. 'And since when do we have bread without crusts?'

'Don't worry William, they weren't wasted,' she assured him. 'I scattered them outside for the birds. And I made finger sandwiches because the bread was too crumbly to cut into quarters.'

'What on earth...,' her uncle spluttered, lifting the top layer of bread. ''Tis only measly bits of cucumber. Where's me cheese?'

'Here, Uncle,' Isabella replied, pointing to another plate where golden cubes decorated with slivers of red tomato nestled on crackers. 'And here's your tea,' she added, passing him a china cup.

'Pah, this thing holds no more than a thimble. Where's me mug? And what's this doing in me drink?' he spluttered, fishing out a slice of fruit with his fingers.

'You said you were parched, Uncle, so I made lemon tea. It's more refreshing than milk, I find.'

'Oh, you do, do you?' he muttered as William gave another snort.

'I'll take Grandmother's in to her,' Dotty said, hastily setting plates and cups onto a tray. 'And I'll have mine in there with her.'

'Like as not she'll throw it back at you when she sees what's on offer,' William scoffed.

'I don't understand what's wrong, Uncle,' Isabella said, frowning down at the table. 'This is how they serve it at Claridge's.' As William rocked with mirth, her aunt shot him a reproving look.

'You'll have to forgive these filling-stines, Isabella,' she said, patting her hand. 'You've made it all look very nice, dear. It's a fine treat for me to have my meal prepared, and I for one am grateful.' She took a sip of her tea and sighed. 'And you're right, this lemon is reviving. 'Tis a long time since I sat down to such a pretty table. Those flowers set my best cloth off a treat.'

'Flowers is for selling not prettying up the meal table,' her uncle grunted, helping himself to a handful of sandwiches.

As silence descended, so did Isabella's spirits. Not wishing to enrage her uncle further, she nibbled on a cracker. The sooner she went home the better, for it appeared she could do nothing right, she thought, blinking back the tears that threatened. There was no way she was letting them see how much they'd upset her.

'Grandmother said that was the best food she's eaten in ages,' Dotty announced, breezing back into the room. 'And she would appreciate more elegant morsels like that in future, please,' she added, giving Isabella a conspiratorial smile.

'Pah,' her uncle snorted, getting to his feet. 'Come on, boy. Some of us have work to do, money to earn.'

'Yeah, some of us understand the value of money,' William snorted, following after him.

'What did I do wrong?' Isabella asked, turning to her aunt. The woman smiled.

'Nothing, dear. Absolutely nothing.'

'But Uncle was really worked up,' she frowned.

'I don't think it was just because you gave him sandwiches without crusts or lemon tea in a dainty cup. Something else is bothering him. Don't know what, but like as not he'll spill the seeds in his own time.'

'But what about William?'

'Coo, take no notice of him,' Dotty told her. 'He's so anxious for Father's approval he copies everything he says and does. Grandmother really tucked into her food, you know. She ate more than usual, too. Quite perky she was when I left her.'

'Then perhaps now would be a good time for me to be introduced? I really do want to meet her before I leave,' Isabella asked, brightening at the thought of seeing her mama's own mama. Her aunt gave her a level look.

'Very well, but be warned, she drifts in and out of the present world very quickly. Dotty, you've just got time to clear the dishes before collecting Thomas and Alice from school.'

'Dotty dishes, that's me,' the girl sighed good-naturedly as she began gathering up their plates.

Butterflies of excitement fluttered in Isabella's stomach as, smoothing down her smock, she followed her aunt outside. A wooden gate led from one back yard into the other, beyond which a sea of violets rippled in the breeze.

'Goodness, more flowers,' she exclaimed. 'Who looks after all these?'

'We do, dear. Father and William will be picking those first thing tomorrow ready for market. It's a never-ending job but it keeps a roof over our heads and pays the bills.'

Recalling how she'd told her uncle that picking a few flowers couldn't possibly take all day, Isabella groaned. Only now was she beginning to understand the extent of their business.

Unaware of Isabella's thoughts, her aunt opened the back door and beckoned her inside.

'Cooee, only me, Mother,' she called, but there was no answer. 'Might be asleep,' she added, leading the way through the kitchen and into the room behind. Curious, Isabella peered around. As in her aunt's home, although the furniture had definitely seen better days, everywhere was spotlessly clean. Orange flames flickered in the grate, brightening the gloom, but curiously the hearth was enclosed by an iron guard fixed to the wall on either side. As her eyes adjusted to the dim light, she spotted the old woman curled up in a comfy chair. She had a rug over her knees and was staring fixedly into the fire, her halo of white curls bobbing up and down as if she was talking to someone.

'Hello, Mother. I've brought Isabella to see you,' her aunt said cheerily.

‘How do you do, Grandmama. I’m so pleased to meet you.’ Excitement bubbled up inside Isabella’s chest as she waited. Slowly, the woman turned her head and stared at her through dark, rheumy eyes.

‘So, you’ve come back then?’ she murmured.

‘Pardon?’ Isabella frowned. ‘I’ve never been here before, Grandmama.’

‘Knew no good would come of all that gallivanting,’ the woman continued regardless. ‘And what you done to your hair? Looks like you’ve rinsed it in clotted cream.’

‘But I…,’ she began.

‘Lovely dark curls you was blessed with. Never happy with what you had, though, was you?’ she muttered. Then her eyes closed and she began to snore.

Chapter 6

‘Come on, dear, no good us staying any longer. She’s lost in her own world again, bless her,’ her aunt explained. With a last despairing look at the old lady, Isabella allowed herself to be led from the room. ‘’Tis sad, but there we are,’ the woman added, carefully closing the door behind them.

‘How long has she been that way?’ Isabella asked, blinking back tears of disappointment and frustration as they made their way back to the adjoining cottage.

‘Since before I came here. Never known her

much different, though she does have the odd good day. There, you's all shook up,' she murmured, her eyes darkening with concern. 'Sit yourself down and I'll set the kettle to boil. A strong cup of tea, that's what you need. I did warn you Mother drifted in and out of life.'

'But she said that I'd come back, yet I've never been here before,' Isabella whispered, sinking into the chair closest to the range.

'I'm thinking she mistook you for her daughter. Father said you has the daps.'

'Pardon?' Isabella frowned.

'It means you has the look of yer mother at that age.'

'But Mama had dark hair.'

'It sounded as if Mother thought she'd lightened it? Oh, I don't know, I'm only guessing.'

'What was my mama like? I was only tiny when she died and I don't remember much about her.'

'That's sad,' her aunt sighed. 'I'm afraid I can't help you, though, for it was backalong and she'd already moved away by the time I met your uncle.'

'But he must have told you something about her?' Isabella persisted, wiping away the tears of frustration that were now coursing down her cheeks. Her aunt patted her hand then looked relieved as the kettle began to whistle.

'You'll have to ask your uncle, 'twer his sister,' she added, jumping to her feet and pouring water into the pot. 'Besides, 'tis not my place to be scandalmongering.'

'Scandalmongering?' Isabella repeated, staring at her in surprise. 'You make it sound as though Mama had skeletons in the cupboard.'

‘Skeletons? That’s a funny thing to be talking about over afternoon tea,’ her uncle said, appearing in the doorway. ‘Just came in for my hat before taking the flowers to Starcross station. Running late today,’ he added staring pointedly at Isabella. ‘You all right, girl?’ he asked, his voice softening when he saw her damp cheeks.

‘We’ve been in to see Mother but she was away with the fairies,’ her aunt explained. ‘Isabella was asking me about your sister.’

‘Ah, I see. Well girl, how’s about coming with me to the station and we can have a chat?’ he asked Isabella, snatching his hat from the hook and placing it firmly on his head.

‘Oh, yes please,’ Isabella replied, brightening at the thought of getting answers about her mama.

‘Best get your shawl and bonnet, it gets nippy when the sea breeze blows in.’

‘Yes, of course,’ she said, jumping to her feet and going up to the room she was sharing with Dotty and Alice.

Taking out her things from the closet, she grimaced down at the smock and shapeless dress she was wearing. Hoping the mantle would cover most of it, she threw it around her shoulders before squinting into the fly-spotted mirror to tie the ribbons on her bonnet. The murmur of voices rose from downstairs, but she couldn’t make out what was being said.

It was evident she’d been the topic of conversation for as soon as she came back into the kitchen, they fell silent.

‘Ready then?’ he asked, seizing the violets from the jug on the table and thrusting them through the hole in his lapel.

'Why do you do that?' she asked.

'What, wear these flowers?' he asked.

'And that funny hat?' she added, then clamped her hand over her mouth.

'I should think you would look embarrassed, girl,' he rebuked, the twinkle in his eyes belying his stern manner.

''Tis the mark of Father's trade,' her aunt told her. 'Diehard the undertaker wears a black topper, Bunty the baker his tall white one, and your uncle wears his straw hat. Everyone recognizes them then, see?'

'And the violets let them know what you sell?' Isabella smiled, gesturing towards his buttonhole.

'That's it, girl. And if we don't hurry we'll miss the train then no flowers will get sold. Come on.'

She followed her uncle outside where William was loading the last of the boxes onto the trap.

'Why you all dolled up like a dog's dinner?' he scowled.

'Isabella's coming to the station with me today so you can get on with the hoeing while we're gone,' her uncle told him in a voice that brooked no argument. Clearly put out, William shot Isabella another glare.

'See you later, William,' she said, smiling sweetly at him. 'Don't forget to watch out for those blue mice.'

'Come along, girl,' her uncle called. Mindful of the stacked boxes, she gingerly climbed up onto the cart. 'Right, Silver, get a move on, we're running behind time,' he called. As the old donkey plodded placidly out into the lane, Isabella turned towards him.

'Why do you call him that? I mean he's grey and moth-eaten...,' her voice trailed away as she realized that once again, she was in danger of appearing rude.

'Full of questions, aren't ye, girl? 'Tis like this. When farming went into decline, I had to sell me horses to pay the bills. Now, you can't bring up a family on fresh air, so I decided to have a go at growing and selling them violets. Did it locally at first but then heard I could get a better price in London.'

'Auntie was telling me about that earlier,' Isabella nodded.

'Right,' he nodded. So, I needed a means of getting them to the station. By chance, I bumped into a man taking this poor creature to the knacker's yard. Did a deal, and for a few coppers I got myself a donkey and he got himself a new life. Reckoned it was our silver-lining day, didn't we, old boy?' he chuckled, leaning forward and patting the donkey's flanks, prompting a loud bray.

'He sounds like he's responding to you,' she laughed.

'That's 'cos he is. Understand each other perfectly, Silver and me, which is more than can be said for some humans round these parts,' he muttered, lapsing into silence.

As they rumbled along, Isabella glanced at her uncle from under the brim of her bonnet. Clearly appearances were deceptive, for beneath his bluff exterior beat a soft heart. Could that be why her father had asked him to look after her whilst he was sorting out his business affairs? She wondered how he was getting on, for already she missed him dreadfully, Maxwell too.

The trap lurched, breaking into her thoughts and she grabbed at the wooden strut as the donkey turned left and began descending a steep hill. To one side was an orchard underplanted with the little mauve flowers that were so abundant around these parts. The branches were devoid of fruit, the leaves the golden hue of autumn.

'Best plums in Devon come from they trees,' her uncle declared, tapping into her thoughts. 'Mother makes a fair few tarts with them, not to mention jars of jam.' Thinking he was referring to her grandmother, Isabella stared at him in surprise then she remembered that was what he called his wife. They certainly had strange ways in this part of the world, she thought, blinking in surprise as a church rose majestically before them. Then she glimpsed a row of headstones to one side and, although she knew her mama wasn't buried there, she shivered.

'Someone treading on yer grave?' her uncle chuckled, as she pulled her mantle tighter round her. 'Be back in the sunshine again soon,' he added. Sure enough, moments later they were out of the shade, passing pretty pink cottages that were spaced further apart than those she'd seen the previous day.

'How do they get the walls that hue?' she asked, thinking how lovely it would be to paint them.

'Gives it a wash of lime mixed with pig's blood,' her uncle told her, laughing as she wrinkled her nose. Then she noticed ornamental birds staring down at her from their thatch.

'Goodness,' she gasped.
'Clever, eh?' her uncle said, seeing her fascination. 'Started when a thatcher decided to put his mark, a biddle – that's beetle to you – on a roof he'd finished. Before long, others were asking him to fashion birds to denote their dwellings. Some think it pretentious but each to their own,' he shrugged.
'Perhaps you should have some blue mice on yours,' she joked.
'Ah, the boy been teasing you, has he? Don't you let him niddle you, girl, it'll do him good to have someone stand up to him. The Sod.'
'Pardon?' Isabella gasped, staring at him in surprise. Certainly, William had been a pain but he hadn't really been that bad. Then she realized her uncle was gesturing ahead.
'That's what they call this harbour. 'Tis the only one in the whole of the country to be on the inside of a railway line,' her uncle told her, grinning knowingly at her expression. Clearly, he'd sensed the atmosphere between William and herself, but before she could pass comment, he was speaking again. 'Now breathe in some more of that ozone, girl, you've got a fair pallor about you this afternoon.'
Isabella gazed out over the expanse of shimmering blue-green water which was flowing out through a tunnel under the railway. Nearby, weatherbeaten fishermen were unloading the day's catch from their boats and stacking the boxes onto the sea wall while gulls swooped and squawked hopefully overhead. It was a world away from the hustle and bustle of the city and for the first time

since she'd arrived, she felt herself relax. She watched as a group of small children, string dangling from sticks, wading in the shallow waters, and wondered if her mama had played here. Just as she turned to ask her uncle, she heard voices calling to him.

'Artnoon, Fred.' Two older men who were sitting on the wall outside an inn raised their jugs of ale in greeting.

'Jim, Ern,' her uncle called, drawing to a halt. 'This is my niece, Isabella.'

'Oh ah,' they chorused, giving her an appreciative look.

'Fancy name for a fancy lady. Heard you'd come to live in the village,' Ern replied, his grey beard bobbing up and down as he spoke.

'Actually, I'm just visiting,' she replied. As the two men raised their brows sceptically, her uncle cleared his throat.

'And it's a pleasure to have my niece here, for however long she decides to stay.'

'She be the spit of your Ells apart from her blonde hair and blue eyes, of course. Suppose that came from 'im,' Jim said, giving a toothless grin. Isabella blinked, trying to associate the appellation with her glamorous mother, Eleanora. Apart from anything else, her father had hazel eyes. Maybe the man's memory was failing. He was old, after all.

'Ah, now Ellie were some looker. No wonder she had all the lads...,' Ern began, keen to continue the tale.

'Time we were on our way or we'll miss the train,' her uncle cut in quickly.

'Heard Furneaux's turned his land over to the

flower growing now,' Jim grinned.

'Be competition for you, eh Fred?' Ern added, his eyes bright with mischief. Isabella saw her uncle's lips tighten but he wasn't about to be drawn.

'Enjoy your drink, gentlemen,' he said, raising his hat.

'Oh ah,' they chorused and promptly returned their attention to their ale.

Her uncle was silent as they resumed their journey, but Isabella was bursting with curiosity.

'How come everyone round here knows who I am?' she asked. He shrugged.

'That's country living for you. News flies quicker than the pigeons.'

'But they thought I was staying,' she persisted.

'Thinks they knows everything that goes on around here. And what they don't, they make up. Gives them something to chat about. Look, there's the open sea over there,' he said, gesturing to their right. 'Be on t'other side of the railway line now.' Realizing he was trying to divert her attention but determined to get some answers to her questions, she turned to face him.

'What was Mama like?'

'Well now,' he murmured. 'She were lively and inquisitive, like yourself.'

'But do I look like her? Grandmother said the strangest thing earlier,' she began.

'Ah, she often do,' he agreed.

'She said I must have rinsed my hair in clotted cream. Auntie thought she'd mistaken me for Mama and it got me wondering. Don't you think it's strange she had dark colouring when I'm fair and have blue eyes?' she asked. He gave her a considering look then shrugged.

'Offspring can take on the colouring of either parent.'

'Yes but...,' she began, about to pursue the subject when she saw a carriage heading their way. Maxwell's was similar, she thought, her heart flipping happily. But even as she leaned forward in her seat, it veered off to the right.

'Oh,' she gasped. Her uncle drew his brows together.

'Something wrong, girl?'

'That carriage, if it's Maxwell, he's gone the wrong way,' she cried.

'Driver's bound to know where he'd be going. Anyhow, that's the visitant route to Powderham Castle,' he replied.

'Oh, I see,' she said despondently.

'If the Earl of Devon is entertaining, it might be an idea to see if his guests want posies for their ladies' fancy frocks,' he muttered, oblivious to her frazzled emotions. 'Got to up the stakes if Furneaux's muscling in on my business.'

Isabella hardly heard him for she was peering along the lane where the carriage had turned off. Already it was just a speck in the distance and her heart sank. Obviously it wasn't Maxwell. Why was he taking so long? Perhaps she should pen him another letter. She could write to dear Papa too. He'd be pleased to know she'd arrived safely.

'Nearly there,' her uncle said, breaking into her thoughts. As the trap slowed, she noticed a peculiar-looking red building towering above them. She was about to ask what it was, when the blast of a whistle sounded. 'Come on, Silver,' he urged, tugging on the rein. As they juddered to a halt in front of the station, two men, smart in their railway uniforms, ran over and began unloading the trap.

'You're late today, Fred. Train's almost here.'

'Been one of them days, Den,' he replied, jumping down to help.

'Bill's flowers are already on the platform. Said you should drop by later. Got something important to tell you, apparently. Probably be about Furneaux and his new venture.'

'Carry on like this and we'll have to put on a train specially for the violets,' the other man chuckled as he lifted the last of the boxes onto his trolley.

The rumble of the approaching engine galvanized them into action and they pushed their loads towards the platform. There was a hiss of brakes and once more Isabella found herself enveloped in a cloud of steam. When it had cleared, she saw all three men had disappeared, leaving her alone in the trap.

Chapter 7

How ill-mannered, Isabella thought, staring around the empty yard. She looked up at the strange-looking building they'd passed earlier and decided that rather than sit waiting, she'd take a closer look. It was quite unlike anything she'd seen before. The walls were built from large blocks of dark red stone with light grey surrounds picking out the window and door openings. Her hands itched to get it all down on paper and, not for the first time that afternoon, she wished she had her watercolours with her. Then she noticed the tall, ornate square tower on the far side of the building and stepped back to see the top of it.

'Ouch,' cried a voice. Spinning round, she saw a young man hopping up and down on one foot. He was wearing a brown high-button sack coat over a waistcoat and sporting a soft cap on his dark hair.

'Oh goodness, I am so sorry,' she cried.

'Don't worry, I expect the infirmary can mend it,' he sighed, gingerly touching his foot to the ground.

'Is it that bad?' she gasped. He looked at her wryly then gave a cheeky grin.

'Not really,' he admitted, mischief glittering in his green eyes. 'It's not often I capture the sympathy of a pretty young lady so I thought I'd capitalize on it. Only you looked so anxious, I couldn't keep up the pretence.'

'I'm sorry for stepping back on you but I was curious about this strange building.'

'Then please let me make amends for my teasing by telling you something about it,' he offered.

'Oh, would you?' she cried. 'I'm only visiting the area and would love to know what it's for.'

'It is a remarkable structure. You will have heard of the great engineer, Isambard Kingdom Brunel, of course?' he asked, looking at her for confirmation.

'Indeed,' she agreed, not wishing to appear ignorant.

'Well, he designed the Atmospheric Railway that originally ran along these parts, and this building with the Italianate tower you were admiring was one of the pumping stations. The pumps in there pushed air through pipes to move the carriages along.'

'Goodness. You said originally, though. Do they not use it anymore?' she asked, eager to appear intelligent.

'Alas, the local rats developed a taste for the leather and grease which formed the seals in the pipes.'

'Rats?' she shuddered, pulling her mantle tighter round her.

'Yep, gobbled them up faster than they could be replaced, so that was the end of that, as it were. This building is all that remains.'

'And splendid it is, too. Thank you so much for enlightening me,' she told him.

'My pleasure,' he said, his eyes twinkling as he perfected a bow. 'You said you were visiting. Might I enquire how long you'll be staying here in Starcross, Miss, er?'

Before she could respond, she heard her uncle shout. Turning quickly, she saw he was sitting in the trap gesturing impatiently for her to join him. Following her gaze, her companion opened his mouth to say something, but she cut in quickly.

'Sorry, I must go,' she said. 'Thank you again for the fascinating lesson,' she murmured before hurrying over to her uncle.

'What the 'ell was you doing talking to young

Furneaux?' he growled, as she climbed up beside him.

'Oh, is that who he was? He was kind enough to explain about the pumping station, Uncle. Do you know...,' she began.

'Stay away from him, you hear?' her uncle interrupted. 'Bad as his father, he is,' he spat.

'Excuse me...,' she began.

'That's an order, Isabella,' he added, tugging on the reins. As the donkey began to move, she stared at her uncle in astonishment.

'Papa would never speak to me like that.'

'Well, maybe he should have, then you'd be more worldly-wise,' he growled.

'How dare you,' she spluttered. 'You can be sure that when Maxwell arrives, he will take issue with you.'

'Oh, he will, will he? Well, I'll look forward to hearing what this Maxwell has to say, if by any miracle he turns up, that is.'

'Stop this minute,' she ordered, but he ignored her. 'I said stop,' she repeated, wanting to be away from this odious man. When he still disregarded her wishes, she peered over her shoulder, hoping to catch the attention of the agreeable young man, but he had disappeared. She stared down at the road passing beneath, wondering if she dared jump.

'Settle yourself down, maid, we're in for a skatt,' her uncle said, pulling his hat further down over his head.

'A what?' Barely had she asked the question when the first drops of rain began to fall. As it became heavier, she stared around for some kind of hood, but although the boxes were protected by a canvas cover, the rest of the cart was open to the elements. She turned to her uncle but he stared resolutely ahead. Simmering with rage, she gazed out over the water where steely clouds now merged with the grey sea. A gust of wind tugged at her bonnet and she put a hand to her head. Her uncle oblivious, or more likely not bothered, continued staring fixedly ahead and the journey back to the cottage was both a cold and silent one. She crossed her fingers and hoped that Maxwell would be waiting for her. However, when they turned into the lane, there was no carriage in sight and her heart sank to her saturated boots. She would write to him tonight.

'Oh my, you're drenched to the bone,' her aunt tutted, pulling Isabella into the warmth of the kitchen. 'Get out of those wet things and warm yourself by the fire before you catch a chill.'

'Stop fussing, Mother,' her uncle said, throwing his hat onto the hook by the door. ''Tis her own fault she took a soaking. If she hadn't spent time blethering with young Furneaux we'd have been back before the weather broke.'

'But I wasn't...,' Isabella began, then seeing his grim expression sighed. 'If you'll excuse me, I've had a busy day and wish to retire for the night.'

''Tain't six o'clock yet,' William scoffed. Ignoring him, Isabella made for the stairs, but halfway up she heard him say: 'Don't know why she's tired, it's not as if she packed many flowers from what I can see. And as for that sparrow food she prepared, no wonder me stomach thinks me throat's been cut.'

By the time she reached her room, Isabella was shivering so violently she could hardly take off her wet clothes. Throwing herself onto the mattress, she huddled under the thin bed cover and let the tears fall. How she wished she was safely back at home where Maisie would be filling her bathtub with hot water and setting out rose-scented soap petals from the cut-glass jar on the shelf. Then she would sink into her soft feather bed and wait for a bowl of Cook's consommé to be brought to her on a tray. Instead she'd spent a horrible day in this godforsaken place where, even though she'd tried to help, nothing she did was right. She hated it here and she hated Uncle and William as well. *Oh Maxwell, where are you?*

Then a thought struck her so forcefully, she sat bolt upright. Instead of writing, why didn't she make her own way home now? If she slipped out whilst the family were having supper, they wouldn't even notice she'd gone. Excitement flooding through her, she made to climb out of bed but a flash of lightning lit up the sky. It was closely followed by a deafening clap of thunder that seemed to shake the whole cottage. She'd hated storms since the violent one they'd experienced the night her dear mama had died. All thought of going outside disappeared as, stifling a scream, she pulled the cover over her head and closed her eyes.

She must have slept, for the next thing she knew Dotty was shaking her awake.

'Come on, Izzie, Father's called a meeting.'

'What time is it?' she muttered.

'Almost five o'clock.' Isabella groaned and

closed her eyes again.

'Please get up, Izzie, or Father'll get mad,' Alice pleaded.

'Yes, do hurry and dress,' Dotty urged. 'I've got your clothes here. They're dry now as I put them on the pulley above the range overnight.' Reluctantly Isabella opened her eyes again and saw the two girls were already dressed, their hair neatly braided. How could they look so awake at this unearthly hour, she wondered?

'All right, I'm coming,' she muttered, taking the proffered garments. Clambering from the mattress, Isabella winced and put her hand to her back. She felt stiffer than the housekeeper's starched petticoats. She couldn't bear to sleep on the floor any longer.

'Girls.' At the sound of their father's roar, Dotty and Alice fled down the stairs. Not wishing to fuel his anger, Isabella quickly donned the coarse clothes, tidied her hair and followed them.

'Are you feeling better, my dear? Come and sit by me, Father's holding a family meeting.' Although her aunt was smiling, Isabella noticed she looked strained.

'Well, if it's a family matter, I'll leave you to it,' she replied.

'Like it or not, you are part of this family now, so sit yourself down. That's an order not an option,' her uncle barked, seeing her hesitate.

'But I've told you, Uncle, I'm only staying until Maxwell comes for me.'

'Not exactly hurrying himself, is he?' William sneered.

'That's enough, William,' her aunt said,

shooting him a stern look. 'Right Isabella, I've poured you a mug of tea and we're having brewis to break our fast. We can eat whilst Father tells us his plan.' Reluctantly, Isabella took her place, but as she stared at the soggy mess in the bowl, her stomach turned over.

'Maybe not what you're used to, girl, but it'll save Mother cooking whilst we're extra busy, so eat up,' her uncle instructed, giving her a stern look. 'Right, pay attention, everyone.' Isabella felt a rush of relief as he turned to address the others. Picking up her spoon, she moved the mush around the dish to give the impression of eating. Not that her uncle was watching, for he was in full flood.

'As you know, Furneaux's going into competition with us. I were right cross when I heard but, as your Uncle Bill pointed out, the man has as much of a right to turn his land over to flower growing as us. We all have a living to earn, after all. But I've worked darn hard to get this business up and running and don't intend to lose my market share.'

'Market share, that's good, Father,' William chortled. 'Market garden, market share, get it?'

'Very funny, boy, but it won't be no laughing matter if the price drops, which it will if the market's saturated with violets. 'Tis all about supply and demand, and from today we are going to double our efforts to provide Covent Garden with the finest blooms at the best price. By the time Furneaux's violets are ready for sale, we will have proved to the buyers that Northcott's can fulfil their needs.'

'But we work hard enough as it is, Father,' Joseph said, waving his spoon in the air.

'I know, boy, and that's why your uncle and I have come up with a plan. But in order for it to succeed, each of you must play your part.' He took a sip of his tea then stared at each of them in turn. 'From now on, we will be working towards doubling our output.'

'But Father…,' Mary began but her husband held up his hand to silence her.

'No buts. As I said, Bill and I have worked out a way. First of all, Joseph, you will team up with your uncle and as it's too far for you to travel there and back each day, you'll move into his cot. Afore you complain, Mother, Bill will bring Joseph for Sunday lunch each week, so you will see him then.' From the grin that met this statement, Isabella guessed that Joseph was happy with the news.

'William, you'll turn the rest of your grandmother's garden over to growing violets. There's a large patch down the bottom going wild and we might even dig up her yard, seeing as how she never uses it now.' He leaned forward and patted William's hand. 'I'm putting you in charge of this part of the business, so it's a good chance for you to prove yourself.

'Dotty, as well as taking violets to the big house on Thursdays then selling the rest in town, you will attend the Saturday market as well.'

'Yes, Father,' Dotty smiled, and again Isabella could see his idea had gone down well.

'Perhaps I could come with you,' Isabella offered, her spirits lifting at the thought of escaping for a few hours.

'Don't take two of you,' her uncle growled. 'You'll stay here and help Mother.'

'But...' She looked at Dotty, hoping she would concur, but the girl stared quickly down at her dish.

'If we've all got to do extra work, does this mean Alice and me don't have to go to school no more?' Thomas asked hopefully.

'No, it does not. Eddy-f'cation's everything,' his mother said.

'Didn't do William any good, did it?' Alice grinned. 'He can't read nor write proper, Izzie,' she told her gleefully. Isabella stared at William in surprise.

'Least I can add up, and the word is *properly* anyway,' William retorted, but Isabella could tell by the way his face flushed that he was embarrassed.

'That's enough,' his father said, banging his fist down on the table. 'We've got enough to do without bickering. Alice and Thomas, you will get up an hour earlier every day to help Mother with the chores then pick the extra flowers we'll be growing.' This was met with groans but their father ignored them.

'Mother, Dotty, and you girl – for the time you are here,' he added as Isabella opened her mouth to protest, 'will have extra flowers to pack. And as Dotty will be out more, you can watch how Mother prepares our meals then take over in the kitchen. I'm sure even you can manage to make brewis,' he added.

'What?' Isabella gasped.

'Of course she can, Father,' her aunt said quickly, smiling encouragingly at Isabella.

'As long as you remember to use the crusts and not just the bread,' William smirked. Knowing it would be foolish to retaliate, Isabella bit her tongue. When he realized she wasn't rising to the bait, William turned to his father. 'So, what will you be doing then?'

'Managing the extra orders and invoices. Then after supper I'll spend the evenings propagating and bringing on fresh plants. Give Furneaux something to really compete with. Now, to work,' he said, getting to his feet and pulling on his hat.

Isabella watched him go then glanced at the clock. It wasn't yet 5.30 a.m. and yet she felt as if she'd been up for ever. She'd go upstairs and write to Maxwell and Papa. There was no way she could stay here with this strident man and his strict routine. As for the food, she thought, glaring down at her bowl ... why, she'd seen Cook put better offerings in the pig swill.

Chapter 8

As the family carried out their father's wishes, knowing her presence on the small holding was temporary, Isabella tried her best to fit in. While she applauded her uncle's determination and tenacity, she was still smarting from the way he'd spoken to her on their journey back from Starcross. If he noticed her coolness he ignored it, treating her the same as the others during the day, then disappearing through the door at the end of the barn after supper each evening.

'What's through there?' Isabella asked her aunt as they stood side by side bunching up the violets a few days later. Dotty, wearing her best bonnet, had departed earlier for the big house, a large willow basket filled with flowers over her arm, and the letters she'd promised Isabella she'd post in her pocket.

'That's Father's domain,' she replied. 'He's bringing on a new strain of plant. Between you and me, it's a bit risky financially but very exciting. He's keeping it under his hat so nobody's allowed inside.'

'You don't mind him taking a chance with your money?' Isabella asked, thinking of all the shabby things in the house that needed replacing. The woman chuckled.

'Once Father gets something in his mind, there's no stopping him. He's no fool, though. Put everything into this market garden, he has, and if he wants to expand the range of flowers he can offer, who am I to stand in his way?' Isabella nodded and concentrated on tying up the posies, but as she worked her mind was busy processing what her aunt had told her. Finally, she had to ask the question that was uppermost in her mind.

'Auntie, when I arrived here, I handed Uncle an envelope from Papa that I'm guessing contained money for my keep?' Her aunt stared at her in surprise.

'He never mentioned it, but then he's had a lot on his mind,' she frowned. 'Not that we expected anything for having you here. You're family, after all.'

'Thank you, Auntie,' she replied, touched by the woman's kindness. The more she thought it about it, though, the more she was convinced that the envelope would have contained money. Quite a lot too, judging by the thickness of it. Could her uncle have kept it for himself? Perhaps to purchase these new flowers?

'Oh, well done, dear. You're really getting the hang of this now, aren't you?'

Isabella stared down at the posy she'd been fashioning and, with a jolt, realized it was true. All the flower heads were facing the same way and she'd even managed to tie their stems neatly with raffia. Feeling ridiculously pleased by her aunt's praise, she beamed and started on another one. It was peaceful in the barn and, as the boxes filled up, she was proud to see the progress she was making. All thought of money forgotten, she let out a sigh of contentment.

'Enjoying yourself?' her aunt asked.

'I am actually,' Isabella replied, surprised to find it was true. 'It's so calm in here, although I still find it funny that you can't smell any of the flowers after a while.'

'Father might have a scientific reason for that, but I like to think it's nature playing one of her jokes on us. I must admit, it's a good time for thinking. Flowers don't criticize or judge, do they?' her aunt said, giving Isabella a wink. 'And it's rewarding to see the results of your labours, isn't it?'

'It is, but you must get tired with everything else you have to do. What with looking after your house and Grandmother's, taking care of the family and teaching me to cook, you never have a moment to yourself, Aunt Mary.'

'And why would I want one? My family and home mean everything to me, Isabella,' she said.

'But you don't have any hired help,' Isabella protested. Her aunt smiled.

'It might surprise you to know that I take a pride in running both homes and bringing up the children. I was raised in an orphanage, you see.' Isabella stared at her aunt in surprise. 'Oh, we were well looked after, but with thirty of us sharing a dormitory and all our clothes cast-offs and hand-me-downs, I soon learned what mattered in life. Having my own home and family is like a dream come true.'

'Goodness, I never realized,' Isabella murmured, her eyes widening in shock. 'Didn't you know your parents at all?' Her aunt shook her head.

'I was left in a chapel porch on Dartmoor. Still, I thank my lucky stars whoever abandoned me knew I'd soon be found by folk that cared. They made enquiries but...,' she shrugged. 'Anyhow, at least I was placed in a home ... of sorts, anyhow,' she added.

'That's terrible,' Isabella frowned.

'Your uncle's the best thing that ever happened to me.'

'How did you meet?' Isabella asked.

'I was in service at a big house on the edge of Moretonhampstead and met him at the town market on my half day. We got talking and just sparked. Couldn't believe it when he called the next day and asked my employer if he would agree to my having a follower. Always been a man who knows his own mind, has Frederick,' she smiled. 'After we wed, he brought me back here with him.'

'How romantic,' Isabella gushed, feeling a sharp pang that her own plans for the future had been deferred.

'Don't mind me and my ruminations, dear,' her aunt said quickly. The rosy flush staining her cheeks made her look softer somehow, and Isabella realized she wasn't as old as she'd thought.

'But I'd like to know more,' she protested, seeing this as an ideal time to discover something about her own family. 'Did you know you'd have to look after Grandmother as well?' Isabella asked, pausing mid-posy.

'Of course. Father told me about the shock...,' her voice trailed off and she quickly resumed her counting. Isabella wasn't going to let the opportunity pass, though.

'Am I right in guessing it had something to do with my mother?'

'Well...,' her aunt began, looking flustered. Then William appeared, two laden baskets over his arms and, looking relieved, she said: 'Oh my, you've picked yet more, I see. Father will be pleased. Good job Mrs Pudge let you have all those boxes.'

Grinning, he carefully placed them in the buckets they'd spent the past few hours emptying and it was all Isabella could do not to groan.

'This little lot are from Grandmother's garden. I'm off to dig over the wild patch at the back so we can plant more. We'll be swimming in blue mice soon,' William said, grinning at Isabella's look of dismay. 'Finding it hard to keep up, are you?' he crowed. 'No sign of your knight in shining armour coming to your rescue then?'

'Now then, William. Your cousin's doing a fine job and I for one am pleased to have her here. It's nice to have a bit of intelligent conversation for once,' she added.

As William snorted and loped from the barn, taking Isabella's good humour with him, her aunt patted her shoulder.

'Don't mind him, dear. He might be my son but he's all the sensitivity of a pumpkin.'

'I've written to Maxwell again, as he might not have received my original note.' Isabella could see the scepticism in her aunt's eyes.

'Well, suppose we'd better get on it like a bonnet,' she joked. Knowing the woman was trying to make her feel better, Isabella forced down her frustration and reached for another box.

'I hope this is the last lot, my back's killing me,' she winced. Having been in here since downing a hasty breakfast at the crack of dawn, she was hot and sticky. What she wouldn't give for a lovely soak in the tub. Even a bowl of lovely warm water would suffice. However, a quick rinse under the pump each evening seemed to suffice for everyone here.

They worked on in silence, but whilst Isabella's hands calmly tied yet more flowers into bunches, her thoughts ran amok. William's remark about Maxwell rankled. However, the more she thought about it, the more she was convinced it was business that was keeping her intended in the City, for hadn't he mentioned there'd been a big takeover in the offing? Maybe he was involved in it and unable to leave his office. Well, she'd soon know when he replied to her note. She hoped dear Papa would respond quickly too, for she longed to find out how he was, and surely by now he would know how much time he needed to sort everything out.

'Come along, Daisy Daydream, as soon as we finish this lot we can break for luncheon.'

'Shall I make a start on it?' Isabella offered.

'Please. There's some of my brawn left so perhaps you could cut some bread to go with it and lay out pickles.'

'Brawn?' Isabella frowned.

'Yes, from the pig's head. I'll show you how to make it if you like.' Isabella gulped, her appetite vanishing completely. Oblivious, her aunt continued. 'You'll find it in a dish on the cold slab in the pantry. And I'm that parched, a nice strong brew would go down well,' she said. Realizing it was her aunt's tactful way of reminding her of her uncle's preference, she forced a smile.

'Don't worry, Auntie, I'll make strong tea in mugs with milk this time. And I'll remember not to cut the crusts off the bread.'

'You're learning, dear,' her aunt chuckled. 'Keep your man's stomach filled and he'll be happy. Dotty won't be back until later so there'll just be the four of us. Perhaps you could make one of those dainty sandwiches for Mother. She so enjoyed hers the other day.'

'I'll take it in to her, shall I?' she asked eagerly.

'Best we go in together, dear, she's that unpredictable,' her aunt replied before returning to her counting.

To Isabella's surprise, when she entered the

kitchen, her grandmother was standing by the range. She was waving a spill in the air above the hob, her white curls bobbing wildly as she chatted away.

'Got to get this lit.'

'Hello, Grandmama,' Isabella said cheerily, looking around to see who she'd been talking to. To her surprise there was nobody else in the room.

'Who are you?' the woman asked, staring at Isabella blankly.

'I'm Isabella, your granddaughter,' she explained. 'We met a few days ago, don't you remember?' The woman narrowed her eyes.

'Never see you afore in me life,' she muttered. Then to Isabella's horror, tears began rolling down her cheek. 'Can't abide strangers in my kitchen,' she sobbed. Isabella moved to put a reassuring arm around her, but the woman backed away and cowered in the corner. At a loss to know what to do, she was relieved when William hurried into the room.

'It's all right, Grandmother,' he soothed. 'You've wandered into Mother's kitchen by mistake. I'll take you home, eh?' Gently he put his arm around the woman and led her towards the door. 'Don't look so worried, she often gets like this,' he whispered as he passed Isabella. 'Put the kettle to boil, eh?'

She stared at William, hardly able to believe this was the terse person who'd delighted in taunting her ever since she'd arrived. Hands trembling, she did as he said then began setting out the luncheon. As she worked she began to feel calmer and couldn't help puzzling over the old lady's outburst. How could her grandmother not remember they'd met? And why was she crying? By the time her aunt came in, Isabella was pouring hot water into the big brown teapot.

'I've just seen William. He's sitting with Mother until I take her luncheon through.'

'I'll come with you,' Isabella replied. Her aunt shook her head.

'Best not at the moment. She's in a bit of a state and needs to settle. What did she say to you exactly?' she asked, scrutinizing Isabella closely.

'That she'd never seen me before, which is strange when you introduced us only the other day.'

'I know, dear, but she'll have forgotten that,' her aunt replied, looking strangely relieved. 'Some days she remembers things, mostly she doesn't. It's the unpredictability that catches us unawares. That's why we keep her door locked,' she sighed.

Just then Dotty breezed in looking happy and carefree. Seeing the table spread with food, her face lit up.

'Oh goody, I'm in time for luncheon. I've had a really good morning, Mother. Lord Lester is entertaining at the weekend so Mrs Pride bought lots more violets than usual,' she announced proudly, sitting down and spreading brawn thickly on a slice of bread.

'Does she arrange them around the house, then?' Isabella asked.

'Some are to be made into posies for place settings, but mostly Cook crystallizes the flower heads for decorating her cakes. You should see them, they're a work of art.'

'Oh yes, I've eaten similar at Claridge's,' Isabella replied, remembering her last meeting with Maxwell.

'Coo, lucky you,' Dotty sighed, staring around the room. 'Where's Father and William? It's not like them to be late for luncheon.'

'Father's checking on his new plants and William's sitting with your Grandmother. You forgot to lock her door before you left and she found her way in here. William said she was trying to light a spill from the range,' her mother informed her, giving her a reproachful look.

'Oh glory,' Dotty said, slapping her hand to her head. 'I was in that much of a hurry to leave, I forgot to check her door was secure. Sorry, Mother,' she murmured.

'Luckily no harm was done this time, but you must be more careful in future, Dotty. We don't want her burning the house down. It's not like you, though,' her aunt said, giving her daughter a searching look. Dotty quickly stared down at her plate. 'I'll take Mother's tray in to her then William can come and get a bite to eat,' Mary sighed, getting to her feet.

'Phew,' Dotty exclaimed, as soon as the door had closed behind her mother. 'That was close.'

'At least no harm came to your grandmother,' Isabella said. 'Did you manage to post my letters?'

'I did. Good job you had stamps, though, 'cos Mother would have known if I used some of the money I got from the big house.'

'Luckily I just had two in my reticule. I'd love to see the manor. Can I come with you next time?'

'No, Izzie, you can't,' she shouted, shaking her

head emphatically. 'And you must promise not to ask Mother or Father either,' she added, jumping to her feet.

'But why?' Isabella frowned. 'I can help, carry extra flowers and...'

'No, I can't risk it, you're far too pretty,' her cousin cried as she flounced up the stairs, leaving Isabella staring after her.

Chapter 9

'Whatever do you mean?' Isabella asked following after her. 'What has my appearance to do with delivering flowers to the manor?' Dotty turned away from the mirror where she'd been arranging her hair on top of her head.

'Everything. And we call it the big house. Look, you must promise not to tell a soul but I've got an admirer,' she burst out, a smile hovering on her lips.

'Goodness, how exciting,' Isabella cried, clapping her hands enthusiastically. 'However, I still don't see why that should stop me coming with you.'

'But Izzie, look at me!' she wailed. 'My hair hangs all straight and I'm dumpy with freckles to boot. You're lean as a racehorse while I look like old Silver.'

'What utter rubbish, Dotty. You're naturally pretty with your dark colouring and you have womanly curves. Obviously this admirer recognizes that fact.'

'But if he sees you, with your golden hair and big blue eyes, he'll have second thoughts about accompanying me to the harvest hop.'

'I still think that's nonsense, but if he did then he wouldn't be worth worrying about, would he?'

'Suppose not,' Dotty sighed, sinking down onto her mattress. 'I wish I was elegant like you, though. I mean you glide into a room like a lady, whereas I sort of bound like a bunny.' Isabella laughed at the girl's description.

'Only because I was made to practise deportment. You should try walking around a room with a pile of books balanced on your head,' she chuckled. 'Each time one fell to the floor, I received a rap on my knuckles from the governess's ruler,' she said, grimacing at the memory. 'What is your admirer like then?' Immediately Dotty's face lit up and she wrapped her arms around her body as if embracing it.

'Handsome as a prince. He's got red hair and hazel eyes that glisten with gold flecks when we ... well, we've only kissed a couple of times, but it was like an explosion. Like sparkles on bonfire night. Coo, me insides go all wobbly thinking about it,' she gushed. 'I expect you feel the same when your fella kisses you?' Isabella thought of Maxwell's chaste kisses upon her cheek or hand but couldn't relate them to Dotty's description.

'So, when is this harvest hop then? And who will be there?' she asked.

'Two Saturdays' time. And that's the trouble, Izzie, everyone will be going. Including Mother and Father.' She let out a long sigh.

'They don't know about ... what's his name, by the way?'

'Alfie, or Alfred when he's being posh. He's the underfootman and in line for a foot up when his boss retires, if you'll pardon me pun,' she joked. Then her eyes clouded. 'And no, they don't know. Father's bound to say I'm too young and...'

'Girls? Why are you upstairs when luncheon is on the table?' As if on cue, her father's voice drifted up the stairs. Dotty turned to Isabella.

'You won't say anything?' she pleaded.

'Of course not. But you'll have to tell them soon if this function is imminent.'

'Function? Oh, the hop. Yes, I know,' she replied, letting out another sigh. 'I was hoping Uncle Bill would have dropped by but he's been too busy turning more of his land over to violets.'

'I haven't met him yet,' Isabella replied.

'You'll like him, he's a sweetie. Really listens to what you has to say and...'

'Girls, get yourselves down here this instant.'

'Best scat, Father sounds ratty.' Privately Isabella thought he was always like that, but she held her tongue and followed Dotty back down the stairs.

When September gave way to October and Maxwell still hadn't appeared – or much less answered her letter – Isabella's spirits plummeted like late-autumn leaves. She couldn't help thinking that William had been right and he wasn't coming after all. Although the idea of taking herself home surfaced from time to time, she didn't want to be a burden to Papa who was obviously still busy as he hadn't responded to her note either. There was also the problem of having no money. Although she'd worked hard every day since her arrival, she had yet to see evidence of any pay.

However, the topic of conversation for everyone was the harvest hop, which sounded to Isabella as if it was the highlight of the year.

'If only I could buy material to make a new dress,' Dotty wailed, her hands automatically tying her posy with raffia. 'I saw some beautiful sprigged cotton in Pudge's last week.'

They were in the barn, bunching up the violets, which to Isabella seemed a never-ending job for as soon as they emptied the buckets William or her uncle would arrive with yet more.

'Sorry, Dotty, we don't have any spare money for luxuries,' her mother told her.

'Surprise, surprise,' Dotty sighed, looking so forlorn Isabella's heart went out to her.

'We could look in my portmanteau and see if anything would suit?' she offered, thinking of her beautiful gowns. Dotty's eyes lit up.

'That's kind of you, dear, but I don't really think chiffons and silks will be appropriate. Those delicate fabrics would soon get snagged on the hay bales,' her aunt replied.

'Hay bales?' Isabella frowned.

'Farmer Furkin lets us use his largest byre. He sets out bales of hay around the walls so the old fogeys can sit and watch us youngsters dance,' Dotty told her.

'Less of your cheek, young lady,' her mother rebuked mildly. 'I'll have you know that as soon as the caller shouts for a do-si-do, Father and I are up like a shot.'

'Don't remind me,' Dotty groaned. 'It's so embarrassing.'

'Never worried you before. Something different this year?' her mother asked, eyeing her shrewdly.

'Well, er, someone might want to dance with me,' Dotty muttered. Then, cheeks flushing like two rosy apples, she bent down to retrieve another corset box.

'Of course, they will,' her mother laughed, turning to Isabella. 'Everyone joins in the circles, squares and lines. It's a very sociable evening. As long as we can keep Father to no more than two jugs of cider. He's not used to the drink, see.'

'Oh glory,' Dotty groaned. 'I'd forgotten about last year.'

'Father works hard and is entitled to let his hair down.'

'Yes, but...'

'That's enough, Dotty,' her mother warned. 'I've a bit of yellow gingham left if you girls can make use of it, for you'll need something suitable as well, Isabella.'

'But I want to look grown up and pretty,' Dotty insisted.

'Pretty is as pretty does, Dotty, whoever you're trying to impress,' her mother said, fixing her daughter with a stare that would curdle even the best pedigree cow's milk.

'Perhaps we could turn a couple of my silk scarves into a top to go with the gingham,' Isabella offered. Immediately, Dotty brightened and the genial atmosphere was restored.

With a bright moon lighting their way, the family

walked together down the dark lane towards the village. Spirits were high at the thought of the evening ahead, although Dotty's mood swung from eager anticipation at seeing her Alfred, to blind panic.

'I feel sick, Izzie,' she whispered.

'Well, please don't be over my best silks,' Isabella replied, holding up her hands in mock horror in an effort to cheer up her cousin. They'd spent the past few evenings sewing the gingham into two new skirts and fashioning her silk scarves into blouses to complement them.

'Do you think he'll like my outfit?' Dotty asked.

'If he doesn't, you'll know he doesn't have good taste,' Isabella whispered, trying not to think of the lavish sum she'd spent on the Eastern-inspired printed stoles from Liberty. Hopefully it wouldn't be too long until she could replace them.

As soon as they reached the farmer's field, Alice and Thomas ran on ahead, shouting excitedly to their friends.

'Remember, girls, best behaviour,' her uncle said, leading the way into a large rustic building. Dotty grimaced at Isabella.

'I hope he doesn't interfere,' she whispered. Isabella smiled sympathetically, then stared around her. The byre was lit by myriad lamps, with candles wedged into an assortment of bottles and jars. As the mix of wax, hay and ale assaulted her nostrils, she wrinkled her nose. The others didn't seem to notice anything, though, as they were either sitting on the bales drinking or gathered in groups chatting. A feeling of anticipation and jollity filled the air. To her surprise, whereas in

London it was a matter of pride to be individually attired, here everyone appeared to be dressed the same. The men were sporting jerkins with red spotted kerchiefs knotted around their necks, while the women wore brightly coloured long skirts and cotton tops. Isabella glanced at Dotty who, having discarded her turnover and puffed up her hair, was anxiously looking around. Suddenly her face lit up as a red-haired young man hurried towards her.

'Oh ah,' Frederick murmured. 'And what do we have 'ere.'

'Let the girls alone, Father,' her aunt reproved mildly. Then as a fiddler began to play, she turned to Isabella. 'Come along, time to dance,' she urged, taking both Isabella and her husband by the arm and leading them towards the empty space in the middle of the floor where everyone was gathering.

A large man with a bright red face was grinning down at them from a platform in front.

'That's the caller,' her aunt told her, raising her voice to be heard over the din. 'Just do as he says and you'll be fine.' Before Isabella could ask what she meant, the fiddler struck up the tune and the caller began issuing instructions in a voice as large as himself.

'In and out, allemande, do-si-do and move on.'

As everyone followed his changing commands, Isabella was swung from one partner to another, sometimes male, sometimes female, it didn't seem to matter. Although everybody was having a good time, all Isabella noticed was the feel of coarse hands that prickled her skin and the less than pleasant odour wafting from some of their bodies.

'Thank goodness,' Isabella muttered, when the music slowed. But instead of stopping, the fiddler was joined by another. As the tempo picked up again, she was pulled into a circle and another frenzy of dancing began. In and out they went, going faster and faster, until they surged so enthusiastically into the middle, she almost touched noses with the gentleman opposite. It was only when he grinned that she realized it was the young man she'd met at the pumping station. However, before she had time to acknowledge him, she was jerked back again.

Just as she thought she would faint from exertion, the music slowed. *Thank heavens,* she thought, making to leave the floor. Feeling a tap on her shoulder, she spun round to find the young man with emerald eyes smiling at her.

'Felix Furneaux,' he announced, perfecting a bow.

'Isabella Carrington,' she replied, surprising herself by dipping a bob.

'Would you join me for the next dance?' he asked.

'Well, I...,' but as she started to refuse, a resounding chord sounded.

'Come on, Country bumpkin,' he grinned, taking her arm and leading her back to the middle of the floor.

'Well, of all the...,' she began but her words were lost in the press of people forming groups and she realized it was the name of a set dance. Then the caller began shouting instructions, and once again she was caught up in the frenzy. As Felix smiled encouragement, she found herself relaxing and following his lead. His touch when he linked his arm through hers was warm, and the look in his eyes admiring so that she found herself losing her reserve and throwing herself into the dance. To her surprise she began to enjoy herself, losing all sense of time as sets followed reels until finally the fiddlers stopped playing.

'Goodness, that was fun,' she gasped, wiping her hand over her brow.

'May I get you a cooling drink? Some lemonade or cider, perhaps?' Felix asked.

'Thank you, a glass of lemonade would be most acceptable.'

'Can't promise cut crystal, but I'll see what I can do,' he winked, leading her over to a vacant bale. 'Make yourself comfortable and I'll be back before you know it.' She frowned down at the makeshift seat but her legs were so shaky, she sank onto it and gazed around.

There was a long line snaking its way beside a trestle groaning with hams, pies, pasties, cheese and pickles, the centrepiece being a huge loaf shaped like a wheatsheaf. She was just admiring it when she noticed her uncle talking to a man who looked so similar that it had to be his brother. At last she'd get to meet her other uncle, she thought. Further along, she saw Dotty standing close to the redheaded man who had to be Alfred, and from the way he was gazing into her eyes, Isabella didn't think for one moment he'd even noticed what she was wearing. How lovely to be adored like that, she mused, realizing that she hadn't given

Maxwell a single thought all evening. She could just imagine his disparaging look if he could see her now. Before she could dwell on the matter, Felix reappeared, grinning triumphantly.

'I don't suppose you've been to anywhere like this before?' he laughed, handing her what looked suspiciously like a jam jar then settling himself beside her on the bale. She was too thirsty to worry, though, and took a long sip.

'Oh, this is delicious,' she murmured, taking another.

'Made by our local brewer, that is. Finest in the land,' Felix declared, downing his drink in one. 'Didn't realize your uncle was Northcott,' he added, waving his empty jar towards the trestle where Frederick was now talking to a group of men. From the animated way he was gesticulating, Isabella guessed he'd probably already supped a cider or two.

'And I didn't realize our families are at loggerheads,' she replied.

'Well, that's a bit strong, surely? Our market gardens might be competitors in trade, but there's no reason we can't go about things amicably,' he pointed out. Isabella raised her brows.

'You try telling that to my uncle,' she sighed, raising her brows. As she did, she noticed a straw spiral shape dangling from the rafters above. 'What is that?' she asked.

'That be the spirit of fertility,' he replied, exaggerating his West Country accent. 'It's fashioned from the last standing stalks in the field where he takes refuge. The farmer twists them together to give him a home for the winter and bring good luck for next year's harvest.'

'Honestly, you do have some funny ways in this part of the world,' she told him.

'I'm guessing from your comment that you are not from around these parts?'

'I'm from London – Chester Square, actually – and I'm biding with my uncle until Maxwell comes for me.' Taking another sip of her drink, she didn't see the frown replace his grin.

'Maxwell?'

'My intended,' she explained.

Just then the music started up again and the caller announced: 'Ladies and Gentleman, Strip the Willow, if you please.'

'Well, it's nice to have met you again,' Felix said, getting quickly to his feet.

'Oh, are you leaving?' she asked, disappointment flooding through her. In truth, she felt comfortable sitting chatting to this pleasant man, who was not only fun but appeared more cultured than the others round here with their strange dialect and weird words.

'Regrettably, propriety decrees I must,' he murmured, giving a tight smile. Before she could ask what he meant, he perfected another of his little bows and walked quickly away. She stared after him but the fiddler struck another chord and, as people surged forward, he was swallowed up in the crowd.

Isabella spotted a flushed Dotty being led onto the dance floor by Alfred, and William laughing with his friends. Realizing the fun had gone out of the evening now Felix had left, she looked for her aunt to tell her she was leaving, but the woman was already forming a set with another couple, ordering her reluctant husband to stand opposite. Isabella couldn't help smiling at her uncle being bossed about for once. As the caller began shouting instructions, Isabella collected up her mantle before she could be coerced into joining in. She'd just reached the entrance when she heard an ear-splitting scream.

'Get the doctor, this girl's hurt,' someone cried. As the crowd parted, Isabella saw Dotty lying on the floor, an anxious Alfred by her side.

'Oh goodness, what's happened?' she cried, hurrying over to her cousin. Her aunt pushed her gently away.

'Give her some air,' she ordered. Isabella stared helplessly down at Dotty who was white as cotton and writhing in agony. Then her uncle appeared.

'You ruddy useless article,' he boomed, glaring at Alfred.

'I didn't mean to drop her, sir. She swung too high,' he muttered.

Chapter 10

With Dotty's ankle declared badly sprained and strapped up, she was unable to help with the flowers. Consequently, the atmosphere around the cottage was subdued.

'One man down will make a difference to my carefully planned operation, so the rest of you will all have to work harder,' Frederick told them, glaring at his daughter. 'With Furneaux in competition we can't afford to slacken our pace.'

Isabella shook her head at his hard-headed attitude. Surely Dotty's well-being was more important than his timetable? They were already working flat out and it wasn't as if poor Dotty had fallen on purpose.

When a penitent Alfred had turned up to see how she was, he was sent away with a flea in his ear and banned from ever calling again. Distraught, Dotty hobbled around with a stick that William had found for her, alternately pleading with her father to reconsider or calling him every bad name she could think of, but he wouldn't be swayed.

Now it was Thursday and they were sitting around the table in the cold light of dawn, eating the brewis that seemed to have become their staple breakfast. What she wouldn't give for a lightly boiled egg with toasted dipping soldiers, Isabella thought, pushing the soggy crusts around her dish.

'Right, Isabella.' She jumped as her uncle's voice penetrated her thoughts. 'We can't afford to let our customers down, so with Dotty out of action, you will take the violets to the big house today then sell whatever they don't buy in the town,' he announced. Isabella gulped. Whilst she'd been longing to accompany Dotty on her visits, she didn't relish going alone. Seeing her hesitate, his steely eyes darkened. 'I take it you can manage?'

'Of course, Uncle,' she replied, determined to rise to the challenge. He gave a loud harrumph then turned to Dotty.

''Tis time you were working again, girl. I've set up a stool by the trestle so you can help Mother pack.' Dotty opened her mouth to protest, but seeing the tic twitching in his cheek, snapped it shut again. 'Come along, William, let's get these violets picked.' Snatching his hat from its peg and the basket from the deep sill of the window, he stalked outside. With a smirk at Isabella, William grabbed his basket and followed.

'Right, now that's settled, it's time I was seeing to Mother,' her aunt said, getting to her feet. 'Alice, you wash the dishes. Thomas, you can dry them – and carefully, mind. We don't want them cracked. Dotty, tell Isabella the quickest way to get to the big house and who she's to speak to. Oh, and you'd best explain where's the best place to stand in town as well. Sure you're up to this?' she asked, turning to Isabella, a worried expression on her face.

'Of course I am, Aunt Mary,' she replied, crossing her fingers behind her back.

'Don't mind Uncle, we're grateful for your help,' she smiled.

As soon as the door closed behind her mother, Dotty called for Alice to fetch her paper and a pencil.

'If I write Alfred a note, will you see that he gets it, Izzie?' she asked, keeping her voice low.

'Yes, if I can,' she agreed, thinking it would be easy to spot the redheaded young man.

'It was my fault I fell and it's not fair he's been blamed,' Dotty sighed. 'While I do this, you'd better get yourself ready. Father will be back with the flowers any moment now.'

Hurrying up to the bedroom, Isabella donned her best mantle and bonnet. Then, thinking it might bring her luck, she snatched up the little silver locket from under her pillow and fastened it around her neck.

When she reappeared, Dotty handed her the folded note addressed to Alfred, along with directions to the big house.

'You need to speak to the cook, Mrs Tripe. She'll tell you how many bunches she requires, then get the housekeeper to pay you. Mrs Tripe is a love and usually gives me one of her nubbies.'

'Her what?' Isabella asked.

'They're her special buns. She makes them with yeast and saffron and they're delicious,' Dotty explained, kissing her fingers with her lips. 'Then you'll need to sell whatever flowers are left. Father'll go spare if you come back with any. Being market day, it's best to go to the Strand for that. Stand outside the stationer's and circulating library, then move on to the linen and woollen draper's later in the morning when the ladies start appearing. But keep your peepers peeled 'cos if you sees a toff coming out of the confectioner's holding a beribboned package, nip over smartish. Like as not he'll be calling upon his lady love and you can tempt him to buy her a posy by holding out your basket and smiling sweetly.'

'Oh, I couldn't,' Isabella gasped, horrified at the thought of approaching a gentleman. But then her uncle reappeared holding a laden basket.

'Right, girl, here's yer flowers. Off you go or they'll wilt,' he urged.

'You mean I'm to walk to the big house?' Isabella asked, staring at him in dismay. Her uncle frowned then pushed his hat to the back of his head.

'Expecting to be conveyed, was yer? Well, sorry to disappoint but Silver has more important work to do. 'Tis only a few measly miles anyhow,' he snorted. Biting down a retort, Isabella took the basket from him.

She'd show him, she vowed as she set off down the lane, the chill of the early-morning air cooling her flushed cheeks. All around, the landscape spread out like an autumnal tapestry of glorious golds, purples and russet, and soon she felt her heart lifting. An on-shore breeze blew up, bringing with it the tang of salt, and she marvelled how even though she was in the countryside, the sea was close by. As the orange-tipped leaves crackled under her feet, memories of playing in the park opposite her home surfaced, and on impulse she kicked up the piles that had gathered, laughing as they fluttered back to the ground. Then spotting the chestnut gleam of conkers on the grass, she gathered up a handful to give to Alice and Thomas later. It was good to be away from the cottage and barn with its endless flowers to be posied and packed.

She could hardly believe she'd been in Devonshire over a month. With a pang, she wondered how dear Papa was. Never having been away from him before, she missed him so much it hurt. As for Maxwell, when would he be free to leave his office? Not having received any communication from him, she thought it must surely be work keeping him from making the journey west.

Although she walked briskly and followed Dotty's instructions, the journey along the winding country lanes took much longer than she'd anticipated and, by the time she'd skirted the woods and turned into the driveway leading to the big house, the sun was already rising above the treetops. Settling the heavy basket onto her other arm, she stared in fascination as a hare leapt down the grassy bank in front of her, closely followed by another. A few moments later, a magnificent white building with a castellated roof loomed ahead, and she quickened her pace. *At last,* she thought, marching up to the front entrance and tugging on the wrought-iron bell pull.

Immediately, the heavy wooden door was opened by a man dressed in a dark jacket and trousers. He stared from Isabella to her basket, his frown deepening.

'Trade round the back,' he intoned, dark eyes heavy with reproach.

'But I...,' she began.

'I repeat, the trade entrance is to the rear of the house,' he sniffed, making to shut the door.

'Don't you dare,' she cried, anxious to divest herself of her basket, which was growing heavier by the moment. Footsteps crunched on the gravel.

'Is something wrong, Somber?' a voice enquired.

'No, my Lord, I was merely directing this, er, person to the correct entrance for her kitchen paraphernalia.' Isabella narrowed her eyes. She had never been spoken to like that before and, being hot and tired, was not in the mood to be insulted.

'Presumably one can walk through this door to reach the kitchen,' she persisted.

'One can indeed,' an amused voice replied at her side. 'Now, turn around. I want to see who dares argue with my butler.' Isabella spun around and found herself gazing into the face of a man of middle years who was holding a shotgun. Her eyes widened in shock. Surely he didn't shoot trespassers? As she stepped back in alarm, he lowered it to his side.

'Don't worry, it's pheasants I shoot, not peasants,' he chuckled. *Of all the cheek,* Isabella thought, then remembered why she was here and smiled graciously.

'Good morning, sir. My name is Miss Carrington and I bring violets for Mrs Tripe,' she said, proffering her basket.

'I'm sorry, my Lord. I did try and tell this person the correct procedure,' the butler said.

'I'm sure you did, Somber. Well, Miss Carrington ... you have a first name, I presume?'

'It's Isabella,' she replied.

'Well, Miss Isabella Carrington, I like a woman with spirit and can see you don't take no for an answer. Perhaps you'd be good enough to take the lady's basket to Mrs Pride, Somber.'

'Mrs Pride? But I was told your cook is Mrs Tripe,' Isabella frowned.

'That she is, my dear. However, I wouldn't risk incurring the wrath of my housekeeper by circumventing her. Now, why don't you come inside and tell me more about yourself,' he invited, his gaze taking in her mantle and dress.

'Thank you,' she replied, stepping into the hallway that smelled delightfully of beeswax and potpourri. He led the way into an elegant room with sunlight flooding through large bay windows and sparkling off the crystal chandelier hanging from the high ceiling.

As she stood admiring the magnificent oil paintings in their gold frames, he asked: 'May I offer you some refreshment?'

'Thank you. I would love to sample one of Mrs Tripe's nubbies,' she smiled.

'Her nubbies?' he echoed, looking bemused. There was a discreet cough behind them.

'I believe they are saffron buns, my Lord,' Somber murmured, from the hallway.

'That's right, they're made with yeast,' Isabella added.

'Are they indeed? Well, perhaps you could ask Mrs Tripe to arrange for some, er, nubbies to accompany our coffee then, Somber. And our guest might like to remove her mantle,' he suggested, giving her a look that sent shudders down her spine.

'I'm fine, thank you,' she said quickly.

'Then that will be all, Somber.'

'My Lord,' he bowed and, with a withering look in Isabella's direction, withdrew. Feeling the need to escape Lord Lester's penetrating gaze, she moved over to the French doors and stared out at the sea shimmering in the distance.

'Oh, what a delightful vista,' she cried. 'It makes one itch to get out one's pastels.' He frowned but before he could respond, a young girl appeared carrying a tray. She looked nervous and skirted the edge of the room, carefully avoiding Lord Lester, before setting the salver down on the table beside him.

'Shall I serve, my Lord?' she squeaked without looking directly at him.

He nodded, and with shaking hands she poured the strong dark liquid into delicate Royal Worcester cups, then proffered cream and sugar. As the glorious aroma of freshly ground coffee beans wafted Isabella's way, she sighed appreciatively. *Real coffee at last*, she thought, grimacing as she recalled the concoction her aunt had brewed the previous day. It had been made from dandelion roots and tasted as vile as it sounded.

'Do help yourself to a nubbie,' Lord Lester invited. Smiling her thanks, she took one and eagerly bit into it. The man was watching her closely, a smile twitching his lips.

'I trust it is to your liking?' he asked.

'It is indeed,' she replied, unable to resist taking another bite.

'You intrigue me, Miss Carrington.'

'How so?' she asked politely.

'Your clothes are a mix of couture and, er, how shall I put this ... well, never mind. Your accent is cultured yet you arrived here like a peasant with flowers to sell to my domestic staff.'

'Oh, that's easily explained,' she laughed to cover her embarrassment. 'I am staying with my Uncle Frederick. Until my intended comes for me, that is. Dotty – Dorothy my cousin – has hurt her ankle and I was asked to make the delivery on her behalf. My uncle didn't wish to let you down,' she added graciously.

'Your uncle being Frederick Northcott?' he asked, enlightenment dawning.

'Yes, he was my mother's brother.'

'Ellie was your mother?' he asked with a quirk of his brow.

'Eleanora, you mean? Yes, she was,' she replied, excitedly. 'You knew her?' She looked at him expectantly, realizing for the first time that he was about the same age as her mama would have been had she still been alive.

'Everyone knew your mother,' he said, giving a little cough. 'I can see the likeness now. Your colouring might be different but you have the same disposition. She was spirited and determined to get her own way, too,' he added, giving her a knowing smile.

'What was she like?' Isabella asked, sitting forward in her seat. He thought for a moment, a mixture of emotions flitting across his face.

'She was fun and liked a good time. Do you like a good time?' he asked, setting down his cup and leaning towards her.

'Well, of course, although since I came here I seem to have done nothing but work,' she frowned and placed her empty plate on the table.

'What a waste of a pretty young thing,' he said, reaching out and stroking one of his long, manicured fingers along her hand. 'Already I see your delicate young skin is reddened and chaffed,' he sighed as if it was the saddest sight he'd ever witnessed. Feeling uncomfortable, though not sure if it was from his touch or the truth of his words, she snatched her hand away.

'You mentioned an intended? I presume he is of comfortable stature?' he asked, carrying on as if he hadn't noticed.

'Of course. Maxwell works in the City. The financial market, you know. He's been very busy lately,' she replied, trying to sound knowledgeable.

Lord Lester nodded.

'And could be tied up for some time. The market's in turmoil with messy mergers and dodgy dealings taking place.'

'You know of these things, living down here in Devonshire?' she asked, staring at him in surprise.

'Even down here in deepest Devonshire we take delivery of the newspapers,' he said, giving a throaty chuckle. 'You, however, are far too pretty to concern yourself with matters of business. I can tell you are used to the finer things of life, so living at the Northcott's hov– house must be somewhat different,' he murmured, leaning closer again.

'Goodness, yes,' she cried, then checked herself. 'I mean, they have done their best to make me welcome, but conditions are cramped to say the least. Why, I even have to share a bed cham–,' she stopped, fearful of revealing too much. A gleam sparked in his eye.

'Well, I have plenty of chambers here. One of your own would be easy to arrange, with the finest scented linen and adjacent facilities, if you get my meaning.' He paused to let this sink in. 'Why don't you spend the day here? We could really get to know each other,' he suggested, leaning forward and patting her knee. Isabella suppressed a shudder. 'Who knows, it might even become a regular occurrence,' he grinned, seemingly oblivious to her reaction.

'A regular occurrence?' she repeated, instinctively leaning further back in her seat as his candid gaze bore into her.

'This house is built for a fine lady like you. I can offer you all the luxuries you are clearly used to, in return for the delight of your company and perhaps a little kindness.' His voice trailed away as he stared at her expectantly. She swallowed hard, aware of the slow, deep ticking of the grandfather clock on the far side of the room.

'I don't really think…,' she began, but he leaned even closer so that she caught the spicy tang of his cologne. Feeling repulsed, she twisted her hands in her lap. 'Of course, I could then tell you more about your delightful mother,' he coaxed. Isabella's thoughts whirled. Her uncle and aunt were always too busy to talk about her mama, and she so wanted to discover more about her. Yet every instinct told her this man, whose gaze seemed to penetrate the very core of her being, was not to be trusted.

'I see you need time to consider,' he sighed, moving away. 'I shall get Mrs Pride to return your basket,' he added, tugging on the embroidered bell pull beside him. Before Isabella could respond, the rustle of starched petticoats heralded the arrival of the housekeeper. She held out the still full basket.

'Cook says these flowers are substandard so she won't be purchasing any today,' she announced, triumph lighting up her dark eyes.

'Substandard?' Isabella echoed, but the woman was already marching straight-backed from the room.

'Oh dear,' Lord Lester murmured as Isabella stared after her in dismay. 'You really should consider my proposal, you know. With Furneaux starting up in competition, it would be a shame if I felt the need to switch allegiance, as it were.' Picking up his newspaper, he motioned for her to leave.

'I'll see you out,' Somber said, appearing by her side. 'And next time, Miss, perhaps you'd remember to...'

'Use the trade entrance, yes, I know,' she replied, vowing there wouldn't be a next time.

Chapter 11

What a repulsive man. How dare he make execrable suggestions like that, Isabella fumed as the door closed behind her. *As for that stuck-up housekeeper. Substandard flowers indeed. There was nothing wrong with them,* she thought, staring down at the perfectly formed violets. She'd been hoping the cook would purchase them all so that she wouldn't have to stand in the town centre like a common flower girl. Stomping back down the long driveway, her thoughts were in turmoil. Even if Lord Lester could tell her every single detail about her mama, she had no intention of returning. However, like others she'd met since her arrival, he'd hinted her mama had led some kind of secret life, and she intended to find out exactly what it was. As soon as she arrived back at the cottage she would tackle her aunt and uncle again, and if they were still not forthcoming, she'd discuss it with Papa the minute she returned home.

By the time she reached the lane, her face was hot and sticky. Reaching into her pocket for a handkerchief, she felt something crackle. It was the letter Dotty had asked her to give to Alfred.

She stared at it in dismay. Although her cousin was relying on Isabella to pass on the message, nothing would make her venture back to the big house. Of course, if she had money she could purchase a stamp and post the letter, but despite working all day every day since she'd arrived in Devonshire, her uncle hadn't paid her a penny and she'd used up her own supply writing to Papa and Maxwell. She let out a sigh. It seemed she had no alternative other than to try and sell the wretched flowers after all. Transferring her heavy basket to the other arm, she trudged on.

It was hot for October and she could feel the sun beating down on her back as it climbed higher in the sky. The trees and hedges that had seemed so picturesque earlier now teemed with clouds of insects, while stray branches caught on her mantle. She was swatting away yet another persistent fly when she heard the sound of hooves and, looking up, saw a dappled pony approaching. It was pulling a smartly painted cart, and as it drew closer she saw Felix Furneaux sitting on the box. Pleased to see him again and certain he would offer her a lift, she smiled sweetly up at him.

'Good morning, Miss Carrington,' he called, returning her smile. 'It's a beautiful day for promenading, is it not?' She was about to tell him where she was bound when, to her chagrin, he tipped his cap and continued on his way. Isabella stared at his receding back, her heart dropping to her boots. Why hadn't he stopped? She'd thought he was different to the other men around these parts, but clearly he was as ill-mannered as the rest.

By the time she reached the edge of the town,

the sun was directly overhead and she was fatigued and thirsty. She skirted the brightly coloured stalls that were piled with produce and fairings spread out before her. It was noisy with vendors shouting their wares, and hefting her basket, she had no alternative but to brave the crowds in order to reach the better side of town Dotty had directed her to. The smell of perspiration mixed with unsavoury street food made her feel nauseous, while the rising dust caught at the back of her throat. Everyone seemed to be eating or drinking as they walked along. *How uncouth,* she thought, yearning to be back in the cultured environs of Claridge's or The Savoy.

She'd just reached the edge of the market when a man unable to see over the pile of garish material he was carrying bumped into her, causing her to stumble into the path of an approaching donkey cart. Although she managed to avoid it, the impatient driver cracking his whip caused the poor beast to relieve itself right in front of her. As the stench from the steaming pile pervaded her nostrils, Isabella's stomach retched. Fearing she was about to be sick, she stared around until she spotted a lane leading off the main thoroughfare, and hurried towards it. Collapsing against the wall of the nearest building, she closed her eyes and waited for her head to stop spinning.

'Oi, off my pitch, you bleedin' bitch.' Something wet splattered on Isabella's chin and she opened her eyes to find an angry woman, vermillion stained lips flecked with spittle, waving a fist at her. She was wearing a top that did little to hide her heaving bosom, while her long black hair hung loose.

'Well, really,' Isabella protested.

'Well, really,' the woman parroted. 'If you thinks being posh tosh gives you the right to nab the best spot, you're bleedin' wrong, you...' Her tirade trailed off, her snarl turning to a dazzling smile as a young man dressed in naval uniform approached. 'Ello 'andsome, lookin' for a good time?' she purred, pulling her blouse lower. Ignoring her, the sailor eyed Isabella up and down appreciatively.

'Nice, very nice,' he murmured, leaning close so that she caught the full force of his beery breath. Recoiling, she pressed herself harder against the wall. 'How about you showin' Ollie here a good time?' he leered. Then he caught sight of her basket. 'Oh, flowers, that's a new one. Always up for learning new tricks, blondey. Spices things up,' he chortled, plucking a violet from Isabella's basket and running it slowly across her chest. Isabella shuddered, and as she tried to move away he let out a lewd laugh. 'Playin' 'ard to get, me lover. Well, Ollie 'ere's just been paid an'...'

'And Ollie can pay me to show him all he wants,' the other woman purred, placing her hand possessively on his arm and fluttering her spider lashes at him. With narrowed eyes, she turned back to Isabella. 'Sling your 'ook and take them furkin' violets with yer, flower girl,' she snarled, snatching up Isabella's basket and hurling it into the road. It landed in front of a passing dray laden with beer barrels, and there was a loud crunch as the wheels rolled over it. As Isabella stared down at the broken remains in dismay, the woman cackled, clapping her hands with glee. 'And yer'll end up the same way if yer don't scat, cat,' she chortled, giving Isabella a shove.

She didn't need telling twice and, leaving the remains of her basket, ran as fast as she could. It was only when she heard the catcalls and suggestive remarks that she realized that, in her haste, she'd headed further up the dingy lane.

'Want some fun, darlin'?' a voice taunted.

'What's the 'urry, lover?' another called.

Ignoring them, Isabella continued running but the lane was narrowing and growing darker. A group of men advanced menacingly towards her, and from the look on their faces, she knew she was in terrible trouble. Blood pounded in her ears as she glanced desperately around for some means of escape, but the only open doors were strewn with drunken bodies.

Suddenly an arm reached out and grabbed her. A scream caught in her throat as she was pulled roughly down another squalid alleyway littered with empty bottles and human detritus. The stench was indescribable and, just when she thought she would pass out, she found herself out in the daylight. As the man let go of her, she felt her legs buckle and sank to the ground.

'Blimmer, girl. Whatever you doin' round there?' he asked. Isabella blinked up at the dark-haired man towering over her. He was wearing a brown smock and looked vaguely familiar but, dazed and disorientated, it took a moment for her to place him.

'Uncle Bill?' she whispered, relief flooding through her as she recognized the man she'd seen talking to her aunt and uncle at the hop the previous Saturday.

'That's right, and you be Izzie, Ellie's girl,' he replied. ''Appen up, you be shaking like a wet dog. Come on, my cart's over there.' He pointed past a row of rickety shop fronts to a rough patch of grass where a pony was grazing. 'Best I take you home. You can tell me what you been about on the way.' He held out his arm and, grateful for his support, she picked herself off the filthy cobbles and allowed herself to be led to his cart.

'Manage the hop up, can you?' he asked in his gentle West Country burr.

'I think so,' she replied, grimacing at the familiar corset boxes that were piled high. Grinning ruefully, he pushed some aside to make room for Isabella.

'My turn to collect them from town. There now, up you go.'

'I suppose that means they will all need filling,' she muttered as he climbed up beside them. Hearing the despair in her voice, he darted her a sympathetic look then called the pony to walk on.

'Hope that brother of mine's not working you too hard?' he asked, taking his briar pipe from his pocket and lighting it. 'He's a good 'un but, like a racehorse, once he gets the bit between his teeth there's no stopping him. This competition from Furneaux has got him in a proper frenzy and no mistake. Take it easy, Fred, I told him. There's violets aplenty round here. Mind you, we've worked hard to build up our business, so I sees his point of view.' She shivered and he frowned.

Clamping the pipe between his teeth, he pulled a sack from behind the seat and handed it to her. 'Here, cover yerself over and get warm. That's quite a fright you had.'

Smiling gratefully and paying little heed to its musty smell, she snuggled under it and, with the man's gentle voice washing over her, finally began to relax.

She must have fallen asleep for when she was woken by a jolt from the cart, they had left the town and were travelling down a country lane. Although the sun had lost its heat, blisters were burning her feet and she felt as stiff as that horrid housekeeper's starched petticoats. The blast of a whistle made her jump, and hearing a train rattling its way towards London she sighed wistfully. What she wouldn't give to be on it.

'Ah, back in the land of the living, are we?' her uncle chuckled.

'Sorry, I must have closed my eyes for a few moments,' she replied. He darted her a worried look.

'Best tell me what you been doin', maid. Did no one say not to venture over that part of town? Fair worried I was when I spied you there in all your finery. Though you're looking a bit draggled now, if you don't mind my saying.'

'Draggled?' she frowned.

'Likes you been pulled through the hedge backers,' he added, puffing on his pipe. Glancing down at her skirts, Isabella saw they were filthy and the hem was hanging down. Her best mantle was snagged and had bits of twig clinging to it, while her boots were muddy and scuffed. Never before had she appeared in public so badly attired. Thank heavens her papa and Maxwell weren't here to see her. Thoughts of them made her heart lurch and she let out another sigh.

'There, maid. Can't be that bad, surely?' her uncle asked.

'It couldn't be worse. Firstly, I had to take flowers to the big house because Dotty hurt her ankle and couldn't. I don't know who was more obnoxious, snooty Somber, the haughty housekeeper or that loathsome Lord Lester.'

'You saw Lord Lester?' her uncle spluttered, taking the pipe from his mouth.

'Yes, he said I was spirited like Mama and offered to tell me more about her if I ... if I...,' her voice trailed off and she stared at him miserably. His lips tightened into a line.

'I can imagine,' he muttered.

'But I so want to find out about Mama and nobody will tell me much about her. Even Grandmama's no help,' she told him.

'No, she wouldn't be,' he sighed. ''Tis only natural you be curious, though.'

'But I'm not going to be nice to that odious man for that,' she burst out.

'Nor should ye, maid. Best yer stay away from him, there's talk of ... well, like I say, best you avoid him. Now, tell me what you were doing on the wrong side of town.'

'That horrible housekeeper returned my basket still full of flowers, so I had to walk all the way into town to see if I could sell them. Then a donkey did his ... well, I thought I was going to be sick so I found a side street. Oh Uncle Bill, it was ghastly. I was accused of stealing this woman's pitch, whatever that is.'

'Look, maid, that street is known as "red-light rhyll". It's where men pay to have fun, and not for the likes of a respectable young lady like you. Promise you'll stay away from there in future.' As the implication of what he'd told her sank in, Isabella's eyes widened in shock.

'Goodness,' she murmured, her hand going to her throat. 'You mean those men in front of me thought they were going to...? Nothing would induce me to go back there, believe you me.'

'Pleased to hear it. Now here we are,' he said. To Isabella's surprise he was already pulling up outside the cottage. As she turned to thank him for the lift, she saw he was staring at her neck. 'I see you're wearing Ellie's locket,' he said gently. 'I was that fond of her and right sad when she had to ... er, when she left. There are things you should be told but this is not the time nor place. Fred'll be out in a moment wanting to unload his boxes and we have important business to discuss. I'll send Joseph over with the trap to collect you one day soon and we'll have a nice old chat, eh?'

'Thank you, Uncle Bill, I'd like that,' she replied, smiling at the kindly man with his sweet tobacco smell. Although his voice had the same West Country burr as her Uncle Frederick, it was softer somehow and his eyes were kinder, too. 'Anything you can tell me would be very much appreciated, although I'm not sure how much longer I'll be staying. My intended has been detained in the City, you see. However, he is bound to be arriving for me soon and Papa will have his affairs sorted by then.'

He frowned and opened his mouth to say something, but just then her Uncle Frederick appeared. He was looking unusually animated, two spots of red flushing his already ruddy cheeks.

'Ah there you are, Bill,' he said. 'And you too, girl. Had a good day? What, no flowers left?'

'No, Uncle,' she replied. *Or basket,* she thought, her heart sinking at his reaction when he found out. But he seemed impatient for her to disappear.

'Get yourself inside, girl. We're having an early supper tonight and Mother needs a hand.'

'Yes, Uncle Frederick. Thank you for the lift, Uncle Bill,' she said, turning back to him.

'My pleasure,' he said jumping off and hurrying round to her side of the cart. As he helped her down, he leaned in close.

'Best not let on you met Lord Lester or that you ended up on the wrong side of town,' he whispered.

It was only later she realized she hadn't asked Uncle Bill what he'd been doing in that unsavoury area.

Chapter 12

Desperate to wash the filth from her body, Isabella went straight round to the pump. For once she relished the cold water tingling her skin and, feeling slightly cleaner, made her way across the empty yard and into the kitchen.

'How did you get on?' Aunt Mary asked. She was standing at the range, stirring something in a large pot. As an appetizing aroma wafted her way, Isabella's stomach rumbled. It was hours since she'd last eaten and, having recovered from her ordeal, she was starving. 'Lory-lor, what's happened to you?' Mary cried when she saw Isabella's dishevelled appearance.

'I didn't sell any flowers at the big house and ended up in the wrong street in town by mistake,' Isabella replied nervously. 'Uncle's going to be furious. You see...'

'Never mind Father, Izzie,' Mary interrupted, putting down her spoon and bustling over to Isabella. 'Just look at the state o' you. Your turnover's all ripped and you're pale as parchment. Sit yourself down,' she ordered, pulling out the chair nearest the range and gently pushing Isabella onto it. 'I'll pour us a cuppa then you can tell me exactly what happened.'

'But Uncle said we were having supper early and...'

'Father and his stomach can wait,' Mary interrupted. 'Anyways, he'll be some time offloading those boxes as William's taken our flowers to the station. Asides, he has things to discuss with Uncle Bill. Cock-a-hoop Father is 'cos them precious new plants of his is thriving,' she added, pouring strong tea from the big brown pot. 'Seems his investment is going to pay off, though he'll need to buy more glass to help with propagation over winter. Not that we usually gets much snow or frost down here, but you never know.' She looked so happy, Isabella didn't like to voice her suspicion about where the money for all this had come from.

'I'm pleased, Auntie,' she murmured, taking a sip of her drink then spluttering when it burned her tongue.

'Well that's put some colour in your cheeks,' Aunt Mary laughed. 'Right now spill.' Isabella put down her mug and, remembering her Uncle Bill's advice, gave an edited version of her day.

'Oh lory-lor,' her aunt clucked. 'I've heard mutterings about the goings-on in that red-lighted place. How dreadful for you and what a blessing you escaped unscathed. You did, didn't you? I mean no one…' She stopped, staring at Isabella as if she hardly dared go on.

'Nobody touched me, if that's what you're worried about,' Isabella reassured her, blinking back the images of the coarse woman, seedy sailor, taunts and menacing faces.

'I suppose Bill happened along when you were making your way home?' her aunt said, breaking into her thoughts.

'Something like that,' Isabella replied, not wishing to say he'd actually been there. 'I'm afraid your basket got crushed, though.'

'Don't worry about that, Izzie, plenty more baskets in the barn,' she shrugged. 'Now, I know it's not Saturday, but if you'd like a bath later, I can heat water and get Father to bring the tub in.'

'Thank you, but I had a rinse under the pump,' Isabella assured her quickly. While she could think of nothing better than a leisurely soak in her bathtub at home, with scented salts to perfume her body, the thought of sitting in an inch of lukewarm water sheltered behind a sheet hanging from the clothes airer, was more than she could bear. Particularly as the family had no qualms about wandering in and out while pretending to ignore her.

'Well, you sit and gather yourself while I go and see to Grandmother. She's having one of her daffy days. Swears blind she saw her Ellie walking down the path this morning. Cors, I told her that wasn't possible, but she insisted it was true and has been fretful ever since. I've made her one of my violet simples to calm her,' she said, getting to her feet.

'You use violets for medicinal purposes?' Isabella asked in surprise.

'Oh yes, we use them for everything. They make fine salves, syrups and sugars as well,' she replied, wiping her hand across her brow. As she picked up a little blue bottle and spoon from the dresser, Isabella noticed how weary she was looking and guessed she must have had a trying day.

'Are you sure I can't help?' she offered.

'Why, bless you, no. You finish your drink. Dotty'll be in soon. It's taking her longer to do the flowers sitting down, though between you and me I think Father's happy she's out there guarding his precious new plantings. Oh, I nearly forgot, this came for you earlier,' she said, handing over a crisp envelope. Isabella's heart leapt. Maxwell had written at last. However, it was written in her father's hand.

My Dearest Isabella *18 October 1892*

I trust this letter finds you well and that you are now

settled with your mama's family.

What strange wording, Isabella thought.

To receive a communication from you was both a delight and blessing, arriving as it did during this most traumatic of times, and I wish you to know how much I treasure your loving words.

I think of you constantly and hope you are happy in Devonshire.

Your loving Papa
Cameron Carrington

Oh Papa, as if I don't know what your name is, she smiled, feeling her insides go all warm at the thought of him. It did sound as though he expected her to be staying a bit longer, though. And if he had found time to write, why hadn't Maxwell? Despite him saying her happiness was paramount, she was beginning to think he didn't care about her at all.

She was just reflecting on everything when Dotty hobbled through the door. Her face lit up when she saw Isabella and, throwing down her stick on the floor, she plonked herself down on the chair beside her without noticing her cousin's dishevelled state.

'You've got a letter, I see.'

'From Papa,' Isabella smiled, replacing it in the envelope and popping it in her pocket to read again later.

'And what did Alfred say when you gave him my letter? Did he reply?' she asked eagerly.

'I'm sorry, Dotty, but I didn't get a chance to give it to him,' she admitted.

'Why not?' she asked, the light going out of her eyes. 'You did go to the big house?' she queried, eyeing Isabella suspiciously.

'Certainly. However, that snooty Somber opened the door and...'

'Coo, Isabella, you never went to the front entrance?' Dotty gasped.

'Well, I never thought to do otherwise, of course.'

'Blimmer, girl, I bet old Pride went spare. Did she buy any violets?'

'No,' Isabella admitted. 'She said they were substandard and even had the nerve to turn her nose up at me when she handed back my basket.' Dotty stared at her cousin incredulously, but it wasn't the slur against the flowers that concerned her.

'You mean you actually dealt with the housekeeper? Coo, you'll be speaking to his Lordship next.' Isabella opened her mouth to tell her she had, then remembered Uncle Bill's advice.

'It was only when I reached the end of the driveway that I remembered your letter, Dotty. I was going to post it from the town centre but ... well, I didn't sell any flowers so couldn't purchase a postage stamp. I really am sorry,' she said, seeing Dotty's dejected look.

'I was relying on you, Izzie, so I won't pretend I'm not disappointed. Still, I guess it can't be helped,' her cousin shrugged. 'Give us it here and I'll think of another way of getting it to him,' she added. Isabella fished in her other pocket and pulled out the creased note.

'I really am sorry,' she repeated, placing it on the table. Dotty shrugged then reached for the teapot and poured tea into her mother's empty mug. Taking a large gulp, she sighed.

'That's better. Dry as dust, I was. Perhaps Joseph will help – if Uncle Bill brings him over for Sunday lunch this weekend, that is. They're that busy. Uncle and Father were grinning like gleeful boys when I came out of the barn.'

'Auntie was telling me he's had success with his new plants,' Isabella said, relieved her cousin had taken the news about her letter so well.

'Yes, if these new cultivars blossom, Father reckons we'll be rich,' Dotty gushed. 'Well, comfortable at least,' she amended.

'That's really good news,' Isabella smiled, happy for the family.

'Cors, Father's happy to have got one up on Furneaux. But I'm just pleased I'll be able to buy new material next time we go to a dance. Oh, I mean, it was kind of you to let me adapt that beautiful scarf but...' Her voice trailed off as she looked at Isabella properly for the first time.

'Coo blimmer girl, you're all bissled and battered, what 'ave you been doing?'

'Let's just say I ended up on the wrong side of town,' Isabella said. Seeing Dotty's shocked face and not wishing to embark on yet another explanation, she got to her feet. 'If you'll excuse me, I'll go and change before supper.'

Upstairs, she grimaced down at her scuffed boots. A visit to her cordwainer would be a priority as soon as she returned to London, she thought, quickly removing them along with her bonnet. Her ruined mantle was fit for nothing other than the rag bag, but knowing her thrifty aunt would find a use for it she set it aside. Stepping out of the torn and soiled clothes, she changed into the spare homespun Dotty had found for her. Although the coarse material prickled her skin, at least it was clean. Combing out her hair in front of the mirror, she frowned to see it had grown and was losing its style. *Oh Papa, thank heavens you can't see me now.* An appointment with her coiffeur was a necessity, as was a manicure, she decided frowning at her reddened hands and chipped nails. As the flash of silver at her throat caught the light, a shiver of excitement bubbled up inside her. Uncle Bill seemed a sweetie and hopefully he would answer all her questions about dear Mama.

Feeling better than she had all day, she tripped lightly down the stairs in her stockinged feet, only to be met by a sombre-looking Uncle Frederick. His usually ruddy cheeks were as white as Aunt Mary's tablecloth, his lips pressed into a tight line. *He's found out about the lost basket and envelope from the big house,* she thought, her heart sinking.

'I can explain, Uncle,' she began, remembering Papa telling her it was better to confront situations head-on. 'I will ask Papa to recompense you and...' Her uncle held up his hand to stop her and it was then she saw he was holding a telegram.

'Sit down, Isabella,' he urged. Her heart flipped over at the gravity in his voice.

'What's wrong?' she asked, sinking into the chair he indicated. Her aunt came and sat beside her, and she too was looking upset.

'It's your father. He's passed on, Izzie,' she murmured, taking Isabella's hand.

'Passed on where?' Isabella frowned. Her uncle cleared his throat and looked uneasy.

'He's dead, Isabella,' he told her.

'Dead? But he can't be, I've just received a letter from him,' she cried.

'I know, but from the postmark it would seem it was delayed.'

'But he's at home sorting out his business.' Silence hung heavy in the air as Isabella glanced from one to the other.

'He's been ill for some time, my dear,' Aunt Mary told her gently. 'That's why he asked us to take you in.' Isabella shook her head.

'He told me he was sending me here while he sorted out his affairs. He didn't say anything about being ill.'

'He knew he hadn't long left and wanted to spare you seeing him suffer,' Mary said, squeezing her hand.

'We think losing his investments hastened the end,' her uncle added.

'When you arrived, we did try to explain you were here to stay, but you would insist it was a holiday.' Stunned by the news, Isabella barely heard her aunt. Poor Papa. Why hadn't he let her remain at home? She could have nursed him, cared for him.

The room began to swim around her and she was sure she was going to faint. A bottle of something strong smelling was held under her nose, causing her to inhale sharply. As the giddiness slowly subsided, she heard her aunt's voice as if from a distance.

'Drink this, Izzie, it'll make you feel better.' A cup was held to her lips and she took a sip. It tasted syrupy sweet, yet scorched the back of her throat and set her insides on fire as it made its way down to her stomach. Moments later she felt the blood in her body start to flow again.

'Thank you,' she whispered.

'Elixir of violets. Never fails,' her aunt assured her.

'Perhaps it would have saved Papa,' Isabella sighed.

'Them plants might be powerful but they ain't no cure-alls. More's the pity,' her uncle replied.

'Oh Izzie, we're so very sorry.' The compassion in Mary's voice was too much and the tears began to well.

'Time enough for that after tomorrow.' Isabella stared at her uncle.

'Tomorrow?'

'Yes, girl. If we catch the first train to London in the morning, we should just make the funeral.'

'The funeral? But you're busy with your flowers,' she replied, staring at him in surprise. He shook his head.

'Family comes first, Isabella. William can take care of things for one day. I'll get him to take us to the station. 'Tis right and proper we pay our respects.'

'I don't suppose a young girl like you has a suitable black dress?' Isabella frowned, her head spinning as she tried to remember what Gaskell had packed for her.

'No, I don't think I do,' she replied. 'I have one

at home, of course. Perhaps we could stop off there on the way?' Her aunt and uncle exchanged meaningful looks.

'Won't have time, I'm afraid,' her uncle said quietly.

'Well, let's see what we can find,' her aunt said, leading the way to a door at the end of the kitchen.

Feeling numb, Isabella followed her into the cramped bedroom with its rickety double bed under the window and a closet and chest lining one wall. Then to her consternation, she saw it was her trunks and portmanteau that were taking up the rest of the space.

'Oh Aunt Mary, I had no idea you had all my luggage in your room,' she cried.

'Don't fret, child, 'tis only a place to sleep,' she replied, sifting through the things in her closet and pulling out a long black garment. 'Now this is a bit worn but at least it's appropriate. I've not got a matching hat but a black ribbon tied round your bonnet should suffice. Besides, 'tis unlucky to wear something new to a funeral.'

While her aunt bustled round, practical as ever, Isabella felt choked and couldn't answer. For once in her life, what she wore seemed of little consequence. All she could think of was her dear papa alone in his hour of suffering. Hot tears welled up and spilled down her cheeks.

'Oh Auntie,' she sobbed, sinking down onto the bed and burying her head in her hands. 'I can't believe I'll never see poor Papa again.'

Chapter 13

On the train to London, Isabella alternated between numb disbelief and feeling sick to the stomach. Poor Papa. Why hadn't she'd stayed at home with him? The question went around and round until her head ached. Her uncle, smart in his black coat that smelled of mothballs and with a bowler replacing his trademark straw hat, watched her sadly but was sensitive enough not to attempt conversation. As soon as they reached Paddington station, he steered her through the crowds and out to a hansom cab. Isabella frowned at the horsedrawn conveyance then stared at the motorized one in front.

'Can't afford that,' he told her. After a brief discussion with the driver, still clutching the box he'd been guarding since they'd left home, her uncle clambered into the seat. Reluctantly, she climbed in after him, staring miserably out at the grey mist that swirled up from the Thames to merge with the leaden sky. Everywhere looked melancholy and depressing, reflecting her mood exactly. In silence, they travelled along busy Park Lane, Hyde Park spreading out to the right where, even on a day as gloomy as this, people were out in their carriages.

'I expect the church will be packed,' she said, turning to her uncle. At the thought of seeing Maxwell and their friends again, the vice-like feeling that had gripped her stomach since the previous day, eased just a little. Before he could reply, the familiar Kentish ragstone building where she'd worshipped with Papa loomed ahead. However, instead of pulling up outside the elaborately decorated Gothic church, the cab veered around the corner and stopped outside a small chapel she'd never seen before.

'But this is the wrong place,' she protested. 'All Papa's friends will be waiting at St Michael's.'

'It's all we can afford, Isabella,' he told her sadly.

'That can't be right, surely...,' she began, but he had turned and was communicating with the driver through the small trapdoor behind them.

'Come along, Isabella,' he said, climbing from the cab. She had little option but to follow him inside.

Isabella stared around the dank and dingy chapel in dismay. It was empty save for a vicar she had never seen before, and four pallbearers wearing black gloves and a crepe band on one arm. It felt eerie and very wrong. A shiver pricked her spine.

'Where is everybody? Why isn't Papa being sent off in style?' she whispered.

'I fear we might be the only mourners,' her uncle told her, sinking into one of the narrow pews at the front. Carefully he opened his box and pulled out a small wreath fashioned from violets and moss. 'Your aunt worked all through the night to have this finished in time. Go and place it on top before the vicar begins,' he murmured, handing it to her then pointing towards the altar. It was then she saw the simple, unadorned coffin set on a bier and had to bite her lip to stop herself crying out.

The sound of her boots echoed around the nearly empty building as Isabella moved forward and, with trembling hands, laid the fragrant tribute on top. Tears welling, she stood there, uncertain what to do next, but the vicar, clearly impatient to begin, signalled for her to return to the seat beside her uncle. The service was short and impersonal and, to Isabella's dismay, other than stating his name, made no reference to her papa. Why, it could have been for anyone, she thought sadly as they followed the men carrying the coffin out to the graveyard.

'Oh no,' she cried, pulling her bonnet lower as the drizzle quickly turned into a downpour. 'That's the last thing we need.'

'Have faith, Isabella, 'tis a sure sign your father will go to heaven,' her uncle assured her. Before she could ask him why, he delved into his rapidly disintegrating cardboard box, this time drawing out a posy of flowers tied with white ribbon, which he handed to Isabella.

'May God receive your soul into his safekeeping, Papa,' she sobbed, throwing it onto the coffin where it landed right beside the wreath. Then with the smell of freshly dug earth mingling with the musky scent of wet violets, she made the sign of the cross as her father was laid to rest.

'Oh Uncle, that was terrible,' Isabella wailed, as they returned to the waiting cab. 'I don't understand why Papa's funeral wasn't held in our own church. At least the vicar would have known who he was. And where were all our friends?'

'I'm sorry, Isabella. It was the best we could afford and at least he was spared a pauper's grave.' She stared at him sharply.

'Papa was no pauper,' she cried. Her uncle let out a long sigh.

'I believe your father did tell you he had money problems.'

'Yes, but he was sorting them out, which was why I was sent to stay with ... oh,' she cried, realization dawning.

'We did try to explain it was to be a long-term arrangement,' her uncle said gently. 'You must remember your father loved you very much and had your best interests at heart. He might have made a mess of his business but at least he ensured his personal affairs were in order. Now, we need to call round to Chester Square and collect some of his effects, then hopefully we'll be in time to catch the evening train back to Devonshire,' he said, taking out his pocket watch and frowning. 'As quick as you can, please,' he said, opening the little door and shouting to the driver.

Before Isabella realized it, they were drawing up outside the only home she'd ever known. Staring up at the three-storey building, she felt as if someone had wrenched her heart from her body. To think she would never hear Papa calling to her from his study, sit opposite him at supper regaling him with details of her day, or retire at night to her pretty bed chamber. Unable to bear it any longer, she threw open the door and jumped out.

'Where are you going?' her uncle shouted.

'Back to my home.' However, before she could ascend the first step, the heavy front door opened and Maxwell appeared, a pretty dark-haired girl dressed in the latest vogue, clinging to his arm.

'Maxwell?' she cried, rushing towards him. To her dismay, he stared right through her, almost pushing her out of the way in his haste to pass.

'Maxwell, wait,' she implored.

'Gracious, don't tell me you are acquainted with that shabby-looking woman, darling?' the girl asked, staring at Isabella curiously.

'Never seen her before in my life,' he replied airily.

'But she knew your name,' the girl persisted.

'I am well known in these parts, Cassandra, darling. Now do come along.'

'Did you see what she was wearing? It looked like something from the servants' rag bag.' Hearing Maxwell's harsh laugh in response, Isabella clutched her hand to her heart, feeling as though she'd been stabbed. Rooted to the ground, she stared wretchedly after them until they disappeared out of the square. What was going on? Why had Maxwell ignored her? And who was that fashionable girl on his arm? She glanced down at the outmoded black dress her aunt had loaned her and grimaced.

'Get back into the cab and wait,' her uncle ordered, appearing at her side.

'But I am home now,' she replied.

'I'm afraid this is no longer your home, Isabella. Now do as I say and I'll explain everything when I return,' he insisted. The steely look in his eye forbade further argument and reluctantly she climbed up inside. Bewildered, she watched as he marched purposefully up the steps and tugged on the bell pull. Immediately Jenson appeared and stared him up and down in the discerning way butlers have. Even in her agitated state Isabella couldn't help comparing the smart cut of his jacket to the ill-fitting coat her uncle was wearing.

Remembering Maxwell's remark, she stared down at her dress again. Perhaps he hadn't recognized her. He was used to seeing her in colourful couture, after all. Yes, that had to be it, she thought, returning her attention to the house where her uncle, after discussion with Jenson, was disappearing inside. What was going on now, she wondered. Just as she was about to climb down, her uncle reappeared carrying a parcel tied with string. Without glancing in Isabella's direction, Jenson firmly closed the door.

'Will you please explain what that was all about?' she asked as soon as her uncle climbed up beside her.

'As soon as we're on the train,' he replied. 'Paddington, quick as you can, driver,' he called.

As the cab made its way back to the station, dodging the clutter of horsedrawn traffic and scuttling pedestrians, Isabella's thoughts were in turmoil. Yet she kept coming back to the same two questions. Why had Maxwell ignored her? And who was that girl on his arm?

While the train steamed its way back through the suburbs towards Devonshire, Isabella listened with increasing dismay as her uncle detailed the events of the preceding months.

'And so, you see, when your father realized the extent of his uninsured losses, he had to sell everything he possessed to escape bankruptcy. He tried every option he knew to avoid it but, as often happens in these cases, his so-called friends didn't want to know, let alone help.'

'Hence none of them attending his funeral,' Isabella murmured. He nodded.

'Of course, if he'd had more time...,' her uncle shrugged. 'But by then he knew he was dying and couldn't continue investing for long enough to rebuild his business.' So that was what her papa had meant about needing more time, Isabella thought, recalling their conversation in his study on that fateful night.

'I should have stayed with Papa and helped him,' she murmured.

'As I've already said, he wished to spare you the disgrace. He wanted you to remember him as he was, and the happy times you'd spent together. If it's any consolation, he wrote saying how relieved he felt knowing you would be looked after and have a roof over your head. He also stated that Jenson had been instructed to advise me when he had, er, passed on.'

'Jenson,' she spat. 'He deliberately ignored me today.'

'He has his position to think of, Isabella. You mustn't think too harshly of him for he did agree to pass on your father's effects. He also apprised me of the current situation regarding the house.'

'So I could have stayed there today,' she insisted. He shook his head.

'No, you couldn't. It's been released to the, er, person who benefitted most from your father's downfall.' Isabella's eyes widened in horror.

'You can't mean... Oh no, please tell me it's not Maxwell,' she begged.

'His father, certainly. And, of course, his son has profited too.'

'But how?'

'They bought out the residue and goodwill of his business for a nominal investment.'

'You mean to tell me that all the time I was waiting for Maxwell to come for me or at least reply to my letter, he was appropriating Papa's business as well as courting my replacement?' she cried, feeling foolish and furious in equal amounts.

'I believe the betrothment between Maxwell Neavesham and Cassandra Blye-Smythe, daughter of Lord and Lady Blye-Smythe, has already been announced in *The Times* newspaper. I also understand the, er, gentleman has moved into the property in Chester Square and is busy preparing it for after their nuptials. His future in-laws are to buy them a house in the country for when they start a ... produce offspring.' He gave a cough then, looking embarrassed, fell silent.

The train swayed as it rounded a bend, and Isabella clutched the armrest for support. '*Someone better, someone better,*' the clatter of the wheels seemed to mock.

'I shall never trust another man again in the whole of my life,' she declared. Her uncle smiled sadly.

'You might feel like that now, girl, but one day you'll see it was for the best. That young man's driven by greed and will do anything to acquire the material things of life. You, on the other hand, have been given another chance to meet someone who values you for yourself.'

'Never,' she declared hotly.

'Never is a long time, my dear,' he told her, patting her arm.

'No, Uncle. My life is over. Everything I have known is at an end.'

'That's as may be, but it could be a chance to turn that end into a beginning,' he quirked his brow. 'Think about it, eh?'

Suddenly, it was all too much for Isabella and she stared out of the window. Instead of the passing scenery, all she could see was the image of the pretty dark-haired girl smiling up at her Maxwell. Except he wasn't her Maxwell any more.

'Not wanted, not wanted,' the train seemed to shout louder this time. As for her uncle's notion of turning an end into a beginning, she would have to think if there could be something in that.

'Sometimes, Isabella...' She jumped as his voice broke into her thoughts. 'Sometimes, you need to revisit your past before you can move on to your future.'

'You sound as though you know about that,' she frowned.

'As a matter of fact, I do,' he agreed softly, a faraway look in his eye. 'And one day I shall tell you about it,' he added. 'Now, it's been a traumatic time, so why not close your eyes and try and get some rest.'

Although she sat back in her seat, she couldn't relax, the events of the day playing over and over in her mind. *Poor Papa, why didn't you tell me you were ill? I could have stayed and helped. If I hadn't gone away, Maxwell might still be mine.* But then, had he just been using her all along?

Staring back out of the window, she saw the light was fading, the passing scenery a shadowy blur as it flashed by. As the train rattled onwards, her thoughts turned to the future. Never would she let herself be used again. The question was, what was she going to do now? The train slowed then jerked to a halt, wakening her uncle. He peered out at the platform.

'Ah, Exeter already,' he said, reading the sign illuminated by a gas lamp. Then as the engine gave a hiss and the train began moving, he turned to Isabella and smiled. 'We shall be home soon and William will be waiting with the cart. I want you to know that Mother and I will be happy for you to stay with us as long as you like. I'm afraid we can't offer the fine things of life you are used to, but you are welcome to share what little we have.'

'Thank you, Uncle, that is kind of you,' Isabella murmured, tears welling at the kindness of these generous family members she'd only recently met.

'As long as you can abide living in a semi-detached property, that is,' he grinned, throwing her own words back at her. Isabella hesitated, uncertain whether to voice something that had been puzzling her.

'Although yours is a semi-detached property, it is joined to the one Grandmama lives in and...' She broke off, not wishing to appear rude.

'And what? Spit it out, girl,' he said. 'If there's one thing we have in our family, it's plain speaking.' Reassured, she continued.

'Why are you all cramped into one half of the building when she has the other all to herself? I mean, it would make sense for you to share all the rooms, wouldn't it?' He nodded thoughtfully.

'It would. Trouble is, Grandmother has her peculiar ways, and at this time of life needs to have her things around her, same as she always has. Gets fretful and argumentative else, and that's no good for anyone. So it's easier for us to stay over our side.'

'But you and Auntie have to sleep in the parlour,' she protested.

'The parlour, eh,' he chuckled. 'Have to tell Mother that one.'

'Talking of Auntie, are you sure she really wants me to stay? I mean, she's been very kind but she already has so much to do.'

'Mother insists on it. Cors, you could muck in more,' he pointed out, returning to his former brusque self.

'But I'm already learning to cook and posy and pack the violets each day.'

''Tis selling the flowers we're falling down on.'

'But you send your violets to Covent Garden each day,' Isabella said, staring at him in surprise.

'True, but with Furneaux setting up in competition, we also need to find regular local custom before he does. That's where you could really help us.'

'What do you mean?' she asked.

'Your pretty looks and genteel voice would go down a treat with the local gents. So, if you really want to help your aunt, you can sell our violets in the town each day. What do you say?'

Chapter 14

Hefting the heavy basket of flowers over her arm, Isabella walked through the town and stopped on the wide street between the stationer's and circulating library. Whilst her uncle hadn't insisted she come here today, he'd made it clear that, with Dotty still unable to put any weight on her ankle, it would assist the household budget if Isabella took her place selling their flowers in town. Although no further mention had been made of the family taking her in, she owed them a huge debt and this was the least she could do.

The early-morning air being chill, her aunt had insisted Isabella wear her woollen turnover and a heavier long skirt she'd found in her closet, which was so voluminous, she'd had to tie it with string to hold it up. In truth, though, she hardly noticed the weather for the tribulations of the past few days had left her feeling quite numb. The death of her dear papa had hit her hard, and she was still trying to come to terms with the fact she'd never see his beloved face again. Catching sight of her reflection in the shop window, she grimaced. She looked like a sack, although the mauve ribbon lightened the beige look somewhat. It seemed wrong to be wearing a bright colour, yet her aunt had pointed out that a sombre figure in black mourning attire would put customers off.

'You can grieve in private and it will mean just

as much. Whatever you wear can't change anything, can it? Besides, mauve is worn by those in half-mourning so it's quite acceptable,' she'd said in her practical way as she sat trimming Isabella's bonnet that morning. Reluctantly, she'd had to agree.

Yet now, as she stood waiting for shoppers to emerge from their homes, she couldn't help her thoughts going back over the events of the past week. If only she'd listened to her aunt and uncle, her papa's death might not have come as such a shock, for on many occasions they'd intimated her stay in Devonshire wasn't a temporary measure. They'd also pointed out that, if Maxwell was coming for her, he didn't appear to be hurrying himself. Maxwell! His deception cut to the core of her very being. To think that all the time she'd been waiting patiently for him, he'd been planning his future with another. Never would she put herself in such a vulnerable position again.

''Ow much, me lover?' She jumped as a man of advanced years stopped in front of her. Leaning heavily on his stick, he peered critically at her flowers. Remembering her uncle's reputation was at stake, she forced her lips into a smile.

'Merely a penny ha'penny for a generous bunch, sir,' she told him.

'Tell yer what, I'll give ye a penny a'perd for two bunches,' he said, giving her a canny grin.

'A penny a'perd? Oh, you mean a penny ha'penny.'

'That's what yer said yer was charging, weren't it?' he frowned. Not wishing to appear dim, Isabella nodded quickly. ''Tis our wedding anniversary, see. Wife would love some pretty flowers but one of these would only half-fill her jug,' he said, picking out a bunch and shaking his head sadly. 'Ah well, not to worry,' he sighed, making to return them to her basket.

'Oh please, do take them both,' Isabella urged, handing him another.

'Well, that be mighty kind, maid,' he said, giving her a broad grin as he handed over his penny ha'penny. 'Wife'll be chuffed,' he said.

What a lovely man, she thought, watching as he carefully tapped his way down the street then crossed over to the green opposite. He was obviously a devoted husband and she hoped his wife appreciated him.

A woman wearing a dark blue dress covered by a starched white apron emerged from the stationer's shop carrying a sign. She placed it prominently on the pavement then turned towards Isabella.

'Don't you be taken in by old Mickey,' she called.

'It's his wedding anniversary and he wanted to treat his wife,' Isabella explained. To her surprise the woman chuckled.

'Aye, and tomorrow it'll be her birthday. Haven't seen you around these parts before. Just arrived, have you?' she asked, eyeing Isabella curiously.

'I am holidaying, er, I mean residing with my uncle,' she replied, swallowing the lump that had risen in her throat, for it still hadn't sunk in that she was here permanently.

'You're Fred Northcott's niece? That explains it,' she nodded, looking Isabella up and down.

'Well, sorry for your loss, I'm sure.' Isabella stared at her in surprise. 'Bill mentioned it when he was in yesterday. All I can say is you'd best be more prudent with those flowers, my girl. Your uncle's not known as Frugal Fred for nothing, you know,' she laughed. 'Well, best get on.'

Mindful of the woman's words, Isabella resolved not to be taken in again. She needed to toughen up and not look gullible, then people like old Mickey and Maxwell could no longer consider her an easy target. Whereas before the mere thought of Maxwell would have made her heart skip, now it felt as heavy as stone. A sudden gust of wind blowing in from the sea whipped at her skirts and she edged back against the shelter of the building.

Determined to show her uncle she could sell, she smiled and held out her basket but, although a few people smiled back, nobody stopped as they went about their business. The early-morning shoppers out to buy provisions gave way to smartly dressed ladies who stared down their noses and made disparaging remarks when they saw her. Isabella could only watch enviously as they scrutinized hats in the milliner's, fabric and ribbons in the draper's and the winter display of footwear in the boot and shoe shop.

'Excuse me, Miss.' She turned to see a smartly dressed gentleman, magnificent white whiskers quivering as he beckoned her from his carriage. 'You are selling flowers?' he added when she hesitated.

'Oh, gracious me, yes. I'd quite forgotten,' she said, hurrying over.

'Do you have any tussie-mussies?'

'No, I'm afraid not,' she replied.

'Well, make me up a corsage while I wait then,' he ordered.

'I'm afraid I only have bunches of violets,' she explained apologetically. The man clicked his teeth in annoyance and snapped shut the window. Immediately, the carriage moved away, a cloud of dust rising in its wake.

How rude, Isabella fumed. Well, she wasn't going to stand around to be treated like some common down-and-out. Aware the apparel she'd brought with her was totally unsuitable for her new life, and loath to continue wearing her aunt and cousin's cast-offs, she went to take a look at the merchandise in the draper's. Perhaps she could find some dark mauve material more suitable for her period of mourning.

The shop with its bow window was a far cry from the grand stores of London, the garments at least two seasons behind the current mode, though even that was a distinct improvement on her aunt's outfit. Fond as she'd become of her, Isabella had to admit the woman had no dress sense.

Purposefully, she opened the door, setting the little bell tinkling. To her surprise, inside was like a treasure trove, and with her anger forgotten she stared delightedly at the silks and satins shimmering like jewels in the soft glow of the fluted-crystal oil lamps. Highly polished shelves reaching from floor to ceiling held bolts of damasks, velvets, brocades, cotton, linen, muslins and flannel. Another cabinet revealed a marvellous array of ribbons, lace, hat pins, needles and beads, in front of which stood glass dishes filled with buttons of every description. Cut-glass ones, twinkling like tiny rainbows, caught her eye and, thinking they would make the perfect adornment for a silk blouse, she reached out to inspect them closer.

'Take your thieving hands off.' As the shrill voice pierced the air, Isabella turned to see who was the unfortunate recipient of the tirade, only to find herself being confronted by an officious-looking woman, hair piled high on top of her head.

'Gracious, I was merely perusing your wonderful merchandise,' Isabella explained.

'Well, you can do it from outside. The likes of you are not welcome in this establishment. I cannot have my clients bothered by a common flower girl,' she sniffed, opening the door. Above the tinkling of the bell, Isabella heard a titter coming from the group of smartly attired ladies she'd seen enter earlier.

'I say, did you see what she was wearing?'

'Fancy, a common-or-garden flower girl daring to show her face in here!'

'Whatever are things coming to?' Swallowing down a retort, Isabella squared her shoulders.

'Believe you me, it will be a pleasure to take my custom elsewhere,' she replied, walking smartly outside. As the door slammed shut behind her, she blinked back hot tears. How demeaning. Never had she been treated so atrociously. Why, only a month or two ago she'd been a carefree young woman, happily shopping for her travels at the best stores in London with her trousseau to plan upon her return.

Now she was an orphan, jilted by her betrothed

and ostracized by the very people who used to serve her. Angrily, she dashed away a tear.

'Oh my dear, how dreadful for you.' Isabella looked up to see two ladies of indeterminate years staring anxiously at her. They were wearing identical black jackets showing ruffles of lace at the neck and long black skirts. Each sported a black velvet hat trimmed with different coloured berries at the front.

'It is distressing to see such a pretty young girl in trouble. Do let us help. I'm Agnes,' announced the woman sporting the hat with cherry-red berries. 'And this is my sister Miriam,' she added, gesturing to her companion who nodded enthusiastically, setting her blue cluster shaking.

'Isabella,' she replied. 'Thank you, but I am not actually in trouble.' They stood surveying her doubtfully through clear grey eyes.

'That's not what it looked like from where we were standing,' Agnes sighed.

'We saw and heard everything, my dear,' Miriam added, placing her hand sympathetically on Isabella's arm.

'We have only recently removed to the area ourselves and will certainly not be patronizing that establishment. I take it from your accent that you are not from around here either?' Agnes asked.

'No, I am residing with my aunt and uncle. My papa has just died and I have no one else, you see. I am meant to be selling these flowers, but I'm not having much luck,' Isabella replied, holding up her nearly full basket. The two women exchanged looks then peered at the violets.

'Oh, what a shame, they seem to be wilting even

as we speak. Look, my dear, maybe we can help you. We have rented a nice little house only minutes from here. Why don't you come back with us and partake of some refreshment while we discuss things?' It was a long time since breakfast and Isabella could think of nothing nicer than a hot drink.

'That would be lovely, thank you,' she replied, her spirits rising.

She followed the two women down an alleyway between the boot maker and a grocer's she hadn't noticed before, then on through winding back lanes, away from the town centre. They came to a stop in front of a smart redbrick house set slightly apart from the rest.

Inside, she was met with the familiar scent of beeswax and rose petals. It was mixed with something else she couldn't quite make out, but was familiar enough to remind her of her home in Chester Square. As Agnes turned and gave her a bright smile, Isabella swallowed the lump that had risen in her throat.

'Make yourself at home, my dear,' Agnes invited, throwing open the door to a large, airy room leading off the hallway. 'Sit yourself down while Miriam makes us one of her restorative tisanes. We haven't had time to hire staff yet so are catering for ourselves. We are quite enjoying it though, aren't we, Miriam?' The woman nodded and disappeared.

'Where have you removed from?' Isabella asked, setting her basket down on the floor.

'Oh, that reminds me,' Agnes said quickly, stooping to pick it up again. 'We will be happy to purchase these from you.'

'What, all of them?' Isabella asked, hardly daring to believe her luck.

'Oh yes, they will be most useful. If you'll excuse me, I'll just put them in water,' she smiled.

Relieved to be sitting down after being on her feet for so long, Isabella sank back in the armchair then stared around the room. It was comfortably if not lavishly furnished, the plain walls relieved by velvet drapes at the lattice window and a scattering of colourful rugs. The little carriage clock on the mantelpiece was the only ornamentation, its gentle ticking soothing her frazzled nerves.

'Well, here we are.' Isabella came to with a start as the sisters bustled back into the room, one bearing a tray with three glasses on it, the other a salver of delightful-smelling pastries. 'Oh goodness, child, did we wake you?' Agnes crooned.

'No,' Isabella lied, a smile quivering her lips, for nobody had called her that since her nanny had left.

'This will soon revive you,' Miriam said, handing her a glass in a silver holder. It smelled unusual and she took a chary sip of the warm liquid. 'It's made to my own receipt,' the woman added.

'It is very nice,' Isabella said, taking another sip so as not to offend her. The liquid warmed her insides and she felt herself relaxing.

'Do have a croustade,' Agnes said, proffering a plate along with the salver. 'You'll have heard of Gentleman's Relish, of course. Well, we call these our sisters' savouries,' she giggled.

'They look wonderful,' she said, her mouth watering at the tempting sight. 'Do you have a pastry fork?' she asked.

'Oh, silly me. Yes, of course,' Miriam said, jumping up and going to the sideboard. After much searching, she triumphantly produced the required cutlery, and Isabella eagerly cut into the pastry. It was filled with fluffy egg and herbs, and so delicious she needed no persuading to take another. As Isabella ate, she became aware of the curious looks the two sisters darted her way as they nibbled on their food. No sooner had they finished than Miriam jumped to her feet.

'Goodness, that must be the lunchtime post,' she cried, hurrying from the room.

'Is everything all right, Miriam, dear?' Agnes enquired when she returned frowning at the sheet of notepaper in her hand.

'It would appear Mrs Davey is too unwell to attend our gathering this afternoon. That means we are one short, which – as you know, sister dear – is totally unacceptable.' She looked at the clock. 'And it is too late to let everyone know, so we shall have to turn them away at the door.'

'Is there nothing we can do?' Agnes asked, clutching her hands to her chest. 'If word should spread that we are unreliable...' She closed her eyes as if finishing her sentence was too much for her.

'What are you one too short for?' Isabella enquired. 'Is it your biritch afternoon because, if it is, perhaps I can assist. I play quite a good game.' Immediately Agnes sat up straight, fixing Isabella with her sharp gaze.

'Would you really be willing to help?' she murmured.

'Of course,' she replied, eager to repay these

two dear ladies for their hospitality. 'Thanks to your kindness I have no more flowers to sell, so tell me what I have to do.'

Chapter 15

Miriam refreshed Isabella's glass, insisting she needed another warm drink after standing in the Strand for most of the morning. Thinking how pleasant it was to have these lovely ladies cosseting her, she duly sipped the fragrant liquid and before long felt a blanket of tranquillity wrap around her. Feeling better than she had for ages, she listened as the two sisters outlined what they actually did.

'You mean you can really make contact with the dead?' she shuddered, staring apprehensively from one to the other.

'Don't look so worried, child. It is all perfectly harmless,' Miriam explained.

'And at this time of year, when the veil between this world and the next is at its thinnest, we feel it our duty to bring the spirits of loved ones through to as many people as we can,' Agnes added.

'Having recently suffered the loss of your father, you will appreciate how devastated bereavement leaves one feeling.'

'Yes,' she murmured, tears falling freely down her cheeks.

'That's it, dear, you let it out,' Miriam said, leaning forward and patting her hand. 'You should see the joy on people's faces when we make contact with their dearest departed,' she added quietly.

'It brings them such comfort,' Agnes added. 'Now finish your tisane, dear, it'll do you good.' Isabella nodded and wiped her tears. They partook of their drinks in companionable silence and Isabella began to feel quite comforted herself.

'What you do sounds marvellous. However, I still don't see how I can assist,' she said, draining her drink and putting her empty glass on the table. The two women exchanged looks.

'Because our meetings are so, er, special, they can only work if the number of participants are divisible by three. All we ask is that you join our guests around the table,' Agnes said.

'Oh,' she murmured. In truth, it sounded scary, and butterflies skittered in her stomach at the thought of joining in.

'This is only the third seance we have arranged since arriving in Devonshire and the delicate nature of our work relies on people being able to place their complete trust in us, so if we cancel...,' Miriam shrugged.

'I see your predicament,' Isabella nodded. 'If you're sure all I have to do is sit there, then I'll do it,' she told them.

'Thank you, Isabella,' Agnes smiled, getting to her feet. 'Whilst Miriam prepares a little welcome for each of our ladies, I'll show you where we hold our meetings.'

Isabella rose to follow but her legs almost buckled under her and she had to grip the arm of her chair to stop herself from toppling over.

'Goodness, I must have been sitting down for

too long.' However, Agnes didn't seem to notice as she led the way back down the hallway. As she opened another door, Isabella saw a rosy-cheeked woman, bonnet askew staring at her. Thinking it was one of the expected visitors, she smiled only to gasp in dismay when she realized it was herself reflected in the mirror.

'Goodness,' she cried. 'I look dreadful, positively scruffy even.'

'I have to confess I did wonder about your appearance,' Agnes murmured. 'It is so at variance with your cultured accent. Not that it matters, of course, for you are here purely to make up the numbers.'

'I haven't always dressed like this. Why, I have silks, chiffons and fine jewels in the trunks stored at my aunt and uncle's cottage.' As Agnes turned and looked at her curiously, Isabella felt the need to explain. 'It just hasn't been appropriate to wear them for packing and selling flowers, hence...,' she grimaced down at her coarse dress.

'Well, don't worry about it, child,' Agnes said softly, taking her hand and leading her into a larger room. It was dominated by a round table set with three candlesticks that were interspersed with bowls of violets.

'Oh, my flowers. They have perked up again,' Isabella cried, breathing in the familiar sweet, musky smell.

'Indeed they have, and their uplifting fragrance will attract the spirits. Ah, and here is the bread and soup for their physical nourishment,' Agnes explained as Miriam came in and set the tray in the middle. 'Now, I'll just stoke the fire and draw the drapes, then we will be ready for their appearance.' A loud rat-a-tat sounded, making Isabella jump.

'Oh,' she cried.

'No need to worry, child, it's only the first of our guests arriving,' Miriam said. 'Keep your eyes lowered when they enter, and on no account say anything to anyone. Understand?' Isabella nodded, taking the seat Miriam had pulled out for her. Trying to anticipate how large the gathering would be, she looked around at the chairs and had just counted the ninth when the guests began filing into the room.

Although Isabella closed her eyes as instructed, curiosity got the better of her and she couldn't resist peeping from under her lashes. The visitants appeared to be elderly ladies, dressed in black bonnets, coats and shawls. Strangely, they were all clutching a tiny posy of flowers which they inhaled at frequent intervals. As someone sat down beside her, the aroma of violets wafted her way. Then she got a whiff of another, stronger scent she didn't recognize. Before she had a chance to think what it could be, the door closed and Agnes took her place opposite Isabella.

'Welcome, ladies, to what I hope will prove a comforting afternoon for you,' she smiled graciously. 'Miriam will now light the three candles on the table to bring warmth and light for our beloved spirits to see their way. Inhale deeply of your nosegays then we will all join hands to complete the circle, ready to summon our first visitor.' There was a rustle of movement around the room as the funny-looking posies were placed on the table. Isabella wrinkled her nose as she caught another trace of that strange essence, but then both of her hands were being firmly clasped and the room was filled with an air of anticipation.

'Firstly, we ask if any life force of our dearly departed is waiting to come through,' Agnes explained, looking at them in turn before closing her eyes. 'Is there a beloved spirit here in this room?' she asked. The tension in the room was palpable but there was no answer.

'Beloved spirits, we bring you gifts from life into death,' Agnes intoned. 'Is anybody ready to come through?' she repeated. Silence. 'I can see someone coming, someone connected to the sea, I think.'

'That'll be my Henry, he were a fisherman here,' an excited voice squeaked. Through half-closed eyes, Isabella watched in astonishment as Agnes's head snapped backwards and her mouth sprang open.

'Hello, Elsie, my lover.' Although the gruff, West Country voice was male, it appeared to be coming from Agnes.

'Oh Henry, I miss you so. Tell me you are happy,' the quavering voice pleaded.

'I am, though I miss ye too. Take care ... of ... yerself.' The last words faded away on a whisper. Agnes expelled a deep breath and an expectant hush rippled round the room. Suddenly her head jerked back again.

'I see a man dressed in a flat cap and smock. He's holding a pigeon and smoking a pipe,' Agnes told them.

'Edward Craib, is that you?' a woman's strident

voice asked.

'We summon our beloved Edward Craib into our midst,' Agnes intoned.

'Our beloved Edward Craib,' the ladies all repeated.

'Commune, Edward, and move amongst us.' There was silence. 'Are you there, Edward?'

'Aye,' a voice grumped, again seeming to come through Agnes.

'Welcome, Edward. Do you have a message for your beloved Ivy? She who has cared for you in your hour of need.'

'Aye, I do. Tell 'er not to be so mean with the money I left.' There was a sharp intake of breath from somewhere close to her, but Isabella's eyes were fixed on Agnes. 'Yer should be ashamed of yerself putting a button in the bowl. I expect better of you, Ivy Craib, and I shall be watching yer.'

'Sorry, Edward,' a woman groaned. 'I'll give properly this time.'

'He has gone,' Agnes sighed. 'Wait, I think I can see something else. A blur is trying to materialize. I see a man with grey hair hovering on the periphery. Oh, he has only just passed and is not yet ready to come through.'

Papa, Isabella thought, the blood pounding through her veins. She held her breath and stared hopefully at Agnes but already the woman was calling for the spirit of Walter Ferris to commune.

'Are you there, Walter Ferris?' she repeated but there was only silence, followed by a strangled sob from further down the room.

'Have faith, dear,' Miriam whispered. 'Perhaps he will come through next time.'

Suddenly Agnes opened her eyes and stared around the table as if wondering what she was doing there.

'I feel no other presence waiting, so let us thank those spirits who joined us today and tell them to go in peace.'

'Go in peace,' the group chanted.

'We may now break the circle,' Agnes told them. As the group dropped their hands, Miriam smiled around the room.

'Inhale deeply of your nosegays so that you too go in peace.' The women did as she said, then leaving their flowers on the table, filed silently out of the room. Agnes was already in the hall, a bowl in her outstretched hands which the women all dropped money into on their way out.

'Don't give up, dear. Walter may well speak to you next time,' Miriam murmured to a woman who was dabbing tears from her eyes. 'Perhaps if you brought something he valued along with you next time, it would help the lines of communication.' The woman nodded and dropped several coins into the dish.

'I'll give double today,' muttered the thin-lipped woman who Isabella guessed must be Ivy, waving a note flamboyantly in the air before placing it ceremoniously into the bowl. 'Gawd knows how 'e found out. Always did have eyes in the back of 'is bleeding 'ead. Don't suppose 'e would have told me where 'e 'id 'is gold watch anyhow.'

'Try looking in all his favourite places, my dear,' Miriam suggested.

'I did that the day he died,' Ivy scoffed.

'Perhaps he left it in his pigeon loft,' Agnes

added, coming into the hall. The woman's eyes lit up.

'I never thought of that,' she cried, scurrying out of the door.

'Let us know if you find it, Ivy dear. We do so like to know we've been of help,' Miriam called after her.

When the last guest had left, Miriam held out the dish to Agnes and smiled.

'Our benevolent fund has done well today.'

'That's good to know, dear. You'd better make sure it's put somewhere safe. We can't have those in need missing out,' Agnes giggled as the two women exchanged looks. 'Now we have kept Isabella here quite long enough, so please can you fetch her basket along with payment for her flowers?' As Miriam scuttled away, Agnes turned to Isabella.

'Thank you so much for helping us out today. I don't suppose our paths will cross again but it has been a pleasure meeting you, my dear. And once again, our condolences for your loss.' At the thought of not seeing these two dear ladies again, Isabella's heart sank.

'Oh, but I had hoped I might attend another seance. You see, I think that grey-haired man who had just passed was Papa and...'

'It might not have been, for most of the men who have recently passed will have been old with grey hair,' Agnes interrupted gently. Isabella's heart plummeted. She'd been sure dear Papa had come to speak with her.

'I could always bring more flowers here for you,' she offered, staring at the woman hopefully.

'Please,' she pleaded. 'You see, since arriving in Dawlish, I have been trying to find out about my mama but nobody will tell me. I thought if Papa came through in spirit I could ask him why everyone around here clams up when I ask about her.' Agnes put a consoling hand on Isabella's shoulder.

'If it means that much to you, then we will try and help.'

'Oh, thank you,' Isabella cried.

'You need to understand I get the best results when I've held a precious possession of the deceased person. It seems to connect with their spirit and bring them through. Don't ask me how,' she shrugged. 'I am merely a medium who tries to use the gift I've been given to best effect.'

'This was my mama's,' Isabella told her, putting her hand inside her turnover and holding out the locket. Agnes scrutinized it for a moment then ran a finger across the silver.

'That won't work, it feels too cold. Have you any other of your mother's possessions?'

'Mama's pearls are in my trunk. Would they be any good?'

'They might well be. Pearls are warm. Look, we are holding another seance on Friday. Fetch them along then and we'll see. You can also bring more of those delightful violets too.' Overwhelmed, Isabella nodded excitedly.

'Ah, here's Miriam with your basket, along with recompense for your violets. Til then, Isabella. One more thing, best not mention any of this to anyone. Unlike you, many have a sceptical nature,' Agnes said, patting her hand.

'Keep your spirits up, Isabella,' Miriam chirped,

closing the door behind her.

To her surprise, daylight was beginning to fade and Isabella knew her aunt and uncle would have been expecting her home by now. Guilt flooded through her, for she knew there was plenty she should be helping with. Carefully placing the coins in her pocket, she put her basket over her arm and hurried along the empty street as fast as her worn boots would allow. She felt hot and bothered, her head still spinning from everything she'd witnessed that afternoon. It hardly seemed believable that male voices could materialize from a female mouth, and yet she'd seen it with her own eyes, hadn't she?

Coming to a crossing of the ways, she stared around in dismay. Which road should she take? She didn't recognize any of the buildings. Remembering her last foray into town, she shuddered. She daren't risk wandering into that red rhyll area again. Yet she couldn't stay here. Not knowing if she was heading the right way, she turned into the widest street but hadn't gone far when she heard footsteps behind her. Heart in her mouth and hand on her pocket, she quickened her pace. And as she did so, the person following did the same.

Chapter 16

Panic fluttering in her breast, Isabella stared wildly around for somewhere to hide, but all she could see were high walls with closed garden gates fronting onto the street. She must have turned the wrong way when she'd left the sisters' house and instead of making her way back into town, had strayed into a more affluent area where the buildings were spaced much further apart. Hearing another shout from behind, this time much closer, she broke into a run, her shawl flapping like a sail in the breeze. The blood pounding through her veins marked time with her paces as she ran until her breath was coming in such painful gasps she feared her chest would burst. Finally she saw a wooded glade ahead and, unable to take another step, collapsed under a tree. Not knowing what else to do, she curled herself into a ball, shielded her head with her arms and waited.

'Isabella?' She flinched as the sound came from directly above her. 'Isabella.' The call was more insistent this time. It was only then she recognized the voice, and peering out from under her shawl she saw Felix Furneaux staring anxiously down at her.

'What on earth do you think you were doing chasing after me like that? You frightened the life out of me,' she cried, jumping to her feet. Relief at seeing a familiar face made her voice sharp and it was his turn to flinch.

'You dropped these,' he said, holding out his hand.

'Oh,' she gasped, staring at the copper and silver coins.

'To be honest, I wasn't sure it was you at first, then I recognized the blonde curls bouncing under your bonnet. I did call out, but you hared off down the road like the devil himself was after you,' he explained. 'I presume you've been selling flowers,' he said, gesturing to her basket. 'So, what were you doing in that part of the town?' She hesitated, not wanting to lie yet remembering Agnes warning her not to divulge anything about their seance.

'I managed to sell all my violets then got lost. I thought, I thought ... oh, I don't know what I thought,' she murmured, realizing it would sound foolish to admit she'd feared she was about to be robbed or worse. He hunkered down on the grass and stared anxiously at her.

'Are you all right? Only your face is all flushed and...'

'Of course I'm flushed, having just been chased halfway around Devonshire,' she snapped.

'Halfway around Devonshire?' he chuckled. 'The length of two streets, more like.'

'It would help if they put signs up on the roads around here,' she retorted ignoring his attempt to humour her. 'Every street in London is clearly named.'

'Would it have made any difference when you don't know the area?' Felix asked reasonably. He was right, of course, but fatigue and fright had taken their toll and she wasn't about to admit it. Instead she busied herself putting the money back in her pocket.

'Best check you don't have a hole in that,' he said, indicating her skirt. 'You were scattering a fair few coins as you went.' Never having worn anything in such a poor state before, Isabella shot him a reproachful look which seemed to amuse him further. Determined to prove him wrong, she got to her feet and marched over to the pavement, only to hear the chink of coins falling to the ground as she went. Hearing a muffled laugh, she spun round, only to see he was walking away from her.

'Country bumpkins, you're all the same,' she shouted. 'Not one good manner between you,' she called. He hesitated then slowly turned back to face her.

'Perhaps you would care to explain that comment,' he said.

'Where I come from it is courtesy to offer a lady a lift, yet the other day when I was walking into town you drove straight by with the merest of waves. And now, knowing I haven't the faintest idea where I am, you abandon me,' she cried.

'My home is over there,' he explained, pointing beyond the trees to where she could just make out a long building. 'As it's a fair hike back to your uncle's farm from here, I was going to fetch the trap and drive you home.'

'Oh,' she murmured, embarrassed at being wrong-footed. She was dog-tired, her feet were aching, and the thought of a lift home was appealing. 'Thank you, that would be greatly appreciated,' she added quickly in case he changed his mind. As a sudden gust of wind tugged at her bonnet and lifted her skirts, she sighed in despair. He smiled gently.

'You look all in and it's getting dimpsy. Might I suggest you put your money safely in your basket then wait for me under the tree? Sea breezes are fickle and, on an afternoon like this, can bring in heavy downpours that will soak you to the skin.' Feeling humbled by his consideration, she did as he suggested then watched as he broke into a run. To think she was worried he'd been after her money when all along he'd been trying to return it. Not that she'd known it was Felix then, of course. She couldn't help smiling at the irony.

He was back with his cart a short time later, and it was only when she collapsed into the seat beside him that she realized just how exhausted she felt. It was growing darker by the minute and Isabella wondered how she was going to explain her late return to her aunt and uncle. As if sensing her impatience, Felix coaxed the pony into a trot.

'I was sorry to hear about your father,' he said quietly.

'Thank you,' she murmured, biting down the knot in her throat. 'It was a terrible shock.' He nodded, then fell silent. Thankful for his understanding, she watched as unfamiliar landscape passed by. There were sheep on one side, cows to the other, while in the distance she could make out the gentle sloping of hills. A whiff of that musky scent she recognized brought her back to the present. Even here, laid out like a patchwork of purple, were field after field of violets.

'Goodness,' she murmured.

'Your uncle isn't the only one to grow them,' Felix laughed, seeing her expression. 'Still, it's a shame he's taken it so badly. There really is a big enough market for us all.'

'These are all yours?' she asked, in surprise. He nodded.

'Well, Father's and mine,' he amended.

'I love that smell,' she sighed. 'It reminds me of Mama. She came from around here, so I guess it must have something to do with that.' He shrugged.

'Violets have always grown around this part of Devonshire. Our mild, mizzly weather does have its compensations,' he laughed. 'Although it's only relatively recently they've been specially grown for the London market. Your uncles are savvy fellows, I'll give them that. Still, it's only fair we should have a chance to expand our business too, although it would have been better if we could have done it without causing a rift between our families.'

'Uncle Bill said the same,' she told him.

'He's a good 'un,' Felix replied. 'It's a shame Frederick's not as understanding.'

'Yes,' she agreed. 'He is totally engrossed in his violets. I must admit, I had no idea how complex growing and selling flowers was until I came here.'

'It's a fascinating process,' he agreed. 'But I'm sure you've heard enough.'

'On the contrary, I'd love to hear more.'

'Well, be warned, it's one of my pet subjects. You say the smell of violets reminds you of your mother. That's understandable because incoming smells get processed by the olfactory bulb in your nose. They then run along the bottom of the brain through the bits most associated with emotion and recall, the amygdala and hippocampus.'

'Gracious, you sound like a scientist,' she exclaimed, staring at his animated face in astonishment.

'Ah well, we country bumpkins do pick up the odd thing here and there, you know,' he drawled. Recalling her earlier words, Isabella flushed. 'Actually, I learned most of this from a man called Armand Millet. When Father realized farming was no longer viable, he arranged for me to spend time at his nursery at Bourg-la-Reine just outside Paris.'

'Fascinating, although I don't see how all that makes me remember Mama,' she frowned.

'Because sight, sound and touch don't take that route, it's our sense of smell that triggers powerful emotional memories. Perhaps your mother wore violets in some form when she was cuddling you?' Isabella screwed up her nose and tried to picture such a scenario but could only recall the fragrance and a snatch of song. She closed her eyes, willing the words to appear, then shook her head in exasperation.

'Don't try too hard to remember,' he said. 'Sometimes these things surface when we're not thinking about them.' Isabella turned to face him.

'You sound as if you're speaking from experience. What's your mother like?'

'No idea,' he shrugged. 'She left when I was five.'

'Oh, I'm so sorry. I didn't know,' she replied.

'It was a long time ago,' he replied, quickly turning his attention back to the pony, but Isabella had heard the bitterness in his voice. She sat back in her seat and watched as he expertly guided the trap down the narrow lane towards a hamlet of thatched cottages she recognized. They were nearing home and she crossed her fingers, wishing for her uncle to be in a good mood.

'Just to clear the air,' Felix said, breaking into her thoughts. 'You looked quite happy striding into town the other day so I didn't think there was a problem. Besides, courtesy dictates a gentleman doesn't offer a lift to a lady who is promised to another. Unless she is in dire need, of course.'

'Well, you needn't bother yourself on that score,' Isabella said, giving a harsh laugh. 'It appears Maxwell is now promised to another.' She saw a spark flash in his green eyes and quickly added: 'I shall never trust another man again for as long as I live.' He raised his brow, but didn't say anything. The threatened drizzle began to fall and Isabella sighed.

'Does it always rain around here?' she asked, pulling her shawl tighter round her.

'Most days,' he nodded. 'But then if it didn't the violets wouldn't flourish and emanate their delicate fragrance.'

'Such eloquence, Mr Furneaux,' she replied, staring at him in surprise. As a flush crept up his neck, she turned away, breathing in the country air. He was right, the smell of violets did seem extra sweet tonight, unlike the pungent nosegays at the seance. She must remember to ask the sisters what they'd added to her flowers.

As Felix drew to a halt outside the little gate, Isabella saw Silver munching at the sparse grass that passed for a front lawn. Her uncle must be back from delivering his flowers to the station, Isabella realized.

'I'm much obliged for the lift,' she said, jumping down.

'My pleasure. I hope our paths cross again,' he said, handing down her basket. As their hands touched, time seemed to stand still as they stood looking at each other.

'Oh, er, yes,' she murmured. Then she gathered her senses. With a polite doff of his cap, he called for his pony to walk on.

Feeling hot and bothered, Isabella made her way round to the pump in the yard. The cold water stung her flushed cheeks like needles and she couldn't help longing for a warm bathe in a tub. Suddenly, the kitchen door was thrown open, spilling light from the indoor lamps onto the pathway.

'Where's yer been, girl? Mother's worried sick,' her uncle called. He was still in his outdoor clothes, the ubiquitous straw hat wedged firmly on his head. 'I were just about to round up William and come looking for yer.'

'I'm sorry. I got, er, delayed,' Isabella replied, drying her face on her turnover as she followed him inside. She was just wondering how to explain her lateness when he spotted the money in her basket.

'Well, I'll be. Will yer look at this, Mother,' he cried, breaking into a grin. 'Our Izzie has sold all her flowers.' Taking the basket from her, he upturned it and there was a jingle as the coins spilled out onto the table.

'Well done, dear,' she exclaimed, putting down her skillet. 'That's more than our Dotty usually brings home.' Feeling pleased with their reaction, Isabella sniffed the air appreciatively.

''Tis stoo and dough balls,' her aunt explained. 'A good meal to reward a good day's selling,' she beamed.

'Perhaps she had some help,' William grunted, banging the mud off his boots on the kitchen step. 'I saw Furneaux dropping her off just now.'

'Felix kindly offered me a lift, but I can assure you he had nothing to do with selling the flowers,' Isabella protested as Frederick turned and glared at her.

'Leave Izzie be, you two,' Mary chided.

'You're so pretty, Izzie, I bet lots of handsome men stopped to buy your flowers,' Alice sighed, staring at Isabella as though she were a princess. Recalling the old man who'd tricked her out of a penny ha'pennny, and the snooty man in his carriage, Isabella shook her head.

'I'm afraid they didn't, Alice.'

'I would have if I were bigger,' Thomas told her, giving her a beaming smile.

'And you won't grow any bigger unless you eat up, young man,' his mother told him.

'You did really well,' Dotty told her grudgingly. 'Where exactly did you stand?'

'Outside the circulating library and stationer's, as you directed,' Isabella replied.

'Well, must be 'cos you talks posh, then,' her cousin pouted, clearly put out that Isabella had sold all her flowers. 'When this wretched ankle's better, I'm going to come with you and see how you do it.'

'Quiet now,' Frederick ordered. 'Sit and savour the good food Mother's cooked for us.'

The rest of the meal passed in silence and Isabella began to relax her guard. It seemed everyone had taken it for granted that she'd sold everything in the Strand. Or had they? Feeling William's gaze on her, she looked up to see him eyeing her speculatively. She turned her attention back to her plate and was surprised to find she could manage the large portion her aunt had given her. If she carried on eating like this, she would have to make allowances when she adapted the dresses she'd brought with her. She was just about to ask her aunt if she could go into her room and open her trunk, when her uncle's voice brought her back to the present.

'That were a lovely drop of stoo, Mother. Alice and Thomas, you can clear away while I go through the list of chores for tomorrow with the others.' He waited whilst they gathered up the dishes and went out to the scullery before turning to face them. 'Now listen ye up, the weather's on the turn so we need to ensure our plants are covered. Boy, you'll help me do that in the morning, after we've picked the flowers for Mother and the girl to posy and pack.'

'I can help with the posy and packing too,' Isabella offered, looking forward to spending a few hours with her aunt and Dotty in the barn. It would certainly be better than traipsing into town again. They stared at her in surprise.

'But tomorrow's Thursday,' Dotty reminded her. 'Mrs Tripe will be waiting at the big house for her flowers.'

'You don't mean I've to go there again?' she asked.

'Give me one good reason why you shouldn't, girl?' her uncle asked, turning his shrewd gaze upon her. Isabella returned his look.

'They didn't buy any violets last week,' she pointed out.

'Ah, but that were before you had the selling experience. We're expecting great things of you after today,' he told her.

Isabella stared at him in disbelief, shivers tingling her spine as she recalled the confrontation with Somber, the sneering look of Mrs Pride and, worst of all, the lewd looks and suggestive remarks of Lord Lester.

Chapter 17

'Right, I'm off to get Mother ready for bed,' Mary announced.

'Do you need any help?' Isabella offered. 'I haven't seen her since I returned from Papa's funer– London,' she amended, feeling the tears begin to well. Her aunt shook her head.

'You look exhausted, dear. I told Father it was too soon to send you trekking into town but he insisted that being occupied would be the best thing. Seems he was right, too. I still can't believe how well you did today, and you not knowing anyone round here, either,' she exclaimed. 'These will swell the coffers nicely,' she added, collecting up the coins and dropping them into the pottery pig on the dresser. Embarrassed by the unmerited praise, Isabella stared down at her lap, then remembered the state of her skirt.

'There seems to be a hole in my pocket, Aunt Mary, so may I retrieve some things from my trunk?'

'Of course, dear. Not now, though,' she said as Isabella got to her feet. 'We'll do it together when I get back, then you can tell me more about your day.' She turned to Dotty. 'You need to put your foot up and rest that ankle, so you can keep Izzie company. I'll expect fresh tea in the pot when I comes back, mind.'

As the door closed behind her, Dotty turned to Isabella, shooting her a quizzical look.

'So, where else did you go today then?'

'What do you mean?' Isabella frowned.

'Oh, come on, Izzie. You can't fool me. You've been gone since breakfast and everyone knows the law moves us on if we spend too long in one place. If you've found a good spot to sell, then it's only fair you share.'

Isabella thought quickly. The sisters had been good to her and, having been asked not to say anything about the seance, it was only right to honour their wishes. Then she remembered the man in the carriage and began relating the incident.

'Coo, you never told him you had no corsages?' Dotty exclaimed, her eyes widening in disbelief.

'Well, I only had the bunches of violets, didn't

I?' Isabella shrugged.

'Blimmer. Isabella Carrington, don't you know nothing?' Dotty cried. 'Corsages command double the price for half the flowers. You takes a small handful in yer fist, wrap leaves around the stems, twist and add a pin. Easy-peasy, lemon-squeezy. Cor luv us, I thought you said you'd worn them on your posh frocks.'

'I have. It's just that I never studied how they were composed.' Dotty gave an unladylike snort then fixed Isabella with her beady look.

'You still haven't said where you moved to.'

'Goodness, I remember now. Oh, it was quite awful, Dotty. I ventured into the linen draper's to peruse their merchandise and this horrid, plain-spoken woman demanded I leave the premises.' She closed her eyes, shuddering at the memory.

'Well blow me, I never known that to happen in Pudge's before,' Dotty whistled. ''Ang on, it was Pudge's you went in, wasn't it?'

'The establishment down from the circulating library and stationer's?'

'That's not Pudge's, silly. They're further back. Friendly in there, they are, help you find the material and corsets you need. That shop you went in is the one the toffs use. It's known for charging fancy prices, and rumour has it there's a room at the back where they lace portly matrons into stays to make them look maidenly. Sometimes even pulling them to fainting point and thinking it funny, can you believe?' Dotty came to a halt, then groaned. 'Oh 'eck, don't tell me you went into the smartest shop in town looking like that?' she asked, pointing to the coarse skirt Isabella had borrowed.

'Well, yes, I did actually.'

'That explains it then, girl. Didn't you notice the fine dresses the other ladies had on?'

'Of course, that is why I thought the establishment would have the appropriate attire I was seeking.'

'Look, Izzie, I don't wish to be mean – especially after all you've been through – but someone's got to point out you're down on your luck.'

'What do you mean?' Isabella asked, wishing the girl wouldn't speak in riddles.

You're working-class like us now.' Isabella stared at her cousin in dismay. Working-class? How absolutely frightful.

'Blimmer, girl, you gone all pale. Still, thank the shining stars you're not stuck indoors like me,' she sighed, staring down at her bound ankle.

'Are you still in much pain?' Isabella asked, remorseful she hadn't thought to enquire before.

'Me ankle's not so bad but me poor heart's sick as a dog. Tomorrow was always me favourite day of the week, see, but you'll be the lucky one going to the big house.'

'Hardly lucky,' Isabella retorted, the mere thought giving her palpitations. 'I mean, how do I approach it after last time?'

'By the back door, I should think,' Dotty chortled then, seeing her cousin's distraught look, became serious. 'Seems to me you should take a large slice of humble pie with you.'

'Has Auntie made some?' Isabella asked, staring around the kitchen hopefully. This time Dotty dissolved into hysterics, tears of mirth running down her cheeks.

'You're a card, Izzie, and no mistake,' she chuckled. 'It means you have to appear all meek, say you're sorry. Look, go around the back and tap on the door. I expect Molly, the scully, will answer. Ask to speak to Mrs Tripe. She's all right, she is. It's always good to enquire about her bunions. Suffers terribly, she does. Then say you've brought the best violets for her cooking and how many would she like?'

'You make it sound so easy,' Isabella murmured.

'That's 'cos it is. And, er...' she fumbled in her pocket and drew out a note. 'Do you think you can see Alfred gets me message this time?' She fixed Isabella with her dark gaze.

'I'll do my best,' Isabella assured her.

'Quick, put it in your pocket, someone's coming,' Dotty hissed, passing it over just as Mary came back into the room.

'I'm sure Mother's getting worse,' she muttered, putting her tray down on the side. 'Oh Dotty, there's no tea,' she cried picking up the empty pot. 'Never mind, I'll make some later when Izzie's fetched what she wants from her trunk.'

'Sorry, Mother, we were busy blathering. I'll brew a pot for when you're done.'

'Thanks, pet. It's time Alice and Thomas were away to their bed, they've school in the morning. Fetch them in, will you, and make sure they have a good wash before they go up? Come on then, Izzie,' she smiled, leading the way to her bedroom and setting a match to the lamp.

The room was cold and appeared even more crowded than Isabella remembered. If she'd thought the three of them were jam-packed into the room upstairs, it was nothing to the confines her aunt and uncle were enduring.

'Look, Auntie, once I've sorted everything out, my luggage can be stored in the barn like Uncle originally suggested. Then you would have more space in here,' she said, conscience pricking. Her aunt smiled.

'Don't you worry about that. Like I said, all we do is sleep in here. Not that we have much time for even that these days,' she sighed. 'Now, is this the trunk you want opening?' she asked, pointing to the largest that was almost hidden under the portmanteau.

'It is, but I don't want to put you to any trouble,' Isabella said, wishing the kindly woman would leave her to her own devices. Although she'd had a cursory look through her things when she'd first arrived, she had yet to discover exactly what Gaskell had packed. 'You look fatigued, Auntie. Why don't you go and have a cup of tea with Dotty whilst I sort out what I need?' she suggested.

'I'm sure you must be tired too, Isabella,' the woman replied, lifting the portmanteau onto the floor. 'Besides, you need company after all you've been through. I know Father and I would wish for someone to look out for our Dotty and Alice if they – heaven forbid – should find themselves in a similar situation. Now, what exactly are you looking for?'

'A lilac dress. I thought it would be more appropriate to wear than...' She came to a halt, remembering it was her aunt's dress she was wearing. 'Sorry, I don't wish to appear rude,' she added, quickly lifting the lid of her trunk.

'No offence taken, dear,' her aunt replied. 'I'm sure it must be difficult adapting to your new life here,' she added quietly. 'How are you really feeling? I thought you were looking a little flushed when you returned earlier.'

'That's probably because I'm only used to strolling around the park, not walking miles to reach the town. Plus, I'm still getting used to washing in cold water,' Isabella replied, burying her head in her luggage. Her aunt watched in silence for a few moments.

'I'm sure you have a lot of things to come to terms with,' she eventually replied. 'Just remember I'm here if you ever want to chat about anything.'

'Thank you, Auntie,' Isabella murmured, swallowing down the lump that once again knotted her throat. 'And I really do want to know more about Mama.'

'What I meant was...,' her aunt began, then shook her head. 'Oh, never mind.'

Isabella continued searching until she found the elusive garment. Jumping to her feet, she shook out the folds of her silk dress. As the soft cloth shimmered in the flickering candlelight, her aunt gasped. Hesitantly, she reached out and gently stroked the delicate material.

'Why, 'tis the finest thing I ever did see, Izzie, but not for the life we live here. Those delicate threads would soon get snagged out in the flower gardens.'

'Yes,' Isabella sighed, throwing it down on the bed and delving back into her trunk. After searching through yet more layers of fine paper – for

Gaskell had been a meticulous packer – she came across a lavender dress. It was made of satin and cotton and had a matching tailored jacket with covered buttons down the front.

'What about this outfit?' she asked, holding it up for her aunt to see.

'That's a bit better, I suppose,' she said. Hearing the doubt in her aunt's voice, Isabella frowned.

'What's wrong with it? The colour is appropriate for lighter mourning attire, surely?'

'Yes, it is and these pastel colours suit you a treat. But...'

'But what?' Isabella asked.

'It's still very grand for round here,' Mary said, shaking her head.

'Well, I think it will do perfectly,' Isabella replied, recalling the sneers of the ladies in the shop earlier. She'd show them. This might have been made back in the summer, but it was more in vogue than anything they'd been wearing. Ignoring her aunt's misgivings, she tossed the garments on top of the silk dress.

'Now, somewhere round here there should be a hat trimmed in a similar material,' she added, scrutinizing the rest of her luggage. 'Ah, here it is,' she cried, holding up a satin-covered creation from a box covered in pink damask. Popping it on her head, she twirled around in front of her bemused aunt.

'That's a fine hat, to be sure, but again very grand for these parts. And you'll still need a turnover, for the wind can be bitter blowing in from the sea this time of year.' But Isabella hardly heard her for she was busy searching for the box containing her pearls. 'Oh Izzie, I thought we'd agreed those should be stored safely away,' Mary groaned. 'In fact, Father said he was going to take them to the bank for safe keeping.'

'Oh, he did, did he?' Isabella cried. 'Well, sorry to disappoint you but I shall be keeping Mama's pearls with me,' she said, slipping them quickly into the pocket of the lavender jacket. No way was he getting his hands on those to fund more of his flower investment, she vowed.

'Well, if you're sure,' her aunt sighed. 'Now, let's get cleared away then you can take your posh outfit through to show the others.'

'I'd actually like to tidy my things by myself, Auntie, if you don't mind. Then I shall retire for the night, for I really am very fatigued.'

'Of course, my dear,' Mary replied. 'Though if you're that tired I can see to all this,' she offered gesturing to the clothes strewn over the bed.

'Thank you, but I'd like to see what else I have in here,' she said firmly. 'You go and have your tea,' she urged, as her aunt hovered uncertainly.

'Well, mind Alice when you go up, for she'll be asleep by now. Oh, and before I go, I just want to ask you how you managed to shift all those flowers today? It occurred to me when I was seeing to Mother that it were strange you selling more than our Dotty. And she never gets that much money for them either,' she added, giving Isabella a quizzical look.

'Must be beginner's luck,' Isabella shrugged, wishing the woman wouldn't keep on about it. 'Thank you for your help, Auntie. Now, if you don't mind, I really am exhausted.' Mary stared at her for a moment then nodded.

As soon as her aunt had gone, Isabella returned her things to the trunk. Then she checked her pearls were safely secreted in her pocket for she daren't risk her uncle getting his hands on them to further finance his business. It seemed he had already used the money Papa sent for his own ends. Which reminded her, he had yet to show her what was in the parcel Jenson had given him when they'd visited her old home in Chester Square. He'd said it contained her papa's effects, which surely meant money. She just hoped he hadn't already spent that as well. It was difficult to equate all this with the man who'd shown such compassion at her papa's funeral yet, as her experience with Maxwell had taught her, men were not to be trusted.

Chapter 18

Despite her aunt's misgivings and the damp, dismal weather, Isabella left the house the next morning wearing her lavender outfit, complete with matching hat. Working-class she might now be, but after the episode in the draper's she absolutely refused to look or act like it. Standards would be maintained at all times, she vowed. Not only that, she would work hard so that one day she'd be in a position to return to the social standing she was used to.

Still unused to being out at such an hour, the

early-morning chill caught her unawares and gratefully she pulled her aunt's turnover tighter around her shoulders. It was the one concession to which she'd agreed in order to appease the woman, and one for which she was now thankful. She hefted the heavy basket over her arm and strode purposefully down the road, giving the appearance of one who had not a care in the world. Her insides, though, were wobbling like one of the jellies her nanny used to make for her birthday.

'Morning, my dear.' Lost in thought, she hadn't seen the cart approach, and looking up she saw Uncle Bill waving at her.

'Good morning, Uncle,' she called.

'Yer looking prettier than ever, though a bit smart for working, I'd have thought. Care for a lift?' he asked, drawing up alongside.

'But you're travelling in the opposite direction,' Isabella said. He grinned then stepped down from the cart and guided the pony backwards into the field he had just passed. Pulling the animal forward again, he turned to Isabella.

'I be going the right way now,' he chuckled. 'Come on.' Climbing back up, he patted the seat beside him, then while he waited for Isabella to settle herself, eased a clay pipe from under his cap and a box from his capacious pocket. Tamping tobacco from pouch to bowl, he expertly lit it. Taking a puff, he sighed contentedly. 'First smoke of the day's always the best. Best not tell Fred, though. He's forever moaning it's a waste of money,' he said, tapping the side of his nose with his finger. 'Now then, how yer feeling this morning?'

'Sick to my stomach, Uncle,' she replied.

'Best to face your fears head-on. Once you done that there's nothing left to dread,' he told her.

'You sound like you're speaking from experience,' she said.

'It's what I do every day, dear,' he sighed and lapsed into silence. His bereft look was such a contrast to his normal demeanour that after a while she felt compelled to ask him what was wrong. He looked at her bleakly.

'Sometimes, things happen in life you just have to overcome,' he murmured. 'Now, here we are,' he added, before Isabella could ask what he meant.

'Oh,' she cried, staring at the boxed hedge he'd stopped beside. 'I should have told you I was on my way to the big house.'

'I know that, dear, and here we are. See that gap there?' Isabella looked to where he was pointing and saw a double green gate discreetly placed in the dark shrubbery where the lane widened.

'That be the back entrance. Only servants and trade use it, so if you go in that way there's no chance of his Lordship seeing you arrive. 'Tis what you're worried about, isn't it?' he asked. Isabella nodded.

'Oh Uncle Bill, you're wonderful. Thank you so much,' she said, jumping down onto the track. 'I can't tell you how much better I feel now.'

'Chin up,' he smiled. She watched in surprise as he turned his cart right around and went back the way they'd come. Clearly he had been on his way to see Uncle Frederick and had altered his route just to give her a lift. Dear Uncle Bill, he'd known she was nervous and set out to help. She couldn't wait to visit him and hear what he had to say about her mama.

Remembering her earlier resolve to maintain standards, she shrugged off the worn turnover and put it over her arm. She lifted the heavy iron latch, walked briskly up the path and tapped on the back door. It was opened by a young girl wearing a white apron and mob cap. She blinked at Isabella in surprise.

'Good morning,' Isabella smiled.

'You needs the front entrance, Miss,' she squeaked, shutting the door in Isabella's face.

Isabella frowned. Last week, she'd not only been chastised for using the front door but commanded to use the trade entrance. Yet now, when she did, it appeared that was also wrong. Well, she couldn't stand here dithering all day, she thought, lifting the knocker and trying again. This time the door was opened by a plump woman of middle years wearing a white apron and cap, a smudge of flour smeared across one cheek. The little maid was peering out from behind her skirts like an inquisitive child.

'Good morning. I have brought violets for Mrs Tripe,' Isabella said.

'I see the flowers but who is bringing them, I ask myself,' the woman replied.

'Forgive me. My name is Isabella Carrington and I am here on behalf of my cousin Dorothy who has hurt her ankle and is indisposed.'

'Well, I be begger'd. You're Dotty's cousin?' she asked, looking Isabella up and down. 'Why didn't you say so? I'm Mrs Tripe, the cook. Come wayin, we're due a skatt,' she said peering up at the leaden sky. 'Molly you chump, didn't you see her flower basket?'

'But she talks lah-di-dah like the toffs,' the maid squeaked. 'And look at 'er posh frock.'

'Stop gawpin' and get back to your work. Them pots won't wash themselves.' She watched as the maid scurried into a room leading off the kitchen then shook her head.

''Bout as much sense as a sausage, that one. Still, it keeps her out of the workhouse,' she said, wiping her hands on her apron. 'Now sit yerself down and tell me how Dotty is,' she added, pulling out a chair.

'Thank you,' Isabella replied, sinking gratefully into it.

'Dotty always has a drink and a nubbie, so I dare say you'd like the same? Or perhaps a glass of elderflower cordial would be more to your taste?' she said uncertainly.

'A cup of coffee and one of your delicious nubbies would be most welcome,' she replied, remembering the heavenly cup she'd been served the previous week.

Whilst the woman bustled about, Isabella stared around the room, taking in the signs of frantic activity. The row of gleaming copper pans above the range, steam rising from a bowl of something delicious-smelling cooling on a work surface, the half-rolled-out pastry on the table beside the floury rolling pin, and a luscious Victoria sandwich awaiting decoration on a shelf above.

'His nibs is entertaining today, so we're up to our eyes in it,' Mrs Tripe said, placing a cup and plate in front of her. Isabella smiled her thanks then lifted the cup, inhaling the aroma in happy anticipation. However, it smelled like the coffee her aunt made. Swallowing down her disappointment, she took a bite of the nubbie.

'Delicious,' she cried. The cook smiled.

'That's what Dotty always says. How's her ankle?'

'It still pains her but she did say this morning she could put it to the ground better,' Isabella told her.

'Good, good. Dare say it won't be long til she calls again, which will be a relief to us all, what with Alfie going round with a face longer than an eel.'

'I have a note for him from Dotty actually,' Isabella said, retrieving it from her pocket.

'I'll see he gets it. Might cheer him up,' she said, giving a wink as she placed it in her drawer. 'Now, Isabella, before we get down to business, tell me how you're settling in?'

'Everyone's been so kind,' she replied diplomatically.

'But you feel like yer wings have been clipped, eh?' the cook replied, staring at her with knowing eyes.

'That's exactly it,' she cried. 'I don't wish to appear ungrateful, but everything is so regimented.' The cook chuckled.

'Long for freedom, eh? Ellie were just the same.'

'You knew my mama?' Isabella stared at the woman in surprise.

'Gawd love us, yes. We was at school together.'

'Really?' she gasped. 'But you're a cook and old

... oh,' she said, her hand flying to her mouth in embarrassment. 'Sorry, I didn't mean to be rude, but I only remember Mama as a young lady.'

'Ah, she always aspired to better things,' the woman nodded with a smile. 'Used to lead his Lordship a merry dance.'

'You were all at school together?'

'Why, love us, no. He were privately tutored. Fancied Ellie something chronic, he did, but she were having none of it. Right sore he was when she told him she'd fallen for someone else.'

'That would have been my papa,' Isabella cried, hardly able to contain her excitement. The woman stared at her for a moment, then nodded.

'Guess it must have been.'

Isabella leaned forward in her seat, eager for more information, but before she could ask anything else the door burst open and the housekeeper strode into the room, starched skirts swishing.

'What is the meaning of this? I'm surprised you have the time to entertain, Mrs Tripe, what with his Lordship expecting a houseful of important guests.' Although her strident voice addressed the cook, it was Isabella she was glaring at.

'That's the very reason I asked for Miss Isabella here to bring extra flowers today,' Mrs Tripe told her. Although Isabella's stomach had flipped at the sound of the housekeeper's voice, clearly the cook wasn't fazed.

'I see. Well, I trust they are of a better standard than last time,' she sniffed. Seeing Isabella bridle, the cook intervened.

'These are perfect.'

‘Tell me how much the girl needs paying then get back to your duties,’ she snapped. Deliberately the cook picked up Isabella’s basket and counted out twenty bunches. ‘That’s an awful lot of flowers, Mrs Tripe.’

‘No doubt his Lordship’s guests will be bringing their daughters so he’ll be expecting an awful lot of cake, all with his signature crystallized violets on top,’ the cook countered. There was a sharp intake of breath and Isabella feared the woman had gone too far.

‘Wait here, girl. I will get your money,’ the housekeeper finally replied, her clipped voice showing her annoyance.

‘Okerd old bissom,’ the cook muttered as the door closed behind her.

‘Thank you, Mrs Tripe, that’s nearly half my flowers you’ve bought there,’ Isabella said, taking back her basket.

‘Don’t you worry, maid. His Lordship’s guests makes short work of my fancies especially when he’s trying to impress them. Cors, now I’ll have to spend all afternoon de-stemming, washing and drying them before beating up egg and sugaring them. Still, it was worth it to see the look on ’er face.’

‘I’d be pleased to help. I can’t believe you went to school with my mama,’ Isabella said, shaking her head.

‘Ah, we had some larks, I can tell yer,’ she said, a faraway look in her eye. ‘You’ve the daps when you smile even though…’ To Isabella’s frustration, the door opened and her voice trailed away.

‘You will find the correct coinage inside,’ the

housekeeper announced, striding back into the room and slapping a brown envelope down on the table. 'Now I'd be obliged if you would let my cook resume her duties.'

'Of course,' Isabella replied politely and pocketed the money. With a swish of her skirts, the housekeeper left and the cook let out a long sigh.

'Always gets her corsets crinkled when his nibs is expecting guests. Fancies herself as the next Lady Lester, I reckon. Can't see him being attracted to a wrinkled old prune like that when it's the young 'uns he likes. Well, I'd best get on,' Mrs Tripe said, wiping her hands on her apron again. 'Tell Dotty I'll make sure Alfie gets her note and I hopes to see her soon. It's been real nice to meet you, maid. Oh, you didn't drink your coffee,' she said, holding out the cup. Isabella stared down at the bitter-looking liquid now coated with crinkled skin and felt her stomach heave.

'Thank you, Mrs Tripe, but I mustn't detain you,' she replied, quickly opening the back door.

It had stopped raining and the air smelled fresh. Even a few birds were singing as, swinging her now half-empty basket, Isabella tripped lightly down the path. She was just closing the gate behind her when a voice sent a shiver snaking down her spine.

'Behold, a beautiful sight to brighten the day.'

'What are you doing here?' she gasped, finding herself face to face with Lord Lester who was holding the reins of a heavily lathered horse.

'I believe I live here, my dear,' he replied, giving a snort of derision. Catching sight of the half-empty basket, he gave her a speculative look.

'From the look of things, you have given one of my suggestions due consideration. I am relieved because, between you and me, I would have hated to switch allegiance, nice chap though I believe Furneaux to be. As for you, Miss Isabella Carrington, you have surely had enough of living in squalor by now, so how about my other proposition?' he asked, eyeing her slowly up and down like she was a prize filly.

Isabella swallowed hard, wishing she'd left a few moments later. If only she'd forced herself to drink that frightful coffee, she would have avoided him. She glanced down the lane, but it was empty.

'Only trade has cause to come around this way,' Lord Lester grinned, clearly enjoying her predicament. 'But then, you know that, don't you. I have to say, despite your circumstances, you are looking far more fetching than you did last week,' he said, moving closer. Realizing she was trapped between him and the gate, she tried dodging to his right, but he anticipated her move, for his hand snaked out and grabbed her arm.

'Not only is the lady spirited, she likes to fight like an alley cat,' he smirked, pulling her close. Desperately, she tried to pull away but he tightened his grip. 'Your mother did too, you know. Such a shame she chose the wrong man. You'd do well to learn from her mistake so you don't find yourself in the same predicament.'

'And what would that have been?' Isabella asked, forcing a smile. Perhaps if she humoured him, he would let her go.

'A rather large one,' he leered, leaning closer. As his lips sought hers, Isabella saw red and her knee came up and delivered a sharp kick to his nether regions. He gave a groan, his legs sagged and he went glassy-eyed. Seizing her opportunity, she snatched her hand away and slapped his cheek as hard as she could.

'Why, you little...' he wheezed but, seizing the moment, Isabella turned and shot off down the lane. 'You'll pay for this, Miss High and Mighty Carrington. And so will your family.'

Chapter 19

Isabella ran until her breath was coming in gasps and the nagging stitch at her side forced her to stop. As she slumped against a tree, trying to regain her composure, her terror turned to anger. How dare the man intimidate her like that? Alley cat indeed. Flowers or not, there was no way she would set foot inside the big house again. If Dotty still wasn't strong enough to make the journey next week then Uncle Frederick would jolly well have to take them himself. 'Hell and damnation to all men,' she shouted but the screeching of the gulls was her only response.

She stamped along, glaring down at the path, heedless of the hedge-banks closing in on either side. Only when she realized it had grown darker did she pause and look up. To her surprise, she had passed through a short dark tunnel and ahead there was water on either side. Where was this place, she wondered, stopping and taking in her situation for the first time. In her haste to get away she must have headed in the wrong direction.

Even though it was the beginning of November, the long grass beneath her feet was dotted with pink and white flowers. A sweep of red sandstone cliffs rose to one side of her and she could hear the shooshing of the waves on the shore close by. The wind blowing in from the sea cooled her flushed cheeks and before long she felt her anger dissipating. After all she'd heard that morning, she had much to mull over and the fresh air would help clear her mind.

All thought of selling the remaining flowers forgotten, she made her way down to the shore and began walking briskly along the sand, which like the soil and cliffs in the area was of a red hue. Fancy Mrs Tripe being at school with Mama, and how annoying that haughty housekeeper had interrupted their conversation. For all the difference in their stations, she'd felt the first real connection with her dear mama since she'd arrived in Devonshire.

As for Lord Lester, she couldn't believe the refined, gentle woman she remembered singing lullabies to her would ever associate with someone so utterly repulsive. Lord Lewd more like, or Lord Lecherous, Lustful, Libidinous, Lascivious. Thinking up as many befitting names as she could, Isabella paid little heed to where she was walking until she heard a shout.

'Watch out, girl, you'll be getting a drenching in a moment.' Snapping out of her reverie, she saw she was right at the water's edge, waves lapping around her boots.

'Oh, thank you,' she called, jumping back and heading to where the woman, basket over one arm, was trudging out of the water and up the compacted damp sand. It was only then that she became aware of other people at the water's edge. They were all bent over, rakes in their hands and wicker baskets by their sides.

'I seen people caught by the incoming tide before, but never the ebb,' the woman tutted, gold hoops at her ears swaying as she shook her head. A red headscarf was keeping her long dark curls from her face, and she had a matching woollen shawl over her shoulders. Her skirt was tucked up around her thighs, exposing bare legs and feet as she rested on the handle of her rake, surveying Isabella with eyes so dark Isabella was reminded of the ebony keys on her piano back home.

'You're not from round these parts then?' the woman asked, eyeing Isabella's attire with great interest.

'No, er, that is, I have recently come to reside here.' For some reason, the woman seemed to think that funny and for the first time she smiled, the weather-beaten skin around her eyes crinkling like a fan.

'What are you doing?' Isabella enquired, gesturing to the net.

'Me and the bairns are cockling. A full pail will fill their bellies and keep the wolf from the door.'

'Shouldn't they be in school?' Isabella questioned, thinking of Alice and Thomas.

'Pah,' the woman spat onto the sand. 'Learnin' won't keep 'em fed. What about you? You don't look like a flower girl and yet you're carrying those,' she said, peering inquisitively into Isabella's basket.

'I was supposed to be selling them, but seem to have lost the town,' she murmured. The woman hooted with laughter.

'My, you're a one and a half. Just so happens, I'm going there myself later. Perhaps I could do you a favour and sell them for you. How much do you charge?'

'Penny ha'penny a bunch,' Isabella replied, her heart soaring at this unexpected piece of luck.

'That's a shame,' the woman shook her head again, sending the hoops swaying. 'I can't afford to buy them from you at that price.' As the woman resumed her cockling, Isabella's heart plummeted. There was no way she could walk all the way back to the town but she could imagine her uncle's look of disdain if she returned home with her basket still half full.

'What could you pay?' she ventured. The woman slowly straightened, then darting Isabella a knowing look, slowly took her purse from her pocket. Frowning at its contents, she sighed.

'Just about manage ha'penny a bunch to take the lot off your hands.' Isabella thought quickly. That might be less than she should get for them but, even if she could face the walk back to the town centre, there was no guarantee she'd sell them all when she got there.

'I accept your offer,' Isabella replied. The woman grinned then, as if worried Isabella would change her mind, hastily transferred the flowers into her own basket.

Coins jangling, and feeling happier, Isabella

made her way off the beach. It was high time she tackled her uncle about her mama's past and asked about her papa's effects. If she arrived back with money in her basket, hopefully he would be more amenable to answering her questions. And she would insist he gave her some answers, too.

Looking around she saw she'd rejoined the lane that ran parallel to the railway line, and knew if she continued her route she would come to the entrance leading to the big house. Loath to risk bumping into Lord Lester again, she darted down a turning to her left instead, passing a couple of whitewashed cottages, where to her surprise chickens strutted around and vegetables grew in the front gardens. How strange, she thought, skirting the woodland that surrounded the big house to her right. Hearing a shot followed by a squawk, she shuddered and quickened her step until she reached a stile beyond which stretched a ploughed field. The church tower rising in the distance was a familiar landmark and she knew she had no option but to make her way across the red furrows that were covered with seemingly hundreds of seagulls.

Her worn boots did little to protect her feet from the stony soil, and wincing she picked her way towards the hedge. She was halfway across when she saw a man with a battered hat ahead. He was staring directly at her, his arms open wide. Heart in mouth, she glanced over her shoulder. Should she make a run for it? Yet she'd come so far, the thought of running back over the sharp earth was more than she could bear. She'd just have to brazen it out. Heart beating wildly, she advanced but strangely the man didn't move, he just stood staring at her with that funny grin on his face. Even the birds weren't scared as they perched on him. It was only when she got nearer that she realized it wasn't a real man but some kind straw-stuffed effigy mounted on a stick. Would she ever understand this strange country life, she wondered, clambering wearily over the stile.

The winding lane with its tumbledown sheds looked vaguely familiar, and it took her a moment to realize it was the one that Uncle Bill had pointed out the day he'd rescued her from the rhyll. Dear Uncle Bill, how kind he was and how sad he'd looked that morning when he'd driven her to the big house. Recalling his invitation to visit, she decided now would be a good time to accept. She could check he was alright and perhaps he would answer some of her questions. Returning to the cottage this early in the day would only further arouse her aunt's suspicions of how she'd sold her flowers.

The way was long and kept snaking back on itself, yet spreading out around her like a beautiful blue carpet were hundreds of violets, their heady aroma filling the air. With Uncle Bill's land laying between Uncle Frederick's and the Furneaux's, these flowers must extend for miles, she realized, taking in the beautiful sight. By the time she reached his farmhouse, she was parched, her feet were aching and she was longing for a cool drink.

Tapping briskly on her uncle's door, she stared around the gardens. Everywhere looked immaculate and it was evident he took great pride in his work. When there was no answer, she walked round the side path and tried the back door. It was opened almost immediately by her cousin Joseph who stared at her in surprise.

'Hello, Joseph. Sorry to bother you but Uncle Bill invited me to call in and as I just happened to be passing, well, here I am,' she smiled.

'You just 'appened to be passing?' he asked, frowning down at her muddy boots. 'Uncle's still up at Father's but you're welcome to come in. We're just having our noontime piece,' he explained, opening the door wider. Kicking the dirt from her boots, she followed him into a large kitchen where the range emanated a welcome heat. Everywhere was neat and tidy, with china stacked on the huge dresser that dominated the room and a picture of a young woman adorning one shelf.

'It's lovely and warm in here,' she said, slipping off her aunt's turnover. Then she felt a prickle creep up her spine and saw Felix watching her from the deal table. Grinning, he jumped to his feet and she couldn't help thinking how good-looking he was.

'Miss Carrington, how lovely to see you again,' he said, perfecting one of his little bows. 'And looking very elegant if I might be so bold.'

'Oh, please don't let me interrupt your luncheon,' she murmured, his emerald gaze making her feel flustered. 'And it's Isabella, as you well know.' He inclined his head in acknowledgement then went back to his meal. There was a fresh loaf, ham and pickles set out on the table, and Isabella suddenly realized how hungry she was. Seeing her looking, Joseph pulled out a chair.

'Want some?' he asked. Before she could answer, he set about cutting a thick slice of bread.

'Thank you,' she said, eagerly accepting the invitation. He added a generous slice of meat then passed over the jar of pickles.

'Lemonade?' he asked, pouring a glass from a pitcher.

'Oh yes, please. This is so kind of you,' she said.

'There's plenty,' Joseph replied politely. 'Haven't seen much of you since you arrived. Liking Deb'n are you?' As two pairs of eyes awaited her answer, Isabella forced a nod. 'Expect you're finding it different to London, though,' Joseph persisted.

'Oh, you've been there, have you?' she asked, her eyes lighting up. He shook his head and pulled a face.

'Nah, too much smoke from them manufactories. I likes the sea air.'

'I've just been walking along the beach actually,' Isabella replied. As they both stared at her in surprise, Isabella realized she'd revealed more than she should have and turned her attention back to her food. As she ate, she was conscious of Felix glancing at her across the table but he waited until she'd finished her meal before speaking.

'Forgive me, did you say you'd been walking along the beach?'

'I did, but that was after I'd visited the big house and sold my flowers,' she replied truthfully.

'I don't wish to appear rude, but don't you think you're a little overdressed for the role of a flower girl. I mean, there are some men who might, er, get the wrong idea if they see you cavorting around looking like that.'

'I'll have you know that I do not cavort, Mr Furneaux. Besides, I am in mourning for Papa and lavender is an appropriate colour to wear,' she told him, wishing he wouldn't stare at her so intently. She took a sip of her drink. 'This is delicious,' she said, changing the subject.

'Was he French?' Joseph asked.

'Who? Oh, you mean Papa? No, he wasn't, why do you ask?'

'Well, you always refer to your parents as Mama and Papa and she were Father's sister so she couldn't be French.'

'Oh, I see what you mean. Do you know I've never really given it a thought? They've always been... I mean I always called them that,' she frowned.

'I expect you're wondering what I'm doing consorting with the enemy?' Felix asked, sensing her discomfort.

'Well, to be honest, I was surprised to see you here,' Isabella replied.

'As you know Father and I recently set up our new market garden venture. Both Joseph and his uncle have been very generous with their advice on how to grow the best blooms to sell,' Felix told her.

'We're 'appy to pass on our tips 'cos Uncle Bill says there's business enough for us all. Best not tell Father, though,' Joseph added quickly. 'I was telling Felix we'd be planting teddies in the spring after we've cleared out the old plants.'

'Why potatoes?' Isabella frowned.

'Violets take no phosphates from the soil but

teddies absorb it, so it be ben'ficial to plant some and rotate everything, like.'

'I see,' Isabella replied, not really comprehending yet not wishing to appear stupid. Feeling Felix's gaze on her once more, she looked up to see him grinning knowingly.

'You needs to really understand the soil,' Joseph continued unaware. 'Uncle Bill grows lots of his flowers between the fruit trees which be good for naturalizing, see. If you're taking them to market, you need to grow great blooms or it's a waste of time,' he smiled.

'You seem very knowledgeable,' Isabella replied, thinking how pleasant he was compared to his taciturn brother.

'Uncle Bill's the best teacher and he says when he's old, even older than he is now, I'll be in charge,' he said, proudly.

'And meantime, Joseph and his uncle are generously passing on their wisdom to Father and I, for which we are extremely grateful, I might add,' Felix told her.

'You'll 'elp us if we ever need it,' Joseph shrugged philosophically. 'We were going to take a look around the gardens and talk about yield. You can join us if you want, Izzie?' he invited, getting to his feet.

'Please don't feel you have to come, though,' Felix added. 'You might prefer to rest whilst you're waiting for Bill to return.'

'I'd love to see them,' she replied, flushing as their gaze met and held. *Steady, Isabella, men are fickle,* she reminded herself. Turning quickly away, she retrieved her turnover.

For the second time that day, Isabella was pleased to feel the breeze cooling her cheeks as she followed them outside. The gardens wrapped around the house and were planted with violets in differing states of growth. They strolled on until they came to an orchard where mauve heads peeped out between the tree trunks.

'We've just picked all the apples and pears and stored them in the shed,' Joseph explained. 'Mother would appreciate some Bramleys if you could take them back with you,' he told Isabella. 'She makes a mean fruit pie and hopefully will have one made by the time we come for luncheon on Sunday,' he said rubbing his stomach appreciatively. Isabella smiled at his expression but he had turned back to Felix. 'What was it you wanted to know?' he asked.

'How much yield we could expect? We're thinking of planting up another two acres.'

'That's a goodly amount,' Joseph nodded, stroking his chin thoughtfully. 'Should get about 100 to 150 pounds' weight of flowers from that, I reckon. Best check with Uncle Bill, though.'

'No need, Joe, you know your stuff and I'm mighty grateful for you taking time out of your busy day to explain everything. Now, I'd better help you finish packing up your violets or you won't have them ready for when Bill returns.'

'I'll help if you like,' Isabella offered.

'Never look a gift horse...,' Joseph began, then looked embarrassed. 'Not that I was suggesting you look like one, of course.'

'I should hope not,' she exclaimed, laughing despite herself.

Joseph led the way into a huge barn which was laid out in a similar manner to Frederick's but much tidier. Pails of violets were lined alongside a long trestle, waiting to be posied and packed and Isabella set about counting out the flowers.

The three of them worked well together and Isabella found herself enjoying the congenial atmosphere. From time to time, though, she caught Felix glancing at her and couldn't help smiling back. By the time the job was finished Bill still hadn't reappeared and Joseph was looking anxious.

'Better pack them onto my cart and I'll give you a lift to the station,' Felix offered.

'Thanks. Can't afford to miss the train,' Joseph replied. 'Go and get your basket, Izzie, and we'll fill it with apples for Mother before we go.'

Isabella did as he suggested, welcoming the kitchen's warmth after the cool air of the afternoon. She stared around the room, marvelling at its order compared with the general clutter of her aunt's kitchen. Then her attention was drawn to the portrait on the dresser and she went over to have a better look. The pretty young woman had her glossy hair falling in waves around her shoulders, and her sparkling eyes seemed to light up the room. Isabella thought how vivacious she was.

'Here's the apples.' Joseph appeared beside her, making Isabella jump.

'I was just thinking how happy the woman looks,' she said, replacing the picture on the shelf.

'That were Uncle Bill's wife.'

'Goodness, I never realized he was married,' she gasped.

'Love of his life, she were. Died in childbirth some years back now. Uncle blames himself,' Joseph told her, dropping the large green fruits into her basket.

'Poor Uncle Bill,' she sighed.

'I know. Sometimes he finds the memories too painful and goes on a bender to forget. Probably what he's done today. Father gets right mad at him.'

'Cart's all packed,' Felix said appearing in the doorway. 'That basket looks heavy. We'll drop you home on our way back from the station, Isabella.'

Isabella nodded, her attention returning to the young woman in the picture. *Poor, poor Uncle Bill,* she thought.

Chapter 20

The journey to the station was bumpy and Isabella clung to her basket as Felix urged his pony on. With the three of them squashed into the seat and the boxes of flowers piled in the back, it was a laden cart that made its way precariously along the winding lanes, swaying down the steepest hill Isabella had ever seen, before passing by a chapel and a school. There was a camaraderie between the two men that Uncle Frederick was evidently not aware of, Isabella thought, as they joked and sparred off each other. They were both looking dishevelled after their exertions and Felix had a dried leaf clinging to his hair. Suppressing the urge to remove it, she stared down at her hands only to discover they were decidedly grubby. Then to her surprise she noticed they were rounding the Sod and turning into the road that led to Starcross. Before she could comment on the way all the lanes seemed to lead into each other, Joseph peered anxiously along the track and let out a sigh.

'Don't worry, we'll make the train,' Felix assured him.

'Hope so or Father'll pickle my plucks. It's Uncle Bill I'm worried about, though. You know what happened last time he went on a bender. Disappeared for days, he did,' Joe said. As they rounded the Sod they heard a blast from a whistle and Isabella could just make out the plume of steam in the distance.

'We'll do it,' Felix assured them again, urging his pony along the lane that ran parallel to the railway line. Minutes later they turned into the station yard, and as the men hastily jumped down, two porters came running to assist.

'Cutting it tight today, Joe,' one said, as he hefted the boxes onto his trolley.

'Your father's flowers are already here,' the other man chirped. Isabella looked over her shoulder and saw Frederick striding towards them.

'What you doing with our flowers, Furneaux?' he growled.

'When Uncle Bill didn't return, Felix offered to drive me here so I didn't miss the train,' Joseph replied, his voice breathless as he continued unloading. There was a shrill whistle and the screeching of wheels on the track.

'Best hurry then. I'll speak to you later, Joseph,'

Frederick muttered. As the men scuttled towards the platform, their laden trollies clattering before them, he turned to Isabella. 'Get yerself into my cart, yer coming home with me.' Isabella opened her mouth to protest, then saw the set of his face and promptly closed it again.

Ignoring the shouts from the other drivers, he drove straight out of the yard and onto the road. Seeing the way his hands clenched the reins, Isabella sat back in her seat and stared out at the rolling waves. Yet again, the steely grey reflected her uncle's mood, she thought.

'What the hell were you doing with Furneaux?' he snapped.

'I went to see Uncle Bill and Felix was there,' Isabella replied.

'And why would you be visiting Bill when you should have been in town?'

'He gave me a lift to the big house this morning.' Ignoring his surprised look, she continued. 'We were talking about facing our fears and he seemed upset about something so I wanted to check he was all right,' she said, giving him an edited version.

'And what fears would a young girl like you have to face,' he growled. Realizing she might as well come clean and see if she could get some answers at the same time, she turned to face him.

'He knew I was scared in case I met Lord Lester again,' she replied.

'Again? You mean you've already met him?' he asked, staring at her in amazement. Isabella nodded. 'When? How?' he barked. Knowing she had no choice, she explained about her faux pas the previous week. When she got to the part about ringing the front doorbell, she thought she saw his lips twitch, but it was gone so quickly she couldn't be sure.

'Let's get this straight. You mean that bast– er, son of a bitch propositioned you?' he snarled, yanking hard on the reins. She nodded but kept her gaze averted. As the cart shuddered to a halt, he turned to face her.

'Why didn't you tell me this last week?' he asked. She shrugged, hardly daring to admit she found his forthright ways intimidating. 'Yet you told Bill? When?'

'He gave me a lift home from town. Knowing I was worried about today, he met me in the lane,' she admitted, dreading him asking about her visit to the big house earlier. However, he had other things on his mind.

'What time was this?'

'Just after I left the cottage. He was on his way to visit you, I think. Why?'

'We haven't seen hide nor hair of him all day,' Frederick declared.

'Joseph told me about him losing his wife and how he goes on benders. What's a bender, Uncle?'

'Nothing for a nice girl like you to worry about,' he muttered, jerking on the reins. Isabella was bursting to ask about her mama but they reached the cottage before she summoned the courage, and then her uncle spoke first.

'You never said what Furneaux was doing at Bill's place,' he said, climbing down and giving her a penetrating stare.

'He and Joe were having their luncheon when I

arrived. They kindly invited me to join them,' she said, trying to be tactful.

'Eating luncheon?' he bellowed. 'What did they talk about?'

'Soil and potatoes. Then...' Realizing she might be about to get Joseph into trouble, her voice trailed off.

'Then?'

'Yield,' she admitted. The narrowing of his eyes told her she'd said too much. 'But Joseph said Uncle Bill assured them there's plenty of business for everyone,' she added, staring at him hopefully. He gave a snort.

'It's taken a lot of hard work to get where we are. We're only just turning a profit as it is, and if Bill doesn't pull his weight, we're in danger of losing our share of the market,' he sighed and pushed his old straw hat to the back of his head. 'Best not tell Mother about meeting Lord Lester, she's worried about you as it is,' he told her.

'Why?' she frowned.

'Them fancy clothes for one thing. She's afraid you might give the wrong impression at the big house. There's been talk, see. Beside people round here have long memories.'

'You're referring to Mama and Lord Lester, aren't you?' she asked. He nodded. 'Why did he refer to Mama as a good-time girl?'

'Because that's what she was. Now take these apples indoors,' he said, handing down her basket. As he turned back to Silver, Isabella saw how weary he was looking, yet needing to know more, she stayed where she was. 'Look, Isabella, I need to go and find Bill. We'll talk more about your mother when I return.'

'You promise, Uncle?'

'Yes, if not tonight then tomorrow,' he assured her. Feeling happier to be getting somewhere at last, she nodded and made her way down the path.

'Coo, look at all them apples,' Dotty said, coming out of the kitchen door with a tray in her hand. 'Did you manage to get my note to Alfie?' she whispered, glancing towards the barn.

'Mrs Tripe promised to pass it on,' Isabella told her. Her cousin's eyes lit up.

'I can walk properly without me stick now, so hopefully it'll be me going to the big house next week.' Isabella felt her spirits soar. She couldn't bear the thought of bumping into his Lordship again, especially after retaliating this morning. Remembering his indignant look and the threats he'd made, she wondered if there would be any repercussions. Best not mention meeting him, she decided. Then she realized Dotty was waiting for an answer.

'That is good news. Although, I shall be happy to take more flowers into town tomorrow,' she said, remembering it was the day the sisters were holding their next seance.

'You've changed your tune,' Dotty replied, staring at her suspiciously. 'Did you shift all of them today?'

'I did. It seems I've got into the swing of this selling,' Isabella shrugged.

'That's good 'cos Mother's relying on the money. Now the weather's getting colder she's taken the little ones to get warmer clothes.'

Isabella felt a pang as she recalled the deal she'd done with the woman on the beach and hoped the coins in her basket would be sufficient.

'Better take Grandmother's tea in to her before it gets cold. She's having a better day so why not come with me?'

'I'd love to,' Isabella cried. 'I'll put my things inside and be right with you.'

Placing the basket on the kitchen table, she shrugged off the turnover and patted her curls into place under her hat. Her hair had grown so much, she really needed to get it cut. She must ask Dotty if she could recommend a good coiffeuse in the town, she thought, hurrying back outside.

'How did you get on today? Did you remember to knock on the back door this time?' Dotty asked as they walked through to the adjoining yard.

'I did, but here's a thing. When the maid answered, she took one look at me and said I should go around to the front,' Isabella exclaimed. To her astonishment, Dotty nodded.

'I'm not surprised. That outfit's gorgeous but hardly fitting for a flower seller.'

'Well, I feel more like myself wearing it,' Isabella retorted.

'All right, keep your hair on,' Dotty laughed, unlocking the back door. 'Cooee, only me,' she called. To Isabella's surprise, the woman was in the kitchen, standing by the unlit range. She was wearing a blue woollen dress and smiling.

'Just going to cook my dinner,' she told Dotty. Then she saw Isabella and her eyes widened.

'Ellie, you've come home,' she cried, throwing

her arms around Isabella.

'But I'm not...,' Isabella began, only to see Dotty shaking her head.

'Oh, you do look grand,' she said, eyeing Isabella up and down. 'Always knew you'd get on.' She spun round and grinned at Dotty. 'I said Ellie would come back, didn't I?'

'You did,' Dotty replied, humouring the woman.

'Well, don't just stand there, come on through and tell me all you've been doing since you was last here.' Trembling with excitement, Isabella allowed herself to be pulled into the living room. 'Sit down, sit down,' the woman instructed. Isabella did as she'd been told then watched as the woman tottered over to her own chair. But to her dismay, no sooner had she sunk into the cushions than she closed her eyes. Isabella watched and waited but within moments the room was filled with the sound of gentle snoring.

'She's gone again,' Dotty sighed, drawing the cover over the woman. As Dotty knelt and banked up the fire then carefully replaced the guard, Isabella stared at her grandmother, willing her to wake up.

'Come on, let's go and start on the supper. We're having raw teddy vry, tonight,' she smiled. Isabella hadn't a clue what that was and at that moment, she didn't really care.

'But she thought I was Mama,' Isabella cried, following Dotty back to their side of the cottage.

'I know. She's been waiting years for her daughter to come home, you see. Apparently, she was about the same age you are now when she left. Mother told her she was dead but ... sorry,' she shrugged. 'Still, that's the best Grandmother's been for ages. Perhaps if she sees more of you it will stir her memory again.'

As Dotty took down the skillet and placed it on the range, Isabella sank into a chair and thought about what she'd said. If only she could have a proper conversation with the old woman, ask what Mama had been like as a child.

'That's right, sit there like lady muck while Dotty does all the work.' Isabella looked up to find William glaring at her from the doorway.

'Oh sorry, I didn't think,' she murmured.

'No, that's your trouble. Didn't think about poor Mother having to work in the cold barn without her turnover either, I suppose.'

'Now then, William,' Dotty chided. 'Mother said she would take a look in the market for another one.'

'She wouldn't have to if her ladyship wore her own.'

'But my mantle got torn...,' Isabella began.

'And you never thought to take a needle to it, I suppose?' William asked, his eyes blazing. 'Besides, you must have more, what with all that luggage you brought with you.'

'Well, I ...,' she began, wanting to explain that Mary thought her clothes unsuitable for around here, but he was in his stride and didn't let her finish.

'And that's another thing, poor Mother and Father can hardly move without falling over trunks and hat boxes,' he scoffed.

'I told Auntie she could move them to the barn but didn't check it had been done.'

'I told Auntie she could move them to the barn,' he parroted. 'Didn't think to do it yourself. Mother and Father have enough to do without sorting out your things. They've bent over backwards trying to include you into our family life and what have you done in return, apart from swanning around wearing fancy clothes and jewels?'

'That's enough, William,' Dotty insisted. 'We're happy to have Izzie here. She's had a tough time and you should be helping her to settle in, not going on at her. Now, call a truce, you two, and help me get supper on the table. Mother and the nippers will be back soon and starving hungry, like as not.' As she turned back to the range, Isabella and William eyed each other warily, like two feral animals sizing each other up.

'Excuse me,' she said, making for her aunt's room. With anger lending her strength, she began pulling the nearest trunk towards the door. It was heavy, but William's words had struck a nerve.

'Whatever are you doing?' Mary cried, coming into the room, a brown parcel under each arm.

'Sorry, Auntie, I hadn't realized my luggage was still stored in here. I was trying to move it to the barn.'

'Fiddlesticks. I told you it was all right where it was. Now come along, Dotty's dishing up, and I for one am thurdlegutted.' Seeing her aunt's look, Isabella knew argument would be useless and followed her back to the kitchen where the children were gathered round the table.

'Me ears is all froze,' Alice announced.

'I'm so hungry,' Thomas cried, sniffing the air appreciatively.

'Here you are,' Dotty told them, passing round plates heaped high with a fried onion and potato concoction. 'Did you get what you needed, Mother?' she asked.

'Got the nips a hooded cape each from Tolley's. Good condition too, but not cheap. Still, it's a start. This is good, Dotty,' Mary told her, tucking into her meal. 'Father not back?'

'He's out looking for Uncle Bill,' William replied.

'Gone missing again, has he?' she sighed.

'What about a turnover for you, Mother?' William asked.

'Not this time,' Mary replied. 'We'll just have to sell a few more flowers.' Isabella stared at her aunt. Surely if her uncle was spending money on his business, they could afford new clothes for everyone? Unless ... once again her thoughts went back to her papa's effects. Well, her uncle had promised they would talk, and she would take the opportunity to ask him all that was worrying her.

'You are welcome to anything in my trunks, Auntie,' Isabella ventured.

'That's very kind, Izzie, but regrettably your flimsy, floaty things are not suited to our kind of life. And please don't concern yourself about your luggage. I really don't know what made you think you had to move it, anyhow.' Isabella stared at William but he busied himself eating and didn't look up. Dotty shook her head.

'I'm sorry, Auntie, I had no idea that having lent me your turnover, you were going without. I shall wear my mantle into town tomorrow,' Isabella told her.

'That's all right, dear, 'tis only just turned cold.

Now, how did you get on today? And where did those apples come from?' she said, eyeing Isabella's basket on the floor. Once again, Isabella found herself relaying an edited version of her day.

'But Grandmother thought Izzie was Father's sister come back,' Dotty cried, taking up the story. Isabella looked at her aunt expectantly, but she looked away.

'Come on, it's been a long day,' she said quickly. 'The dishes can wait until tomorrow.'

Exhausted, Isabella fell onto her mattress. Although gentle snores soon emanated from her cousins, the events of the day played over and over in her mind. The cook's comments about her mother had been interesting but she sincerely hoped she'd never have to encounter Lord Lester again. The thought of him trying to kiss her sent shudders down her spine. Her reaction might have been justified but she knew enough about life to know people would think there was no smoke without fire. And Lord Lester wasn't the kind of man to take kindly to rejection so would there be any repercussions?

William's outburst had stirred her conscience and she resolved to help her aunt more. It had been good seeing Felix again and getting to know Joseph, too. Poor Uncle Bill, she hoped he was all right and that when Uncle Frederick returned he would keep his word about their discussion. She had so much to ask him. It had been a surprise seeing her grandmother so lucid, albeit for a short time. Hopefully, she would soon have another good day, for although she kept hearing bits about her mama, fitting them together was proving to be more difficult than the most complicated jigsaw puzzle.

Chapter 21

The next morning, Isabella took her customary place between the circulating library and stationer's. William's words had struck home and, having recovered her mantle and smoothed it as best she could, she was now wearing it over the lavender outfit. It certainly wasn't in the condition she was used to, yet she couldn't bear to think of her aunt being cold. Vowing that from now on she'd be more considerate of the needs of the family who'd taken her in, she intended to sell as many bunches of violets as she could for their full price. She would then take the rest to the sisters' house – if she could find her way, that was.

Putting her hand inside her collar, she ran her fingers over her mama's pearls, comforted as ever by their presence. Knowing her aunt wouldn't have approved of her wearing them into town, she'd concealed them under her jacket before leaving the cottage, and hopefully today they would prove a tangible link to her past. Patting her collar back into place, she smiled at the early-morning shoppers in an effort to entice them to stop and buy.

It was to no avail as everyone hurried by without even acknowledging her. A bitter wind blew up, bringing with it the strong smell of salt and seaweed, and before long she was so cold, she could hardly feel her feet.

'Here you are, dear.' The woman from the stationer's appeared at her side, holding out a steaming mug.

'Oh, er, thank you,' Isabella replied. She was about to say she never partook of refreshment in the street but the delightful aroma of coffee proved too tempting. Taking it gratefully from her, she glanced left and right then drank it quickly. The hot liquid tantalized her tastebuds and warmed her insides. 'That was delicious, and most welcome. Thank you again,' she said, handing back the empty mug. The woman grinned.

'You looked as though you needed it. Winter's certainly blowing itself in with a roar, isn't it? Look, why don't you stand behind my sign? It'll help keep the wind off you. Not having much luck with the flowers, then?' she said, gesturing towards Isabella's overflowing basket.

'I guess it's too cold for people to stop,' Isabella sighed. The woman eyed her doubtfully.

'Perhaps if you looked a little less affluent they'd find you more approachable,' she suggested. 'Tell you what, I'll take a bunch. A spot of colour will liven up my counter,' she said, producing a couple of coins from her pocket. Isabella smiled gratefully and handed over the violets. Then, as the woman turned to leave, she remembered her uncle.

'I don't suppose you've seen Uncle Bill, have you?'

'Gone off again, has he? Let me think now,' she murmured, staring out over the green opposite. 'I do recall seeing him hurrying in the direction of the rhyll, stupid man. Still, if it helps him forget, you can't blame him, can you? Oops must go, customer waiting.' The woman bustled off leaving Isabella to ponder what she'd been told.

What on earth was he doing at the rhyll, Isabella wondered, remembering the seedy place he'd rescued her from. As three smartly dressed ladies approached, she smiled and held out her basket. Despite her fine clothes, they raised their immaculate brows, tutted to each other and crossed the street and began walking along the green. 'Stuck-up toffs,' she muttered. Then, realizing what she'd said, she laughed. Goodness, what had Dotty said about her now being working-class?

As another gust of wind lifted her skirts and tugged at the ribbons on her hat, she turned to take shelter behind the sign. Just then someone tapped her on the shoulder.

'Hello, dear.' She spun round to see the two sisters beaming at her. They were dressed in their customary black outfits, the berries on their hats bobbing up and down as they greeted her.

'Good morning, Agnes, Miriam,' she cried happily.

'My, you are looking pretty today,' Agnes gushed, taking in Isabella's outfit. 'Is that new?'

'Goodness me, no. It's one Gaskell, my chaperone, packed for me.'

'Ah, I thought it had the style of the city about it,' Agnes nodded. 'Actually, my dear, we thought we'd come and see if you still wanted to join our little meeting this afternoon?'

'Indeed, I do,' Isabella told them. The sisters

beamed again then exchanged a look.

'I see you've still got lots of flowers left,' Miriam remarked, glancing in her basket.

'We nearly bought some yesterday from a woman with black curls and gold hoops in her ears. Quite insistent, she was, but we know violets don't last long and feared they might wilt before our meeting today,' Agnes added.

'You would have purchased them cheaper, though,' Isabella replied, recalling the lady from the beach.

'Oh no, dear, she was selling them for the same price as you,' Miriam frowned. *Well, of all the cheek,* Isabella thought, but the sisters were linking their arms through hers. 'Come along, we've a seance to arrange,' they cried.

As they hurried her through the streets, Isabella tried hard to remember the way. The last thing she wanted was to lose her bearings again. However, the sisters moved at such a pace that all too soon they were letting themselves into the house they were leasing. Isabella was ushered down the hall with its familiar smell of beeswax, rose petals and that other fragrance she couldn't discern, then into the same room as before. This time a fire was blazing brightly in the hearth.

'Now, let Miriam take your basket then we'll have a nice drink to warm up. It's certainly bitter out there,' Agnes told her, holding her hands to the fire. 'Miriam has made a special tart for our luncheon, with Naples bisket grated over egg yolks and cream, all seasoned with nutmeg, cinnamon and sugar.' She touched her fingers to her lips and kissed them theatrically.

'But I couldn't finish it without these,' Miriam cried, holding out the violets.

'Goodness, you put flowers in your tart?' Isabella frowned.

'It is the pièce de résistance,' Miriam nodded. 'We put flowers in everything.' The sisters looked at each other and giggled. 'I'll drop these into the kitchen and make us a nice tisane.'

'And I'll take your mantle, dear, or you won't feel the benefit when you leave.' As Agnes held out her hand, Isabella shrugged off the garment and gave it to her.

'I can't get over how different you look,' Agnes enthused, her eyes settling on the pearls at Isabella's neck. 'Quite the young lady. Although that worn mantle doesn't do you justice, if you don't mind my saying. And this lovely necklace was your mother's?' she asked taking a step closer and scrutinizing the ropes.

'Yes, these are the pearls I mentioned last time. Do you think they will help Mama to, er, come through?' she asked, trying to remember the term Agnes had used.

'They might,' Agnes nodded. 'Of course, I shall need to feel them, hold them, soak up their aura.'

'They have an aura?' Isabella asked, unfastening the clasp and placing them in her outstretched hand.

'Of course. They will have absorbed your mother's life force,' the woman explained, running her fingers over the stones. 'Such lustre and size, so nearly perfectly round,' she murmured. 'These pearls must surely be natural?' she asked, giving Isabella a keen look.

'Goodness, yes. Papa adored Mama and would only give her the best. Why, does it make a difference then?'

'Oh yes,' she said, a gleam sparking in her eyes. 'Now, hush for a moment while I try to capture their essence.' Agnes closed her eyes and slowly ran her finger over each pearl.

'Will they make Mama come through, then?' Isabella asked, too excited to be quiet.

'You'll need to be patient, child, sometimes it takes longer than others.'

'But Papa nearly came through last time, didn't he?' Isabella persisted.

'Have you brought something of your papa's as well?' Agnes asked, her eyes snapping open. Isabella shook her head.

'I don't really have anything, although I know Uncle brought some of his things back from Chester Square after his fun–' As the tears begin to well, her voice trailed off. 'Sorry,' she whispered, taking out her handkerchief and dabbing her eyes.

'No need to apologize, my dear. Grief can hit at the most unexpected times and yours is still very raw. Ah, here's Miriam with our tisanes,' she said.

'Just what the doctor ordered,' Miriam smiled, handing her a glass in its silver holder. Isabella smiled her thanks, inhaling the heady aroma which seemed stronger than she remembered.

'Now, drink up, it will make you feel brighter,' Agnes instructed. Isabella duly sipped the fragrant liquid and before long felt that blanket of tranquillity wrap itself around her once more. In fact, she relaxed so much she hardly noticed the conversation going on around her. Then she became aware of the sisters staring at her.

'Feeling better now?' Agnes asked. Isabella smiled for her spirits had lifted and she was feeling quite insouciant.

'I'm pleased to see you have a much better colour,' Miriam told her. 'Now, we need to partake of luncheon if we are to be finished before our dear ladies arrive,' she added, handing her a plate upon which nestled a delicate tartlet. This time she was also given a pastry fork. 'I made this especially for today so do let me know what you think.' As Isabella cut into it, the pastry flaked and the filling smelled sweet-scented and quite heady.

'Goodness, I didn't know bisket could taste so exquisite or have such an effect. You said you added flowers, which did you use?' she asked. The sisters looked at each other and giggled again.

'Sorry you must forgive us. Not many people appreciate our culinary skills. We use violets, primroses, poppy tears, even strawberries, whatever's in season at the time,' Miriam told her. Isabella blinked, did she say tears? Before she could check, the woman got to her feet. 'Talking of flowers, I must go and finish my nostr– er, nosegays.' As she left the room, Isabella looked over at Agnes but the woman had her eyes closed and was stroking the pearls again. The room was quite hot now and, feeling her own lids growing heavy, Isabella sat back in her seat. She must have dropped off for, the next thing she knew, Agnes was patting her shoulder.

'Time for our meeting.' Groggily Isabella got to

her feet. Then she saw Agnes was holding out her pearls.

'Do you think Mama will come through?' she asked again.

'One can never be sure,' she sighed. 'I haven't had much time to really absorb the pearls' spirit, but we can try. Now, do you have the case for them?'

'Oh, don't worry, I can fasten them back on now,' Isabella said. Agnes shook her head. 'Sorry, dear, I make it a rule never to have material goods of the deceased in the room in case it interferes with the spiritual energy.'

'I understand,' Isabella replied, delving into her pocket and drawing out the satin-lined case.

'Thank you, dear. Now, don't get your spirits up,' she gave a titter at her own joke. 'Your mama may or may not come through this time. We shall have to wait and see,' she said, leading the way into the room where the meetings were held.

It was set out the same as before, the three candlesticks interspersed with the large bowls of violets emitting their musky scent. Miriam carefully set down the bread and soup then bustled away while Agnes drew the drapes and lit the candles. Isabella's heart fluttered, whether from nerves or anticipation she couldn't be sure.

'Good luck, dear. Now, close your eyes,' she whispered as the door opened and the visitors began filing in. Once again Isabella couldn't resist peeping and saw they were all inhaling the tiny posies of flowers. As they passed her chair, she caught a trace of the stronger scent she didn't recognize. She really must remember to ask the sisters what it was.

As Agnes instructed them to hold hands, Isabella's curiosity was replaced by excited anticipation, and she found her heart racing. The seance proceeded exactly the same way as before but, to her dismay, although several spirits made their presence known through Agnes, none were those of her dear mama or papa. She closed her eyes tightly and focused on their images as if, by doing that, she could conjure them up. It was to no avail, though, as when the final thanks were given and everyone rose to leave, she was left with acute disappointment and a crashing headache.

'You mustn't be disheartened, my dear,' Agnes said, closing the door behind the last guest and turning to Isabella. 'This is only your first real participation.'

'But I so wanted to hear from one of them at least,' she cried.

'As I said earlier, I didn't have long to really absorb your mama's essence. Perhaps if you were to leave her pearls with me, I could concentrate my powers?'

'Here's your basket with our payment for the violets,' Miriam said, appearing in the hallway.

'I was just suggesting Isabella leave her mother's necklace here until next time then I would have time to work my magic on them,' Agnes laughed softly.

'As long as Isabella feels she can trust us with her precious pearls,' Miriam said, looking at Isabella for confirmation.

'Of course, I do. Until next week then.'

'Oh no, dear, we won't be holding another until the last Friday in December. That's the downside to our success rate, you see. Once we have satisfied our existing clients' needs, we have to find new ones.'

'Oh, I see,' Isabella murmured. Although she was trying to follow their conversation, her head was spinning and she felt in desperate need of fresh air. Giving the sisters a shaky smile, she wrapped the proffered mantle around her shoulders and slowly went out through the open door.

Although the wind had dropped, rain was falling in sheets. Feeling slightly unsteady on her feet, she remembered to turn right then carefully made her way through the puddles, back towards the town. At least the route was familiar this time and with the lamplighter already about his work, the streets would all soon be lit. She put her hand to her head and wiped her brow, wondering how she could be feeling hot when the air was cold. Perhaps it was the tart she'd eaten, for although it had been delicious, she was no longer used to rich food. Her heart was beating rapidly and the blood pounded round her veins, which was at variance with her low mood. She'd been so sure her dear mama or papa would come through.

Making an effort to concentrate on where she was going, she finally found herself back in the Strand. The place was deserted apart from the lady from the stationer's, who was taking in her sign. Hearing Isabella approach, she looked up, her welcoming smile quickly replaced by concern.

'Are you all right?' Isabella went to nod but the ground seemed to be swaying. 'There now, I've got you,' the woman said, putting one arm under hers and leading Isabella into the shop. 'Gracious girl, you're all flushed,' she said, pulling out a chair from behind the counter and easing Isabella into it. 'Looked out of the store at luncheon time but you were nowhere to be seen. Thought you must have gone home or been moved on.' Before Isabella could reply, the doorbell jangled and the woman turned to see who had come in.

'Hello Felix, I was just closing but...,' she began.

'Good afternoon, Mrs Spink. I was returning from the station, when I saw Isabella stumbling along the pavement. Are you all right?' he asked, staring anxiously at Isabella. She took a deep breath and realized the wooziness was gradually beginning to clear.

'Yes, thank you,' she whispered. 'I think it must have been something I ate.'

'Could well be, you're that green about the gills. Have a sip of water then take it easy for a few moments,' the woman said, holding out a glass.

'So, you took your flowers to the station here, then?' the woman said, eyeing Felix curiously.

'Yep, thought it better after yesterday. Give Frederick a chance to calm down,' he replied. 'Though it looks like I'll be seeing him after all, for as soon as Isabella feels able to stand, I shall of course take her home.'

'There really is no need,' Isabella protested, struggling to her feet then promptly collapsing in a heap on the floor.

Chapter 22

Isabella's head throbbed and she felt disorientated. Gingerly opening her eyes, she blinked in the bright light. She tried to sit up but the room spun around her and she fell back against the pillow. Gradually, as the world righted itself, she realized she was back in the bedroom she shared with Dotty and Alice. How had she got here? The last thing she could remember was slumping to the ground in the stationer's and Felix gathering her up in his arms. Feeling warm and protected, she'd sighed and nestled into his chest. Oh glory, what must he have thought of her, she shuddered, growing hot at the recollection. Then she saw her dress was on the floor beside her. Peering under her cover, her eyes widened when she saw she was only wearing her silk combinations.

Not daring to think any more, she pulled on her dress and ran a comb through her tangled hair. Then knowing she had to face the music, slowly descended the stairs.

'Are you feeling better?' her aunt asked, looking up from the dough she was kneading.

'I think so,' Isabella replied, but the effort of getting up had left her weak and she sank into the nearest chair.

'Well, that was a fright you gave us and no mistake. Gibbering about spirits coming out of human mouths and all sorts you were. Hot as a poker one moment, shivering the next. That nice Felix was so concerned he insisted on carrying you right up the stairs.'

'Oh,' Isabella whispered, her hand flying to her mouth.

'Cors I was right behind him,' her aunt went on, oblivious to the relief flooding through Isabella. 'Said he thought you must have caught a chill standing out in the cold and wet all day. Now, what you need is something warm inside you,' she said, putting the dough to prove by the range then dragging down the skillet. Moments later a dish of egg scramble was placed in front of Isabella. 'Now, get that down you.'

The pungent smell emanating from the yellow mound made her stomach heave. Hastily, putting her hand over her mouth, she dashed outside to the privy and retched until there was nothing left inside. Heedless of the falling rain, she forced her jelly-like legs over to the pump where she splashed cold water on her face until she began to feel better.

'Sorry about that,' she murmured when she went back indoors.

'Sit down, Isabella,' her aunt instructed, looking grave. 'I take it you can't manage this?' she asked, removing the untouched food before taking a seat opposite.

'Where are the others?' Isabella asked.

'Being Saturday, Father's taken Alice and Thomas to help Joseph. The poor boy's doing his best to keep things going, but needs all the assistance he can get. Dotty insisted she was well enough to sell and so she hitched a lift into town with them. Mind you, the poor girl's been itching to get out. Anyway, Father should be back soon to help William who's trying to keep things together here. So,' she paused and looked straight at Isabella, 'this seems the perfect time for us to have a chat.'

'Oh, er, that's nice,' Isabella replied, although from the set of her aunt's face, she had a feeling it was going to be anything but.

'Now, young lady, this isn't the first time you've come home looking flushed and out of sorts. What I want to know is why. You're looking better now you've been sick, so do you have something to tell me?'

'Tell you, Auntie?' she asked, her heart thumping as she wondered if the woman had found out about her visit to the sisters.

'Look, dear, we're your family and here to help. If you've got yourself into trouble then you has to tell us.'

'Trouble? I don't know what you mean.' Her aunt sighed.

'Before your papa died, you were walking out with someone called Maxwell, and soon to be betrothed.'

'Yes, but I don't see what that has to do with my feeling queasy earlier,' she said, toying with the spoon on the table. To her surprise her aunt reached across the table and took her hand.

'You haven't had a mother to advise you about things, dear, and men can sometimes take advantage of a girl's innocence. If you're expecting an arrival, then I'll do all I can to help.'

'No, I'm not expecting Maxwell, Auntie. As you

know, he's already found another,' she replied, realizing to her surprise, it didn't seem to hurt nearly as much.

'Blimmer, girl, can you not see what I'm getting at? A baby's what I mean.' Isabella stared at her aunt aghast.

'You mean you think I am, I would ... oh no, Auntie, I can assure you I most certainly am not,' she cried, jumping to her feet. 'And how you could even suggest such a thing is...'

'Don't blame Mother,' Frederick said, coming into the room and staring at Isabella. 'It's a natural assumption under the circumstances.'

'Oh, you think so, do you? Well, let me tell you my morals are intact, which is more than can be said for yours.' There was a deadly hush and her uncle's lips tightened.

'I think you'd better explain what you mean,' he said, his voice low.

'I'm talking about the money from Papa that you have spent on your precious garden,' she told him.

'What?' he thundered, his face turning purple. He stared at his wife in astonishment then stormed into their bedroom.

'Oh Izzie, you've got things so wrong,' Mary whispered, shaking her head sadly.

'You mean there wasn't money in that envelope from Papa?'

'Yes, there was. Your father intended us to use some of it for your keep, but...' Mary began.

'But you used it for your own ends instead,' Isabella supplied.

'We wouldn't do that,' Mary exclaimed, looking horrified.

'See this, Miss High and Mighty Know-all,' Frederick barked, striding back in and slapping a paper down on the table in front of her. ''Tis a bond in your name. We invested all the money your father gave us and were going to present it to you next year, when you become of age.' As tears of shame welled, Isabella stared unseeingly at the certificate.

'But you said you'd invested in your business, buying glass and...,' she cried, her voice trailing away as the enormity of her assumption hit her.

'And so I have, using the money I've earned through sheer hard graft,' he hissed.

'Our family works for anything we want, Izzie. We'd never steal from anyone,' her aunt whispered. As they both stared sadly at her, Isabella realized how dreadfully she'd insulted these kind people who had taken her in.

'Now, unless you have some other heinous crime to accuse me of, I have work to do,' Frederick muttered. As the door slammed behind him, rattling the window panes, Isabella turned to her aunt in dismay.

'I'm sorry, Auntie,' she began. 'I had no idea.'

'No, and perhaps we should have told you,' the woman sighed. 'It just seemed a good idea, what with you attaining your majority so soon after losing your father and home. But I must apologize too, for jumping to the wrong conclusion as to why you've been queasy. Now, I'll just put this back,' she said, picking up the bond. 'Unless you'd prefer to keep it?' she asked, holding out the certificate.

'No, I feel dreadful enough as it is.'

As her aunt bustled into her bedroom, Isabella sank into a chair and put her head in her hands. She'd never felt so bad in all her life. This wonderful couple had opened up their house to her and all she'd done was thrown their kindness back in their faces.

'Right, dear, I'm off to pack the flowers. Make yourself a hot drink and when you feel better perhaps you could give me a hand? No, not now,' she said, as Isabella started to get up. 'Best for us all to have some breathing space. A cup of tea wouldn't go amiss when you come out, though.' Isabella nodded then watched as her aunt threw her turnover around her shoulders and disappeared outside.

For a long time, she sat listening to the November rain slapping at the windows and slithering down the chimney to hiss and spit on the crackling logs in the range. Hadn't her papa always told her not to jump to conclusions?

'Hello, anyone home?' She jumped as Felix appeared in the doorway, dripping rain onto the coir mat. 'I did knock but there was no reply.'

'Do come in,' she murmured, her face growing red.

'Can't stop. I hope you're feeling better today?' he asked, remaining on the mat. 'You gave poor Mrs Spink a turn, dropping to her floor like that.'

'Sorry, but I am a lot better now. Thank you for bringing me home and, er...,' her voice trailed off.

'Don't worry, your aunt was standing right behind me,' he replied, mischief sparking in his eyes. 'Anyway, can't stop, I just called by to say that

Father and I found Bill earlier. We took him home and put him to bed. Seems to be my vocation these days,' he quipped. Seeing Isabella flush, he grinned. 'Perhaps you could let your uncle know?'

'Yes, of course,' she stammered, and before she could say anything else, he'd gone. As the kettle began to sing, she cursed, realizing the least she could have done was offer him a hot drink. Well, she could take some tea out to her aunt then help her pack the flowers, she decided, pouring hot water into the big brown pot. She'd thought it crude after the silver ones she was used to, but now it seemed homely somehow.

Her aunt smiled as Isabella carried the tray into the barn. She was standing at the trestle, counting flowers, and Isabella felt a pang when she saw all the pails of violets still to be packed. Shaking the raindrops from her hair, she pulled out a stool, picked up one of the bunches and began tying it with a length of raffia. Her aunt watched from over the top of her mug. 'Sure you're up to this?' she asked.

'Yes, I'm feeling better now, thank you. Although I still feel bad about earlier.'

'Me too,' the woman agreed. 'Still, no good dwelling on words that can't be taken back, so we'll move forward, eh?' Isabella nodded, grateful for the women's philosophical attitude. They fell silent, listening to the rain drumming on the roof as they posied and packed. Before long the soporific effect of the flowers began to take effect and Isabella felt her nerves calming.

'Oh, I almost forgot. Felix Furneaux called by to say he and his father found Uncle Bill and have taken him home.'

'Funny he didn't pop in here to tell me,' her aunt replied. 'Guess he must have wanted an excuse to see you. Quite smitten, he is, if you ask me.' Ignoring her knowing grin, Isabella frowned.

'Well, I'm off men for life,' she declared heatedly, ignoring the memory of nestling against Felix's chest that popped unbidden into her mind. To her surprise her aunt chuckled.

'That's a long time to be lonely, dear. And, to my way of thinking, that Felix is a handsome fellow.'

'It's good news about Uncle Bill, isn't it?' Isabella asked, determined not to be drawn. 'He'll be able to help the others now.'

'Not for a few days, he won't. It'll take him that long to sleep off the effects of all the liquor he's doubtless consumed along with goodness knows what else.' Hearing the disapproval in her aunt's voice, Isabella placed the posy she'd just tied into the half-filled corset box then asked the question that had been on her mind since she'd visited her uncle Bill's house.

'Joseph told me Uncle's wife died in childbirth and that he blames himself. I don't understand. I mean, it's tragic but not uncommon.'

'No, even in these enlightened times, it still happens. Meggie was frail but refused to listen when the doctor warned her she wasn't strong enough to carry a child. She loved Bill so much that, despite his objection, she was determined to give him a son. They both died during the birthing.'

'Oh, that is tragic,' Isabella cried.

'It is, and whilst Bill can cope most days, on

others his grief and guilt get the better of him and he has to escape.'

Lost in their own worlds, they continued their work. Compared to Uncle Bill's problems hers paled into insignificance, Isabella thought. She still missed Papa desperately but whilst her dear mama had been young when she'd been taken, at least they'd enjoyed time together and known the joy of being parents. She looked up to see her aunt staring at her across the trestle.

'I'm pleased to see you're wearing your locket again, dear. Those pearls are beautiful, but undoubtedly valuable and I do worry about you wearing them around the place. Are you sure you don't want your uncle to put them in the bank's safety box?'

'Now then, Mother, if Isabella thinks us capable of stealing her money she's not about to trust us with her precious jewels,' her uncle said, dumping more flowers into the pails they'd just emptied.

'I'm really sorry about the misunderstanding, Uncle,' Isabella said, turning to face him.

'Misunderstanding, were it?' he snorted, raindrops dripping off his hat and jacket onto the floor.

'Now then, Father,' her aunt chided. 'We should accept Izzie's apologies and move forward.'

'Is that so?' he muttered. He ran a hand over his stubbly chin and stared at Isabella thoughtfully. 'Trust is a big thing in this family, girl. How about you show yours by letting me put those pearls in the bank? It'd save Mother worrying you're going to be robbed at knifepoint every time you go out.'

'Oh, er, well I...,' she began, wanting to comply yet knowing she couldn't until she collected them from the sisters.

'Clearly you don't have any faith in us,' he muttered when she hesitated. Turning on his heel, he stomped back outside.

'Felix Furneaux called to say they've found Bill and taken him home,' Mary called after him but, if he heard, he gave no indication.

'Don't worry, dear, he'll come around. Although it would help if you could show him you trust us. Sets a lot of store by that, he does. Now, what did you think of Uncle Bill's place? Looks after it a treat, doesn't he? Well, most of the time.'

'It was beautiful and Joseph was really kind showing me around,' she said, bending to reach another box. 'He said they would be growing potatoes next year. Will you be sending them to Covent Garden instead of violets?' Hearing a snort, she turned to find William rocking with mirth.

'Oh yeah, we're going to sell teddies and eat violets,' he said, dumping yet more flowers into water. 'You still have no idea what running these large market gardens for a living entails, do you?'

'Well, I...,' but she was talking to his retreating back.

'Don't worry, Izzie. William doesn't understand you've only been here a couple of months. Anyway, you're doing well there,' she added, nodding approvingly at the flowers Isabella had packed. 'At this rate, we'll be in time for the train after all. It's a bit different to trying to sell them in town, isn't it?'

'Goodness yes, I hate that,' Isabella cried. 'All those snooty women looking down their nose at me as they pass by.'

'Well, you've been coming back with an empty basket, so if they haven't been buying your flowers, who has?' her aunt asked, giving her a searching look.

Chapter 23

Isabella stared at her aunt, trying in vain to come up with a reasonable explanation, but then the woman shrugged.

'No, don't answer, Izzie. Having spent the morning speaking about trust, it's time I put it into practice.' Knowing she should admit she'd been selling her flowers to the sisters, Isabella flushed and stared back down at the posies on the trestle. Despite her aunt's understanding, Isabella knew she wouldn't approve of seances, and being desperate to hear from her mama or papa, she didn't dare risk being forbidden to attend. Besides, she had to collect her mama's pearls.

Racking her brains for something to steer the conversation away from selling, she remembered one thing she'd been meaning to ask.

'A gentleman stopped his carriage and enquired if I had any tussie-mussies. What are they?' she asked.

'Small nosegays decorated with a lace doily,'

her aunt replied, looking thoughtful. 'Suitors use them to convey messages to their loved ones.'

'How? I mean flowers can't talk, can they?' she asked, trying not to laugh.

'Oh, but they can, my dear. Each bloom has its own meaning. The language of flowers, they call it. Our dear Queen was a staunch advocate, until her beloved Albert was taken. Though these violets have always been a favourite of hers,' she said, picking up the bunch she'd just counted out. 'They mean faithful love. To assure a lady of his devotion, a gentleman might ask you to wrap them in lavender-coloured lace. A red rosebud in the middle signifies ardent love, while a sprig of myrtle would add strength to that.'

'Goodness, how fascinating,' Isabella cried. 'Maxwell bought me the odd corsage but never anything like that. Still, I don't suppose there's a flower for him finding another,' she muttered.

'Well, the yellow sweetbriar denotes the decease of love,' her aunt told her. 'But bitterness is a waste of energy so why dwell on such unworthy thoughts on a lovely day like this?' Hearing the rain drumming even harder on the roof, Isabella stared at her in amazement. Then she realized the woman was humouring her and smiled.

'Does it always rain here?' she asked. 'I'm sure I don't remember it being this wet in London.'

'Ah, come to lovely Devon where it rains six days out of seven,' Mary chortled. 'Not completely true, but near enough. Still, if it wasn't for our moist climate the violets wouldn't flourish, so it's a small price to pay. 'Tis good for the complexion, too. Talking of rain, those boots of yours are less than useless for this weather. I'll see if I've got something more suitable in my chest.'

'Oh, please don't go to any more trouble,' Isabella said, glancing at the sturdy, lace-up boots her aunt favoured. Never could she wear anything so unsightly; she'd rather suffer wet feet until she could have replacements made for the button boots she favoured.

'It's no trouble. I've already found some grey woollen material in the closet which would make a serviceable warm dress for you. It worries me, you going around selling flowers all dressed up like a lady. Don't argue,' she added holding up her hand when Isabella opened her mouth to protest. 'That frock of yours, pretty though it might be, is too flimsy for winter. Besides, people have been talking and, as your guardians, it is up to Father and I to make sure you act and dress properly.'

'Who said you were my guardians?' she cried.

'Your father, my dear, and we would be doing him a disservice if we didn't take our responsibility seriously.'

'But I attain my majority in February.'

'And until then you are in our care. Father and I had a long chat after Felix brought you back from town in what can only be described as a state quite unbefitting of a young lady. We decided that from now on you're to be treated exactly the same as Dotty and Alice, which means abiding by the rules of the house. Now, it's nearly noon so I'm going to prepare our luncheon then see to Mother.' Seeing Isabella's hopeful look, she shook her head. 'She's having another of her mad and muddled days so I won't suggest you come with me. Finish packing the flowers in here then you'll be ready for something to eat.'

Isabella watched through the open door as her aunt dashed across the puddled yard and into the cottage. As far as she could make out, abiding by the rules of the house meant doing as she was told. It was all right for the others, Dotty was only seventeen while Alice was still an infant. She, on the other hand, would be twenty-one in February and whilst it was only three months away, for someone used to doing what she wanted when she wanted, it sounded like a life sentence. Frustration lending energy to her work, she continued posying and packing, but soon the violets worked their magic and she felt calmer and focused again. She was just placing the last of the bunches into the box when Frederick strode into the barn.

'Well, girl, you've done a grand job here and no mistake,' he said, pushing his hat to the back of his head so that raindrops slid down the back of his coat and onto the floor. 'Getting the hang of things are yer?'

'It took a while, but now I'm actually enjoying it,' she told him, surprised to find it was true. He nodded and stared at her for a moment.

'Want to see the new cultivars I'm nurturing?' he asked. Shocked by his praise and offer, she followed him to the other side of the barn and waited while he unlocked the door. Ushering her in, he proudly gestured to the rows of earth-filled boxes covered with sheets of glass that were set out on another trestle. Peering inside one, she saw little green shoots which, although healthy, looked different to the plants outside.

'Goodness,' she murmured, not knowing what else to say.

'You should have seen them a few weeks ago,' he chuckled, mistaking her surprise. 'Tiny they were. Now look at them,' he said proudly. 'And, with some tender loving care, they'll be ready to be transplanted come spring. Be the making of this household, they will, put our name on the map and money in the bank. But until then they'll need lots of kind words.'

'Kind words?' she asked, certain he was jesting.

'Of course, plants need nurturing and encouraging just like people,' he said, giving her a knowing look. 'Mother thinks I was too harsh earlier but I was saddened you had no faith in us. She says it's a failing of mine being hot-headed,' he sighed.

'It is I who should apologize, Uncle. My accusation was unforgivable.'

'Well, water under the bridge, as your aunt always says. Don't think I've forgotten our discussion about your mother either, but what with Bill taking off, things have been hectic. This is where I come to think things out, so perhaps we'll have our talk in here, away from flapping ears, eh?'

'Could we start now?' she asked eagerly only to hear William calling them.

'Best go in for luncheon. But soon, Izzie, I promise. Remember, though, not a word about my new babies to anyone outside this family.'

It was a simple meal of cheese and oatmeal biscuits, but Isabella was so hungry she tucked in with relish.

'Forgot to put the dough in to bake,' Aunt Mary admitted as she sat munching her food while scribbling a shopping list.

'That was my fault,' Isabella admitted.

'Surprise, surprise,' William muttered only to receive a stern look from his father.

'We need a fair few things,' Mary said, running her finger down the page.

'Right, William. Mother and I have things to discuss, so you take the flowers to Dawlish station today. Isabella, some fresh air will do you good so you go with him. He can drop you at the grocer's then pick you up on his return journey.' Ignoring William's scowl, Frederick continued: 'Dotty's visiting a friend this afternoon and Thomas and Alice are staying over to help Joseph so you won't have to worry about them.'

'That'd certainly be a help, if you don't mind,' Mary said, looking askance at Isabella.

'Of course, Auntie,' she replied, eager to atone for her earlier behaviour.

'Pudge's is opposite the grocer's, so you could pop in there and pick up a length of mauve ribbon. Sewn onto that grey material, you'll have a dress suitable for wearing during your period of mourning.'

'I didn't know you had money to spare for furbelows, Mother,' William frowned.

'Isabella has been earning her keep same as you, boy, and will receive equal allowance. 'Tain't much, mind,' Frederick said, pushing a couple of coins across the table, 'but it's yours to spend as you wish.'

'Goodness, thank you, Uncle,' she murmured.

Was there no end to his surprises this day?

William was sullen as they drove into town. Despite the rain falling in sheets, everywhere was busy and he stared purposefully ahead, dodging traffic, pedestrians and the debris that littered the wet roads.

'Saw you coming out of Father's private potting area earlier. You might think you've got your feet well and truly under the table, but I'm the oldest son and Father's market garden will be mine one day, so don't you go getting any ideas,' he grunted, drawing to a halt outside a row of shops at the seaward end of town.

'I wouldn't dream of it. Muxy hands and thoughts are not for me, thank you,' she told him, smiling sweetly as she climbed down and collected her basket. Resisting the urge to make an unladylike gesture, she turned her attention towards the draper's shop. Bales of materials filled one window whilst the other displayed lace collars, scarves, hat pins and a miscellany of other accessories. Pushing open the door, Isabella looked around in surprise. It certainly bore little resemblance to the smart linen draper's she'd previously visited. Here the merchandise was piled haphazardly and covered every conceivable space.

'Can I help you, my dear?' a pleasant voice asked. Isabella made her way to the counter where a plump woman stood smiling at her.

'Good afternoon, madam. I'm looking for mauve ribbon to trim a grey woollen dress,' she asked.

'We got ribbons of all sorts. Have a gander at this little lot,' she invited, pulling out a wooden drawer and placing it on the counter. Isabella cast her eye over the various spools, selecting the one she thought most appropriate. While the woman measured it out on the rule that ran the length of the shiny wooden counter, Isabella stared idly around. At the back of the shop hung the ready-made corsets Dotty had told her about. She couldn't help grimacing at their wrinkled forms which reminded her of the chicken carcasses she'd seen swinging from hooks outside the butcher's. Did women really wear such ugly garments?

'Settled in at the Northcotts', have you?' the woman asked, handing over the ribbon wrapped in brown paper.

'Oh, er, yes, thank you,' she murmured, dropping the correct money into the woman's podgy hand and heading for the door. 'Tell Dotty I got what she wanted,' the woman called. Shaking her head at the woman's familiarity, Isabella began making her way across the road just as a heavily laden cart swung around the corner, swaying and shedding straw on the road. She jumped back but was too late to avoid its wheels spraying mud over her skirts. The driver, a boy in a tattered shirt collar and fraying cuffs, shook his fists at her as he went past.

'Really,' Isabella fumed, dabbing ineffectually at the marks with her handkerchief. Muttering crossly under her breath, she pushed open the door of the grocery shop with such force, it set the bell jangling violently.

There was a stunned silence as the grocer and the line of waiting customers turned to stare at her. To her chagrin, she saw one of them was

Felix Furneaux. He gave a slight lift of his brow.

'Good afternoon, Miss Carrington. I trust all is well?' he enquired, his lips twitching.

'Quite dandy, thank you, Mr Furneaux,' she told him, forcing a smile. Then, not wanting him to see her in a dishevelled state yet again, she moved away to take a look around.

The store was well stocked with haunches of smoked ham hanging from hooks in the ceiling. Glass-fronted counters were covered in baskets of pulses, and other dried goods were displayed on a ledge beneath. Shelves lined the walls from floor to ceiling, holding an assortment of jars, canisters, multi-coloured packets of food and household commodities.

The babble around her subsided briefly as two customers bustled out of the shop together, then her attention was caught by the grocer's voice.

'Not great weather for lifting the ladies' skirts, eh Felix?'

'It certainly isn't, and some of them are crying out for attention, too,' he replied. 'You wouldn't believe how frustrating it is having to bide my time.' Hardly able to believe what she was hearing, Isabella turned away again, feigning an interest in the large bins containing oatmeal, barley and flour. Only when she heard the tinkle of the bell as Felix left, did she move towards the counter.

'Good afternoon, Miss,' the grocer said.

'Good afternoon. I have been asked to collect these items,' she replied, handing over the list her aunt had made. He nodded, removed the pencil lodged behind his ear and began plucking things from the shelves, crossing off each item as he put it on the counter.

She watched as he expertly sliced cheese, placed it on greased paper and weighed it. Then he picked up a pair of wooden paddles, went over to where a mound of golden butter glistened from a stone slab. He cut off a piece, shaped it into a neat pat before wrapping and tying it with string. Finally, he weighed out broken biscuits from a jar, added them to everything else, then quickly tallied his row of numbers.

'Tell Mrs Northcott, end of the month as usual,' he said, handing it back to Isabella. He was about to say something else but the little bell tinkled again and William entered the shop.

'Good afternoon, William. Everything's neatly packaged ready for transport.'

'Thank you, Mr Cox,' he said, picking up the parcels. 'Perhaps you could manage to bring the biscuits,' he said airily to Isabella. Fighting down her irritation at his patronizing attitude, she nodded to the grocer and followed him outside.

'How was your afternoon's shopping?' he asked, stowing the groceries in the back of the cart. 'Saw Furneaux's cart parked outside when I went past earlier. Bit of a coincidence, being as he called by the cottage to see you this morning.'

'I don't know what you mean,' she replied, still reeling from what she'd heard in the shop.

'Oh, come on, it's obvious he's got a thing for you,' William smirked.

'Well, I do not reciprocate this thing, as you put it. Anyway, a man who goes around lifting the skirts of ladies is disgusting and certainly of no interest to me,' she snapped. William stared at her for a moment, then a light sparked in his dark eyes.

'Oh, so you've heard,' he said gravely. 'Hardly surprising really, for he is well known around here for his weird ways.'

Chapter 24

'Are you awake?' Dotty whispered, sinking down onto her mattress and pulling the cover over her.

'Yes,' Isabella admitted, for although she'd pleaded tiredness to escape her aunt's cheerful questions and William's sneering looks, she hadn't been able to sleep. The storm raging outside only reflected the turmoil seething inside her.

'You was in a right old state when you came back yesterday. Felix was that worried about you. I reckon he likes you, Izzie. You know, I mean *really* likes you,' she said.

'Well, I really don't like him,' Isabella replied. No matter how hard she tried, she couldn't get Felix's bizarre revelation out of her mind. To think she'd considered him honest, candid even.

'Can't think why not. He's good-looking and fun. Father used to like him too, before they started growing flowers for the market. Cors, he's not as handsome as my Alfie.'

Realizing she wasn't going to get any peace, Isabella sighed inwardly and turned towards her cousin. Even in the dark, she could tell the girl was beaming.

'You've seen Alfred then?'

'How did you guess?' she giggled. 'It was his afternoon off and he treated me to coffee and cake in that smart café on the front. Lovely, it was.'

'The cake, you mean?' In spite of her own low mood, Isabella couldn't help smiling at the girl's enthusiasm.

'Yeah, that an' all. Oh Izzie, I do love him so,' she cried, rolling over to face Isabella. 'We've got this understanding. And guess what? He's going to speak to Father on his day off. Promise him he'll look after me better in future, even though we knows it wasn't his fault I fell and hurt me ankle. And,' she paused dramatically, 'then he's going to ask permission for us to walk out together. I'm so happy I could burst.'

'I'm pleased for you, Dotty. He seems like a nice young man.'

'Nice? He's blooming fantastic,' Dotty gushed. Isabella shook her head at the girl's fervour.

'Oh, by the way, Mrs Pudge said to tell you she's got what you asked for.'

'Goodie. I showed her this dress in a periodical and asked if it would be possible to make one like it. She said there was a paper pattern for a similar one and would get it in for me. Alfred wants me to be his partner for the Christmas party the big house put on for the staff. Can you imagine?' Isabella could, but luckily Dotty was chattering on. 'I so want him to be proud of me. Cors, it'll mean being good to get all me allowance but it'll be worth the effort if I can buy the gorgeous red material I've seen.'

'Sounds lovely,' she murmured. They fell silent,

each lost in their own thoughts. Isabella recalled last year, when she'd been invited to so many balls, she'd had to write a list detailing what she'd worn to which so that she didn't do the unforgivable and wear the same dress again. A sudden rattling of the window panes made her jump.

'In for a right old squall by the sound of it,' Dotty murmured as hail spattered against the glass and a gust soughed down the chimney, bringing with it dust and a sprinkling of soot. 'Good job we only lights the fire in here when it's bitter or we'd be black as the coal man.' Isabella shuddered at the thought, but Dotty smiled. 'I likes it on nights like this when we're snug as bugs in bed.' Bugs? In the bed? This time Isabella's shudder didn't go unnoticed.

'Oh Izzie, you are a one. Bet you found Pudge's a bit different to that posh draper's.'

'Yes, I did,' Isabella agreed, thinking of the hotchpotch of merchandise scattered around the shop.

'Will you come and see the material I like, when I've saved up?'

'Me?'

'Yeah, I want to look classy like you. It'll probably be expensive but Mrs Pudge said not to worry if I couldn't save enough in time, 'cos I can let her have the rest in the New Year. She's such a dear, isn't she?'

'Actually, I thought her manner quite familiar,' Isabella admitted. 'Where I come from, proprietors of shops know their place and keep their distance.'

'Blimmer, girl, that sounds 'orrible. I'm not sure

I'd like city life. It's much nicer when people are friendly and help you.'

'Goodness, I hadn't thought of it like that, I must admit,' Isabella conceded, shivering as another gust of wind whooshed down the chimney with an eerie wail.

'Perhaps you should relax, give folk a chance to get to know you,' Dotty said. 'Like poor Felix, for example,' she added.

'I couldn't imagine being friendly with someone who, who...,' her voice trailed off.

'Who what?' Dotty persisted, moving closer so that Isabella could feel her breath on her cheek.

'Well ... goodness, this is so embarrassing,' she admitted. 'When I was in the store, Felix told the grocer he was frustrated because he couldn't lift the ladies' skirts,' she said, in a hushed voice. To her astonishment, Dotty shrieked with laughter.

'And you thought...,' she lay back on her pillow, struggling for breath as tears of mirth rolled down her face.

'I don't find it in the least bit funny, especially as William said he had a reputation for doing it,' Isabella huffed.

'And so he has, being as how he has a dozen or more to deal with,' Dotty said, propping herself back up on her elbows.

'A dozen or more,' she gasped putting her hand to her mouth.

'Oh Isabella, you should see your face. Clearly you don't understand, and by the sound of it, my dear brother didn't intend explaining. The ladies he was referring to are the trees that border his land. Lifting the skirts is simply how they describe pruning the lower branches to allow planting underneath.'

'Oh,' Isabella murmured, her face growing hot at her assumption. 'Well, how was I to know? Wait until I see William. First it was blue mice and now this.'

'I think he...' The rest of her sentence was lost as a flash of lightning and an ear-splitting crack rent the air. It was followed by a tortured tearing sound then a loud crash which shook the cottage and rattled the windows louder than before. 'Blimmer, what was that?' Dotty cried, running over to the window and peering out. 'Coo, the blooming elm's come down and landed on the barn roof.'

Throwing her mantle around her shoulders, Isabella followed Dotty down the stairs where Mary was already standing on the kitchen doorstep holding a lantern. As Dotty went to push by her, she shook her head.

'No point in you getting wet too. Father and William have gone to investigate. Put the kettle on to heat, they'll need something warm when they come back in. I must go and check on Mother,' she told them, pulling her shawl up over her head and disappearing outside. Dotty waited until the light she was carrying was swallowed up by the murk then turned to Isabella.

'You make the tea. I'm going to see what's going on.' Before Isabella could reply, she'd stepped into her boots and was scurrying over to the barn. She was back moments later, hair plastered to her head and dripping water onto the floor.

'Blimmer, it's bad,' she cried, kicking off her boots and snatching up a towel. 'Father and William are shoring things up best they can but there's not much else they can do til it's light. Got a right yelling at from Father for going out, though,' she muttered, wiping the rain from her face.

'Mother's still asleep, would you believe?' Mary cried, coming into the kitchen and placing the lantern on the sill. 'Oh Dotty, can you never do as you're told?' she sighed.

'Just wanted to see if I could help. Oh, there's the kettle,' Dotty said as the whistle sounded. 'I'd better riddle up the range a bit more, too, it's perishing out there.'

They were slumped at the table, hands round their mugs, when the two men strode into the kitchen. Both had mud-streaked faces and were soaked to the skin.

'Is it very bad?' Mary asked, jumping to her feet and taking Frederick's sodden coat from him.

'Won't know exactly until morning,' he sighed. 'Me new plants and glass are smashed to smithereens, though.'

'And the ones out in the fields are saturated,' William muttered.

'I thought they liked the wet,' Isabella ventured, trying to lighten the atmosphere.

'A drinking not a drenching,' he snorted.

'Well, at least we're all right, thank the Lord. I mean, it could have crashed down on the roof of the cottage. Come and sit down, the pair of you. You look all in.'

'Think I'll hit the hay, Mother. In fact, we'd all better get some rest. God knows there'll be enough to do come morning. It'll be all hands on deck,' he said, shooting Isabella a challenging look.

'Of course, Uncle. I'll do whatever I can to help,' she replied.

The next morning, the storm had abated and, with a watery sun breaking through the clouds, they trooped outside. Isabella, at her aunt's insistence, was wearing a pair of pattens over her worn boots.

'They might not be pretty but they'll save your feet getting muxy,' she said. Isabella tried not to grimace at the clumpy contraptions as she clattered over the yard. However, when she saw the fallen tree sticking out of the barn roof, and the havoc the storm had wreaked on the plants, all thought of her attire disappeared.

'Poor Uncle,' she murmured, seeing the set of his face as he stared at the mangled mess that had once been his potting and propagating room.

'It'll take an army to lift that tree,' William grunted. Just then they heard the clatter of hooves and rumble of wheels and saw Joseph at the reins, with Bill, Thomas and Alice all peering anxiously at the barn.

'Seems the cavalry's arrived,' Mary said, waving as they clambered down from the cart. 'As you can see, we've a bit of a problem,' she told them as they all stared at the damage.

'You suffered much in the storm?' Frederick asked Bill.

'Nothing like this,' he replied with a shake of his head. His voice sounded raspy and Isabella saw he was looking pale, but whether that was from the shock of seeing the barn or his recent absence, she couldn't tell.

'Think the hedging gave us protection from the prevailing winds, Father,' Joseph told him. 'Bottom field's a bit waterlogged but other than that we seem to be all right.'

'Good. Well, let's take a walk around, see what we can do,' Frederick said.

'Best thing we can do is get some breakfast on the go while the men work out the safest way to tackle things,' Mary told them.

'Goody, more food,' Alice grinned, seemingly oblivious to the seriousness of the situation. 'We had some porridge but I'm still hungry.'

'Seems like a fry of eggs and teddies is needed, then.' Mary smiled and ruffled her daughter's hair, clearly pleased to have her home again.

Although Isabella had heard the phrase, cooking up a storm, she'd never seen it applied before. On went the kettle, out came the skillet and pan, and the loaf that had finally been baked the previous day was sliced and buttered. Soon the kitchen was filled with the aroma of cooking. Isabella could hardly believe her aunt could concentrate on domestic affairs when there was evidently so much that needed doing outside.

'We'll all think better with a satisfying meal inside us,' she said, seeing Isabella's frown. 'Ah, here come the men. Perhaps you can pour tea whilst Dotty helps me serve up?'

Heedless of their muddy boots, everyone squashed around the table or perched on the windowsill and tucked into the food. As their plates were cleared, grim looks and muttered moans gave way to hopeful smiles and helpful suggestions so that, by the time the men disappeared back outside, a plan of action had been drawn up.

'Call if you need us,' Mary told them. 'We'll be in here preparing luncheon.'

'I know it's Sunday, Mother, but in view of what needs to be done, I think we'd better eat at supper time. Give us longer,' Frederick said, putting on his bedraggled straw hat and going out of the door. The others nodded and followed.

'But surely we should be helping outside,' Isabella ventured.

'Don't worry, Izzie, there'll be plenty of cleaning up for us to do once they've lifted that tree.' Seeing Isabella frown, she added: 'Being a family means working as a team. If we take care of the day-to-day things in here, it frees the men up to attend to the immediate problem. Like the clearing away,' she said, gesturing to the dirty plates and mugs littering the table. 'I'll take Mother's tray in and see how she is today.'

They'd just finished preparing food for the evening meal when William popped his head around the door.

'Father says he could do with a hand from everyone now. As long as you don't mind getting yours muxy, Izzie,' he said, his dark eyes challenging.

'I'd be delighted to help,' she said smiling sweetly at him.

'Best put them pattens on again,' Mary said. 'I've a feeling we are going to get really dirty this time.'

Her aunt was right. Having decided that before the tree was lifted the barn should be cleared, he ordered them to form a chain, and they passed pails, tools, pots and packets from one to the other, with Alice and Thomas running around to place them in their grandmother's shed.

'Right, now we need to see to the plants,' Frederick said, but Bill shook his head.

'Sorry, Fred, got to go. Feeling a bit sick, like,' he explained, looking shamefaced. Frederick nodded grimly but Isabella found herself feeling sorry for her uncle. How sad that his past life should have such a profound effect on him all these years later.

'Isabella, you take care of the plants over there,' Uncle Frederick told her, pointing to the patch just beyond the yard. 'You need to hoe carefully round each one, then use your hands to gently sweep the soil from the leaves. The fine hairs on their underside trap the dirt and block the breathing pores. At least it'll give the flowers a fighting chance. Mix the tailor's clippings in this pail with some of the dung in that one and lay it around the stems. Think you can do that?' he asked. To be truthful, she wasn't sure, but hearing William snigger, she nodded.

'Of course, Uncle.'

'Good. The rest of you collect more clippings and dung and follow William,' he ordered. 'I've things to see to in the barn before we lift that trunk.'

Determined to do her bit, Isabella set about her work. It was back-breaking and she found the mud and stench nauseating at first. After a while, though, she was pleased to see the difference she was making by freeing the leaves from the splattered soil, leaving the buds free to blossom. As she laid the clippings she'd gingerly mixed with the dung, she recalled her uncle telling her that she needed to free herself from the past before she could move on to the future, and suddenly she understood what he'd meant. What a wise man he was, she thought, automatically reaching up and tucking a stray lock of hair behind her ears.

'Now there's a sight I never thought to behold. Isabella Carrington with muck all over her face.'

Being so absorbed in her work, she hadn't heard the crunch of footsteps on the path and, startled, she looked up to see Felix grinning down at her.

Chapter 25

'What are you doing here?' Isabella asked, then noticed another man standing behind him and hastily rose to her feet.

'Good afternoon, my dear. Matthew Furneaux at your service,' he smiled, and gave a little bow. 'Don't take any cheek from my son,' he added, the gleam in his hazel eyes belying his sharp words.

'Father, this is Miss Isabella Carrington,' Felix told him. She held out her hand, then saw it was coated in dirt and dung.

'Oh, I do apologize,' she added, quickly withdrawing it.

'No apology needed, my dear. It's heartening to see you tending to the needs of our dear princesses.'

'Pardon?' she frowned.

'These violets are called Princess of Wales,' Felix explained. 'Although in France they go by the title *Princesse de Galles.*'

'Goodness, I just thought of them as violets,' she said, frowning down at the flowers.

'Don't mind Felix, my dear, he absorbs facts like a sponge,' Matthew told her. He looked around then shook his head. 'That storm hit you badly, I see. Still, at least everyone's pulling together,' he added, gesturing further down the garden where the others were all bent over the flowers. 'We met Bill earlier and he told us about the tree coming down, so we've come to offer our services,' he added, stroking his walrus moustache thoughtfully as he stared at the trunk protruding from the damaged barn.

Felix turned to Isabella and their gaze met and held. A delicious feeling of warmth washed over her and she felt as though time was suspended. Then footsteps crunched up the path behind them and the spell was broken.

'Morning, Mr Furneaux, Felix,' William said, eyeing them suspiciously. 'What can we do for you?'

'I think perhaps it's more a case of what we can do for you, William,' the older man replied cheerfully. 'You're going to need extra strength to lift that brute,' he said pointing towards the fallen tree.

'Ain't that a fact,' Frederick muttered, coming out of the barn to join them. 'Come to gloat have yer?' Hardly able to believe his rudeness, Isabella stared at her uncle in surprise.

'Far from it, Fred. We've brought a strong rope with us. Tell us exactly what you want doing,' Matthew replied, ignoring the hostile reception. He stared up at the lowering clouds, his forehead wrinkling into a frown. 'Looks like it'll turn nasty again soon, so it'd probably be best to get on with it now.' Frederick eyed his competitor keenly for a moment, then with a curt nod led the way over to the barn.

'Seems hostilities have been suspended,' Felix murmured, as the two men strode away. 'Perhaps we could have a chat later,' he suggested, turning back to Isabella. 'You appeared somewhat pre-occupied in the grocer's yesterday.'

'She was fascinated to hear about your need to lift the ladies' skirts,' William smirked.

'Indeed I was, Felix,' she replied, ignoring the gleeful grin on her cousin's face. As Felix quirked his brow quizzically, she smiled. 'After hearing you talk about yield the other day, I understand your frustration at not being able to get your trees pruned to allow for extra planting.' William's face was such a picture, she had to bite her lip to prevent herself laughing out loud.

'Can't stand here gossiping all day,' he snapped, stalking over to the barn.

'Well, you are full of surprises, Miss Carrington,' Felix said, giving her an appreciative smile that sent her insides fizzing.

'How so, Mr Furneaux?' she asked coyly.

'First I find you digging around in the mud, wearing those most, er, interesting-looking contraptions on your feet,' he said, grinning down at her pattens. 'Then I learn you have a good understanding of our business. I'm impressed and, if you're agreeable, would like to further our discussion another time.' As he stood looking at her expectantly, they heard his name being called. 'Must go,' he added and she watched as he ran over to join the others, coat-tails flapping behind him like a ship in full sail.

'Said he liked you,' Dotty chuckled, putting down her pail on the low wall that edged the yard. 'And despite all your protestations last night, I'd say you're more than a mite struck. Mother says we should go in and make everyone a hot drink. Me back's killing me and me ankle's aching, so can't say I'm sorry to stop digging in the dirt.'

'Right, I'll just wash my hands first,' Isabella said.

'Better do your face an' all, muxy moppet,' Dotty laughed. 'Never seen you look so dirty, yet you're glowing like a lantern.'

'Must be the fresh air,' Isabella blushed, her glance straying to where Felix was helping cut off the broken boughs. As she watched, he shed his jacket and began pulling on the rope, his biceps rippling through the sleeves of his shirt. Her heart began thrumming a tattoo, and she quickly turned away and headed for the pump.

Later that afternoon when the tree had been sawn up, removed to the boundary hedge and a tarpaulin lashed over the gaping hole in the roof, the weary but jubilant men tramped into the kitchen to be greeted by the fragrant aroma of rich gravy.

'That smells good, Mrs Northcott,' Matthew said, sniffing the air appreciatively. 'Are you sure there's enough for all of us?'

'Cors there is, Matthew. And it's Mary, as you well know,' she chided, ignoring the glare her husband shot her. 'The least we can do is feed you after you've kindly helped us out like that.'

As they all tucked hungrily into the casserole that had been simmering on the range for the best part of the day, Isabella darted a covert glance at Felix across the table, only to find he was doing the same. She stared quickly down at her plate before anyone else saw, but could feel his eyes still watching her. As soon as the plates were empty and talk turned to the day's operation, Felix got to his feet.

'Thank you, Mrs Northcott, that was a superb meal,' he said, then turned to Isabella. 'I see the rain has stopped and wondered if you would care to take a stroll around the garden. With your permission, sir,' he added, looking askance at Frederick.

''Appen, if the girl wishes,' her uncle shrugged.

'I'd love to,' she stammered, quickly getting to her feet to avoid their curious stares.

'Good idea,' William said, jumping up. 'Bit of a walk'd be good after all that grub.'

'Sorry, William, but in this case three would be a crowd,' Felix told him. Ignoring his glower, Isabella snatched up her mantle and opened the door. As they stepped outside, Felix leaned over and drew the material gently around her, the touch of his fingers on her neck setting her pulse racing.

'Can't have you getting cold,' he murmured, his voice husky. 'Come on, let's take that walk.'

It was a beautiful if breezy evening with the moon curling above them in a silver arc and myriad stars twinkling like sequins in the inky heavens. The air was filled with the heady fragrance of violets, and Isabella sighed contentedly as they strolled side by side down the length of the garden.

'You look more relaxed tonight somehow,' Felix said, breaking the silence. 'As well as beautiful, of course.' She glanced down at the coarse material of the dress she'd borrowed and grimaced.

'Regrettably none of the clothes I brought with me are suitable for this life,' she sighed.

'You'd look lovely in a sack, Isabella. Why, your hair is positively gleaming in the moonlight.'

'Gaskell would have a fit if she saw me without a hat,' Isabella laughed. 'But then life here is so very different,' she added, jumping as an owl hooted and swooped out from the barn next door.

'Have you settled in well here?' he asked.

'Apart from the wildlife scaring me half to death, you mean?' She pondered for a moment and then nodded. 'Actually, I am beginning to, thank you. Auntie and Uncle have been most welcoming. Although the privations take some getting used to.' He raised a brow but didn't say anything as they continued walking.

'You sounded very erudite about the pruning of trees earlier. If your knowledge of plants and flowers is anything like equal, you will be a great asset here.'

'I'm learning all the time,' she replied, not wishing to admit what she'd actually thought lifting the ladies' skirts had meant.

'And enjoying it too, if the look on your face when I arrived is anything to go by.'

'Surprisingly, I found it therapeutic tending to the plants,' she admitted.

'Well, they do say green is the colour of renewal,' he said, stooping to pluck the flower from a broken plant and inspecting it. 'Though this poor little maid has had it.' As his long finger gently caressed the petals, a shiver tingled down Isabella's spine.

'Come on, let's get moving before you catch a chill,' he murmured.

'Did your flowers suffer much in the storm?' she asked.

'Not really. Luckily the trees afforded protection. Unlike here, which is more exposed,' he said, gesturing around. 'Did your uncle have anything of value stored in that big barn?' She bit her lip, remembering the new plants her uncle had shown her.

'I'm not sure really,' she hedged, not wishing to reveal any family secrets. 'You were telling me the names of the violets earlier. Did you learn them from that man in France?' she asked, eager to change the subject.

'Armand Millet? Fancy you remembering that!' he replied, looking pleased. 'Yes, I did. He is one of the most successful and respected commercial violet growers. It was a fascinating experience and I learned so much. For example, did you know this humble flower is unique?' he asked, holding up the violet he'd been carrying.

'Really? How so?' she asked, for apart from colour and smell, surely all flowers were the same.

'As well as its scent, it generates a property

called ionine which dulls the sense of smell.'

'Aunt Mary explained about that when I told her the flowers I was packing had no fragrance. Of course, the sisters use violets at their se–' Realizing she was about to reveal details of her visits in town, she stammered to a halt.

'Sorry, you were saying?' he asked, staring at her expectantly. Even in the shadowy light she could make out the earnest expression on his face.

'Nothing really, just thinking aloud,' she laughed. 'Please, do tell me more about ionine, it sounds fascinating.'

'Very well, but I think we should turn back now before you get cold,' he suggested as they reached the second field of plants and a gust of wind whipped round them, sending the flowers rippling. 'You must promise to tell me if I become boring,' he said, taking her arm. Even through her mantle she could feel the warmth of his touch. If this was boring, long may it last, she thought.

'I promise,' she replied, coming back to the present and seeing him staring at her expectantly.

'I warn you, this is a subject I could talk about all night. As you probably know, the scent comes back if you hold the flower away for a time before inhaling it again, whereupon, lo and behold, the ionine effect kicks in again. This is proving a nightmare for skilled perfumiers in France.'

'You mean they make perfume out of violets?' she asked, staring at him incredulously.

'Indeed they do,' he conceded. 'However, in order to make a longer-lasting fragrance, they need to mix it with the recently discovered synthetic notes to enhance and sustain the violet's capricious aroma without overpowering it. Oh, I do apologize, Isabella, here we are nearly back again and all I've done is rabbit on.'

'It's been fascinating,' she assured him. 'I find it quite astonishing that delicate little flowers like violets should pose problems for accomplished experts. You make the subject sound so interesting, I would love to hear more.'

'Perhaps you would like to visit our market garden then, say next Saturday afternoon?'

'I will have to check with Uncle but I'm sure that will be fine.'

'Excellent, and after the grand tour, maybe you would permit me to take you out for afternoon tea.'

'Oh, but I don't have a chaperone,' she protested. He gave a chuckle, which echoed round the quiet of the garden.

'My dear Miss Carrington, I was only suggesting we had a further discussion not ... not that I wouldn't like, well...,' his voice trailed away.

'I'm sorry, Felix. I'd forgotten I was in Devonshire and that things are different down here.' She glanced sideways to find he was doing the same. As their gaze met and held for the second time in as many hours, she felt her heart skip.

'I'd love to accept your kind invitation,' she murmured. He nodded and moved closer so that she could feel his breath on her face. For one moment, she thought he was going to kiss her but then he pulled back.

'Look, a shooting star,' he cried pointing towards the sky. She stared at the tail of light flashing across the heavens then closed her eyes and made a wish. When she opened them again, he was smiling gently at her.

'I hope it comes true for you,' he murmured. 'Now, we really must go in before your uncle sends out a search party,' he said, his voice husky once more. Slowly he leaned towards her and this time he didn't hesitate. His lips lightly brushed her cheek and again she saw stars, though this time they were shooting around her head.

That night as she lay in bed, listening to her cousins snoring, she held her hand to her still-burning cheek and sighed contentedly. What a charming man Felix was. Handsome and fascinating too. Who would have thought such a disastrous day would end so happily? She closed her eyes and, for the first time in ages, her dreams were of the future instead of the past.

Chapter 26

The next morning, Isabella floated downstairs on a haze of happiness, only to be met with the grim faces of the family as they sat hunched round the table.

'What's wrong?' she asked, taking her seat and noting they were back to having beastly brewis again.

'William and I have been out to assess the storm damage and it's much worse than we feared,' her uncle told her. 'The whole of the big barn has been affected, which means we can't do any work in there. Not that there will be many flowers worth picking for a while anyhow. Can't send bedraggled blooms to Covent Garden,' he added gloomily. 'Completely ruin my reputation, that would.'

'Which will leave the way clear for lover boy to take our share of the market,' William spat. 'No wonder he was looking so jubilant yesterday.'

'What does jubilant mean?' Alice asked, but Isabella hardly heard her, for she was remembering Felix examining the damage to their flower fields and asking about the contents of the barn. Had he been using her as a foil for his own plans, she wondered, her dreams turning to dust.

'Why, you didn't think he was looking so happy because of your company, did you?' he taunted.

'William, that's not nice,' Mary chided.

'I shall ask Felix when I see him on Saturday,' she said.

'Oh?' Frederick asked.

'He was telling me about making perfume. When I expressed a desire to know more, he invited me to see his gardens,' she admitted, ignoring her uncle's disapproving look.

'Makes a change from etchings,' William snorted.

'That's quite enough of that, William,' Mary scolded. 'Come along, Izzie, eat your breakfast. We've a lot to do today.' Isabella stared down at the mush of milk and crusts and felt her throat constrict.

'We need to have a chat before you next meet him, girl. There's things you need to know and things you mustn't tell,' Frederick told Isabella.

'Like what?' she asked but he was already

studying the pad he'd been scribbling on.

'Right, Alice and Thomas, get yourselves off to school now. There'll be plenty for you to do when you get home, so no dawdling,' Mary ordered. 'Don't forget your lunchtime pieces, and put your capes on, it's raining again,' she told them, ruffling Thomas's hair affectionately as he scrambled down from the table.

'Aw, Mother,' he groaned, flattening it again with his hand.

The door closed behind them then opened again as Dotty came in carrying a tray.

'Still blooming raining,' she moaned, setting it down on the sill and shaking the drops from her shawl. 'Grandmother's feeling better today. She even asked me to wind up her music box so she could listen while she ate. Said a little melody was good for the soul, can you believe.' Frederick nodded distractedly, then gestured for her to take a seat.

'Right, listen up,' he ordered, staring at each of them in turn. 'I've been working out the cost of the storm damage and it's not good. Mother's come up with the helpful idea of using the damaged heads for making jam and tablet to sell, which will bring in some money as well as not wasting the violets.' Dotty brightened.

'I'll take them into town and sell them after I've been to the big house. There will be flowers for them, won't there?' she asked anxiously.

'Might be enough by Thursday,' Frederick replied. 'William, I want you to go out now and pick all the violets that can be used for cooking. You girls will help Mother in the kitchen,' he said, looking at Isabella and Dotty.

'What will you be doing, Father?' William asked.

'Seeing the bank manager for a loan,' he replied grimly. 'Money'll be tight for the next few weeks until we're back on our feet so there will be no allowance for anyone,' he added, getting to his feet and pulling on his hat and coat. Isabella noticed that for once he didn't put a bunch of violets in his buttonhole.

'But Father, I'm trying to save for new material...,' Dotty began.

'And I'm trying to save our business and home,' he snapped. 'Now, Isabella, do you have your pearls?' Isabella stared at him in dismay. What could she say? If she told him she'd left them with the sisters she'd have to come clean about the seances. 'I don't intend pawning them, if that's what you're worried about,' he snorted. 'With Mother fretting about them being secure, I was going to deposit them in the bank's safe but I can see from your face you still don't trust us.' As Isabella opened her mouth to protest, he turned and stormed out of the room, slamming the door behind him.

'But I didn't mean...,' she began.

'He was only trying to help,' Mary said quietly.

'Wouldn't hurt you to let him pawn them anyway, being as how he saved you from the workhouse,' William muttered, scowling at Isabella before slamming out of the door behind his father. Bewildered, Isabella stared after him. That she might have ended up in the workhouse had never occurred to her.

'Would it help to pawn them?' Isabella asked,

turning back to her aunt.

'We wouldn't dream of it, dear, so don't even think about it,' she replied, patting Isabella's hand.

'But William's right. You did take me in and... ,' she began.

'We did it willingly,' Mary cut in. 'Father'll get things sorted out. He always does. I looked out that grey material earlier,' she added, turning and taking a length of woollen fabric from the dresser. 'As it's so wet outside, why don't you cut it out and sew that dress we were talking about?'

'But shouldn't I be helping you with...'

'I need to find my receipts and gather everything together, so you can use the table while I'm doing that. Believe you me, dear, I'll feel much happier when you have a respectable frock to wear out. And I can't tell you how relieved I am you're wearing that locket instead of them pearls. I take it they're in a safe place upstairs?' she asked, fixing Isabella with her gimlet stare.

'Yes,' Isabella replied, crossing her fingers behind her back.

'Now, if you're not finishing that breakfast, go and get your lavender dress to use as a pattern. Dotty, clear away then you can help me take the stalks off the flowers.'

As Isabella went upstairs, she could hear her cousin bewailing the lack of allowance. Poor Dotty, she thought, remembering how the girl wanted to impress Alfred. Perhaps she had something suitable in her trunk. She would suggest they took a look later. There might even be things she could give the family, she thought, still upset that the pearls had caused such a bad atmosphere. As soon as she got them back she'd suggest her uncle take them. Feeling better about her decision, she took her dress from the closet and went back downstairs.

'Just look at the state of that,' her aunt said, pointing to the mud stains. 'You should be ashamed of yourself, Isabella. Why ever didn't you sponge them off?'

'I never thought,' she admitted.

'Well, girl, it's time you did. Regrettably for you, the days of having servants to do these things are over. Brush off the worst then you can wash it in the outhouse later,' her aunt told her, placing the clean dishes back on the dresser.

Isabella did as her aunt suggested, then spread the grey material over the table. Using her dress as a guide, she began pinning out the shape.

'Right, I'm off to see if Mother needs anything,' Mary said, grabbing her turnover. 'Although it's good she's having a better day, it does mean she requires more attention. While I'm gone, Dotty, you can get out the stone mortar and sugar loaf from the pantry.'

'I'm never going to save enough in time for the party now,' Dotty moaned as soon as her mother had gone.

'We could take a look at the things I brought with me. See if there's anything you'd like to wear or adapt,' Isabella told her.

'Coo, that'd be great,' Dotty cried, brightening.

'Perhaps you should have this material instead of me,' she suggested, gesturing to the table.

'That'd hardly be festive, would it?' she snorted. 'Now, if you've got any more like this?' she added, running her finger over the satin fabric.

'There's a matching jacket which could be fashioned into a blouse,' Isabella mused. They jumped as the door opened and William stomped into the kitchen carrying two baskets.

'I see Madam High and Mighty's looking after herself, as usual,' he muttered, dumping the flowers on the floor. 'Shouldn't you be helping with the cooking rather than making something fancy to wear when you go out with lover boy?'

'Actually...,' she began, but found she was talking to his back. 'Oh dear.'

'He never used to be like that,' Dotty said. 'Reckon he's got a thing for you, Izzie,' she grinned. 'Oops, here comes Mother,' she added, scuttling over to the pantry.

'Well, Grandmother's in good spirits today, Izzie,' Mary said. 'You can take her luncheon in later if you like. Ah good, William's picked the violets, though the poor things look so draggled, cooking's all they're good for. Have you got everything else ready, Dotty?'

Isabella smiled at her aunt's seemingly endless energy, then carefully began her cutting out. It'd been ages since she'd done any needlework, or painting come to that, and she realized she missed being creative. Whilst she'd employed dressmakers for her couture outfits, she'd always enjoyed making her own things for informal wear.

'Oh, you have made a good job of that,' Mary said when she'd finished. 'Now, you sit by the window to catch the light while you sew it up. It's time I got on with the jam. Have you finished that sugar yet, Dotty?'

To the sound of stems being snipped from flower heads, Isabella began to stitch. As she sewed, she thought how much her life had changed since she'd left London. Although she desperately missed dear Papa and still thought of him often, her days here were so busy that the time just flew by. Her new family had made her so welcome and she was determined to have that conversation about her dear mama soon. Her thoughts turned to Maxwell but instead of steely grey eyes that analysed and assessed, a vision of warm, green ones that listened and encouraged popped into her head, making her heart flip. Despite her vow never to let another man into her life, she realized Felix had found his way into her affections. Now she'd had time to think about William's earlier words, she couldn't believe Felix would use her in the way he'd suggested. However, she'd be on her guard not to let out any family secrets. Not that she knew many, she thought with a shake of her head.

A wonderful aroma wafted across the room and she inhaled appreciatively. Although similar to the smell at the seance, this was sweeter and more appetizing. It was a shame she had to wait so long to see the sisters again for she really was impatient to find out if Agnes had absorbed her mama's aura from the pearls and would be able to invoke her spirit.

Turning the material to sew the other seam, she began humming softly. As ever, the music of a cradlesong evoked snatches of words and that elusive fragrance from the past which, even in this violet-growing place, she'd yet to find. Lost in her memories, she began to sing:

Goodnight, sleep tight, while the angels watch o'er
My darling delight, scent of violets will soar
All mingled with dum, de dum

Oh, why couldn't she remember all the words? She gave a sigh of frustration then realized her aunt and Dotty had stopped what they were doing and were watching her curiously.

'Sorry, I know my tones are anything but dulcet,' she said, grinning sheepishly.

'No, it wasn't your voice, more the words,' Mary murmured, looking uncomfortable. 'Oh heck, me jam's boiling.' Quickly, she turned back to her pan, stirred furiously, then took a spoonful and placed it on a cold plate.

'Why do you do that?' Isabella asked.

'To see if it's reached setting,' Dotty answered, lining the jars along the table. 'You wait a moment then push it with your fingers and if it crinkles, like this, then it's done. If you boil the mixture too long it'll go bitter then no one will eat it.'

'Are you sure there's nothing I can do to help?' Isabella asked, conscious that they'd been toiling while she'd been sewing and musing.

'You can pen the labels if you like. Dotty's writing's worse than mine,' Mary laughed, pushing her hair back under the day cap she was wearing. 'But that can be done this afternoon. While Dotty helps me bottle this lot, you can prepare luncheon and take Mother's into her. She's asking for more of them tiny bite-sized morsels. It's funny the things she remembers,' she added with a smile. Isabella stared at her aunt in surprise, for usually she insisted they went in together.

Although the rain had eased, the yard was filled with puddles and Isabella gingerly made her way round to next door and let herself in. As she carried the tray through to the living room, she heard music playing. It couldn't be, she thought, staring at her grandmother in surprise. The music came to a stop and she was just thinking she must have imagined it after her recent reminiscing, when the woman turned the key of the box on her lap. Sure enough, it was the same tune and Isabella nearly dropped the tray as the woman began singing the lyrics. When she reached the words Isabella had forgotten, she felt the tears welling up. As the music box ran down again, the woman stared at Isabella and smiled.

'Violets and roses, that's what my Ellie used to mix. Used to love that scent, she did. Cors, when she went to London, she had it made up proper. Only came back once after, but she smelled like a field of flowers,' the woman beamed.

'She was my mama,' Isabella prompted, excitement fluttering in her breast.

'I know that girl, I'm not daft,' she tutted. Then her eyes dimmed and she stared into the fire. Scared she was about to retreat into her own world again, Isabella knelt down and took her hand.

'She used to wear that all the time. Weren't worth much but he give it her, see,' her grandmother sighed as she pointed to the locket at Isabella's throat. 'It were all so long ago.' As she lapsed into silence again and closed her eyes, Isabella bit her lip and waited. *Please come back,* she willed. The rain started again, lashing the window and trickling down the chimney where it landed on the glowing embers with a hiss. Suddenly, the woman's eyes snapped open.

'What's your name?' she asked, her rheumy eyes focused on Isabella.

'Isabella,' she replied.

'That figures,' the woman laughed. 'Always had grand ideas, did Ellie. That's why she married who she did.'

'Papa was a good man,' Isabella assured her grandmother.

'You're the spit of him, you know.'

'Really?' she asked, frowning. Nobody had ever commented on that before. Quite the reverse, in fact.

'Roger, that were 'is name. Roger the Dodger,' she snorted then closed her eyes.

Chapter 27

'Everything all right, dear?' Mary asked as Isabella came back into the room. 'Did Grandmother eat her luncheon?'

'No, she didn't even look at it. She was playing her music box. Then she spotted Mama's locket and seemed to understand who I was, saying I looked like Papa.'

'That's good, isn't it?' Dotty asked, pushing her plate aside.

'I thought so, but then she got muddled again because she called him Roger,' Isabella sighed.

'Oh,' Mary gasped, 'I knew I shouldn't have let

you go by yourself.' Then as Isabella looked askance, she quickly began clearing the dishes. 'Sadly, that's how she is these days, in the past most of the time, then something triggers her memory and back she comes, albeit fleetingly. It was probably that music this time.'

'When I went in, she was singing along to it and they were the same words Mama used when she sang to me. Do you think it was hers when she was a child?'

'I don't know, Izzie. You'll have to ask your uncle. Oh, I do wish you'd hurry up and have that chat,' she sighed. 'I'd better slip next door and make sure everything's all right. Dotty, you get those lemons squeezed ready for steeping the rest of the flowers William's picking. Izzie, perhaps you could make a start on those labels.' Before Isabella could ask any further questions, Mary had disappeared out of the door.

'At least the juice will clean all this blue off,' Dotty grimaced, staring down at her stained hands. 'Did Grandmother get a spark in her eyes when she spoke about your mother? I love it on the days she comes back to life, if you get my meaning. You get a glimpse of what she used to be like, don't you? I reckon she was a right character.'

'I just wish she'd been with it for longer,' Isabella sighed, wondering why her aunt had been so furtive. Why shouldn't she see her grandmother by herself?

'Grandmother might have another good day tomorrow, you know,' Dotty said, giving her a smile. 'We'll both take her breakfast in and play her music box again. Must dash outside before I start on the tablet.'

'What is tablet exactly?' Isabella asked.

'Candy cake, and it's scrummy,' Dotty replied. 'Have you never tasted it?'

'No, I don't believe I have. And I still can't believe you make all these things from violets.'

'Beg a piece from Mother when it's set, then you can see for yourself. Now, I definitely must go.'

As Isabella settled down at the table and began penning the labels, she couldn't help humming the cradlesong. She was so engrossed in her task that when William appeared and stared over her shoulder, she jumped.

'Might have known yer writing'd be as fancy as yerself,' he sneered, putting the baskets of wet flowers on the table right beside her writing paper. 'S'pose you 'ad some posh governess eddy-f'cating yer.'

'Can you put those on the floor before water drips over the labels?' she asked.

'Anything else, my lady?' he sneered, grudgingly placing them on the floor.

'Yes, can we stop this continual backbiting? I can't help how I was brought up. Besides, I didn't get taught anything about market gardening,' she told him.

'And your point is?' he muttered.

'That we all need to be shown how to do things, and we find some subjects harder than others. You, for example, are obviously a competent flower grower.'

'And you're definitely not,' he grinned.

'Well, I still haven't spotted any blue mice

roaming the gardens,' she murmured. The gleam in his eyes encouraged her to continue. 'However, I'd love to learn and if you were to help rather than hinder, then perhaps I could repay the favour.'

'Don't see how,' he replied, staring at her suspiciously.

'I could show you how to write your letters, if you'd like me to,' she offered. He stared at the pen and paper on the table then nodded.

'Suppose I could see what you know,' he conceded, then clammed up as Dotty returned.

'I see you've brought in the flowers, William. Help me tail the stalks then I can steep the heads in the lemon juice so Mother can boil them up with sugar.'

They set to work but minutes later heard the cart clattering to a halt outside. There was the sound of voices and then Frederick and Bill strode into the room closely followed by Mary. They were looking sombre and Isabella feared the meeting at the bank hadn't gone well.

'As we've a full house, you might as well know the bank would only grant a loan if I put the cottages and gardens up as collateral,' Frederick muttered.

'And did you?' Mary asked, worry clouding her face.

'Did I heckers, like. Risk losing our home? Over my dead body, which is useless anyway as I'm not insured.'

'Father please,' Mary cried. 'We'll manage, we always have.'

'Exactly what I told that old buffoon of a manager,' he added, throwing his hat onto its peg on the wall. 'Bill here offered to put his house up as surety but, of course, I refused.'

'Don't know why,' Bill shrugged. ''Tisn't as if I've a wife and family of me own to care for.' As a heavy silence fell, Frederick stared at Isabella.

'Hear Grandmother's been back so it's high time we had that chat, girl. Mother says she's sleeping now, so we'll go next door where it's quieter. You'd best come too, Bill.'

'You'd better sit in the kitchen so you don't disturb her,' Mary suggested. 'Take your mantle, Izzie. It'll be chilly as we daren't light the range in there.'

For the second time that day, Isabella found herself in the adjoining cottage with butterflies skittering in her stomach.

'Sit down,' Frederick said, indicating the ladder-back chairs placed round the scrubbed table.

'Now girl, what we have to tell you will come as a shock but, as you've already gathered, there are things you need to know about your mother.'

'First of all, I think we should say how much we loved her,' Bill said, smiling at Isabella. 'Being the girl in the middle of us two lads, Ellie had us wrapped around her little finger. She adored your uncle here – worshipped him, in fact – and used to follow him about.'

'Til she got older and took to following others about,' Frederick growled.

'Whilst I, being the youngest, got bossed about something awful,' Bill smiled, ignoring Frederick. 'It will probably help you understand if you realize Ellie always aspired to the nice things of life, Isabella.'

'Is that why she called herself Eleanora and associated with Lord Lester?'

'She was always known as Ellen round here, although I understand she changed her names after she moved to London,' Bill smiled sadly.

'Names?' she frowned.

'Look, let's just tell you what happened or we'll be here all night. You can ask questions later,' Frederick sighed. Seeing how uncomfortable he looked, Isabella nodded.

'Lord Lester always had an eye for the ladies and Ellen thought she was in with a chance. She fancied herself as lady of the manor, but of course he was just toying with her. A man of his standing marries someone of his own class and wealth, not the daughter of a poor farmer like your mother was.'

'Poor Mama, she must have been heartbroken,' Isabella cried.

'Ellie were made of sterner stuff, and he was only one of her targets,' Frederick laughed. 'Loved a good time, she did, and went out with anyone who'd provide it. Until she fell in love, that is.'

'With Papa, you mean,' she smiled, feeling her heart flutter. 'And then I suppose they married and he took her to London, where I was born.'

'That would have been the idyll,' Bill agreed, looking serious now. 'However, life's not like that.' He stared at the empty range and Isabella knew he was thinking of the wife he'd adored.

'The man your mother fell for was also out for a good time,' Frederick said, taking up the story again. 'There were those who said that Ellen got her just desserts when he upped and left her in the family way.'

'You mean, I have a brother or sister?' Isabella gasped, her hand going to her chest.

'No, Isabella, you were that child. As you can imagine, Grandmother couldn't bear the shame of having a bastard in the family, especially around these parochial parts. Your grandfather had friends in London and arranged for Ellen to stay with them until after you were born. The plan had been for her to return under the guise of a widow and raise you here.' He stopped and cleared his throat.

'Only she never came back. She met the man you knew as your father and that was that. Grandmother never got over the shock of it all,' Bill said. Isabella stared wide-eyed at both her uncles, trying to take in all they'd said.

'Are you saying that Papa wasn't really my father?'

'Not biologically, no,' Frederick agreed. 'But there's more than one way to be a father. To my mind, the man who raised and protected you is the true paternal figure. And Cameron Carrington did all those things, did he not?'

'Yes,' she agreed, tears welling at the thought of the wonderful man she'd adored.

'Did you never wonder why he was so much older than your mother?'

'I can't say it ever occurred to me. I was so young when she died, my memories of her are hazy,' she murmured. In truth, until recently, all she'd really been concerned about was a plentiful wardrobe and full social life. How futile it seemed now.

They sat in silence, pondering on the past, until

they heard the faint strains of music coming from the next room.

'Grandmother's awake. Do you want to see if she's still lucid?' Frederick asked.

'Oh yes,' Isabella cried, jumping to her feet. 'For nothing's really changed, has it?'

'Well,' Frederick began. The men exchanged looks then Bill declared he needed to get back to work and hastily left.

Isabella rushed into the next room to find her grandmother sitting in her customary chair, muttering away to the now silent music box.

'Hello, Grandmama,' she cried. When the woman didn't respond, Isabella gently eased it from her hands and turned the key. As the music began to play, the woman looked up.

'Ellie?' she asked, her eyes widening in surprise.

'It's me. Isabella.' The woman's eyes brightened for a moment and Isabella's heart leapt, but instead of saying anything, she started singing the lullaby. Isabella joined in, tears rolling down her cheeks as the familiar words from long ago rang around the room. When the music died away, Isabella looked at her grandmother expectantly. The woman stared back blankly before turning towards the fire, the music box still clutched in her hand.

'Oh Grandmama, please don't go now,' she cried. But there was no reply.

As her uncle tentatively patted her shoulder, Isabella turned to him. 'Do you think she'll come back?' she asked.

'No telling,' her uncle said, bending and tucking the blanket back over the woman's knees.

'We'll let her rest for now. Mother will come and check she's all right later.'

'Auntie really takes care of her, and all of us, doesn't she?'

'Yes, she does,' he replied, staring thoughtfully at the old woman.

'Thank you for telling me about Mama,' she added.

'I'm sorry if it came as a shock but you need to know the truth especially...,' he broke off as Mary hurried into the room.

'Just came to make sure everything is all right,' she said, looking anxiously from one to the other.

'Yes, thank you, Auntie,' Isabella replied, trying to smile.

'And what about you, dear?' Mary asked, her voice soft as she took hold of her husband's arm. He nodded, staring at his wife as though seeing her for the first time.

'Talking about Ellen made me realize just how much you do for Grandmother, and all of us,' he replied, clearing his throat.

'Oh Fred,' she whispered. 'That's what I'm here for.'

Not wishing to intrude on such an intimate moment, Isabella crept from the room. Dotty looked up as she entered the kitchen, her eyes burning with curiosity.

'You all right?' she asked.

'I think so. Just a lot to take in,' Isabella replied.

'Mother said you could have this,' Dotty smiled, holding out a square of tablet.

'Thank you,' she murmured, taking it and staring at it unseeingly. 'Do you mind if I have it upstairs? I've so much to think about.'

Throwing herself down on her mattress, she stared at the ceiling, trying to make sense of everything. Her uncles' revelations went around and round in her head like a carousel. That Papa – dear, dear Papa – wasn't her real father was hard to believe. But that horrible-sounding Roger man was. As for dear Mama, she clearly was not the gentle, sweet woman she remembered. Of course, Isabella had been very young when she'd died and her memories were muddled to say the least. Yet her dear papa must really have loved her or he would have sent her away, wouldn't he?

And poor Grandmama, how terrible it must have been for her to discover her unmarried daughter was with child. Clearly that was the shock that had sent her doo dally, as Dotty called it. Then there was her aunt who cared for her, and her uncle who worked all hours to make his business a success to provide for his family. The loving way they'd been looking at each other when she'd tiptoed out moved her to tears. It was evident her uncle had only just realized what a treasure he'd married.

Exhausted, she closed her eyes, then remembered her uncle had been about to tell her something else before her aunt walked in. She would have to ask him about that in the morning. With hot tears staining her cheeks, she fell into a troubled sleep.

Chapter 28

The next morning, to Isabella's surprise, apart from enquiring if she was all right, no reference was made to the events of the previous day.

'You've had a shock, dear, and need a few days of peace and quiet to recover. Well, as much as you can get in this noisy household,' Mary said quietly.

'Where's Uncle?' she asked, remembering their unfinished conversation.

'Out with his precious plants, where do you think?'

'And how's Grandmama today?' Isabella asked.

'In her own little world, as usual. The good news is the rain's eased and we can get outside and start putting the barn to rights, ready to pack the flowers – as soon as Father deems them fit for Covent Garden, that is. I suggest you stay in here, dear, and finish sewing your grey dress. You can add that ribbon you bought the other day. It'll be nice for you to have something new to wear when Felix calls.'

But after the shock of the previous day, even the thought of seeing Felix failed to raise her spirits. As Isabella tried to settle to her stitching, her mind kept wandering back to the past, especially one question. Why had her papa, the man who'd always stressed the importance of honesty, led her to believe he was her real father? Finally, when she'd had to unpick a sleeve for the third time, she threw the dress down in frustration.

'Not in the mood for it?' She looked up to see William staring at her. For once there was a look of compassion on his face.

'I am finding it hard to concentrate,' she admitted. 'What are you doing? It's not like you to be indoors at this time of day.'

'Done everything I can outside. Plants are beginning to dry out, so they need to be left alone. Mother and Father are discussing the best way to lay out the barn. It'll be some time before they can afford to have the roof repaired properly so they've decided the tarpaulin should suffice over the winter. Means they can only use half of it, though, and Father still needs space for his propagating and cultivating.'

'Yes, I can see that,' she replied, remembering how he'd carefully protected his new plants.

'Cors, all the time they're doing that, the paperwork's mounting up and I can't help with that, can I, not understanding me letters properly?' He stood staring at her and Isabella detected the hopeful glint in his eye.

'Would you like me to show you whilst it's quiet in here?' she volunteered, knowing his pride wouldn't permit him to ask. She really did want to get on with her cousin and this would be a good opportunity to begin building bridges between them. When he nodded, she went over to the dresser, took out some paper and a pencil then picked up the periodical Dotty had left on her chair.

'Come and tell me what words you know,' she

said, sitting down at the table and opening the magazine. He stared down at the page and shook his head.

‘’Tain’t no good, just looks like ants scattered everywhere,’ he sighed. Isabella looked at the letters and saw a lot of them were in italic.

‘Yes, I see what you mean,’ she conceded. ‘Can you write your name?’

‘Not really,’ he grunted. ‘Can only do the letters in straight lines.’

‘Ah, I see,’ she said, carefully writing out his name in capitals.

‘Yeah, I get them, they look like sticks,’ he said jubilantly.

‘Then that is what we will use,’ she told him. ‘Now, you watch carefully and I’ll show you how to write your name in stick language.’ Deliberately, she wrote WILLIAM across the top of the page. ‘Now all you need to do is practise until it comes easily.’

‘You really think I can do it?’ he whispered. ‘Old Beaky was always vustlin about proper letterin’ and said I was less than useless.’

‘Mr Beaky was your teacher?’

‘Yeah, but he were only interested in the clever ones.’

‘I see. Well, you’re bright enough when it comes to all things violets. Do you think Mr Beaky could grow things?’

‘Wouldn’t get his ’ands dirty,’ he snorted.

‘Well then, if you learn your letters like you have your plants, you’ll be more knowledgeable than him, won’t you?’

‘Yeah,’ he cried, his eyes lighting up with pleasure. 'Oh 'ere comes Dotty. No tellin' her, right? Can't be doing with her gawkin' over me shoulder.'

'It will be our secret,' Isabella assured him. 'Practise in your room, and when you can write your first name as well as I have, we will move on to your surname.'

'Thanks,' he cried, snatching up the pencil and paper and running up to his room. 'You'd make a better teacher than Beaky,' he shouted over his shoulder. Isabella stared after him. A teacher? Now there was a thought, but before she could ponder further, the door clattered open.

'How are you, Izzie?' Dotty asked, throwing her turnover down on the chair. 'Oh 'eck,' she cried, putting her hand over her mouth. 'I wasn't meant to say anything.'

'That's all right, it's kind of you to ask. I'm still feeling shaky to be honest but...,' she shrugged. Her mind was still so muddled, there wasn't much she could say. 'How's Grandmama and everything outside?'

'Grandmother's back to her silly self – silent one minute, gibbering the next. As for the violets, I'm hoping there'll be enough to take to the big house on Thursday so I can see Alfie,' she winked.

By Thursday, although the violets weren't up to Covent Garden standard, Dotty insisted they would be good enough for Mrs Tripe to use for crystallizing. When her father looked doubtful, she told him it would be a waste not to take the rest to the local market, along with the jam and tablet she and her mother had made. Isabella couldn't help smiling at the girl's persistence, knowing she was desperate to see Alfred.

'Very well,' Frederick agreed. 'But I want you back here as soon as everything's sold.' With indecent haste, Dotty filled her basket then hurried off before he could change his mind.

'Right, Isabella, Mother has things to do in the house so you can help me in the barn,' her uncle told her, as soon as Dotty had left.

'If you're feeling better after your shock, that is?' Mary asked, giving Isabella one of her searching looks.

'I am, thank you,' Isabella replied, knowing she had to come to terms with the fact that her life had been based on a lie.

'Come along, we can chat while we work,' her uncle said, snatching his hat from the hook and striding from the room.

'If you find it too much, you can always come back and finish your dress,' Mary said, smiling kindly at her.

It was the first time Isabella had been into the barn since it had been damaged by the storm, and she was shocked at how much darker it was with the tarpaulin covering the roof. The trestles and empty pails were lined up ready, but without the violets, everywhere looked drab and smelled of damp.

'Right, this is now my potting place,' her uncle said, leading the way into a partitioned area to one side. 'Bit smaller but adequate.' Isabella stared at the table on which sat boxes covered with sheets of broken glass that had obviously been pieced together. 'Don't touch anything, it's all a bit precarious but it will suffice for me little cultivars.'

'They're all right?' she asked. He nodded.

'Managed to save quite a few, which is a blessing being as how they cost me an arm and a leg. Be worth it when I see them Furneaux's faces in the spring,' he chuckled.

'Felix was telling me about the plants of France,' she ventured.

'Pah,' he spat. 'Italy be where the best plants come from,' he said, carefully lifting a sheet of glass and running his finger gently over the leaves.

'So what exactly is a cultivar?' she asked, thinking it prudent to divert attention away from his rivals.

'You really want to know?' he asked, staring at her in surprise.

'I do,' she replied, surprised herself to find she really was interested.

''Tis a variety of plant produced from a natural species, see, and maintained by cultivation. These little babies could have come from as far away as Asia Minor or the Levant and are thought to have been brought to Europe by Genoese or Venetian merchants.'

'And you went all the way there to get them?' she asked incredulously.

'Gawd love us, no,' he laughed, replacing the glass and turning to stare at her. 'Couldn't afford that, nor Italy either. Bought them from a man who'd been cultivating them from ... well, never you mind. Like I said, cost me a fortune but 'tis an investment. When these bloom, they'll have double petals and be so colourful Furneaux'll have to wear dark glasses,' he chuckled, then looked stern. 'Can't say I'm happy you associating with them, to be honest, but Mother says 'tis your business. Just promise you'll say nothing about any of this.'

'Of course not, Uncle,' she assured him, staring down at the plants. 'Those leaves are different to the ones outside, aren't they?'

'Well spotted. We'll make a flower girl of you yet,' he chortled. 'If things pan out as I hope, this family will have a more comfortable way of life, and in due course it will be William's inheritance. Which reminds me, I'm pleased to see you two getting on better. Mother tells me you are helping him to write.'

'That was meant to be a secret,' she murmured.

'Not when Mother makes his bed and finds his things under his pillow,' he chuckled. 'It'll be a right help if he can learn. Apart from getting rid of that chip on his shoulder, it'll give him a better understanding of how this place runs. 'Tis not just about picking and selling a few flowers,' he grinned, repeating the words she'd uttered when she first arrived.

'I'm sorry, Uncle,' she replied. 'I had no idea how much work was involved.'

''Tis like anything, you only get out of life what you put in. A lesson I'm afraid your mother never learned.'

'I've been thinking about everything you and Uncle Bill told me,' she admitted. 'You both seemed to have differing ideas.'

'Bill adored his older sister and has a rosier recollection of her. I, on the other hand, remember only too well the lengths she'd go to in order to get her own way. More importantly, when I think back to what a lively and spirited woman Mother was before Ellie got into trouble ... well, I'm sad for a life wasted. She's never really known Mary or our children, and that hurts.'

'That is very sad,' Isabella agreed.

'Yes,' he sighed. 'As I've said before, your grandmother never recovered from the shock, so her life's been blighted by my sister's selfishness. I realize she was your mother and I'm sorry to be speaking about her like this, but it might go some way to explaining my bitterness towards her.'

'I can tell Aunt Mary is the love of your life, though,' Isabella smiled.

'She is, but I'm ashamed to say I've only just realized it.' Isabella stared at him in astonishment.

'But...,' she began then remembered their conversation on the train journey back from London. 'You loved someone else before?' she guessed. He nodded and stared down at his beloved plants.

'I was infatuated with ... well, it doesn't matter who. Her father threw up every reason why we couldn't wed and she listened to him. Months later I met Mary and her adoration was balm to my wounded pride. I could give her a home and the family she yearned for and...,' he shrugged. 'Talking about Ellie with her self-centred, hard-hearted attitude made me appreciate what a wonderful woman Mary is. I shall spend the rest of my days making it up to her,' he sighed. 'And that's another reason these plants have to succeed. I want her to live out her days in comfort, not struggling like she does now. I know this has all been difficult but your aunt and I are both here for you,' he told her.

'Thank you, Uncle.' She stared at him, thinking this was the time to bring up the idea she'd be toying with. 'About the bond, Uncle. I'd really like you to use that money for repairs to the roof,' she told him, staring up at the dark tarpaulin. 'And to purchase new glass.'

'No, Izzie,' he replied sharply. 'It's kind of you, but that is for your future. Whilst it's true your father sent money for your keep, he wanted the rest of it to be invested in your name. It was his way of ensuring you'd have a good start when you marry.'

'But I'm not even betrothed,' she protested. 'Besides, you haven't taken anything for my board and lodging, have you?'

'Don't worry, girl, you be earning that,' he grinned. 'Now, do you have anything else you want to ask me before we begin working?'

'One thing that's really been puzzling me is why Papa led me to believe he was my real father.'

'Because that's how he thought of himself. He might not have been your biological father but he loved you dearly, and after your mother died he did everything he could to give you the advantages of a privileged upbringing.'

'I hadn't thought of it like that, and I did love him so very much,' Isabella whispered, the tears which never seemed far away welling again.

'Look, Izzie, the past few days have been traumatic for you but you need to build on what you've learned,' he said, lifting up the glass and taking out a little plant in its pot. 'Like this little chap here, the offspring of other parents who started off life in sunnier climes. He's already set down roots, but needs nurturing and encouragement in order to fulfil his potential in his new life. You began life in London and moved here. Your aunt and I have offered you a new home and encouragement, but only you can fulfil your potential,' he said, brushing a tiny speck of soil from the leaves before placing it back in the box.

As he began tending his other cultivars, Isabella thought about what he'd said. For someone normally brusque, he had shown astonishing sensitivity, and knowing she was still wanted here was an enormous relief.

'Thank you, Uncle. Now what can I do to help?' she asked as the door opened and William came in, bringing with him that sweet musty smell of damp earth. He was carrying an armful of spindly little plants which he carefully deposited on the remaining space on the trestle.

'Mother wants a word, Father,' he said.

'Right. Perhaps you'd like to start showing Izzie how we propagate,' Frederick replied.

'Are these more of those cultivars you were telling me about?' Izzie asked, frowning down at the trestle. 'Only they look really spindly, if you don't mind me saying.'

'That's 'cos they're cuttings,' William said, shaking his head.

'Our native violets grow wild but seldom set down seeds, or if they do them bloomin' mice get to them first,' Frederick told her. 'In order to increase our stock for next season we need to plant these cuttings. You'll see William has chosen those with tiny rootlets attached. We'll prick them off, pot them up then place them under glass. Hopefully they'll grow into sturdy plants ready to be transferred back to the garden come late spring. It's a bit late in the year to be doing this now, of course, but the first lot got crushed to smithereens by that damned tree so we've got to try again. Can't have blessed Furneaux taking over our share of the market,' he snorted.

Despite his scathing expression, the mention of the Furneaux name made Isabella's heart flip. Her uncle's chat today had helped her get things in perspective. He was right – she did need to move on with her life, and in two days' time she'd be seeing Felix. Of course, her excitement was because she wanted to see around his garden and hear more about ionine, she told herself, vowing to have her grey dress completed in time.

Chapter 29

'You're looking lovely, if I might be so bold,' Felix remarked, proffering his hand to help her up beside him. As waves of pleasure rippled up her arm, Isabella smiled demurely. In truth, she was feeling pleased with her appearance. Having stitched the mauve ribbon to her dress, there'd been enough left to trim her bonnet and, whilst not as grand as the outfits she'd brought with her, it was a distinct improvement on Mary and Dotty's cast-offs. She felt she'd managed to retain her identity whilst being more suitably attired for her life here.

'How are you?' Felix asked after calling to his pony to walk on. 'Heard you'd had a chat about your mother. I wanted to come and make sure you were all right, but Father reckoned it would be unseemly under the circumstances. Said you would need time to adjust.' Isabella turned to him in surprise.

'How on earth do you know that?' she cried.

'Uncle Bill let something slip when I met him for a jar,' he murmured, glancing sideways at her.

'And they say it's women who gossip,' she said, laughing.

'That's better. You're much prettier when you smile,' he grinned, then fell silent as he concentrated on guiding them down the steep lane. Isabella looked around at the mauve flowers peeping under hedgerows that glistened with drops from the recent rain. Now the autumn tints had faded they lent a welcome splash of colour. For the first time since Monday, she felt herself beginning to relax. It was good to be away from the cottage, for Dotty had been like a broody hen earlier, fussing around and making sure everything was tidy for Alfred's visit. Knowing how her cousin felt about him, Isabella hoped her uncle would agree to them walking out.

'I'm looking forward to seeing your gardens and hearing more about your business,' she told Felix, coming back to the present.

'Ah,' he replied, looking awkward for a moment. Then he smiled. 'And I'm looking forward to our walk and hearing more about you, Miss Carrington, or should I say...,' his voice trailed away and she could see the flush spreading up under his collar.

'Oh Felix, it's Isabella, as you well know,' she chided.

'Yes, of course,' he murmured. 'I thought we'd take the quickest route through the woods then meander back the scenic way along the coast. I'd love to show you the nature reserve as this time of year it's a haven for wildlife,' he added, pulling on one rein, whereupon the pony obligingly turned. 'Now we are entering Beechnut Wood.'

'What a curious name,' she murmured.

'This is like one long canopy in the summer when the beech leaves are out,' he explained, gesturing to the tall trees that rose on either side of them.

'I suppose we are by the beach,' Isabella replied, staring in fascination at their lofty branches so that she didn't see Felix shake his head. Sometime later, he turned into a driveway bordered by more beeches, with manicured lawns spreading out on either side. As a large, elongated building with a neatly thatched roof loomed before them, Isabella's eyes widened in amazement. With its eyebrow windows at the first floor and three doors at the front it was a magnificent sight.

'Goodness, I had no idea you lived in such a grand house, Felix,' she gasped. 'I thought you were farmers originally.'

'We were. And this is a Devon longhouse. In Grandfather's day, the animals lived alongside the family in that part,' he said, pointing to the door at one end. 'Called it the shippen.' Seeing her shudder, he chuckled then jumped down. Hurrying round to her side of the cart, he held out his hand to help her.

'Father's indoors if you would like a chaperone. Otherwise permit me to escort you around the flower gardens,' he said, sweeping his cap from his head and perfecting a bow. She hesitated for a moment, then smiled.

'I'm sure your intentions are honourable and I would very much like you to show me around,' she replied, linking her arm through the one he proffered.

He led her round to the back of the house, where row upon row of violets stretched as far as she could see. The breeze rippling through their blue heads gave the impression of waves on the ocean, while the air was heavy with their fragrance. She inhaled delightedly as she gazed around. Then it struck her not only was this much larger than her uncle's garden, despite it only recently having been turned over to flowers, the abundant plants were all in perfect condition. Now she understood why he felt threatened.

'Hello, my dear.' She turned to see Matthew striding down the path towards them. 'I hope my son is behaving himself,' he said, pretending to frown at Felix.

'Yes, he is, Mr Furneaux,' Isabella assured him. 'And may I say what delightful gardens you have.'

'You may indeed,' he replied, looking pleased. 'Of course, we were lucky to have been sheltered from that storm. How is Frederick doing?'

'Fine, thank you,' she assured him. 'He's decided to manage with the tarpaulin as a temporary cover and has been busy repotting his cult– oh sorry, wrong name,' she said quickly, putting her hand to her mouth. 'I mean propagating. There are so many gardening terms to learn, I get muddled.' Matthew raised a brow, but nodded politely.

'You are welcome to join me for afternoon tea indoors,' he invited.

'Thank you, Father, but I have arranged to take Isabella into town,' Felix told him.

'Perhaps another time then,' Matthew smiled before, stroking his walrus moustache, he wandered further down the garden.

'Come on, let's go before he finds something he just must show you,' Felix urged.

'I don't mind,' she assured him.

'But I do. I'd like to show you our delightful park. We can walk along by the stream and watch the antics of the ducks and spend time really getting to know each other,' he said, gazing at her so intently her pulse raced. 'Dusk falls early this time of year, so we won't have that long in any case,' he said as they made their way into town. She stared up at the watery sun peeping out from behind the clouds and prayed for the rain to stay away.

'You promised to tell me more about ionine and the perfumiers of France,' she reminded him.

'That was a ruse to get you here,' he replied, green eyes gleaming with mischief. Then, seeing her indignant look, he became serious. 'Well, let me see now, the violet has a single-note scent and perfumiers use top, middle and base notes to make a fragrance that's not only balanced but will last. As I said before, our dear little flower has a capricious aroma and it takes great skill to enhance and sustain it without overpowering it. Hence, the need to mix the real thing with synthetic notes. Did you know the violet was the Greek goddess of love Aphrodite's chosen flower?' he asked, turning to look at her.

'Goodness, really?' she stuttered, for his gaze was making her feel quite hot. 'You are a mine of information,' she told him.

'Mostly useless,' he grinned, jumping down and tying the reins to the horse ring by the side of the green. 'Come on, let's explore,' he said, once again holding out his hand to help her down. This time he didn't let go of it and as they wandered the lawns alongside the wide stream with its ducks and waterfalls, she could feel the warmth of his fingers through the material of her gloves. Then a vision of Gaskell's disapproving look popped into her mind.

'Goodness, what's that building with the big wheel on the side?' she asked, using the excuse of gesturing across the street to remove her hand. Whilst she loved the feel of it, she couldn't help thinking it wasn't respectable to be seen holding hands in public.

'That's Strand Mill,' he told her, seemingly unperturbed. 'Probably where your bread comes from on the days Mrs Northcott doesn't bake,' he added.

'You mean that wheel makes loaves?' she asked staring at it in surprise.

'In a manner of speaking,' he laughed. 'Come on, all this talk of bread is making me hungry.'

He led the way from the green, across the street and through a side road until they came to a thatched property with shutters at the window. The sign on the wall proclaimed it to be the Lake Hill Tea Cottage and a little bell tinkled as he pushed open the door and gestured her inside.

'Good afternoon, Mr Furneaux,' said the rotund lady who waddled over to greet them. Dressed in a long black skirt with a crisp white apron that barely covered her middle, she stared at Isabella curiously then showed them to a table in the window. 'What can I get you? We've got scones just out of the oven, lemon sponge, or perhaps you would prefer sandwiches?'

'What takes your fancy, Isabella?' he asked. In truth, she could have eaten the lot for she'd been so nervous waiting for Felix to arrive that she'd skipped luncheon. As if reading her mind, he grinned and threw up his hands.

'It all sounds splendid, Mrs Veale. Perhaps you could bring us an assortment?' he replied.

'How you youngsters can eat so much and stay slim is beyond me,' she said, her smile belying her words.

'Actually, I could eat a horse,' Felix declared.

'Well, we don't have any of those, young man, so you'll have to make do with my fancies,' the woman said, waddling away.

'Knew I should have bagged one of those ducks from the stream,' he sighed.

'Felix, really,' Isabella chided, looking around, although they were the only customers.

'So, how are you feeling about everything now?' he asked, his green eyes darkening to olive.

'Well, everyone's being very kind. Uncle had a chat and made me see the rest of my life was just beginning, as it were. All I need to do now is decide what I'm going to do with it.'

'That's easy,' he grinned. 'You can marry me.'

'Felix, I'm being serious,' she cried.

'So am I, Isabella. In fact, I've never been more serious in my life,' he said, his gaze boring into her.

She couldn't make Felix out, Isabella thought as she walked up the path. He'd insisted she was the woman for him, yet how could he know when they'd barely met? Raised voices coming from inside the cottage roused her from her reverie then, as she went to lift the latch, the door burst open.

'Perhaps you can talk some sense into the girl, Izzie,' her uncle growled, stalking past her. Isabella's heart sank. She'd had a lovely if strange afternoon and all she wanted to do was take herself upstairs and reflect on it.

'Hello,' she said, brightly. Her aunt, looking stony was sitting opposite a tear-blotched Dotty, and they were so engrossed in their conversation that they didn't respond.

'But why can't Alfred walk me out?' she wailed.

'You heard Father,' Mary sighed. 'Oh Dotty, if only you'd had the sense to ask before sneaking out with the boy, Father might have been more amenable. Now you've got to show a sense of responsibility.'

'I shall die if I can't see Alfie,' Dotty sniffed.

'I doubt that,' Mary smiled wanly, shaking her head. 'Did you have a good afternoon, Izzie?' she asked, finally turning to Isabella.

'I did, but what's going on here?' Although she

asked the question, she had a suspicion what the answer would be.

'We let slip we'd been to the tearooms a couple of times before Alfred officially asked Father if we could walk out, and he went mad. How old-fashioned can you get? I'll show him. They want a maid at the big house so I'll apply. Then I can see Alfie every day,' Dotty declared, staring at her mother defiantly.

'Good idea. You can live in and send home a decent wage,' Mary replied mildly. 'Of course, Lord Lester has a strict policy of his staff not walking out together, but if you think it's worth it...,' she shrugged, leaving Dotty to draw her own conclusions.

'Well, I shall take the flowers to Mrs Tripe on Thursday then,' Dotty told them, flouncing up the stairs.

'She usually does,' Mary murmured, shaking her head. 'Unless you'd like to?' Isabella shook her head emphatically. Then, seeing her aunt's questioning look, she smiled.

'Although I would like to go into town too. My boots have worn right through and Felix offered to take me to a cobbler he knows.'

'So that's the way the wind blows, is it?' Mary declared, giving Isabella a look. 'Best take some money out of the pig, but keep it under your bonnet. Father heard Furneaux's secured the order with Powderham Castle and he's hopping.'

Chapter 30

When Isabella saw Felix waiting for her on Thursday morning her heart flipped. She'd wondered if things might be awkward after his proclamation, but he gave his cheeky grin and she felt herself responding.

'Come on, lovely lady, let's get you shod,' he declared as she clambered up beside him.

'You make me sound like your horse,' she murmured.

'Well, both my girls need feeding and grooming,' he joked.

The day was grey with soft mizzle falling and Isabella was relieved she didn't have to walk, for even with wodges of paper lining her boots, moisture still penetrated them.

'It's so open around here,' she enthused, staring at the passing landscape.

'Sounds like you're getting used to your new life,' he commented, giving her a sideways look. It was true. Considering she'd only been here three months or so, it was amazing how everywhere already looked familiar. As they approached the outskirts of Dawlish, Felix turned into a side street she'd never seen before. Here the buildings were sprawled together, their little windows latticed.

'This is the old part of town where the craftsmen have their businesses,' he told her, pulling up outside a whitewashed property, identical to the others in the terrace. 'Come on, Todd'll mend your boots good as new,' he grinned, leading the way through a stable door. Isabella grimaced down at her scuffed feet and thought that would take a miracle. Still, she couldn't afford to be choosy these days.

The cobbler was a wizened old man who took her boots and studied them.

'Unusual to see such fine leather this badly worn,' he said, eyeing Isabella curiously.

'Can you do anything with them, Todd?' Felix asked.

'Does it rain in Devon?' he laughed. 'Take a seat while I sort thee out.'

'I need to go and collect more boxes for our violets,' Felix murmured to Isabella. 'I'll be back shortly then we can stop for a bite to eat on the way back.'

'Thank you,' she smiled, setting down her basket and taking a seat. She heard him mutter something to the cobbler then, with a doff of his cap, he was gone. Isabella stared around the little room, wrinkling her nose at the smell of leather and glue as she took in the lasts, tools and nails. The cobbler looked up from his hammering.

'You be Ellen's girl. Settling in, are yer?'

'Yes, thank you,' she smiled stifling a yawn.

'Bit different from London, eh?' he added, going back to his work. It certainly was, she thought. Before Felix had called, she'd been out in the garden cutting the flowers that were beginning to flourish again. Determined to outdo his rival, her uncle had them all working longer hours tending the plants, and the opportunity to relax was welcome. She must have dozed off, for the next thing she knew the cobbler was shaking her arm.

'Frugal Fred getting his pound of flesh, is he?' he quipped. 'Here ye are. I put on some new, heavier soles and blacked the uppers so they should last.'

'Thank you,' Isabella smiled, slipping them on. 'How much do I owe you?'

'Felix said he'd take care of that,' he said, narrowing his eyes. 'Good chap, that. Seems fond of thee. Hate to see him get hurt, 'specially by a snooty vurriner,' he said, giving her a warning look as he slapped another shoe onto his last.

'I'll have you know even we snooty vurriners pay our own way,' she said, tossing a handful of coins down on his bench. 'Do keep the change,' she added, sweeping from the shop. Thank goodness her aunt had insisted she take that money from the pottery pig on the dresser.

Luckily Felix was waiting outside, the cart laden with boxes.

'Gosh, you do look cross. Didn't Todd make a good job of your boots?' he asked, as he helped her up beside him.

'Yes, he did,' she admitted. 'Just a little misunderstanding when I insisted on paying him,' she added, not wishing to relay the rest of the conversation.

'There was no need...,' he began.

'There was every need. I thank you for your kind thought, Felix, but a girl has her pride.'

'Not too much to refuse luncheon at Mrs Veale's, I hope?' he grinned, but Isabella was heartened to see the glimmer of respect in his eyes.

The Lake Hill Tea Cottage was only a few minutes' ride away and, although it was busy, Mrs Veale insisted on showing them to the seats in the window they'd occupied before.

'No horse today, I'm afraid,' she joked, prodding Felix with her pencil.

'Ah well, we'll just have to make do with its liver then,' he sighed, gesturing to the menu on the table. Then seeing Isabella's expression, he shrugged. 'Perhaps not. How about homemade pie?' Isabella nodded, her stomach rumbling in anticipation, for the delicious aromas wafting her way made her realize she was very hungry indeed.

As the woman waddled away, Felix turned to Isabella and smiled. He leaned forward so that the other diners couldn't hear.

'I'm surprised your uncle allowed you to come out with me today.'

'Well, he couldn't really stop me, could he?' Isabella replied.

'I guess not,' he grinned. 'Still, it doesn't help when the feud between our violet farms looks set to escalate.'

'Oh?' Isabella frowned.

'Father and your uncles have begun competing for the Christmas market,' he sighed.

'Christmas? Not already, surely?'

'Oh yes, it comes early here in Devon. Something to do with being so far west,' he joked.

'You do talk drivel, Felix,' she smiled.

'Aye, I second that,' Mrs Veale said, placing steaming plates of steak pie and mashed potatoes in front of them. 'Although you do have good taste in lady friends,' she added, winking at Isabella as she waddled away again.

They ate their meal in companionable silence. The pastry was crisp and the meat melting.

'Well, I was ready for that,' Felix said, pushing aside his empty plate.

'That was delicious,' she replied. 'Thank you.'

'You're welcome. Now, going back to our earlier conversation. Despite what you say, Christmas will soon be upon us and I for one intend to enjoy the festivities,' he said, staring at her intently. 'The hotel on the green always hold a celebratory dinner dance on Christmas Eve and I wondered if you would do me the honour of accompanying me?' As his gaze held hers, waves of anticipation washed over her.

'I'd love to,' she replied, her heart thumping excitedly.

Isabella entered the cottage on cloud nine, only to be confronted yet again by a sobbing Dotty.

'I didn't know about it, honest,' she wailed. 'I just went to the big house as usual and was handed this note to give to Father and then the door was shut in me face. It was the only way I could see Alfie.'

'What's going on?' Isabella asked.

'Got a letter from Lord Lester, haven't I?' her uncle replied, stabbing the embossed sheet of paper in front of him with his finger.

'As my wishes haven't been complied with, I have no alternative other than to rescind my custom with your company. Henceforth, Furneaux will be supplying my flowers,' he read. 'Has this anything to do with you?' he asked turning to Isabella.

'I didn't mean to slap his face or ... but he was going to kiss me and...,' hearing them gasp, her voice trailed away.

'He was going to kiss you?' Mary asked, her brows disappearing under her cap.

'Well, he don't say anything about that here,' her uncle grunted. 'Merely that he'd requested you deliver the flowers to Mrs Tripe instead of our Dorothy.'

'Oh,' Isabella murmured, wishing she'd kept her mouth shut. 'Well, Lord Lester did mention this to me when I last delivered the violets but never for one moment did I think he was serious.'

'Obviously he was,' Frederick snapped. 'You don't ignore the orders of someone like that. Not only have I lost custom at Covent Garden, but Furneaux's got his nose in at Powderham and, if that's not enough, now he's to supply the big house. What do you say about that, eh?'

'I can only apologize for not conceding to Lord Lester's wishes that I deliver his flowers but ... you see, well ... that was only part of the bargain,' her voice trailed away and she felt her cheeks flush as she remembered her last meeting with the onerous man.

'I see,' her uncle sighed. 'He thought like mother like daughter, eh? Might have guessed.'

'If he was taking liberties then you was within your rights,' her aunt declared. 'There's been talk in the town. Don't concern yourself, Izzie, a man like that will get his come-uppance sooner or later, lord or no lord. I'd love to have seen his expression when you slapped him,' she chuckled.

If only you knew, Auntie, Isabella thought.

'It ain't no laughing matter, Mother,' Frederick grunted.

'No, of course not,' she replied, composing herself. ''Tis only weeks til Christmas and you girls can help me get things ready for when Father secures his orders. You'll be supplying all the big hotels and restaurants with table arrangements and corsages, won't you, Father?' she said, turning to her husband.

'Yes, I will,' he agreed, looking mollified.

'Well then, girls, what do you say?' she asked. Isabella nodded her agreement. Although she was dying to tell her aunt about Felix's invitation, this wasn't the time. Dotty, however, had no such qualms.

'As it's not all my fault about the flowers, can I walk out with Alfie and go to his Christmas do?' she asked.

'I'll think about it,' Frederick grunted. 'I'm going to see to my cultivars. At least they don't answer back,' he added, plonking his straw hat firmly on his head.

'You'll never guess what? Father's had a change of heart,' Dotty whispered. They were lying in bed, Alice snoring gently beside them. 'He says as long as I don't go sneaking behind his back again, I can walk out with Alfie. He wasn't sure about me going to the Christmas do at the big house, but Mother put in a good word, saying Lord Lester wouldn't lower himself to put in an appearance. Just as well 'cos I'll never have enough money for a new outfit.'

'As I said before, you can choose one of mine,'

Isabella reminded her. 'Felix is taking me out to dinner at a local hotel on Christmas Eve, so I shall need to adapt one as well.'

'Coo, we'll look like real toffs,' Dotty sighed happily.

'Indeed we will,' Isabella smiled.

'Everyone's talking about the feud between our families. Father and Uncle Bill are making plans to outdo Furneaux. All seems stupid to me. Cors, Father having earned less means we won't have many treats for Christmas. It's the kids I feel sorry for but, as Mother says, you can't pull a rabbit out of a hat when you've got no hat in the first place.'

Isabella recalled the Christmases of her childhood. The china doll dressed as a fairy, the doll's house made specially for her, and she'd always had a new outfit to wear. Perhaps she could find something suitable for Alice and Thomas, she thought.

However, despite the events of the day, it was emerald-green eyes and a cheeky grin that filled her dreams.

The next weeks were manic as they picked, posied and packed the violets ready for Covent Garden as well as preparing tussie-mussies to be assembled at the last moment. Determined to outdo his rival, Frederick was out securing orders from the many hotels and restaurants in the local towns and villages which were hosting Christmas celebrations.

'It'll mean working over the festive period,' he told them. 'But it'll give us the opportunity to make up for the business we lost after the storm.'

'We can still celebrate with a nice meal in the evening,' Mary told them stoically. 'Though don't you young 'uns go expectin' much in yer stockings,' she told Alice and Thomas.

Seeing their looks of dismay, Isabella and Dotty exchanged smiles. As well as altering gowns for their forthcoming parties, they were secretly making a dress and shirt for the youngsters. Isabella had even found a jacket she could make into a turnover for her auntie and appropriate items for her uncle and William. She had in mind something she could give her grandmama but alternated between thinking her idea brilliant or stupid.

Although they were tired after long days working in the barn, anticipation lent enthusiasm to their long evenings of sewing. Dotty was so excited about the burgundy dress she'd found to alter that Isabella was surprised she could sit still long enough to stitch.

'I'll look like a princess,' she kept saying. 'Just wait til my Alfie sees me.'

Isabella smiled, hoping Felix would be equally impressed with her outfit and that the fine weather, which had been surprisingly warm for December, would continue. Although she was becoming used to travelling in an open cart, she couldn't help thinking longingly back to the days when she'd been conveyed by covered carriage.

Chapter 31

Christmas Eve arrived at last and excitement filled the little bedroom as they changed into their finery. Isabella stared at her appearance in the fly-spotted mirror. The satin silk in sapphire blue suited her colouring and she'd turned her favourite velvet cloak into an evening wrap to cover her shoulders. Unable to afford getting her hair coiffured, she'd pinned it up in a chignon with an ornate comb and, despite her aunt's protestations that her feet would get cold, was wearing her silver sandals.

'Coo, me 'air's frizzed up grand,' Dotty exclaimed delightedly, throwing down the brush on her mattress. Isabella smiled, still not able to equate the expression with pleasure. If her curls frizzed they were a nightmare to tame.

'You look beautiful, Dotty,' she told her cousin, for she did indeed look grown-up with her hair styled in ringlets instead of being tied in its usual braid.

Having dropped a very excited Dotty off at the big house with instructions not to leave until they collected her, Felix and Isabella continued their journey to the hotel.

'You look stunning,' Felix told her when she emerged from the cloakroom.

'Not looking too bad yourself,' Isabella smiled, thinking that was an understatement. In his dark tuxedo and waistcoat, white winged-collar shirt and white bow tie, he looked every inch the man about town. He'd even tamed his dark wavy hair with spicy-smelling pomade.

The evening, programmed to be a lavish and leisurely affair with dancing between the courses, was something Isabella had been looking forward to. Streamers festooned the high ceilings and a tall Christmas tree scenting the room with pine and lit with myriad candles twinkled in the corner. As the other diners greeted Felix warmly, he proudly introduced Isabella but, although everyone was polite, she couldn't help sensing their reserve. She was pleased when they were shown to a table for two in the bay window, from which they could look out over the lantern-lit green. The centre-piece, a tiny cluster of violets, was tastefully decorated with silver baubles.

'There are violets on every table. I wonder who supplied them,' Felix said, raising his brows.

'To be honest, I don't really care. For one night, I'd like to enjoy myself without worrying who secured the order for the flowers,' Isabella told him.

'Your wish is my command,' he said, staring appreciatively at his first course of venison pâté adorned with cranberries. As the waiter poured their champagne, Felix gave her an outrageous wink.

'Hope this is as intoxicating as you,' he whispered, raising his glass to hers. Not knowing how to respond, she smiled and turned her attention to her plate. The food was delicious and she savoured its richness after the simple fare she'd become used to.

'Would my lady care to dance?' he asked, jumping up as the music began.

He was surprisingly light on his feet and Isabella effortlessly followed his lead. As he gazed tenderly down at her, she felt her pulse race. Whether from the bubbles or the tang of his cologne, she felt lightheaded and happy.

The fish course was followed by roasted goose, and Felix persuaded her to indulge in another glass of champagne.

'It's been a hectic few weeks so let's push the boat out,' he laughed. 'Hopefully, come the New Year, things will ease up and we can spend more time together.'

'That would be nice,' she agreed, for he was attentive and amusing and she hadn't enjoyed herself so much in ages.

'Well, what do you think of our little hotel? Not a patch on the swish London ones, I'll be bound,' he said.

'Actually, I feel quite at home here. The food and service are excellent,' she admitted, only to be rewarded by a broad grin.

'Phew, that's a relief. I was worried you'd find we yokels wanting,' he replied, exaggerating his accent. 'Come on, they're playing our tune.'

When she looked askance, he grinned, holding out his hand to lead her onto the dance floor. As their fingers touched, little arrows of pleasure shot up her arm once more. The music was slower this time and he held her tight, leaning in so she felt the warmth of his breath on her hair. Her heart was beating so loudly, she was sure he must hear it.

'Gracious, who'd have thought it? A Furneaux with a Northcott,' a lady muttered as she glided past them.

'Matthew and Frederick would be shocked if they knew their offspring were associating, and so closely too,' her partner replied.

'Ah, but that's Ellen's girl, and you know what she was like. He's probably hoping for a bit of fun tonight.'

'Well, of all the ... besides my name's Carrington,' Isabella cried, the magic evaporating like dew in the morning sun.

'Don't let them spoil our evening, Isabella,' Felix murmured, as the music came to a stop. 'Come on, dessert next,' he added, leading her back to their table.

Determined to ignore the barbed comments, they tucked into an ice-cream confection decorated with a sprig of holly, but it wasn't until Isabella was sipping the aromatic strong coffee that she felt her hackles subside. Sensing Felix watching her, she looked up to see him frowning at the neckline of her dress.

'You're not wearing your silver locket?'

'No, it doesn't feel right somehow, after all that's happened. I'm really not bothered about trimmings and trappings anymore.' Felix stared at her for a long moment.

'Do you know something? I really like this new Isabella. She's softer, more approachable somehow. Just the sort of woman I want to marry in fact.'

'But Felix, we haven't known each other for

long,' she protested.

'I've always known what I wanted, Isabella, and I want you,' he replied, holding her gaze until she grew so hot she had to look away.

'This coffee is absolutely gorgeous,' she murmured, taking another sip.

'And so are you,' he whispered. 'I wish we could spend tomorrow together but Father's insisting we work. Strange when he's always taken half the day off before. Mind you, he wasn't happy I was bringing you here tonight.'

'Uncle Frederick's the same,' she sighed. 'Although he doesn't mind me walking out with you as long as I don't tell you any family secrets,' she assured him. To her surprise, Felix stared down at the table. 'What is it?' she asked. 'Doesn't your father like me because I'm your rival's niece?'

'It's not that, Isabella.' Seeing the turmoil playing out on his face, she waited. 'Father heard your uncle's got hold of some cultivars and wants me to find out what species they are,' he admitted.

'Well, I can't enlighten you, I'm afraid,' she smiled apologetically. Instead of smiling back, he continued to look troubled. 'There's something else?' she persisted, the babble of voices around them receding.

'If I don't find out, he's threatening to disinherit me,' he admitted. 'Not that I'm worried for myself, but I can't ask you to marry me without being able to offer you a decent standard of living. Not that it will be anything like the one you've been used to. However, I intend working hard to build up the business.'

'But Felix, that was my old life,' she sighed.

'A man has a duty to provide the best he can for his wife, Isabella,' he said. 'I can't understand Father, though, he's never been like this before. It's since he and Frederick started competing.'

'Yet Uncle Bill doesn't seem to be affected, does he?'

'He loves the actual growing process, as does Joseph. What they don't know about violets is nobody's business. Forgive me, Isabella, I didn't intend mentioning any of this tonight. Listen, they're playing the last waltz. Shall we?' he asked, holding out his hand.

As their bodies melded together, his closeness sent shivers of delight shooting all round her insides, and when he nuzzled the back of her neck she thought she'd died and gone to heaven. She really didn't want the evening to end, but when the music faded away, he reluctantly released her and led her to the cloakroom to collect her wrap.

Outside a sliver of silver moon lit their way to the cart. As soon as he'd helped her up, he reached into the pocket of his great coat and handed her a tiny package.

'Happy Christmas, Isabella sweetest,' he murmured.

'Why Felix,' she cried delightedly, tugging at the ribbon.

'No, wait until tomorrow and when you open it, remember this.' Then he kissed her lips, sending stars shooting across her universe. 'And don't forget to make a special wish,' he added, his eyes blazing with emotion. Biting down the lump in her throat, she nodded and turned away before he could see her tears.

Shrieks of excitement woke Isabella the next morning. She'd lain awake half the night, thinking back over her wonderful evening, Felix's revelation and the decision she'd reluctantly made. Thankfully Dotty, who'd chattered excitedly all the way home then fallen asleep as soon as her head had hit the pillow, was unaware of the torment churning Isabella's insides. Ignoring the cries of delight coming from downstairs, Isabella reached for the little box and tugged at the bow. As she gazed at the silver star shining from its satin lining, hot tears tumbled down her cheeks. Remembering her promise to Felix, she made the wish she knew could never come true.

'Come along, Izzie, we've got a present for you,' Alice cried. Quickly placing the brooch in her pocket, she wiped her eyes and hurried down the stairs.

'Happy Christmas,' the family chorused.

'Look at my posh frock,' Alice exclaimed, twirling around in front of Isabella.

'Goodness, you look just like the Christmas fairy,' she smiled. 'And can this handsome young man really be Thomas?' she added, seeing the boy stroking the soft material of the shirt she'd fashioned.

'I've made you violet soap,' Alice said, handing her a small parcel wrapped in paper. 'Well, Mother helped, of course, but I did the stirring,' she added proudly. 'We had to wait ages for it to harden, though.'

'Thank you. It smells gorgeous,' Isabella said, putting it to her nose. 'Even better than that I used back home,' she added delightedly, for it was the first luxury she'd had since arriving here. 'You'll have to show me how to make it. Now, I have gifts for the rest of you too,' she smiled, handing over the presents she'd secreted in her share of the closet.

'Coloured pencils. Blimmer, never had none of them before,' William cried.

'These paint brushes be perfect for cleaning the leaves of my cultivars,' Frederick said, looking pleased.

'Why, if this isn't the finest turnover I've ever had,' Mary declared, pulling Isabella close. 'Are you all right, dear? You look a bit pale,' she whispered. ''Tis only natural you'll be remembering your father.'

'I'm fine,' she replied, swallowing down the lump in her throat. 'Can I take Grandmama her breakfast? I have something for her too.'

'We'll both go, shall we?' Dotty said, jumping up and grabbing the tray from the table. 'I can tell her all about my lovely night at the big house. Not that she'll understand, but that's not the point, is it?'

'No, it isn't,' Isabella agreed, smiling gratefully at her cousin, who unknowingly had just solved her dilemma. It wouldn't matter if her grandmama didn't understand her gesture; it was the fact she was making it.

'Don't be long, then. It might be Christmas but we've still got work to do,' Frederick reminded them.

'Slave-driver,' Dotty muttered as they made their way outside. 'Did you have a good evening,

Izzie? You was very quiet on the way home.'

'Couldn't get a word in edgeways with you chattering on about Alfred,' Isabella teased, as she carefully unlocked the door and led the way into the front room.

'Happy Christmas, Grandmother,' Dotty cried, placing the tray on the little table beside the woman.

'Happy Christmas, Grandmama,' Isabella added. The woman nodded but didn't look up from staring into the fire.

'I made a new dress and wore it at the big house last night. Alfred said I looked beautiful,' Dotty gushed, two pinks spots flushing her cheeks.

'Big house,' the woman repeated, but when she turned to face them her rheumy eyes were blank.

With a last look at her locket, Isabella took the music box from the shelf and carefully placed it inside.

'I think this has come home,' she whispered, holding it out for her grandmama to see.

'Home,' the woman nodded. Isabella waited, hoping for some sign of recognition, but the woman picked up the cup and sipped her tea. *Oh Grandmama,* she thought, *how I wish I'd known you before you retreated inside your own world.* But then, if it wasn't for the shock of Isabella being born illegitimately, the woman would probably be living a normal life. For the second time that day, she felt the tears welling and had to blink them away.

They spent the rest of the day posying and packing in the barn before trooping back to the kitchen to be greeted by the delicious aroma of roasting meat.

'I was going to bring Mother in,' Mary told them, 'but she was sleeping so peacefully, I didn't have the heart to wake her.' Then Bill and Joseph arrived armed with candies and cider and the family celebrations began.

Although Isabella tried her best to join in, her heart was heavy as she remembered the last time there'd been a gathering round the table. Felix sitting opposite, their gazes meeting, holding hands whilst strolling around the moonlit garden and wishing upon the shooting star. Running her fingers over the little silver brooch in her pocket, she let out a long sigh. If she'd thought her life complicated then, it was nothing compared to how she was feeling now. She just hoped the next time she saw him that he'd listen and respect the decision she'd made.

Chapter 32

To her surprise and dismay, the end of December came and still Felix hadn't called to see her. Although she dreaded what she had to tell him, perversely she was disappointed he hadn't taken the time to visit as he'd promised.

'Are you sure you want to stand in the Strand by yourself?' Aunt Mary asked. Isabella looked at her in dismay for today was the day of the seance. Luckily, though, her uncle intervened.

'Don't question the girl, Mother,' Frederick said.

'We've enough violets blooming to fill the whole of the Strand, never mind one basket. It were you who gave Dotty permission to go walking out with Alfie on a Friday, after all. Though it does seem strange you offering, girl?' he said staring suspiciously at Isabella.

'Just want to help,' she replied, picking up the laden basket.

'At least you look more the part of a flower girl in that grey dress and woollen turnover,' her aunt smiled.

It was a cold and bright morning as she made her way to her customary place in the Strand. It seemed an age since she'd last been here and, determined to do her bit, she smiled and held out her basket invitingly. To her surprise, people began returning her greeting, some even stopping to purchase a bunch of violets.

She was on tenterhooks waiting for the sisters to appear, for she was sure her mama's spirit would come through this time. After all, Agnes had had ages to pick up her aura and essence from the necklace. The first thing she'd do when she returned home was give the pearls to her uncle for safe keeping. Whilst he'd been true to his word and not mentioned them again, she knew he was waiting for her to hand them over.

The church clock chimed noon and she stared around in surprise. Usually the sisters had appeared by now. By the time it got to half past one, knowing the seances always started promptly at two o'clock, she began making her own way to the house they were renting.

'Oh, there you are,' Agnes said, frowning as she

opened the door. 'We began to think you weren't coming,' she added, taking the basket of flowers from her.

'You've always collected me before and...,' Isabella began.

'Silly girl, we told you we couldn't today,' Miriam clucked, handing her a nosegay. 'Now, breathe deeply of the flowers, dear.' She waited whilst Isabella inhaled and then, after exchanging looks with Agnes, ushered her into the front room where the curtains were already drawn and the candles lit.

This time the smell of flowers seemed overpowering and Isabella just had time to register that the violets in the glass bowls couldn't be the ones she'd just brought, when Agnes instructed them all to join hands. Breathing heavily, she asked if there were any spirits waiting to come through. As Agnes went through the same sequence as before, Isabella felt her pulse racing. *Please come through, Mama and Papa,* she willed. She waited impatiently whilst a couple of spirits, through Agnes, spoke to their relatives, then all went quiet. Just when Isabella feared the meeting was at an end, the woman's head jerked back again and her mouth opened.

'Isabella, darling, it's your mother.' Her eyes widened in astonishment. Mother? Mama never called herself that. 'I want you to know I'm happy now your dear father is with me.' Isabella stiffened in her seat. Now she knew this wasn't right.

'Do you wish to respond, Isabella?' Agnes asked.

'What was my biological father's real name?' she asked, staring at Agnes intently.

'Fancy you needing to ask that. You know he is called Cameron,' the voice stated.

'But...,' she began.

'She's fading ... oh, she's gone,' Agnes murmured, her eyes snapping open. Smiling sweetly, she announced that the seance was over.

As the others filed out, handing over their nosegays along with their money, Agnes turned to Isabella.

'There, didn't I tell you I would be able to reach your mother through her pearls? I hope it brought a measure of comfort to you at this sad time.'

'I suppose you'll be telling me that if I leave my father Cameron's solid-gold pocket watch with you, I can expect to hear from him next time?' she retorted.

'You have it on you?' Agnes asked, a gleam sparkling in her eye.

'No,' Isabella replied. 'However, I would be pleased to have Mama's pearls back.'

'You're sounding very sceptical. Surely you didn't think we'd be holding onto them?' Miriam said, holding out her basket. 'You'll find them in there along with the money for your flowers as usual,' she said stiffly.

'Now, if you'll excuse us, we are very busy today,' Agnes said, almost pushing her out of the door.

As the fresh air hit her, Isabella began to sway. *Not again,* she thought, clutching at the railings as she began making her way unsteadily down the street.

'Isabella, are you all right?' Felix? He'd come to her rescue, she thought. Then, as if staring through a haze, she saw it was her uncle Bill who was staring down at her from his cart.

'I'm fine,' she assured him as her head slowly began to clear.

'Something you ate?' he asked.

'Actually, I haven't eaten anything since breakfast.'

'That might explain it then,' he said, sounding doubtful. 'Come on, I'll take you home.' He took her basket then helped her up beside him. The swaying of the cart brought on another bout of dizziness and she closed her eyes.

She must have fallen asleep for the cart shuddering to a halt woke her. To her surprise they were back at the cottage and, although it was almost dark, she could still see the concern on her uncle's face.

'Sorry about that, but I'm feeling better now.'

'Really? You look just like I do the day after the night before,' he chuckled. 'If I didn't know better, I'd say you've been on the sauce. Come on, I'll see you safely indoors. I need to speak to Fred anyway.'

'Oh Isabella, what have you been doing?' Mary cried taking the basket from her.

'Found her wandering down Carlisle Gardens. All of a daze, she was. Hope she's not coming down with something,' Bill said, looking worried.

'It's not the first time she's come home like this,' Mary said. 'For the life of me, I don't know what she gets up to.'

'Me neither,' he said, shaking his head. 'Fred in his shed?'

'Where else?' Mary sighed. 'I'll just see to Izzie

then I'll dish supper, if you'd care to stop.'

'I would, thanks,' he replied, going back outside.

While her aunt and uncle were talking, Isabella retrieved the jewellery case from the basket and put it in her pocket. Then, before her aunt could say anything, she tiptoed up the stairs. She had too much to think about to answer the questions she knew were coming.

Something about the sisters was niggling her, but her head was still woozy and she couldn't think straight. Slipping the jewellery box under her pillow, she undressed and was asleep in seconds.

'Father wants to see you in the barn,' her aunt greeted Isabella when she went downstairs the following morning. She was looking grim-faced, which was not surprising since Isabella was late up, and for once she didn't offer any food to break her fast. Not that Isabella was hungry, but she was desperately thirsty and her head ached.

'I'm sorry about yesterday,' Isabella said, pouring herself a mug of tea.

'We'll talk about that later,' Mary replied. 'Now, please don't keep Father waiting any longer,' she added, staring pointedly at her drink.

To Isabella's surprise, when she entered the earthy-smelling interior, she saw a uniformed man standing beside him. Both men looked grave and Isabella's heart sank.

'Ah, Isabella, Constable Good here would like to speak to you about your movements yesterday. I told him you were selling flowers in the Strand, but he seems to think otherwise.' Isabella's stomach did a double flip and she swallowed hard.

'Miss Isabella ... er?'

'Carrington,' she supplied, trying to keep her voice steady.

'Right,' he said, snapping open his notebook and frowning.

'We have reason to believe you attended number thirteen Carlisle Gardens, temporary residence of two ladies calling themselves the Misses Honesty and, under the guise of a seance, participated in black magic.'

'Oh no...,' Isabella began.

'You mean you weren't at the said premises between the hours of two o'clock and three thirty?' he asked narrowing his eyes.

'Well, yes, I was but...'

'Then please answer my questions. Did you meet with the aforementioned?'

'Yes,' she whispered, aware of the anger sparking in her uncle's eyes. 'But it was in order to make contact with my mama and papa.'

'And did you?'

'Well, Agnes, one of the sisters said she had a message from Mama but she got the name wrong and I knew she was pretending and it was terrible,' she groaned.

'Perhaps you could start at the beginning,' Constable Good suggested. 'When and where did you meet these women, and what exactly happened?'

Knowing she had no choice, Isabella began relating the events from the time she'd first met Agnes and Miriam in the Strand, to the seances and nosegays.

'Nostrums,' Constable Good corrected. 'An elixir or substance designed to cure or alter the state of one's mind. Did those clients attending the seances inhale from them at all?'

'Oh yes, they were encouraged to frequently.'

'And yourself?'

'Only yesterday. On my two previous visits I was given tisanes and dainties for luncheon.'

'Did you notice any after-effects?' he asked, watching her closely.

'I did feel lightheaded and suffered the most terrible headaches.'

'Came home looking like she'd had a night on the town. Flushed in the face, muttering gibberish,' Frederick snorted.

'That would fit in with our findings, sir,' the constable nodded. 'One of the women is, er, how shall we say, conversant with opiates. Was there any mention of flowers, poppies in particular?' he asked, staring directly at Isabella.

'Funnily enough, they did say they dealt with all things flowers,' she nodded. 'Oh yes, and they also mentioned poppy tears,' she said remembering back to their conversation before Christmas.

'That would account for the altered perception and illusionary effects,' the constable muttered, writing furiously in his notebook.

'My God, what the 'ell have you been involved in?' her uncle cried. 'Only sent you into town to sell a few violets and...,' he spluttered.

'And did these women use violets?' the constable interrupted.

'Yes, they put big bowls of them on the table,' Isabella admitted.

'Blimmer, girl, you mean that's who you sold our flowers to?' her uncle roared. Isabella nodded and, feeling ashamed, stared down at her feet.

'Am I right in thinking these violets would have a soporific effect, sir?'

'They would, but more soothing than sedating,' Frederick explained.

'Would this smell mask other aromas?'

'Might well do,' Frederick replied, still staring at Isabella in dismay. 'I can't believe you'd get involved in something like this.' Anxious to explain, Isabella hurried on.

'It was just after Papa died. I was so unhappy, Uncle. Agnes said Papa was trying to come through but that it was too soon after he'd passed.'

'Utter tosh,' Frederick muttered.

'I know that now,' Isabella cried. 'She said if she had something personal of Mama's to absorb her essence, she could get her to come through.'

'So, you gave her your pearls?' her uncle sighed. Isabella nodded.

'I offered her my silver locket first, but she said it was too cold,' she explained.

'Too cheap more like,' Constable Good muttered.

'I suppose that was the last time you saw the necklace,' her uncle growled.

'Oh no, I got it back yesterday,' she cried, anxious to prove she hadn't been taken for a complete fool.

'Continue explaining about the seance, if you would,' the constable requested, pencil poised.

'It was strange because Agnes said Mama was coming through. It really seemed as though a different voice was coming out of her mouth, but it didn't sound anything like Mama at all. So I asked her a question and she got the answer wrong.'

'And what happened then?' the constable asked.

'Agnes said her spirit had gone and the seance was over. They seemed anxious for everyone to leave.'

'And you all went?' the constable prompted.

'The others did but I asked for Mama's pearls.'

'And they gave them to you, just like that?' he asked, staring at her intently.

'Yes, they put the box in my basket and almost pushed me out of the door.'

'And did you check your pearls when this, er, Agnes gave them back to you?'

'No,' Isabella frowned. 'I was feeling woozy and then Uncle Bill brought me home and ... why?' she asked, feeling she had missed something important.

'These women have a reputation for replacing items of jewellery with counterfeit,' the constable replied.

'What?' she gasped. 'I'd best go and check right away,' she said, rushing out of the barn before they could stop her.

As Isabella barged through the kitchen door, her aunt looked up from the pan she was stirring.

'Izzie, whatever's the...,' she began but Isabella ran past her and up the stairs. Scrabbling under her pillow, she pulled out the box and opened it.

'Oh,' she gasped, letting out a sigh of relief. There, nestling on the velvet pillow, was the pearl necklace she knew so well.

'It's all right,' she shouted, running back past an openmouthed Mary and down to the barn. 'They're here, see,' she cried handing over the box.

'You're sure they're the same ones, miss?' the constable asked.

'Well, yes, I think so,' Isabella stuttered, staring down at them again.

'Check carefully now. How about the clasp?' Isabella took up the necklace and studied it closer.

'Well, it looks the same, oh...'

'What is it?' her uncle asked.

'There was one pearl by the clasp which had a sort of mark on it. A lucky mark, I used to call it, but it's gone. Perhaps they cleaned it off?'

'I doubt it, miss,' the constable said. 'I'll need to have these checked out, sir,' he said, turning to Frederick.

'Of course, and thank you for coming here today, Constable.'

'There's one more thing before I go,' he said, turning back to Isabella. 'Now Miss, you say your name is Carrington?'

'That's correct,' she replied.

'I'm afraid it isn't,' Frederick sighed. 'Sit down, Isabella,' he added, extracting a paper from the parcel on the trestle in front of him.

'Oh, those are...,' she began, recognizing the package.

'The papers I collected when we visited your old home in Chester Square. You'd better have a look at this,' he said, passing over an official-looking piece of paper.

'It's my birth certificate. Oh!' she gasped, sinking onto the stool beside her. 'There's no ... the surname says Northcott.'

'Your natural father disappeared before you were born and your mother used her name. She never married Cameron Carrington, the man who raised you, so...,' he shrugged.

'Well, you have been most helpful, Miss, er, Northcott,' the constable said, looking uncomfortable. 'I shall be making further enquiries and most insist you don't leave the district.'

'Isabella will be staying here, Constable,' Frederick assured him, showing the man out of the barn.

So she wasn't Carrington at all. Her true name was Isabella Odorata Northcott, Isabella mused, rereading the certificate.

'What a strange middle name I have,' she muttered, as her uncle returned.

'Viola Odorata is the name by which the sweet-scented violet is known. Your mother always had a thing for them, making perfume and what not. Used to mix them with water and rose petals.'

'Oh yes, Grandmama told me that. Apparently when Mama went to London she had the real perfume made up, which I suppose is the smell I remember,' Isabella replied. 'I'm sorry for causing you all this trouble, Uncle,' she added. 'When I was offered the chance to make contact with my parents, well, it seemed too good an opportunity to miss. And now I find out I'm called Northcott.'

'Cheer up, girl, there are worse names,' Frederick smiled. But Isabella frowned.

'I'm illegitimate,' she gasped, as the truth hit her like a sledgehammer. 'How frightfully dreadful.'

Chapter 33

'You're not the first and won't be the last,' her uncle said, patting her shoulder. 'You do realize those pearls you brought back are probably fake?'

'Funnily enough, it doesn't seem important somehow,' she said, realizing just how true it was. 'I suppose those other ladies were duped too?'

'I'm afraid so. It appears those so-called sisters prey on vulnerable widows, extracting as much as they can from them before moving on to another town and starting all over again.'

'That's terrible.'

'It is. Whilst I understand you wanting to make contact with your parents, I hope you've learned your lesson. Those mind-altering substances cause serious problems, especially to those of a sensitive nature.'

'Don't worry, Uncle, I shall never get involved with anything like that again. Those sisters seemed so kind, and up until yesterday they had me fooled,' she shook her head.

'Charlatans, that's what they were, Isabella. Now, let's forget them. You've had a terrible shock, girl, but amongst these papers is a letter for you,' he said, passing her a cream envelope addressed in the hand Isabella knew so well. 'I'll leave you to read it in peace.'

As her uncle closed the door behind him, with trembling hands, Isabella slid out the single sheet of paper.

My Dearest Isabella,
You are reading this, because sadly my time here is at an end. Knowing your aunt and uncle to be fine, upstanding people, I requested they give you a home when I no longer could. You can believe me when I tell you how it grieved me to send you away at the time I most wanted you by my side. However, that wouldn't have been fair, and one day, in the fullness of time, you will come to understand a parent has a duty to put the wellbeing of their child before their own wishes.

You have been the best daughter a man could ever have wished for. You might not be of my blood but no father could have loved you more. My one regret is that I was unable to give you my name but, of course, that was your mama's decision. She was a fine woman and I loved her dearly, so it is one I had to respect.

I have left the money put by for your dowry with your uncle. Regrettably, dear Isabella, it is nowhere near as much as I had planned, but I hope you will be understanding of the circumstances.

Dearest Isabella, be happy in your new life. You have been the most delightful daughter and it has been both a joy and a privilege raising you as my own.

Your loving Papa,
Cameron Carrington

'Oh Papa,' she whispered, the tears coursing down her cheeks. 'I wish you'd told me you were ill.'

'He wanted you to remember him as he was. Is that such a bad thing?' her uncle said, putting his arm around her as he slipped back into the barn.

'I suppose not,' she sobbed. 'And he says he loved me.'

'Of course, he did,' her uncle agreed. 'He gave you a fine and privileged upbringing. 'Fraid you'll have to rough it here with us now, though,' he said. 'Put that letter in your pocket and dry those tears. When you're ready, we've work to do.' He turned away and began tending his plants.

Knowing he was giving her time to compose herself, Isabella read the letter again and, with a warm glow in her heart, put it safely in her pocket. It was something to treasure and reread when she wanted reassurance.

'Right, what shall I do?' she asked her uncle.

'We need to make sure these cuttings thrive to increase stock in the spring. Then there's our new cultivars to nurse so we can outsmart Furneaux. Probably not the time to mention it, but there's something I need to say,' he said, looking at her gravely.

'What's that, Uncle?' she asked, her heart sinking as she wondered what else was coming.

'I can't stop you walking out with that Felix but I need you to assure me you won't pass on anything you see or learn in here,' he said, staring at her fixedly.

'I've already promised you that, Uncle,' she replied. 'Not that he's called to see me recently.'

'No, I've noticed he's not been round. Why would that be?' her uncle grunted.

'He can't afford to go out with the likes of me,' she muttered. 'His father said if he didn't find out from me the name of these cultivars then he'd be disinherited.'

'He's got a blimmer nerve, given his past,' he roared. Then a spark gleamed in his eyes. 'Ah, but I never told you what they're called,' he added.

'No,' she admitted. 'And even if you had, loyalty to you and Auntie would have prevented my letting on. But...,' her voice trailed away as the tears threatened to spill over.

'But? Come on, girl, you've been going round with a face as long as them steam trains, so spit it out.'

'Mr Furneaux owns a large property with extensive grounds and Felix has so much to lose, I decided it would be best not to see him again.'

'And he accepted it just like that?' Frederick persisted, his eyes narrowing.

'I haven't actually told him,' she admitted. 'But he must have come to the same conclusion, for he hasn't called to see me since, has he?' Her uncle stared at her thoughtfully.

'Well, girl, I'm proud of you,' he said. 'A few short months ago, you wouldn't have concerned yourself about other people's feelings, taking the opportunity of a good standard of living as your right.' Isabella frowned, realizing what he said was true. 'Not that my opinion matters, but the best thing you can do is keep busy. Work through your worries, as it were.'

'Yes, of course, Uncle. What would you like me to do?' she asked, staring at the plants he was watering.

'Go and help your aunt in the kitchen. She's come up with a ruse to get one up on Furneaux. Something she says we men would never think of,' he laughed.

The next morning Isabella and Dotty, both with laden baskets, made their way to the market. Isabella had been surprised both of them could be spared until her uncle grinned and rubbed his hands together.

'Double the sales, double the money. And of course, we're expecting good things from you with Mother's added value,' he winked.

'Coo, it's lovely to be away from the house and all that talk of beating Furneaux,' Dotty cried, swinging her basket happily as they made their way down the lane. 'Now we has to pick and pack as fast as we can, I swear I blimmer well pick and pack in me sleep. Talking of which, haven't seen Felix around recently.'

'I expect he's busy,' Isabella replied, quelling the flutter in her chest at the mention of his name. 'How's Alfred?' she asked, knowing how easy it was to divert her cousin.

'Fantastic, wonderful an' bloomin' great,' Dotty gushed, grinning widely. She went on to expound his qualities, leaving Isabella to her own thoughts. Rereading her papa's letter the previous evening had warmed her numbed heart. Although it still hurt that Felix hadn't called, she'd have to respect his wishes and move forward in her life. She was so lost in her musings that before she knew it, they'd arrived at the Strand.

'Happy New Year, girls,' Mrs Spink called, setting down her sign behind them. 'You could be lucky with corsages today, there seems to be some competition going on as to who can host the best “at home” to celebrate the coming of January.’

‘Coo, thanks, Mrs Spink,’ Dotty said. ‘Right, Izzie, remember what to do?’

‘I think so,’ Isabella replied, watching closely as Dotty set down her basket, snatched up some violets and began winding leaves around the stems. ‘Look, customers heading our way. You deal with them while I fix the pins, it’ll be quicker.’

‘Good morning, my dear,’ a woman of middle years said, smiling at Isabella. ‘Two bunches, please. Oh, and what’s this?’ she asked, pointing to the packets her aunt had added to their baskets.

‘’Tis violet tablet,’ Dotty called. ‘Mother makes the best.’

‘Haven’t had that in years,’ the woman replied. ‘Just the ticket to keep the cold out. I’ll take some.’

Business was brisk, and by the time the ladies in their furs appeared for their morning promenade, one basket was empty and the tablet had proved popular. Just as Mrs Spink had predicted, they descended upon the girls, requesting corsages but declining the tablet.

‘Gracious, one must watch one’s figure,’ one woman, thin as a reed, commented in her haughty voice.

‘Oh, must one?’ Dotty muttered under her breath. ‘Rather be happy and plump.’

‘Ssh Dotty, she’ll hear you,’ Isabella whispered. ‘Would madam care for a bow to be added?’ she asked, turning back to the woman.

‘Oh yes,’ she replied, looking on eagerly as Isabella added one with a flourish.

By the end of the morning, they’d sold nearly all their flowers and Isabella’s head was spinning with names. It appeared everyone knew Dotty and she'd been introduced to seemingly the whole of Dawlish.

'Do yer recognize them biddies over there? Only they've been eyeing yer for ages?' Dotty asked. Looking up, Isabella saw two ladies swathed in fox furs, watching her intently.

'I don't think so,' she replied but Dotty had turned away to serve another customer.

'Isn't that Northcott's niece whom we saw dancing with Felix Furneaux at Christmas?' one lady said in a voice intended to carry.

'It is,' her companion sniffed, taking out her lorgnette and studying Isabella. 'Nice fellow, too. I'm pleased he's seen sense and dropped her. He's been seen out with that nice Miss Swanson recently.'

'His father will be so relieved. They do say bad blood will out, don't they? And now there's all that talk about his Lordship.' Smiling benignly, they continued on their way, leaving Isabella staring after them in dismay. That's why Felix hadn't called, then. And what was that about Lord Lester, she wondered, turning back to Dotty who, unaware of the exchange, was chatting as she handed over the last of their violets.

'Coo, you've gone all pale. Are you all right, Izzie?' she asked as they started for home.

'Yes,' she replied. 'Never better.'

'Those old biddies didn't upset you, did they?' Dotty frowned.

'Of course not,' she lied.

'Good, 'cos you seemed to be enjoying yourself and I was hoping we could do this again. If we can persuade Father, of course.'

'It has been fun,' Isabella said, forcing a smile. 'I've never spoken to so many people in my life before.'

'Yea, you even had a way with them toffs. Probably 'cos you speaks in their hoity-toity way,' Dotty grinned. 'Adding them silver bows so we could charge extra was genius.'

'Well, they've only been languishing in my portmanteau. I'll see what other accoutrements I can find when we get back.'

'Accoutie what?' Dotty cried.

'Trimmings,' Isabella replied.

'Well, why didn't you say? It's like Aladdin's cave in your trunk. Hope Mother's got something tasty for luncheon, I'm starving,' Dotty replied, quickening her pace.

Her cousin's non-stop chat on the way home left Isabella time to ponder on the remarks the two women had exchanged. While her heart was heavy, at least she knew where she stood, she thought.

Mary and Frederick were astonished when the girls emptied their money onto the kitchen table.

'Blimmer girls, that's a good morning's work,' Frederick cried.

'Well done, you two. I thought the tablet would bring in extra but that's astonishing,' Mary cried, scooping up all the coins and placing them in the pottery pig on the dresser.

'Well, the toffs didn't want any tablet in case it ruined their figures,' Dotty told her, rolling her eyes. 'But everyone else was happy to buy it. Mrs Spink told us there would be a run on corsages for their fancy parties and she was right. Izzie tied them with some of her silver ribbon, which went down so well we were able to add a halfpenny to each one,' Dotty crowed. Her aunt smiled.

'Well done, Izzie. I hope Dotty introduced you to everyone.'

'Cors I did, though not the toffs. But here's a thing, when Izzie spoke to them they smiled and looked almost human.'

'Dotty!' Mary chided. 'Now, sit down. Luncheon's ready.'

'I found most people friendlier with Dotty there,' Isabella explained, trying to dismiss the triumph on the two women's faces as they'd spoken about Felix.

'Perhaps it's you who has become more approachable,' Mary replied, looking at her shrewdly. 'I always thought that grey dress would help.'

'Come along, William,' Frederick urged, as the boy came thundering down the stairs. 'Want you to take the flowers to the station this afternoon.'

'Yes, Father,' William replied before tucking into his bread and ham.

'You not hungry?' Mary asked as Isabella toyed with her food.

'I was thinking,' she smiled. 'The tof– I mean, the ladies might not desire tablet but they could be interested in purchasing items for beautification, like the violet soap Alice made for Christmas. It smells divine...,' she trailed off as William gave a loud snort.

'Only use soap if I has to, and then not that female-smelling stuff.'

'Philistine,' she laughed. 'You wait until you get

a lady friend, you'll feel differently then.'

'Pah!' he scoffed, a flush creeping up under his collar.

'Anyway, it's not only about speaking the same way as the ladies; it's about understanding their requirements. With the right products, it would be easy to capitalize on them,' Isabella said, turning back to her aunt.

'You might have something there, Izzie,' Mary nodded. 'I'll do some costings of the ingredients.'

'I'd really love to learn how to make soap, especially if it would help the family budget,' Isabella said eagerly.

'Seeing as you're so willing to help, me new plants need tending so yer can give us a hand, girl,' her uncle told her, getting to his feet.

'We'll talk more about your idea later,' her aunt called as Isabella followed after her uncle.

'You dust, I'll water,' he joked, handing her one of his new brushes, and carefully lifting the glass from the pots on one side of the trestle. As the earthy aroma filled the air, Isabella began sweeping the minute particles of soil from the leaves. In the peaceful atmosphere, her thoughts began to roam from making soap to the two ladies and their comments about Felix and Miss Swanson. So he'd found another, had he? She hadn't intended seeing him again, so why did the idea of him walking out with someone else hurt so much?

Distracted, she paid little heed to what she was doing and, turning quickly, knocked the edge of the glass. As the tray of precious plants crashed to the ground, she stared at her uncle in horror.

'Oh no,' she gasped, her hand flying to her

mouth. 'I'll clear it up,' she muttered, gathering up the shattered shards mixed with bits of pot and soil.

'Leave it,' he barked. 'Sit down and stay out of the way. I'll see to it,' he ordered.

She watched as, with a shake of his head, he hunkered down and began plucking the plants from the debris, carefully placing them on the trestle.

'I'm so sorry,' she murmured, tears threatening as she waited for him to berate her clumsiness. There was silence while he seemed to gather his thoughts.

'Could 'ave been worse,' he said eventually. ''Tis only the ones William brought in so a few missing's neither here nor there. Thought a trip out might have cheered you up but you still seems jittery. Didn't see young Felix, by any chance?' he asked, raising his brow enquiringly.

'No,' she replied truthfully.

'Hurting, eh? Well, given time, you'll heal and bounce back, just like our plants here will,' he said, gesturing to the sorry-looking cuttings that now required repotting.

'I hope so, Uncle,' she sighed. 'And I really am sorry for the damage.'

'Accidents happen. Now, to cheer you up, I'm going to tell you all about our little cultivars here.' Carefully he removed the glass covering the other plants. 'These lovelies are called Parma violets, which, as far as I can tell, have never been raised round here before.'

'Apart from the leaves, how will they be different from the Princess of Wales variety you already grow?' she asked, surprising herself by really wanting to know.

'These beauties will be double-petalled, like pom-poms, see?'

'Goodness,' she exclaimed, staring at the little shoots in fascination.

'Not only that, they'll be multi-coloured,' he grinned.

'Really?'

'Yep, they'll be white going into pale blue and mauve with flecks of carmine red. People everywhere will flock to buy them from Frederick Northcott,' he announced grandly. 'We'll beat those Furneaux, then Mrs Northcott will be able to take it easy at last.'

'I can't imagine Auntie sitting with her feet up, somehow,' Isabella smiled.

'Maybe not, but she deserves the chance,' he declared, studying each leaf intently. 'You should give young Felix a chance too. I've a feeling he's got a reason for not showing up.'

Indeed he has, Isabella thought grimly, her spirits plummeting once more.

Chapter 34

Although no further mention was made of her faux pas, Isabella couldn't help noticing she hadn't been invited back into the potting area. In fact, she'd been encouraged to go out more.

'Fresh air will do you good,' Aunt Mary said,

handing her a basket full of flowers and tablet to sell. 'Getting to know people will help you settle in,' she insisted. 'You can ask the ladies if they'd be interested in purchasing violet soap. If they are, we'll look at that receipt this afternoon.'

'I'll do that,' Isabella smiled, for the idea really interested her. 'Do you have a sample I could show them, only I've already used mine so much it has worn down.'

'Good idea,' her aunt said, going to the dresser and taking a tissue-wrapped bar from the drawer.

While Dotty skipped off to meet Alfie, Isabella, sample soap in her pocket, took up her usual place in the Strand. It was too early for the ladies of the town to be out, but business for flowers and tablet was surprisingly brisk. She was beginning to recognize many of the locals and, to her delight, they greeted her like a friend, even asking if she knew about the violet ball that was held in May. Although it was months away, it appeared to be the highlight of the year.

The day was warm and dry for January, and later in the morning the ladies began appearing for their constitutional. Many stopped to purchase corsages and Isabella, now adept at making them, smiled as she added the bows which had proven popular. Then she showed them her soap and enquired whether they would be interested in placing an order.

'It smells divine,' she told them, holding it up for them to test themselves.

'I agree,' one lady said, nodding so enthusiastically the ostrich feathers on her hat fluttered and flapped. 'However, it does look rather plain.'

'Yes,' her companion agreed. 'I prefer something more decorative, myself.'

'We will, of course, be adorning each tablet with pressed flowers,' Isabella assured them, wondering where the notion had come from.

'Well, in that case, I may well be interested,' the first lady replied.

'We are repairing to Bath tomorrow but will return in a fortnight, so will drop by to inspect some samples. Good day to you.'

Isabella watched as they crossed over to the green opposite, excitement fluttering in her chest. Most of the ladies were pleasant when you got to know them, although she was mindful that these days she needed to remember her place. To her surprise, she rather enjoyed the challenge of trying to secure orders, although the extra enquiries took time and it was mid-afternoon before she could make her way back to the cottage.

Thankfully the two malicious gossips hadn't shown up, for she couldn't bear hearing any more of their tittle-tattle. As far as Felix Furneaux was concerned, he could string himself up by his violet stems. She would concentrate on learning how to make soap.

Just then she saw white little drops like pearls clustered under the hedgerow. Snowdrops meant hope and consolation, her governess had told her on one of their walks around the park. Well, she could certainly do with some hope in her life.

To her surprise, she arrived home just as her uncle was returning from the station. With a jubilant grin on his face, he ushered her inside. Throwing his hat on its peg, he turned and kissed

a surprised Mary on the cheek.
'Well, Mother, divine justice has been done,' he cried.
'Don't tell me you've been wagering on a horse, Frederick Northcott?' she snorted.
'Better than that,' he grinned, rubbing his hands gleefully. 'Furneaux's got red mite all over his plants.'
'Oh, the poor man,' Mary murmured.
'What is this red mite?' Isabella frowned.
'Red spider, the most dreaded pest of all,' Mary replied. 'It results in mottling of the foliage, which disfigures and discolours the flowers.'
'In severe infestations, the whole flower is covered in a mesh of webbing,' Uncle Bill said, coming into the room with Joseph.
'Can't think where it came from. You don't usually get red mite in winter,' Joseph added, shaking his head.
'Perhaps Furneaux's brought in diseased specimens from outside,' Uncle Bill said. 'We've checked all our violets and thankfully there's no sign of red spider yet, but we'll be keeping a regular eye out.'
'Ours seem all right too,' William announced, arriving with Alice and Thomas hanging onto his arms.
'Well, we must be vigilant, 'cos it spreads rapidly,' Frederick told them. 'It'll mean ruination for Furneaux, of course.'
'Can't anything be done?' Isabella asked.
'The only way is to strip all the affected leaves, burn them and spray the rest with a solution of soft soap and water,' Uncle Bill told her. 'Trouble

is, Furneaux's got so much land, it'll take him longer to do it than it takes those darn mites to spread.'

'Not if everyone assists, surely,' Isabella replied.

'What? Help our rivals?' Frederick roared. Isabella stared at him in disbelief.

'I can't believe you said that, Uncle. When Papa's business was in trouble, none of his so-called friends lifted a finger to help. They disappeared and let him sink. You can't let that happen to neighbours, rival or not, surely?' she cried.'

'She's right, Fred. And they did help here when that tree came down,' Bill pointed out.

'Mary?' he asked, turning to his wife.

'You're a good man ... underneath all that bluster,' she told him, patting his shoulder. He let out a long sigh.

'Very well, we'll take both carts and see what can be done,' he muttered.

'Where do you think you're going?' he asked Isabella as she snatched her mantle from the hook.

'I'm coming with you,' she insisted. 'Even I can check the leaves, if I know what I'm looking for.' She stared meaningfully at William, who flushed.

'Make sure you wear thick gloves,' Frederick told her. 'Alice and Thomas, you stay here. Doubtless Dotty will be back soon, when she can tear herself away from that Alfred. Explain what's happened and that you're all to check the plants hourly.'

'Oh, must we?' they groaned.

'Yes, you must,' he insisted.

'I'm sure Father will find some pocket money

for you this week,' Mary assured them. 'I'll come too. You'll need hot drinks and something to eat,' she added, packing bread and cheese into her basket.

It was growing dark by the time they reached the Furneaux residence but flashes of light moving up and down the garden revealed the two men frantically tearing up plants and tossing them onto a growing pile ready for burning.

Lantern in her gloved hand and hood over her head to keep out the wind, Isabella followed the men while Mary went inside the house.

'Don't worry, Furneaux, the cavalry's here,' Frederick called.

'I'll show you what we're looking for, Izzie,' William offered. 'Although, by the state of these leaves, it'll be obvious.'

Methodically, they worked the rows of violets, checking, stripping and throwing affected foliage onto the ever-growing pile. From time to time, the moon peeped out from behind the clouds, but Isabella hardly noticed as she followed her cousin. Even when her back was aching, such was the sense of urgency that she refused to give up.

Then the fire was lit and a cheer went up as the devastated plants began to burn. It was only a brief respite before they moved onto another section of the gardens.

'Bet Furneaux wishes he didn't have so much land now,' William whispered. 'By the way, now you showed me them other letters, I can write both me names now.'

'That's wonderful,' Isabella smiled. 'Next I'll show you how to write your address.'

'Father'll be gobble smackled,' he grinned.

They worked their way to the bottom of the garden by the orchard, where they found healthy-looking plants unaffected by the mite.

'I'll dig a trench round these, Furneaux,' Frederick called. 'You light the other fire.'

'Will do,' Matthew replied. 'Think we've got the worst of it stripped now.'

'Right, Izzie, you look all in. Go up to the house and tell Mother to prepare hot drinks and som't to eat,' Frederick said, coming over to where Isabella was still searching for signs of the dreaded red mite.

'I can't see any more here,' she told him, putting her hand to her back and easing herself into a standing position. Amazingly the sky was lightening to grey, the moon a fading crescent as she plodded up the path. Her eyes were hot from squinting and she felt as if she was covered in dirt. Goodness only knows what she looked like, she thought.

'Isabella, is that you?' Felix cried, crunching up the gravel behind her. 'I had no idea you were here. Why, I hardly recognized you,' he gasped. Isabella fixed a smile on her face.

'No reason why you should after all this time,' she said tightly, although her pulse was racing. 'Now, if you'll excuse me, I have to relay a message to my aunt.' As she turned and continued her way towards the house, he hurried after her.

'What's the matter, Isabella? I'm sorry I didn't come and see you as soon as I returned but the past few days have been a nightmare.'

'Really? And where, may I ask, have you come

back from?'

'Up country. Father dispatched me on Boxing Day.'

'And how is Miss Swanson?' she asked.

'Ruth? Fine when I dropped her off, why?'

'So, you admit you've been seeing her, then?' Isabella said tightly, hardly able to credit his insouciant manner.

'Yes, I did see her. Why?' he asked.

'Oh, somebody mentioned it,' she shrugged, not wishing to show how much it bothered her. 'Have you known her long?'

'Years. We went to school together but she moved to Plymouth after she married. She came up on the train to visit her grandmother and when I saw her laden with provisions, I offered her a lift.' So this Ruth was married, she thought, her spirits rising.

'You said you'd been away?' she asked, the ice around her heart beginning to thaw.

'Father dispatched me to collect more of the plants he'd ordered. Only it seems they were all diseased. We had one hell of a row on Christmas Day because I hadn't found out the name of your uncle's cultivars. I told him to go ahead and disinherit me because nothing would stand in my way of seeing you.'

'Really?' she cried, her heart singing. He nodded.

'He finally admitted he'd been irrational and agreed to back down if I went and collected his plants immediately,' he sighed, and even by the dimming light of her lantern she could see how fatigued he looked.

'I didn't even know you'd been away,' she murmured.

'You mean you didn't get my note?' he asked, frowning. 'I asked Father to deliver it, but by then I suppose he'd had a few,' he groaned.

'But surely you could have come and told me what you were up to?' she insisted.

'Father said a bit of space would give me time to reflect on my feelings for you,' he admitted.

'So you weren't sure?' she goaded, conveniently forgetting her own decision.

'Of course, I was, positive in fact. But I thought if I went along with him, he'd be more amenable. I told him this feud between our two families was infantile and had to stop, you see. He said there was more to it than I realized.'

'Oh?' she asked, intrigued despite her tiredness.

'It began when Frederick was courting the girl who eventually became my mother. Apparently, her parents thought he wasn't a good enough prospect. My father on the other hand had a much bigger farm, and she was encouraged to receive his attentions instead. It didn't work out, of course, as you know she left when I was young.'

'Oh, poor Auntie Mary. She has no idea,' Isabella cried.

'It was long before she came on the scene. She's a shrewd biddy, though, so I wouldn't be surprised if she didn't suspect,' he replied. 'I told Father I had no intention of being held to ransom. But of course, all this is irrelevant because you had no idea I'd gone away. Oh Isabella, what must you think of me?'

Seeing his anguished expression, all she could

hear was the thumping of her heart, feel the racing of her pulse. *Be still my beating heart.* Unbidden the lines she'd learned by rote popped into her mind and she smiled wearily.

'At this precise moment, Felix Furneaux, I think you're one muxy man.'

'While you, my lady, are pristine,' he countered, a gleam sparkling in his eyes. 'Oh Isabella, I've missed you so much,' he groaned, leading her to the veranda. He held out his arms and for a moment she hesitated but then, as she moved towards him, footsteps crunched on the path.

'Come on, you two,' Frederick called, and their moment was lost.

'I don't believe it,' Felix groaned.

'Ah well, Mr Furneaux, you know what they say about good things coming to those who wait,' she teased. Feeling happier than she had for weeks, she hurried inside.

'Oh, so that's the way things are, is it?' her aunt said when she saw Isabella's flushed face. 'And here's me working my fingers to the bone while you're canoodling outside. Go and wash yourself, then help me get these hungry men fed. And as for you,' she said, wagging her finger at Felix. 'I'll not ask where you've been hiding these past weeks but again, please be more considerate of my niece's feelings. She's been going around like a wet weekend in high summer.'

'Of course, Mrs Northcott. You can rest assured I have no intention of ever letting her out of my sight in future,' he replied solemnly.

'Now you're being stupid,' she snorted. 'Make yourself useful and pass these round,' she added, handing him a tray of drinks as the men stamped wearily back into the house.

As they tucked into the breakfast Mary had prepared, Felix and Isabella grinned at each other across the table. The atmosphere around them was almost convivial. Relief that the crisis had been averted mingled with awareness that they needed to be vigilant the mite hadn't spread to their neighbouring gardens. At one end of the room, Frederick and Matthew were deep in conversation.

'They seem to be getting on well. Do you think their feud over the flowers might be at an end?' Isabella asked.

'Not sure about that,' Felix mused. 'But I think they might have buried the hatchet after all these years.' He gestured to Mary who was watching them, a smile hovering on her lips. 'She knows she's his real true love, as I hope you know you are mine.'

'Shh, Felix,' she demurred. 'Everyone's listening.'

Chapter 35

'I see you're wearing your brooch,' Felix smiled, gesturing to the silver star on Isabella's lapel. 'Did you wish when you opened it?'

'Yes, I did. It's a lovely present,' she replied, running a finger over the shiny surface.

'And significant, I hope. Did you remember

our kiss?

'Felix, really,' Isabella protested, staring around the little café. It was two days after the discovery of the red spider mite and they were celebrating their victory over afternoon tea at Mrs Veale's.

'Everyone's too busy discussing their own affairs to worry about ours,' he grinned. His unfortunate choice of words rankled, immediately transporting her back to her relationship with Maxwell. 'What is it?' he asked, seeing her stiffen. 'What have I put my clumsy size tens in now?'

'Nothing,' she replied. 'I guess I'm still a bit tired after the other night,' she added.

'Too tired to discuss your birthday? It's only a couple of weeks away and being your twenty-first, I thought we could use it to announce our intent, if you get my meaning. With your permission, I should like to speak with your uncle. Father has come around and...'

'Please stop, Felix,' she urged, feeling a dreaded sense of déjà vu. 'You're taking things for granted. I mean everything's happened so quickly and...' Her voice trailed away as she saw his hurt expression. Ever the gentleman, he nodded.

'Forgive me, Isabella, I've obviously assumed too much too soon.' Grateful for his understanding, she nodded.

'I do like you, Felix,' she admitted.

'Glad to hear it. Wouldn't want to waste good money buying cake for a lady who didn't like me,' he quipped.

'Oh Felix, so much has happened recently,' she sighed. 'And you need to know something about me.'

'I know you're beautiful, intelligent, if a little too serious at times, caring and...'

'Illegitimate,' she broke in. 'My mama never married my papa and so my name isn't Carrington but Northcott. I'm a bastard, Felix,' she whispered.

'Ah, well, a rose by any other name,' he smiled.

'Don't make light of this, Felix. It's important.'

'But does it change anything?' he asked. 'I mean, when we marry you'll be taking my name anyway. Don't glare at me, you know I'm hoping you'll agree one day. Although I must confess patience is not one of my virtues.'

'Oh Felix,' she groaned. 'I just need time,' she said, unconsciously echoing her papa's words from the previous year.

'Well, you can't ignore your birthday. I expect you'll be celebrating with your family, along with all those new friends you seem to have made. Honestly, it took us ages to get through the park this afternoon with everyone stopping to greet you.'

'Really, Felix, you do exaggerate,' she laughed. Privately, though, she was pleased she seemed to be fitting in at last. Selling flowers wasn't nearly as bad as she'd thought, and the soap they'd made the previous day was already hardening nicely. Her aunt had even showed her how to press the flowers ready to decorate each tablet.

'Felix to Izzie,' Felix said, clicking his fingers and bringing her back to the present.

'Sorry, Felix, what were you saying?' she asked.

'I was asking about the plans for celebrating your birthday.'

'Nothing's been said, but you know Auntie, the more the merrier round her kitchen table,' Isabella smiled.

'She's a great woman, and a superb cook,' he agreed, rubbing his stomach appreciatively. 'Come on, it's growing dark and it's time I took you home.'

That night Isabella lay on her mattress, her thoughts spinning like the top she'd had as a child. She did like Felix a lot. He was warm, kind and funny and his touch sent shivers rippling all through her body. Which Maxwell's never had. However, Felix talking about future intent and celebrating her coming of age birthday with an announcement had chimed too closely with the last conversation she'd had with Maxwell in Claridge's. Of course, Felix was nothing like the avaricious, opinionated man Maxwell had turned out to be. But she hadn't known him very long. Staring down at the little silver star clutched in her hand, she closed her eyes and wished.

'Well, Isabella, for someone with a special birthday to celebrate, you don't look very happy,' her aunt announced. She was standing at the table kneading dough when Isabella finally surfaced the next morning.

'Sorry I'm late getting up. I had a sleepless night,' she admitted. Her aunt gave her a knowing look.

'Well, I'm parched so why don't you pour us a cuppa whilst it's quiet for once,' she suggested, placing the bread to prove. 'You should be learning how to do this, you know,' she added, gesturing to the mixing bowl. 'Now things have calmed down a bit, it's time we taught you to cook properly. A man can't live on fresh air, you know. He likes a decent meal in his stomach.'

'Hmm,' she agreed, not wishing to be drawn.

'I know Mr Furneaux has that big house, but Felix isn't a rich man so you'll not be affording servants, my girl.'

'Aren't you assuming rather a lot?' Isabella sighed.

'Well, unless I've been reading the signs wrong these past days. You know, shining eyes at the mention of a certain young man's name, singing to yourself as you get ready to meet him, pinning back your hair in a new style...'

'All right, Auntie,' she conceded, holding up her hand. 'I do like him, but is that enough? I mean, I thought I was going to marry Maxwell but he found another. Matthew Furneaux's wife left him. It's all too risky.'

'All life is a risk,' Mary told her. 'As for Maxwell, it sounds to me like he were an opportunist and you're better off without him. And Matthew's wife, well, we all know he wasn't the love of her life, don't we?' She shot Isabella another knowing look. 'I'm not stupid, Izzie,' she said quietly. 'I loved Frederick from the moment I met him, and I honestly believe he's come to return my feelings over the years. But nobody can tell you what's right, you have to go with what you feel in here,' she said, thumping her chest. As Isabella nodded, her aunt smiled gently. 'And don't forget that money your father left you. Not a fortune, but enough to grant you a certain amount of independence, if you decide that's what you'd prefer.'

'Thank you, Auntie,' she whispered, getting to her feet and throwing her arms around the woman. 'For that, and for taking me in.'

'Oh, my dear Izzie,' Mary murmured. 'You've become a daughter to me, just like Dotty and Alice. Now, it's time we did some work. There's a jar of dried fruit in the pantry. I'll show you how to bake a birthday cake.'

True to his word, Felix didn't mention their relationship again, and when he arrived at the cottage on the evening of her twenty-first, he produced a bunch of bright crocus from behind his back with a flourish.

'To celebrate your birthday and the return of spring,' he said.

'Why thank you, Felix. They're beautiful,' she smiled. 'Oh,' she said as he handed her a brightly wrapped package.

'Gift number two. And now for my third,' he murmured leaning forward and kissing her cheek. As warmth radiated around her entire body, Isabella found herself locked in his gaze.

'Ooh, what you got?' Alice asked, breaking the moment as she hopped up and down with excitement. 'I made her some special scented violet water,' she announced proudly to Felix, who made a big show of sniffing the air around Isabella.

'I thought she was smelling nicer than usual,' Felix told her, his eyes twinkling mischievously.

'Oh you,' Isabella sighed, punching him playfully.

'Typical, I buy the lady a present and get thumped for my efforts,' he groaned, rubbing his arm.

'This is beautiful, Felix,' Isabella gasped, staring at a silver star with a tiny diamond set in the centre.

'Well, the more stars you have to wish on, the more I can hope,' he whispered, gazing at her intently. 'May I?' he asked, taking it from her and fastening it around her neck.

His touch sent delightful shivers spiralling down her spine and, feeling her face growing hot, she took a step backwards. He gave her a knowing smile, then turned to Mary.

'Something smells appetizing, Mrs Northcott.'

'Mother's cooked two long-tailed rabbits, 'specially,' William said.

'Really?' Izzie asked, thinking it a strange choice for her birthday.

'You don't like rabbit?' he persisted.

'I shall make you write the letters out if you're not careful,' she chided.

'What, after I wrote you that birthday card?'

'Stop teasing the girl,' Mary chided, placing a large platter of pheasant on the table. 'Well, sit yourselves down. Father will serve.'

It was a convivial meal and when Mary brought out the cake, everybody cheered.

'Made by Isabella's fair hands,' she announced. Felix took a bite then pretended to choke, much to everyone's amusement.

After they had eaten and the table had been cleared, Felix thanked Mary for the meal then turned to Frederick.

'It's a lovely evening, sir, would you mind if I took Isabella for a stroll around the garden?' When he nodded his assent, Isabella's heart began racing. Surely Felix wouldn't, wasn't, going to ... but his face gave nothing away as she snatched up her mantle and hurried outside.

Holding out his arm for her to take, they walked slowly down the path, breathing in the heady fragrance of violets.

'I still love that smell,' she smiled.

'And now, courtesy of Alice, you're wearing it too,' he grinned.

'I'd love to be able to make it properly, like those perfumiers you were telling me about.'

'Well, you have another star to wish on,' he said, gazing at her intently.

'I'll have to make sure I use it wisely,' she told him.

'Indeed you will,' he murmured, the look in his eyes making her shiver with delight. 'Come on, let's get moving. Can't have you getting cold now you're an old lady,' he quipped.

'Felix Furneaux,' she protested. They continued their walk and, anxious to fill the silence, Isabella said: 'I'm glad our families have stopped that silly feud.'

'Me too. Although we'll never stop them competing for business. It's ironic to think that all the while they were fighting, coachmen were driving their Lords and Ladies' guests past our farms to see the carpet of blue and smell the soft scent of violets. If only they'd known what was going on behind the scenes, eh?'

'Indeed,' Isabella nodded, thankful he didn't

suspect what she'd thought he'd been up to behind the scenes.

'How are the new plants coming along? It's all right, Father's given up the idea of competing,' he said, seeing the look on her face. 'He's talking about cultivating another strain, but that won't be until our natural plants have recovered.'

'How are they doing?' she asked.

'Coming on well. Violets are a hardy stock despite their fragile appearance. With nurturing and encouragement, they'll bounce back from what life has thrown at them. A bit like humans, really,' he said, pulling her close. 'You have to give them time.' As his lips grazed hers, a delicious tingling flooded her body so that when he drew away she was left wanting more.

As February turned to March, and the new Parma violets flourished and bloomed, so did Isabella's feelings for Felix. She went about her work filled with a sense of contentment and purpose she'd never before experienced. To her delight, she'd been accepted by most of the locals, and her flair for adorning the corsages with bows of ribbon and lace made her popular with the ladies, who were now clamouring for her bars of soap.

One day in April when the sky was filled with puffball clouds and the air sweet with the fragrance of flowers, Dotty turned to Isabella and grinned.

'Well, girl, we've been that busy, poor Furneaux won't stand a chance now,' she chuckled, shaking her basket so that the coins jingled. 'Mother said as we've done so well, we can look in Pudge's for new material.'

'What for?' Isabella asked.

'The violet ball. You can't have forgotten.'

'No, of course not, how could I?' she replied for it been the topic of conversation around here since the beginning of the year.

''Tis only a few weeks away and we need new dresses. It's the high spot of the year and I want my Alfred to be proud of me. Cors, I'll not be standing next to you for the judging.'

'What judging?' Isabella asked, wishing her cousin wouldn't talk in riddles.

'For the Violet Queen, of course. Come on, let's see if old Pudge has got anything new in,' Dotty said, grabbing her by the arm and leading her around the corner.

Minutes later they were staring at the bales of materials piled haphazardly inside the draper's.

'If I had my own emporium, I'd make sure the merchandise was laid out more enticingly,' Isabella murmured.

'Coo, get you. Sell a few bits of soap and yous planning to have your own shop,' Dotty scoffed. Isabella felt a frisson of excitement. Why shouldn't she have her own place? But her thoughts were interrupted by Dotty, who'd been sifting through the materials. 'Ooh, look at this white frothy stuff. It'd suit you a treat, Izzie,' she squeaked, pointing to a bale of imitation organza. Isabella ran her hands over the material.

'Hmm,' she murmured, not liking to say it was gawdy and rough to the touch. However, it had given her an idea. 'Let's go home and look at the rest of the gowns I brought with me. If we find something suitable we can use our allowance for new accessories.'

'Oh let's,' Dotty cried. 'Although I do like this green satin. I could use the same pattern as Christmas. Alfred said the shape made me look all womanly.'

Isabella stared at Dotty in astonishment. Beau or not, that he should have commented on her shape seemed very forward. But, undaunted, her cousin hurried from the shop. Back home they searched through the remaining dresses in the trunk.

'Coo, this is the bee's knees,' Dotty said, holding up a ballgown in rose with ivory silk underskirts.

'It's a good shape for you, Dotty, and if we add lace at the neckline you could get away with the colour. Try it on,' she said but Dotty was already pulling her smock over her head.

Leaving her cousin to it, she rummaged through her now somewhat depleted wardrobe of clothes. Right at the bottom, she found the dress she'd worn to a charity ball she'd attended with Maxwell. She was about to put it back when she had second thoughts. The soft lilac chiffon shot through with silver was the ideal colour, while the draping neckline edged with tiny seed pearls was decorative without being ostentatious. All she needed was a wrap to cover her shoulders and perhaps a matching band for her hair, she thought, delving back into her trunk.

'What do you think?' Dotty asked, pirouetting in front of her.

'You look beautiful, and with a lace panel to

protect your modesty, it will be perfect.'

'But I likes showing me bosom,' Dotty protested. 'It makes me feel womanly and Alfred will...'

'Alfred won't want other men staring at his young lady,' Isabella told her firmly. 'Now, what do you think?' she asked, holding her dress up in front of her.

'You look like a princess, Izzie. But then you always does,' she pouted. 'Can I really borrow this dress?'

'If you promise to sew this piece of lace here onto the front, it's yours to keep, Dotty,' she laughed. 'Now, I think I've got some slippers to match that dress so let's see what else we can find.'

Each evening, as soon as supper was cleared away, Isabella and Dotty worked on their outfits, planned what accessories would go with them and how they would wear their hair.

'What about you, Aunt Mary? What will you wear?' she asked. To her surprise, the woman smiled and put her finger to her lips. 'Wait and see,' she teased as the door opened and Frederick came in.

'Such fuss for one night,' he muttered. 'And talking of fuss, Lord Lester's been arrested.'

'About time, too,' Mary cried. 'Got away with everything for far too long.'

'What has he got away with?' Isabella asked, looking up from her sewing.

'Taking advantage of poor young girls. Ruins their reputations then abandons them. Obsessed with young flesh, he is.'

'Mother, really,' Frederick remonstrated.

'Well, they don't call him Lord Leper for nothing,' Dotty sniffed.

'What do you know about that?' he frowned.

'Alfie told me he lures the young maids to his room with promises of fine clothes and jewels. Mrs Tripe tries to warn them to stay clear but they don't listen.'

'I suppose it's his word against theirs,' Isabella mused.

'That's right. It seems this time he set his sights on one of his visitor's daughters. Unfortunately for him, it turned out to be the offspring of no other than a judge from up country. They reckon Lester will go down for such a long stretch that by the time he gets out he'll be so old he'll be past it.'

'Praise be,' Mary cried.

'Cors, me and William have had the real excitement, planting out the new cultivars. Strong and healthy they look, too. Won't be long til we realize our fortune, Mother.'

'Well, I'm pleased for you, after all that time and effort you've spent on them,' Mary replied.

'It'll be a carriage and pony for you soon, my love. Did you see young Felix earlier?' he asked, turning to Isabella.

'No, why?' she asked, looking up from her sewing.

'Well, girl, he called by to ask me something,' he said giving her a broad wink.

'Something to do with your beloved flowers, no doubt,' she murmured, returning her attention to the intricate pattern she was stitching onto the front of her wrap. Although she was delighted about Lord Lester, the ball was only the following day and she was determined to have it finished in time.

'Oh ah, it were definitely about one of my blooms,' he chuckled.

Chapter 36

At last, the day of the much-anticipated violet bail dawned. As the sun shone brightly from a clear blue sky, the excitement was palpable and they hurried through their chores, eager to change into their new dresses.

Finally, Frederick and William left for the station, leaving Isabella and Dotty free to get ready.

'Of course, to prepare properly you should have bathed in the dew of the May dawn,' Mary said as she filled every available container with water and placed them to heat on the range.

'Not blinking likely,' Dotty cried, helping set the tin bath in front of it.

As the fragrance of the violet soap wafted around the room, Isabella relaxed back in the warm water and almost forgot she wasn't in her bathtub back home.

'Hurry up, Izzie, we'll be late,' Dotty cried, impatient for her turn. 'You will do me hair, won't you? I'm that nervous me 'ands have gone all shaky.'

'Calm down,' Mary soothed. 'You're going to look bonny.'

'Bonny?' she screamed. 'I want to look beautiful.'

'And you will,' Isabella assured her, wrapping the scrap of towel round her. 'There you are, your turn.'

'Alice and I will get ready in my room so you'll have more space upstairs,' Mary told them.

'I'm wearing my new dress too,' Alice grinned. 'And Mother's made me a matching band like yours, Izzie.'

'You'll look even more like a fairy than ever,' Isabella told her.

Taking it in turns to use the looking glass, they arranged their hair, changed into their outfits, then bit their lips and pinched their cheeks to give themselves some colour.

'How do I look?' Dotty asked.

'Pretty as a princess,' Isabella assured her. 'And if I'm not mistaken, Alfred has just arrived.'

As the girl clattered down the stairs, Isabella took one last look in the mirror. Who would have thought she'd be taking so much care for a local hop, she thought, smoothing down the folds of her dress.

To Isabella's surprise, when Felix called for her the seat of his cart was draped in purple material.

'Can't have you getting that beautiful dress muxy, my lady,' he said, helping her up. She stared down at the soft lilac gown shot through with silver and wondered again if it wasn't rather grand for a local function. Still, her aunt had assured her it would be perfect, so she would have to trust her judgement. Felix was wearing the same evening attire he'd worn before, and as the soft rays of the setting sun illuminated his face, she marvelled again how good-looking he was.

The ball was held at the same hotel as the Christmas Eve dinner dance, but this time a raised dais had been placed at one end of the large room. Candles flickered and everywhere was a sea of mauve, with violets covering seemingly every surface. Soft music was playing as waiters circulated with trays of drinks.

'Do you mind if we sit here for the moment?' Felix asked, gesturing to a table set in an alcove. 'We can join your folks later, but I'd like us to have some time to ourselves. That is, if you ever stop greeting all and sundry,' he said, as she smiled at another girl she'd recently become friendly with. However, his grin belied his stern words, for Isabella knew he was pleased she was fitting in to life here in the West Country. He took a sip of his drink, and she was surprised to see his hand trembling.

'Are you feeling quite well, Felix?' she asked. 'Only you seem a little on edge.'

'Me? Never,' he grinned, jumping to his feet. 'Would you care to dance, Miss Northcott?'

'Why, thank you, Mr Furneaux,' she replied, 'I thought you'd never ask.' He took her hand, sending shivers of delight shooting up her arm. As they circled the floor, pressed ever closer together by the throng, Isabella couldn't help thinking how lucky she was to be in the company of such a wonderful man. She caught sight of Dotty dancing with Alfred and noticed how radiant she looked. Then, with the excitement in the room at fever pitch, the music stopped and a gong sounded.

'Will our prospective Violet Queens please take their places,' the compère announced.

'Come on, Izzie,' Dotty laughed, grabbing her arm. Before Isabella could protest, she was being pulled onto the stage.

'What am I supposed to do?' she asked, feeling self-conscious as she gazed at the assembled guests.

'Beam beautifully at the judges, of course,' Dotty chortled. 'Oh Izzie, you look like a stranded fish gaping like that. Come on, it'll all be over in minutes. Once they've made their choice, there'll be more dancing and we can snuggle up to our men again.' She waggled her eyebrows so outrageously that Isabella couldn't help but laugh.

'Ladies and gentlemen, silence please,' the compère requested. 'May I ask all our delightful contestants to parade along the stage, please.' Isabella swallowed hard as she followed the other girls. All were smiling widely, some even performing a wiggle as they passed in front of the judges. 'Thank you, ladies. You all look so delightful, it's going to be a difficult decision.'

'Smile, Izzie. It's only a bit of fun,' Dotty hissed as she took her place beside her. Fun? Why, she'd rather put pins in her arm.

'Ladies and gentlemen, the judges have reached their decision. The Violet Queen's first attendant is...,' he paused for the roll of drums, 'Dorothy Northcott.'

'Coo, blimmer, girl, that's me,' Dotty shrieked, jumping up and down so that the judge had difficulty in placing the purple sash over her head. As the crowd applauded, a delighted Dotty gave a curtsy.

'And the second attendant to our Violet Queen is...' Another pause was followed by a roll of drums.

'May Anning.' Again, the room erupted into cheers and applause until the gong sounded once more. The room fell silent and this time the tension was tangible.

'And now, ladies and gentlemen, the moment you have all been waiting for. Our Violet Queen for 1893 is...' The compère paused and held up his piece of paper.

'Isabella Northcott.'

'What?' she gasped, but already she was being ushered to the front of the stage, where a circlet of violets was placed on her head.

'Ladies and gentlemen, before I ask you to give a rousing cheer for our new Queen, I have received a special request,' the compere announced. 'As if your evening hasn't already been exciting enough, it is about to reach new heights,' he announced dramatically. He turned and nodded to the floor where, to Isabella's surprise, Felix stood waiting. Suddenly, in front of everyone, he threw himself down on one knee.

'Isabella Odorata Northcott, would you please do me the honour of agreeing to become my wife?' he asked, gazing up at her adoringly. Isabella stared at him in astonishment. How could he do this, she wondered, shaking her head. It was only when a groan rang around the room, that she realized what she'd done.

'I mean, yes, I will be honoured to,' she cried.

As a tumultuous roar went up, Felix leaped onto the dais and took her hand. Placing a star-shaped diamond ring on her finger, he whispered: 'You had me going there, Isabella. I thought you'd rejected me again. And in front of all these people, too.'

'Not this time, Felix. But in future please could you spare my blushes and do things a little less publicly,' she scolded, her smile belying her words.

'Your wish is my command,' he grinned. Then right in front of everyone, he kissed her lips.

As the band began to play, seemingly hundreds of violets were released from the net suspended overhead, cloaking them in a confetti of perfumed purple blossom. Felix took Isabella in his arms and stared lovingly into her eyes, and she knew that for ever more she would associate the musky fragrance of violets with this magical moment.

Acknowledgements

Grateful thanks to:

Carol Lockton, who answered my endless questions on violets and provided me with so much information.

Grove Nurseries, Bridport for explaining about Parma Violets and how they first came to this country.

Dawlish Museum for showing me pictures of 'Old Dawlish'.

My friends at BWC who patiently listened to my unfolding story and gave invaluable feedback.

Teresa Chris for her insightful comments and sterling support.

Kate Mills and her wonderful team for making me so welcome at HQ and helping me with the editing and production of this book. Your ideas have been invaluable, your enthusiasm heart warming. I hope I have repaid your faith in me.

The publishers hope that this book has given you enjoyable reading. Large Print Books are especially designed to be as easy to see and hold as possible. If you wish a catalogue please ask at your local library or write directly to: